NICOLETTE REED

Daemon Rising

NICOLETTE REED

First edition

ISBN: 978-0-9905617-1-2

This book was professionally typeset on Reedsy.
Find out more at reedsy.com

This book is dedicated to the memory of Juli-Ann Williams who was one of the most vivacious woman I've ever known and who left this world too soon.

Other Titles by Nicolette Reed

Fae Hunter (The Soulstealer Trilogy, Book #1)
Mane Attraction (A Soulstealer Novella, Book #1.5)
Fae Guardian (The Soulstealer Trilogy, Book #2)
Mane Chance (A Soulstealer Novella, Book #2.5)
Fae Warrior (The Soulstealer Trilogy, Book #3)

Praise for Fae Hunter

"*Once you start reading Fae Hunter, you won't be able to put it down. The action starts on the first page and never lets up for the entire book. Just when you think you can take a deep breath and maybe even put the book down for the evening, a new twist erupts that makes you keep reading for one more chapter and one more chapter and one more chapter...*"

–Romance and Mystery Author and Editor Sally Berneathy

"*This book has so many surprises, twists, and turns, I couldn't put it down.*"

–Paranormal Romance Guild Reviews

"*I think it's this love triangle that made the book for me.*"

–Fantasy and Romance Author J.F. Jenkins

"*Great world-building, engaging characters that quickly draw you into the story, and enough twists and turns to keep you flipping the pages.*"

Chapter One

The sweet, tangy scent of Miss Chow's Orange Chicken arose from the container that rested precariously between Cat's thighs. Usually, the to-go box found a place in one of her many cup holders, but work had been busy and she'd little time to clean up the coffee cups and water bottles that occupied every crevice of her tank-like Mercedes Benz wagon.

Cat reached for the radio and turned the dial in search of an oldies station. The salesman had told her about the presets, but there was only so much tech a girl could swallow, and she was already up to her ears with this latest project. Thankful to have a job, but already wishing it was Friday. And it so wasn't even close.

Another twist and static changed to music as a Temptations song blared. The 60s. What a decade. From The Beatles to Johnny Cash, to Elvis Presley. She approached the bridge that spanned the River Rouge and led to the rural side of Ashton. From here on out it was only farmland and a winding road that ended at the Iron Forge Mine. Cat had procured a small piece of property with lots of land on all sides. A buffer from people, and other things.

She took the last turn and crept along the narrow drive to the small cottage she called home and sighed. God, she loved this place, her — far from the world — place of peace. Her headlights shone across the vast expanse of her front yard and struck the barrier of forest that bordered the backyard. Her cheer at being home deflated. "Damn, I told Thalia not to have them mow."

In the fall, the grasses grew chest high and stalwartly survived the winter frost. At least that had been her experience in the past year. She liked to keep the wall of grass, a shield that stopped the neighbors from becoming, well, too neighborly.

The golden light of the sunset splashed across the sky, bouncing off the gathering of storm clouds in the distance. The purplish-pink haze reflected off the whitewashed siding making her house appear like a hippie dream. "Glad that was one era I missed."

Cat inhaled another whiff of the orange sauce and imagined the first salty cashew crossing her lips. Her stomach growled but maneuvering over the rutted road made it impossible to eat without making a sloppy mess out of her favorite outfit, a pair of jeans and a white t-shirt. These guilty pleasures were all she had to live for these days. Miss Chow's Orange Chicken and remotely rebooting servers for Iron Forge. At least she didn't have to fake any pleasantries with her co-workers.

She glanced down and slid a finger under the lid, dipping it into the sauce and drawing it into her mouth. Nirvana. Another great band, another decade lost. Pushing the regret from her mind, she looked up and spied the glowing yellow eyes of some nocturnal creature staring straight into her high beams.

"Shit!" Cat slammed on her brakes and wrenched the wheel to the left. The front end dove into a hill of grass clippings that cushioned the impact. *Way to overreact, Cat.* "I'm never going to hear the end of this from Thalia."

Orange sauce oozed down her leg, the hot, fragrant liquid

puddling at her feet. *Damn it.* She let her head fall onto the wheel, and the horn blared. Should she give it up and go inside, or head back to town for round two?

A gentle knocking on the window caught her attention, and she groaned at being found in such a pathetic position.

"If you wanted to thank me for the yard clean-up you could have picked another way." Her one and only friend, Thalia's stunning green eyes peered at her over the top of her horn-rimmed glasses. She opened the door and sniffed. "So this is the reason you left the house? You knew I was coming over, why didn't you just ask me to pick it up for you? Here, let me help."

Thalia reached for Cat's leg and moved her foot. She retrieved the container but left the remaining contents on the floor. While Cat knew it was unsanitary, she wanted to scoop up the lost food and devour it. Years of not having anything will do that to a person.

"You know how I am about the fortunes." Miss Chow's fortunes were uncanny, but only when she handed them directly to Cat. "Besides, I didn't expect the weasels would be out already. The seeds have barely sprouted."

Staring out across the fields, Cat inspected Ash Farms which occupied the entire south side of Ashton east of the River Rouge and also bordered her property. Last year she'd arrived at the same time. Back then the fields were already beginning to show signs of a bountiful harvest. This year, brown grass still littered the fields, like winter forgot it was only a few months long and spring hadn't visited yet.

"Are you blaming the weasel for this mess?" Thalia gestured to the already sticky stains on Cat's jeans and the confetti of clippings strewn over the yard.

3

Cat climbed out and tucked the small paper bag holding the fortune cookie into her purse. "I only saw its eyes. It seemed kind of big. You didn't see it when you came out?"

"Nope. Let's get you inside and cleaned up. And I swear I'm not making a pass at you." Thalia hooked her arm around Cat's waist and directed her toward the house. She leaned forward and licked a small spot of sauce off the tip of her nose. "Maybe just a little."

Cat smiled at the bold nature of her friend. At one time she was the same way, unafraid of anything but boredom. It gave her comfort that Thalia felt safe to be that way with her because the teasing remained a boundary that wouldn't be crossed. Couldn't be crossed. Being a recovering succubus means no nookie. In her own way, Cat was recovering too, but her ailment was a whole lot more complicated than just being a demon spawn.

Cat ascended the stairs and surveyed the yard from the porch. Darkness had fallen, and the comfort of nightfall wasn't coming with it. To the north were the rickety pilings of Iron Forge where she worked. Once thriving, the mine now struggled to remain active.

She scanned the border between the open field and the tree line, a pit of uncertainty in her gut. Something was out there, watching. A sensation she could never shake, which seemed to be getting worse, no matter how much she tried to isolate herself from the outside world.

The trill of her phone from inside the cottage brought her back to the present.

"Want me to pick it up?" Thalia asked.

Cat glanced at the glowing hands of her Timex. "No, I'm still on call for another 30 minutes. I'll get it."

4

The stench inside the sparse one-room cottage hit her like a brick wall. Cat ran to the phone as it hit the third ring and yelled out to Thalia. "Can you open the windows? Smells like something died in here."

"Hello?"

"Hi, hello. Is this Catherine James?"

She hadn't been Catherine for many years. "Cat."

"Cat. This is Aidan from Iron Forge." The nervous male voice didn't make her cringe, she was used to people calling and acting like the world was about to end if their system froze. He didn't sound overly dramatic like many of the callers who had no idea how fortunate they were. She had actually experienced having her world end.

"Well, Aidan from Iron Forge, you have exactly twenty minutes for me to solve your problem and then your department will have to approve my overtime." There was at least a quarter of that container of Orange Chicken left, and she wasn't above licking her own pants to get her fix.

"Sorry, I know it's late. Norm told me to call. You know Norm?"

Speaking of weasels. "Yes, I know Norm." And she also knew that he couldn't get through a conversation without a hint of innuendo, and that was over the phone. She hoped to never experience him in-person.

Cat heard the pounding of keys and the shuffling of paper at the other end of the phone. "He said you might be able to recalibrate the system I am working on."

"Re-calibration requires me to be on-site. I don't do that. You'll have to call the firm and get someone else." Cat pressed her thumb into the stain on her knee and mourned the loss of her favorite meal.

5

"I did. They sent some kid that doesn't know a PC from a Mac. You're the only one I can ask without getting approval for another vendor. Is there any way you can stop by tomorrow?"

"There's a good reason why it smells like something died in here." Thalia stood at the window and pointed behind the couch with the chopsticks in her hand. She poked around the bottom of the take-out container and plopped a piece of chicken into her mouth.

"Hey, I was going to eat that," Cat spoke into the receiver as she placed it back on the cradle. "Sorry Aidan, I can't help you."

"You can't even watch Nightmare on Elm Street with me. Trust me, you'll lose your appetite after you see this." She poked around the container and Cat snatched it out of her hand.

"The reason I can't watch that has nothing to do with the gore. It's just I've seen too much." Cat stared into the container and eyed the last piece of chicken sitting in the bottom, one cashew stuck to the side. Whatever was behind that couch couldn't be as bad.

She leaned over the side and caught the coppery scent of blood before seeing what remained of the creature. Long pointed ears sprouted from its small head. Thick wiry black hairs dotted the surface of its greenish skin. Its mouth was pulled back in a broad grin and revealed a row of sharp incisors that ran the length of both the top and bottom of its jaw.

"The window was already open, that must have been how it got in. I'll get rid of it. Glad to know the perimeter spell I bought works," said Thalia.

The amorphous outline of the creature began to come into focus. Cat knew precisely what she was looking at. Not a good sign. It meant he might still be after her. Goosebumps rushed along her arms and legs, and she swallowed hard. "Goblin."

Thalia snapped open a plastic sack and disposed of the remains before tying it shut. "It was probably living in the field and got stirred up when they cut the grass today. Nothing to worry about. No harbinger of doom."

Cat slid back down onto the couch and reached into her purse. She paused as her fingers brushed by the wax paper bag inside and she drew out the cookie. She cracked it open and ate a small bite before pulling out the fortune. Ritual was important.

"I'm screwed."

Conquer your fears, or they will conquer you.

* * *

"I'm so screwed." Aidan raked his hand through hair, well overdue for a trim, and tugged at the ends. He slammed the phone down on the receiver and let his face fall onto his keyboard.

"Eeeeeeeeee. I'm not sure the boss is going to understand your memo."

Aidan raised his head and glared at Norm who was holding a mug that advertised "Mustache Rides Only 50¢." He twisted the end of his lip sweater and took a swig.

"I called Catherine James like you recommended and she totally blew me off. Why didn't you tell me she goes by 'Cat'? I think I made her mad." Aidan squinted at his screen, which was covered in gibberish. Gibberish only Cat James could help him with, and she'd hung up on him. Pretty rude on her part, especially since he was desperate for her help. "There is no way I am going to make this deadline unless I can get this system bug figured out. It's the only explanation for why all these numbers are off. Are you having the same problem?"

Norm rubbed his buzz cut. "Yeah, she totally blows me off too. Glad to know it isn't just me."

"I didn't mean the girl."

"Oh, right." Norm rocked on his toes and back on his heels again. "Yep, I have the same problem. Except the boss isn't paying attention to my stuff, so it doesn't really matter."

Aidan watched the digital timestamp on his computer turn from 7:29 to 7:30 p.m. "Well, I can't call her back tonight without risking overtime. I'm already working for free past five. I don't need anything coming out of my check."

Aidan swept the papers from his desk into a leather satchel and switched off his monitor. The bank of fluorescents that lit up their temporary workstations powered down leaving only the safety strips which directed them to the exits. A handful of bulbs hung down from overhead and emitted a soft glow.

The core mines of Iron Forge shut down twenty years ago. It had been repurposed and for that Aidan and everyone else in the town was grateful. Jobs were hard to come by in the small town of Ashton.

"What are you still doing here anyway?" Aidan stood and let his eyes adjust to the low lighting. He surveyed the sea of cubicles which sprawled out from the center of the room. All dark. Despite the commandment from his boss that everyone had to stay to figure out why they couldn't separate this one particular mineral from their soil readings, he was the only one who remained. Well, him and Norm.

Norm jostled his arm. "Waiting for my buddy to get off...work. Oh man, that sounded bad."

"Only to you, Norm. Look I'm a little spent, can we do it another time?"

"You blew me off last week. You owe me." Norm set his mug down and flipped up his collar. "Besides, I finally got the Tato sisters to agree to meet me for a drink. I told them I was bringing a friend."

Aidan pointed towards the door. "Before I change my mind."

"Don't worry man, you can call Cat tomorrow. I'm sure you just caught her at a bad time."

"She can't possibly be having as bad a time as I am right now. Or as I am about to."

"Conquer your fears, man. Two girls." He held two fingers up to his lips and snaked his tongue between them. "Two."

No sooner had Aidan's foot touched the exit when he heard a door slam from the opposite side of the room. It echoed off the cold concrete and traveled up into the blackness above. The snake had slithered from his perch. A disembodied voice, oily and full of malice, reached them.

"Mr. Ash, a word before you leave. Mr. Bigsby, leave. Now."

Norm spoke between his fingers. "Man, I'd love to help you out here but..." He stuck his tongue out again.

"I'll catch up with you later." Aidan searched for the man behind the voice, but the twenty-foot perimeter of light around him couldn't reach far enough into the darkness. He braced himself, feet apart and chest out. His boss might outrank him, but he'd be damned if he let the man physically intimidate him.

The stiff soles of Victor Niro's leather Ferragamos reverberated through the open space. An expensive name brand the man tried to impress Aidan with. He could care less about such trivial things. Victor stepped under the nearest bulb. Aidan met his boss's flinty gray stare head-on.

"So, you must have good news for me if you are going to

have drinks with your bud-dy." The syllables of the last word popped out of his mouth, and he crossed his arms over his chest. His navy blazer was still crisp, the half Windsor of his tie drawn tight at his collar. Pretentious didn't begin to describe the guy.

Aidan reached into his pocket and clutched the check he had folded and shoved in there this morning. Every time he felt his temper snap, he reminded himself that this job was only temporary. He needed it, and so did his father, but it didn't define him, not by a long shot.

"The variables are sorted out. I've set the program to run overnight and should have those results before the week is out."

Victor took a step forward, coming within arm's reach. Aidan raised his own chin and stood straighter, refusing to cower in front of this bully.

"We've had our differences. Mostly me wondering how a farm boy could be of any use to a project of this caliber. But you had good scores, so I allowed you to be on my team. My team." He tilted his head to the side. "Don't make me regret giving you this position."

Fists clenched, Aidan swallowed every ounce of pride he had, which wasn't hard considering all the blows his family had taken of late. But he needed to get the seed in the ground quickly if the farm had a single chance of making it through the season and that meant he needed money. The money tucked into his pocket.

Victor chuckled and reached for his phone in his back pocket. He cracked it open and made a show of flipping through the bills. He pulled out a crisp twenty and handed it to Aidan. "Here, go do some conquering tonight."

Calling on his newly honed acting skills, Aidan kept the distaste from his expression and accepted the cash. He shoved it in his pocket alongside the check. They had played this game before, and there was no use refusing Victor's "generosity." The twenty didn't make Aidan any more indebted to Victor and the Iron Forge than he already was. And he didn't plan on spending the money on booze anyway.

"Today is Monday. Find a way to separate that red mineral shit from my soil by the end of this week." Victor pocketed his wallet and got in Aidan's face. "If I have to go through Hell because it's not done, you're the one who is going to feel the fire."

Suddenly that drink sounded a lot more tempting.

Chapter Two

The doorbell woke Cat from her fitful sleep. Thalia had offered to stay the night, but Cat knew better than to lead her friend into temptation. She had met Thalia at the community center where all the addict groups meet up on Thursday nights. Sometimes it was nice to be in a room where everyone was supportive, and no one asked you the gory details of why you were there, because that meant they'd have to reciprocate. And no one, not even Thalia, had ever heard all the gory details of Cat's past. But she, and two other people who resided Earthside knew enough.

The bell rang again, and Cat looked over the top of the couch towards her driveway. Jeremiah Harper, the teenage son of her closest neighbor, jumped off her porch and ran north toward his home.

Jeremiah seemed to have an odd fascination with Cat. Sometimes his presents were a collection of lilies or a hand-carved set of chopsticks and other times he would leave flaming cow pies. Mom always said the boys who liked you the most treated you the worst. She hoped Jeremiah was feeling unusually indifferent today.

She flicked the coffee pot on as she passed by the kitchen and stopped to read a note taped to the front door. "I'm going to ask my sources about the goblin. Please don't worry. Call me if you need anything. P.S. You are adorable when you are sleeping. xoxo, Thalia."

So much for not tempting her. Cat cracked the door open and sniffed at the air before deciding it was probably safe to open it all the way. Or not. At her feet lay a beautiful wooden bowl. Ashton was once graced with fields of Black Walnut trees. That's what the history books claimed. After the Iron Forge Mine started operation, the trees had all died out. Except for one. One tree remained in the center of town, circled on all sides by an iron fence, kind of like a slap in the face of the forge. Take our land, but you won't take our life. Now the forge was the only thing that pumped life into this place.

Cat's fingers shook as she bent down and cupped the sides of the blackened wood. The familiar nutty aroma was unmistakable. But the fact that this crazy teenage hick had probably chopped down the symbol of this town wasn't even the worst thing on her doorstep. Inside the bowl, piled high, was shimmering red dust. A mineral she was all too familiar with. The goblin may not have been a sign, but this undoubtedly was. It was starting all over again.

"Dammit." Leaving the stuff out on her porch wasn't an option. Any beastie within a half-mile radius would be attracted by the cinnabar dust. A mineral common in volcanic soils, but she didn't think it was common here anymore. She was either wrong, or someone was playing a cruel joke.

She set the bowl inside the door and scanned the yard, pulling her orange comforter tighter around her shoulders. In early spring the morning temperature didn't get much above forty degrees and this morning felt even colder. Movement from the corner of her eye drew her attention to her wagon parked fifty feet from the bottom step of her porch.

13

Outside Thalia's circle of protection spell. One which she bought off some VooDoo Priestess she met while passing through Louisiana. It had proved useful last night, reducing the intruder to a pile of goblin goo right inside her cottage, but the fact that the thing had even gotten that far unnerved her.

"Hello? Is anyone out there?" Jeremiah was long gone, but something was still hiding nearby. A creature attracted by the bowl and its contents. As soon as she dealt with whatever it was, she was going to have to have a stern talk with Jeremiah and his overprotective mother.

Cat was answered by a high-pitched screech, like the sound of a nail being drawn slowly across a chalkboard. Or the side of her wagon.

She jumped down the stairs and flicked open her pocket knife, a weapon she kept close to her side, even in sleep. The six-inch blade tended to jab her in the thigh too much, but it was worth the occasional discomfort to know she was protected. The screech stopped when she reached the driver's side of her car. A thick, penetrating scar marred the jade finish along the entire length.

"Whatever you are, you're dead. That's going to be expensive to fix." Cat skirted around the side in time to see a squat form disappear around the back of her cottage. She raced after the creature, immediately regretting not stopping to put on shoes as the sharp stones and pebbles cut into the bottom of her feet.

Her prey ran south towards the forest line and disappeared into the dense brush. She followed it in, and the canopy of trees swallowed the approaching daylight. Limbs whipped by her face as she dove further into the overgrowth. To the east was the River Rouge and to the west, a sharp drop off into the Culvert Canyon. Even though she couldn't see it anymore, there was only one direction it could have gone.

Light pierced through the brush, temporarily blinding her as she broke free of the forest floor. An errant root snagged her ankle, and she went down hard, tucking her body as she fell. A few somersaults later her forward progression was stopped by something very hard.

"Holy crap, are you okay?"

In a split second, she realized the voice came from something human and that if whoever he was had seen her with the knife, then she would have a heck of a lot more explaining to do than just, "I was on a jog through the woods." She palmed the pocket-knife, discreetly using her pinky to depress the latch to close and tuck it into the waistband of her shorts.

The initial adrenaline rush wore off, the extent of her injuries, and the pain associated with them began to make itself known. She rolled over to face the witness to her embarrassing tumble. The critter was long gone. If it had wanted to attack her, then it would never have run off. Most beasties who aren't from around here don't like direct confrontation. They'll fuck with you, but they don't want to be fucked with. And since most people can't see them, they get away with a lot. Cat could see them. She could see more than she ever wanted to.

She looked up into the concerned stare of the man hovering over her, his brow furrowed as he knelt down beside her. Sunlight shown from behind him, shrouding his features.

Cat put her hand up to shield her face. "I think I'm fine. Just didn't expect whatever that was."

"Brambles." The man reached out his hand and offered to help Cat to her feet. "They can help keep the deer away from the crops, but they can also become a nuisance, which you found out the hard way."

Cat surveyed the damage. Her calves were splotched with purple berry stains, her shirt was still speckled with Miss Chow's orange sauce from last night's mishap, and her feet were definitely cut up. She tried to put weight on her right foot, and a sharp shooting pain ran up to her knee.

The man caught her under her right arm and steadied her. She stared into his sky blue eyes, wide with concern. Sun-kissed strands of blond were woven through his dark brown hair. He swept his bangs out of his face and smiled. A dimple appeared in his cut chin. "Paul?"

"I, uh, no my name isn't Paul. Can I help you get back to your house?" She expected this adorable man to start belting "Silly Love Songs" at any moment. After she got back from her sojourn into Hell, she caught up on all she had missed. The Beatles had gone on to make a lot more music, and for a month she shut herself up inside a room and only exited to use the bathroom. She may have been slightly obsessed, but McCartney's upbeat tunes had finally convinced her to start interacting with the present day. It didn't hurt that he was still alive. And he certainly wasn't in his 30s like this man was.

"I think maybe I hit my head." She saw a wooden post sticking half out of the ground where she had come to rest. "Did I do that?"

The man shoved a hammer into his belt. "No, I was out here fixing the post. Good thing I guess. You must live in the old Hamsby cottage. It's the closest thing around. Unless you appeared through a magical portal or something."

"No. No portals." Cat quickly shut down the rising panic in her chest at the mention of otherworldly travel. He was kidding of course. Had no idea. Couldn't have any idea. "I mean, you're right. I moved into the Hamsby place about a year ago. I would appreciate the help." Cat tested the ankle again, and although the pain was less sharp, there was no doubt she had done some damage.

"Funny we haven't met before." The man let Cat put more of her weight on his shoulders, and they started to limp back towards the cottage. "You must not come out a lot."

"I like to keep to myself. See what happens when I go outside." Cat feigned a laugh that didn't sound convincing even to her. Thalia was going to kill her for going after a beastie without any back-up. But dealing with an angry Thalia was better than being taunted all day by some otherworldly creature. If it were another goblin, she'd be scrubbing cow pies off the side of her house all summer. They liked to cause trouble more than anything. And now she had a pile of goblin attractor right inside her door.

Her door. She had left it open when she ran down the stairs. *Shit.*

Cat hobbled a little quicker. "Can we hurry back? I think I might have left my door open."

"No need to worry out here. Folks are pretty honest. You must come from the city."

"Detroit." Her last year there had been the worst for the former bustling metropolis. The 1967 riots. Whole swathes of the city destroyed in the mayhem that spread its fingers out and put a stranglehold over everyone for many years to come. At least that was what she learned. She had been a casualty of the real reason Detroit fell. Demon invasion. Try telling that to a shrink.

"Oh, then, of course, you don't know about small town living. What brought you up here?" He matched her speed as they broke through into the backyard. She scanned the grounds quickly, seeing no signs of her visitor.

"A job. And some peace and quiet." They rounded the front of the house and Cat stopped. The front door was wide open, the wooden bowl upside down on her welcome mat.

He removed his arm from around her waist and gestured to the open door. "Can I help you inside?"

She stuttered a response that wasn't yes or no. It wasn't safe for either of them if the goblin got hold of the mineral. Think troll on steroids and sometimes visible even to those not usually inclined to see demon spawn. She hopped up the stairs and bent down to gather the bowl.

"Let me get that for you." He grabbed it before Cat could. He turned the bowl over. It was licked clean. Too late. Dammit, she needed to get rid of him, and quick. No evidence that anything had ever been there. "Is this made of walnut oak? That's pretty rare around here, you should keep this safe." He pressed the bowl into her hands.

"Yeah, well thanks, I appreciate your help."

The inside of the cottage held a wealth of equipment. "You've got quite the set-up in there. No wonder you want to keep your door locked. Not that I think most people would know what to do with all that stuff."

Cat turned and followed his gaze to the bank of servers she had against the back wall. She liked to keep everything in the living room, maintaining the one bedroom in the house the sole exclusive property of her bed, and sleep when she was able to shake the dreams loose.

"It's how I can work from home and not have to deal with the commute." Iron Forge was fifteen minutes up the road, but they didn't need to know how close she was. As far as they were concerned, she was contracted through a third-party vendor and worked offsite.

"Oh, wait. You're not Cat are you?"

Cat hesitated. She was careful not to interact with the townsfolk, other than Miss Chow and a few of the regulars at the community center. Thalia helped shield her from most conversation, and she'd remember having met this Paul McCartney doppelganger. Nostalgia alone would have made her stomach do the flips, and that didn't happen anymore. Not with the emotional walls she had successfully erected over the years.

"Yes, I'm sorry, do we know each other?"

"Not exactly, but you hung up on me yesterday." He held out his hand. "I'm Aidan, I work at Iron Forge."

* * *

She shook his hand like it was a slimy, wet noodle, quickly withdrawing herself from the social gesture at the edge of what would be considered polite. Behind her, an alarm sounded three times from the kitchen. Aidan had interactions with their onsite tech support before, and none of them looked like this woman. He expected a woman who barely brushed her hair and wore pajamas all day. Cat had a long, lean figure. Her tawny eyes peered at him from behind a curtain of mahogany hair.

Without taking her eyes off him, she pointed a thumb over her shoulder. "Coffee is ready, would you like some? I just need to check my ankle really quick."

"Can I help? I don't mean to intrude, I really had no idea who you were." The last thing Aidan needed was for her to think he was some kind of stalker. Good thing Cat had fallen at his feet and not the other way around.

"No, I insist." She ushered him inside and shut the door, a slight limp in her step. The door had an old peep window which she briefly peeked out before latching the deadbolt. She was either married or paranoid. Or both.

"I hope being here isn't going to get me in trouble with your husband."

She turned and stared at him, incredulous. "I would need a husband before that would happen, and even then, any husband I would have wouldn't be so insecure and untrusting."

Great, he had managed to piss her off even more than he had before. "I'm sorry. It's just small-town politics. You have to be careful where you step around here. Everyone knows the business of everyone else, and it only takes one whiff of impropriety to get the gossips going."

"You mean the Harpers?" Cat grabbed an ice pack from the freezer and then stood on her tiptoes to grab two mugs from the top shelf of the cabinet above the coffee pot. Aidan couldn't help but notice the smooth skin of her stomach as her shirt rose up briefly. Nor the knife tucked into her waistband. "You take cream and sugar?"

"No, black." He buried his face in the mug and tried to hide the rising panic in his face. He was no stranger to the wilderness survivors who lived in the areas surrounding Ashton. Was Cat one of them? Considering her reclusiveness and the knife, she might be one of the crazies. He tried to swallow a large mouthful of coffee and quickly realized that was not what he was drinking. Before his sense of propriety could catch up with him, his reflexes had forced the stuff back into his mug. "I'm so sorry, that's not coffee is it?"

Cat laughed and held the back of her hand to her face. She

fought to swallow what was in her mouth. "I'm so sorry, I didn't even think. I brew my own, it's dandelion root coffee. No use wasting all the weeds out there. Here, this will make it better."

She reached out one long, slender arm, her lithe body stretching like a cat emerging from a warm cocoon. Rich brown hair tangled down her back and her belly pulled taut. As if reading his thoughts, she tugged at her shirt. Disappointment simmered inside him when he no longer spied her pale flesh as she came back with a small jar. She pinched the contents inside and hovered her hand over his mug. "Are you okay with cinnamon?"

"Yes, and I promise I'll be better prepared this time."

She dropped the spice into his mug and locked eyes with him, pausing before gesturing to a small sitting area next to the bay windows at the front of the house. The sun was starting to rise to the mid-point of the sky. Although Victor knew Aidan was going to be late for work because of scheduled fence maintenance, he hated to be indebted to the man any more than usual. But he did need her help, which in turn, would help Victor. Not that Aidan really wanted to do anything for the selfish bastard.

To get on her good side, he'd drink her concoction and pretend to enjoy it. Sipping the brew, he was surprised to notice the subtle flavors in his cup. Chicory and beetroots, barley and rye grains, crops which his family farm used to churn out at the same rate the Iron Forge now processed the waters of the River Rouge for minerals. It was earthy and natural, like the woman in front of him appeared to be. But now both the farm and the mine seemed to be drying up.

"So, you're not a total hermit if you have met Ms. Harper.

21

She makes the best cherry pie in Ashton."

"Actually, I haven't met her. Her son likes to play jokes on me. I was chasing him away from the house when I stumbled upon you." She propped her foot up on a chair and put the ice bag on her ankle. "He won this time."

A bitter taste formed in Aidan's mouth that wasn't from the strange dandy brew. Jeremiah Harper had been a problem for years, and he hated to hear that a newcomer was being terrorized by him. His family standing was the sole reason Ms. Harper made sure Jeremiah stayed far away from his property line.

"I'll have a word with his mother."

"I have to admit, I appreciate the chivalry. You don't see a lot of that these days, but I would rather not draw any more attention to myself. Honestly. I think after today he probably won't be coming around. I might have scared him a little."

Aidan remembered the knife at her waistband. She could certainly take care of herself. "How's your ankle?"

"Feeling better already. So, Aidan, you work at Iron Forge, and you fix fences? How is that?"

"A man has to pay the bills somehow. I'll do any odd job I can." And that was the honest truth. If he could work full time on the farm and bring it back to its former glory, he would. But no amount of man hours could resurrect the past. After the accident, they lost too much. Money and time. Money could be replaced, but time was running out. The only thing still blooming on the property were the cherry trees. The Iron Forge was a necessary evil.

"I understand that. This wasn't really my first choice either. But I heard being in IT was a good job and one you could do from anywhere, so...we all make sacrifices." She repositioned the ice pack and looked out the window. The rays of the morning sun make the flecks of gold in her eyes sparkle. Somewhere inside those eyes, he could feel the pain of some unknown sacrifice.

"What is it you would rather be doing?" She stared down at her lap, and his eyes circled around the room, searching for a clue as to why she was hiding out here all alone. What she had to be afraid of. Ashton was quirky, but the folks were mostly harmless. The gossips never drove anyone out of town. No one took them that seriously.

The sparse room yielded no secrets.

"I once had this dream I would become a painter." Cat lazily swirled her finger across the top of the bright yellow linen tablecloth. Her hands were slender, her nails blunt and unpolished — delicate hands able to sweep a canvas with a bold stroke. Or better yet, stroke his own body. He shifted in his seat and pushed his thoughts from where they had no right to be at the moment. "But I also like to eat and have a roof over my head."

She set the cup down and removed the ice pack, pressing into the injured area with care. "I think it's doing a lot better. Just a mild sprain." She stood up and walked a few steps. "I'll be back to chasing down trespassers in no time. Thanks again."

Aidan realized she was trying to get him to go. He hadn't even gotten her to agree to help him, let alone leave her cottage. There had to be some way. He pointed out the window towards his farm. "You see those trees out there."

Cat stared out in the direction of the Ash Farm's one remaining crop. Yesterday the cherry blossoms had come into full bloom. Bright pink petals in stark contrast to the evergreens and dead wheat fields surrounding the rest of the area.

She inhaled a sharp breath. "I've never seen those before."

"You must have come last year after the bloom. It only lasts a few weeks, and then the petals fall, making room for the fruit. It's a special time of year."

"Now that would be something I would love to paint." Something else caught her eye, and she quickly turned, blocking both their view from the outside. "Were you coming to a point? I'm sorry, it's just that I need to get to work."

Cat pointed to the clock above the doorway. In twenty minutes Victor would be walking into his office and if Aidan wasn't at his desk at least pretending to slave over something he was in a lot of trouble. Victor knew he would be late, but any later and he may as well not show up. And the last thing he needed was more heat. Hopefully, all his words would come out right.

The door banged open two inches stopping as the chain caught the door. Aidan watched Cat's hand go to her waist and then relax as another female voice came from outside. "What the heck Cat? Why do you have the chain on? I said I'd handle it."

Cat quickly unhooked the chain, and the door swung open. Standing in the doorway was a curvaceous woman with stark black hair that came down to her shoulders. Her short bangs stopped right above her horn-rimmed glasses. Green eyes bore into him in an instant, and he felt like he was under a spell he couldn't control. She sauntered across the threshold, hips swaying back and forth against a fitted pencil skirt and heels. He shook his head trying to clear the spell he had fallen under. The woman wasn't even his type.

"Well, excuse me. I didn't know you had such delicious company." Her smile invited him to step a few inches closer, and that's what he did before he even realized it.

"Thalia, Aidan. He works at Iron Forge." Cat stepped between them and whispered something in her ear.

Thalia put her hand to her forehead as if she were shielding her eyes from the sun. "Sorry to interrupt, but I wanted Cat to see this. I know you don't ever like to leave the house, but this seems really interesting."

Aidan scanned the paper Thalia was holding. A flyer for the Cherry Blossom Festival. The exact thing he wanted to invite Cat too. "That's perfect, I was just about to mention that. It is entertaining, and you'll really get to see what Ashton is about."

Thalia pointed to a corner of the flyer. "And besides there is a freak show, says they have real goblins and ghouls. Sounds very interesting." Thalia peered over the top of her glasses at Cat and pointed again to the flyer. "Goblins."

"Yeah, I'm not sure who arranged the acts at the fair this year. Usually, they save the scary things for Halloween, but it does keep the teenagers entertained. Better that then having nothing to do but harass the neighbors," he said.

Cat took the paper from Thalia and turned to Aidan. "How about tomorrow night? And Thalia comes with."

If she wanted to bring her buddy all the better. He definitely didn't need the town to start talking about who Aidan Ash was dating and who was going to be the next Mrs. Ash. He had bigger things to worry about.

"Sure, I'll bring my co-worker. Norm. I owe him one for bailing on him the other night when I had to work late."

Thalia gave a little hop, her hand still shading her eyes. "Yay, double date."

Aidan and Cat both said at the same time, "Not a date."

25

"So I'll stop by and pick you up at 8 tomorrow night? We'll have to take two vehicles. Both Norm and I drive two-seaters."

"I'm not so sure that's a..."

"Great idea!" interjected Thalia.

The best thing to do at this point would be to leave before things got any weirder if that were even possible. "Mind if I give you my number in case you need to call me?"

She grabbed a pen from the coffee table and handed him the flyer. "You can write it on here."

He scrawled his number on the back of the flyer. He felt like he was in high school again, all thumbs. He went back over his writing and made sure his chicken scratch was legible. "Take care of that ankle. I'll see both of you tomorrow."

"Bye-bye," said Thalia. Cat waved and rolled her eyes at her friend.

Aidan walked down the steps and towards the street. He glanced back towards the house and noticed a long ugly scratch down the side of Cat's car. Like someone had keyed it. Jeremiah Harper and his mother were going to hear from him. The last thing he needed was Jeremiah's fool antics ruining his chance of collecting his bonus from Victor. Aidan needed Cat's help, he didn't need some hooligan chasing her out of town. If he could make his quota at the mine, then he would have enough to afford the seed. He hoped the workers would agree to work on credit until his next payday. The Ash family name was still worth something in this town, but if he didn't turn things around, that wasn't going to last for long.

Chapter Three

"Don't pull so hard." Cat held tight to the sides of her head. Thalia had decided that she needed a makeover which included a ponytail.

"Believe me, you don't want your hair in the way when you are making out." She twisted the rubber band onto her hair. "You'll thank me later."

"This is not a date, it's an investigation," Cat muttered curses under her breath. Going to the fair was bad on so many levels. The idea of being around all those people made her uncomfortable, but the thought of being with Aidan terrified her. The image of his earnest eyes filtered through her reluctance and she felt a sense of obligation, although she wasn't sure why. He was a perfect stranger. *A hard-bodied, sexy mouthed stranger.* She pushed the image aside and reminded herself of the other reason she had accepted. The devil's dust would draw the goblins, and the only place that produced a significant amount of it was the Iron Forge Mine. She had forgone visiting the site in person for that very reason.

"Okay, but can I call mine a date? I haven't had one in years." Thalia patted the curls at the end of her bob and readjusted her glasses in the mirror. Off-white piping swopped across the chiffon-like dark cobalt fabric of her tank dress. The 60s-inspired detailing on her belted frock was sure to turn heads

27

at the fair. *Not like she needed help in that arena.*

"Are you sure you can control yourself?" Cat fussed with her white cardigan, attempting to align the V-neck to hide as much cleavage as possible. Thalia had insisted on dressing her as well.

Thalia undid the top button of Cat's sweater and readjusted her necklace. Lacquered red beads and shiny green leaves graced a gold chain, giving the impression of ripened cherries. "I think I'll be fine." She trailed her finger just along the line of Cat's white lace bra and adjusted the strap before squeezing her arms and stepping back.

Thalia had come a long way since they first met at the group. Cat knew immediately that she had demon energy. After asking her back to the cottage so she could figure out what kind, she quickly learned first-hand that Thalia was a succubus. That night had ended most interestingly. Cat tried to dampen Thalia's sex drive, and Thalia attempted to do the opposite. Regardless, they remained friends ever since.

"These polka dots are right over my nipples, I swear it just calls attention to my boobs." She ran her hands down her black capri pants and bent down to buckle her Mary Jane stiletto heels. "And I don't know how appropriate these are for a fair."

Thalia handed Cat a small clutch. "Your six inch is in there. Look, these people don't have horse races, they have this Cherry Blossom Festival. They get all dolled up and sip cherry wine, eat cherry pie and spray on cherry perfume. We'll fit right in."

Cat tucked the clutch under her arm. If there was one thing that she was convinced of, it was that she didn't fit in with these people. A simple fact that she was okay with. While many most probably thought they were well versed in the ways of the world, they had no clue what evil beings existed out there just beyond their line of vision. Let them continue being innocent. No one should have to have gone through what she had, and she wouldn't wish it on her worst enemy. "You forgot to mention they also invite goblins to their event."

"Which is why we need to figure out what is up. None of the locals I talked to seem to remember that ever being a part of the event. Everyone wants to blame the person they like least in town. So everyone is a suspect."

The roar of an engine followed by the trumpeting sound of an air horn playing La Cucaracha announced the arrival of their dates for the evening. Cat leaned out and saw a powder blue 1979 El Camino and a Scrambler. Her heart skipped a beat. The last time she had 300 ccs of horsepower between her legs was in 1967. Upswept exhaust pipes ran along the bike's left side. The painted aluminum fenders and alloy tank confirmed it was definitely from Cat's era.

"If Norm is the one on that bike we are switching dates." The man straddling the machine wore tight faded jeans, frayed at the edges. His black leather jacket had zippered cuffs and matched the boots that rose to his mid-calf. He flipped up the face shield on his helmet and pulled it over his head, shaking out his dark locks. "It's Aidan."

Thalia leaned next to Cat as she stared out the window. "So, that's my date." She pointed to the man exiting the car, who could only be Norm.

He was clearly of Japanese descent, but that couldn't be the only cultural mix running through his veins. Asian men did not grow the kind of impressive mustache that graced his face. Combined with the buzz cut, Hawaiian print shirt, and the sexual remarks he always made, he embodied pretty much every bad cliché.

"I'm really sorry, Thalia."

"What are you talking about? They don't call it a womb broom for nothing."

"Thalia!"

"What?"

The door knocked, saving Cat from having to endure any further explanations of the anatomy of Norm's lip foliage. Thalia scurried over and swung it open.

"Hello, ladies." Norm gave a half bow. "Name's Norm Bigsby, but my friends call me Mr. Big."

Aidan pressed by Norm, and his mouth fell open. He stared incredulously at Cat.

"Hi, I'm Thalia." Thalia broke the awkward silence and extended her hand to Norm.

"Enchanté." Norm planted a kiss on the back of her hand.

Thalia giggled. "Tickles."

Cat buttoned the top button on her cardigan. "I know I'm over-dressed. It's all Thalia's fault."

"No, you look great. It's just you looked so different yesterday," Aidan stammered. He stepped over the threshold and ran a hand through his mussed hair. He half smiled, and a dimple appeared on his cheek. She hadn't noticed that before.

"She cleans up well doesn't she?" Thalia smiled, Norm practically glued to her side. "Mr. Big this is Cat."

"The Mistress of Mystery. We finally meet." Norm held out his hand and Cat shrank away. She wasn't about to let those whiskers touch her hand. There's no telling where they had been.

She crossed her arms over her chest. "Nice to meet you, Norm."

Norm half laughed and stepped back beside Thalia. "Shall we go? Your chariot awaits my Goddess."

Thalia giggled again and followed Norm outside.

"I've got an extra helmet." Aidan pulled a half helmet from behind his back. "Are you going to be okay on the bike? I should have warned you."

Cat undid her ponytail, sliding the rubber band over her wrist, and shook her hair loose. She reached for the helmet and tightened the buckle under her chin. The distinct musk of leather rose up from the soft strap beneath her fingers. It had been a long time since she had been this excited about something so seemingly mundane. "Let's ride."

She wrapped her arms around his waist and clutched onto the soft cotton t-shirt that clung to the tight body underneath his jacket. He definitely must spend more time helping out at the Ash Farm than he does sitting at a desk at the Forge.

Cat laid her head against his back and took in an exotic blend of cherry and red musk that she could smell on Aidan now that they were close. La Cucaracha sounded, and Thalia waved from the open passenger window. The four-seater car was made into a two-seater because of the huge subwoofers in the back.

Norm leaned across her lap and yelled out, "Hey, check this out." He pushed a button on the dash, and the front end of the car hopped a few feet off the ground and bounced up and down.

"Rodeo, baby!"

"He's quite the show-off, but he's harmless. You don't have to worry about your friend." Aidan flipped the visor down on his helmet. "Are you ready?"

Little did Aidan know it wasn't Thalia she was worried about.

Cat clung tighter to his waist, not because she needed to, but because she had a good excuse. "Whenever you are."

Aidan turned the ignition key on and tickled the carburetors. His abdomen muscles flexed under her fingers as he stood up and kick-started the bike. It ignited on the first kick. He twisted the throttle and revved the engine. The muffler rattled against her leg, and she hooked the heel breast of her stiletto on the passenger footrest. All four cylinders were firing, vibrating the padded seat between her legs.

Aidan let go of the brake pedal, and they lurched forward down the dirt road. Recent rains kept the road moist and perfect for high speeds without creating any dust clouds. As they reached the bridge crossing the River Rouge, Cat closed her eyes and pretended she had somehow warped back the fifty years that she had missed. Fifty years that had been stolen from her. If she could somehow find a piece of herself then maybe it wouldn't feel like she had lost so much.

* * *

Aidan pulled into the Ashton Fairgrounds and felt a swell of pride. A rainbow of lights spiraled from the center of an enormous Ferris wheel, the sound of roller-coaster riders screamed past, and the smell of livestock reminded him of home. He could almost taste the fried goodness of the cherry fritters he waited for every year. His only regret was that the cherries had not come from his farm this time. But that would all change, hopefully with the help of the woman whose arms still circled his waist.

"You doing okay back there?" Aidan patted her arm, and she released her grip, leaving comforting warmth across his mid-section. He turned and watched her staring at the stream of residents entering the gates, small children in hand who jumped up and down at the sight of the fluffs of pink cotton candy stuck onto paper cones.

She took off her helmet, a flyaway piece of glossy hair whipping in front of her face. Without thinking, Aidan reached up and tucked behind her ear. She looked up at him, her green eyes liquid in the dim light. His attention fell to her lips, and he fought the urge to kiss her. A scream from someone on a nearby ride followed by laughter broke the spell, and he dropped his hand, flustered by the surge of lust that burned through him. She cleared her throat. "This is incredible. How many people live in Ashton?"

Damn, he'd made her uncomfortable. "415 last count, though that was probably before you came into town and Mary Evondale had her baby, so I would put that at 417. Though the Cherry Blossom Festival does attract visitors from the surrounding towns." He stowed their helmets and offered his arm, hoping she would take it. "Can I escort you inside?"

Norm skidded into the parking lot and pulled to a stop next to Aidan's motorcycle. He hung out the window and patted the side of the car. "Why you gotta make me look bad in front of the ladies, homeboy?"

"Don't think that's possible," said Cat under her breath.

Aidan laughed, but sensed her unease with his well-meaning but sometimes over the top friend. "How about we catch up with you two at the show? I want to show Cat the stables."

Norm looked slightly dejected and suddenly perked up as Thalia let loose a cascade of giggles that felt almost contagious. "Catch up with you later my man."

Aidan swept by the ticket booth and waved to the man inside.

"You get in free? You must be pretty famous around here."

Cat smiled up at him, and he could tell she was sincere. She honestly had no idea. He wanted to keep it that way, even if only for a little while. The last thing he needed was for her to think he was some spoiled trust fund baby. He was anything but.

"I do some work around here, being let in free is one of the perks." He steered her toward the stables which tended to be quiet late at night. The animals got a lot of attention during the day, but at night the corrals were pretty quiet.

"So you work at the Forge, fix fences, and clean stables? How do you find the time?" Aidan was sure she was making polite conversation, and while he wished he could be honest, he wasn't ready to admit the truth of his situation to her or anyone else.

"You always find time for things that matter the most." He hoped maybe seeing his prize stallion would help him steer the conversation in the direction he wanted. Away from him. "Come see Angel Eyes. He's the famous one around here."

They turned the corner and found two teenagers making out on a pile of dry hay. They were so involved with what they were doing that they didn't even notice Aidan and Cat.

"The two of you better get your cotton candy. I heard they are about to run out," said Cat. She grinned and folded her hands across her chest. The girl yelped and hopped up, hay sticking out of her hair.

She ran over to Aidan, "You won't tell anyone will you Mr. A..."

Aidan put his hand up before she could finish. "Just make sure I don't catch the two of you doing this again."

They raced out of the barn and the horse in the stall nearest them gave a snort. "I think this horse thinks you were too easy on those two," said Cat. She peered in and squealed as the horse's muzzle poked out from the darkness.

"This is Angel Eyes, and I'm sure you are right. But we were all young once." Cat stroked the white stripe on his forehead and patted Angel's mane. "Have you ever heard of horse sense?"

Cat stepped away from the corral. "You mean that horses can sense the good or bad in people?"

The warmth he had felt from her since the moment she got onto his motorcycle suddenly chilled. She kicked at the hay at her feet and stared beyond him towards the sound of the bustling fair and vendors who were trying to con passersby to join in a game no one could win. He was starting to feel like he was playing the same game and Victor was his biggest adversary.

"No, not that. Honestly, I think horses just reflect what they feel from the person. If you're scared, it will set them on edge, like any animal...or human." Aidan immediately regretted adding on that last word. Cat crossed her arms back over her chest, and this time it wasn't in mock disappointment like she had moments before with the teenagers. "I mean horse sense, the ability to make good judgments or decisions."

Cat relaxed slightly, pulling her hair back into a ponytail at the top of her head and securing it. The curve of her neck drew in his attention more than he cared to admit. "This hay isn't too good for these stilettos. They're borrowed. What did you say about meeting Norm and Thalia at a show?"

Aidan had barely recovered from his verbal blunders. He was walking a thin line with her and not even sure what was considered good or bad. It was nice talking to someone who didn't already know who he was and yet utterly frightening at the same time. "The creep show. It's the first year they've put it on, and it seems pretty interesting. I'm sure it's not too scary. They know we have lots of kids here and it's on the main stage."

She perked up at the mention of the entertainment. "Right, the flyer said goblins. Should be some great special effects. Let's go." She hooked her arm through his, and now she was the one doing the steering.

Between the main stage and the stables were some fifty or more stands selling everything from new age crystals to fried gelato on a stick.

"Step right up, step right up. Win the lady a stuffed puppy. Come on son, you look like you have a good arm." The vendor, Willy Forrester, knew who Aidan was and that he had spent all his elementary school and teenage years playing football. And Aidan knew Willy was always running some game in town. The County Fair offered him a legal way to take money from people. And Aidan was a sure target.

"No thanks." Aidan rubbed his arm. "Arm is not feeling so good tonight."

"Come on, Aidan. Don't you want to impress your lady friend?"

Cat wrapped her arm around Aidan, her soft body flush against his side. The faint scent of her shampoo and woman drifted to his nose, and he inhaled. "Maybe I'm the one who wants to win a stuffed puppy for my man, ever think of that?"

Her man, he liked the sound of that. However, he was also getting Cat embroiled in the town drama which she had apparently been trying to avoid by isolating herself. First, stick foot in mouth, and then make sure to do the other one too. Just so you're even on both sides.

Willy put three baseballs down on the fake green. Aidan bent down to whisper in Cat's ear. "If Willy is running the booth the game is rigged."

"Watch me." Cat stepped up and set down a five dollar bill she pulled from her clutch. On a raised platform about six feet away sat a 10-gallon metal milk container that was obviously rigged. Ash Farms once had dairy cows, and Aidan could tell this can wasn't standard. It didn't take much to see that a concave piece of steel was welded to the rim of the can. There couldn't be more than a one-sixteenth difference between the hole and the softball Cat bounced in her hand.

"One ball wins you a Cherry Blossom Frisbee, two wins you this stuffed puppy. Make all three, and you get my phone number little lady."

Cat smirked and tossed the ball, flicking her wrist, so it got some backspin as she released it. The ball hit the rim and spun around twice before sinking inside. Willy reached up to get the Frisbee.

"Not so fast, I've still got two balls."

"Yes, you do." Willy sat on a nearby stool and gave Cat a once over that made his skin crawl. He didn't like the sleazy look the man cast her way. "Take your best shot."

The second ball sunk with the same ease as the first. "Be careful Cat, you might end up with Willy's phone number."

Cat smiled over her shoulder and turned back to take aim.

Aidan rested his hands on his hip, and a diamond encrusted hand slid through the opening. "Aidan Ash, I told you to call on me if you were coming to the fair. As the newly crowned Miss Ashton, the town's namesake must escort me to my seat for the show."

The ball hit with such force against the steel milk container that it toppled to the ground. "Whoa! Take it, easy lady. Two is good for a puppy." Willy handed the stuffed mutt to Cat and foisted a slip of paper in her direction. "And with an arm like that, you can have my number as a consolation prize."

Cat waved away the come-on. "Save it. Did she say your name was Aidan Ash? As in Ashton? Ash Farms?"

Acting oblivious to the sudden tension between him and Cat, Violet adjusted the sash across her dress and extended her hand dripping in jewels which Aidan wasn't sure were all real. Violet's family had made their own fortune, but since Violet was always throwing herself at Aidan, he didn't suspect that it was enough to keep her satisfied.

"Well hello. I don't believe we have met. My name is Violet Chanterelle. Or Miss Ashton. Aidan and I go way back. Are you new to town or like some third cousin?"

"Chanterelle, isn't that some kind of fungus?" Cat shoved the stuffed puppy into Aidan's arms. "I'm going to see if I can find Norm and Thalia. Nice to make your acquaintance Violet."

If Aidan was worried that he had said the wrong thing, he didn't have to worry anymore. Now the rest of the town was doing it for him.

"Violet, I'm really sorry but that was one of my co-workers, and I really need to make sure she finds her way okay."

"Certainly, sweetheart. You and I can catch up later." She looked from the stuffed puppy and back in the direction Cat had fled to before sauntering back to wherever she came from.

* * *

"How could I have been so stupid?" Cat jostled past the thickening crowd that waited in line for the Freak Show. She intended to make some excuse to detach herself from Aidan to give herself time alone, but he had done that for her. Feigning anger wasn't necessary. Of course, she felt stupid for not realizing that the most handsome man she had seen in a very long time was the heir of Ashton. And the fact that he worked at the Forge meant she was going to have to act friendly. She wasn't off to a good start.

Her stilettos sank into the grass, impeding her progress and she cursed herself for allowing Thalia to dress her like some supermodel on steroids. The ankle she twisted earlier in the day began to throb again. She pushed back the pain and focused on her mission. She had to have a look backstage before the show started.

Cat climbed a small rise that dropped down into a half bowl dotted with metal chairs and picnic blankets. Sodium vapor lamps were spread throughout the area and focused on the stage. Most people in this small town had probably never seen anything like it. To Cat, it screamed "not normal."

Gleaming mirrors and richly painted wall panels made up the set while endless yards of red and purple plush velvet drapery framed the stage. Illuminated globes ran the length of the platform which dripped with golden filigree. Colossal twin Corinthian columns acted as the trussing for the roof. To the left of the stage, Cat saw what she was looking for, a lighted arched staircase leading back into the shadows.

She passed the front row and laid a hand on the railing. Power hummed through her fingers, and there was no telling if it was good or bad. Though surprise shows of power usually don't manifest in a good way. Cat wasn't sure the audience was ready for whatever entertainment this cast had in store.

"Cat, over here." Thalia waved from her seat in the front

row. Norm leaned back in his chair, his legs crossed in front of him and his arm slung over the back of Thalia's chair. "I saved you guys seats."

Cat crooked her finger, beckoning Thalia to come to her. The last thing she needed was to fend off Norm's advances while trying to sneak into demon territory. She barely knew him, but she knew his type. Thalia patted Norm's knee and leaned over to whisper in his ear. She removed the sweater over her shoulders and draped it across the seats before coming to Cat's side.

"I told him we were going to find the lady's room. I don't think we have more than twenty minutes before the show starts." She looked beyond Cat into the crowd. "Where did Aidan run off to?"

"You mean Aidan Ash, the pride of Ashton?" The man who had conveniently forgotten to tell her who he really was. Exactly like her ex-boyfriend.

"So you figured that one out, huh?" Thalia searched through her purse and took out her lipstick, expertly reapplying her red lips without the help of a mirror. "Looks like you have your hair back up in that ponytail. Does that mean you were making out?"

"No, it means I don't need my hair falling in my face when I am hunting demons. And why exactly didn't you tell me you knew who he was?"

"I didn't want you to get nervous." Thalia put her hand on Cat's shoulder. "It's been a long time since you've gotten out there and I didn't want any more pressure on you."

"Tell me you also didn't happen to notice the power coming from this thing." Cat gestured to the stage, staring for the first time, into the mirrors lining the walls. They were polished to such a shine that the surface almost looked liquid, as if you could step through them into another world. "Oh shit."

Thalia followed her gaze. "I know. I'm hoping they don't have enough power to turn them on. Can't possibly right?"

"Did I mention the bowl of devil's dust I found on my porch the other day? I think they do."

Previously unnoticed speakers warbled to life. Preshow music piped through the sound system, an oppressively dark score heavily reliant on the low end of the orchestra. Wagner tubas and contrabass clarinets produced a somber and noble motif. It sang of both the fate of the audience and their captivator's vanity.

"The show's going to start soon," said Thalia. The lights dimmed and brightened, beckoning the townsfolk like moths to a flame.

Cat got halfway up the stairs and faced the crowd, counting in her head the number of children sprinkled throughout the venue. Images of what could be flashed through her mind. Beads of sweat formed on her brow.

"Did you guys already get the backstage tour?" Aidan appeared from behind a family of 80s head-bangers, all of them with matching teased-up hair, the boys, and the girls. "I wanted to introduce you to the stagehand. Arnold practically raised me when Dad was busy on the farm."

"Actually, I was looking for the bathroom, and Thalia said that she saw one back here." Thalia made an impatient motion and tapped on her wrist. "She's just going to show me."

"Okay, look I wanted to talk to you about..."

"Later." Cat ran up the last few steps and swept open the curtain that covered the entrance to the backstage. She reached into her purse and grabbed the six-inch blade, feeling

41

a wash of confidence return as she snapped the blade into place. The darkness behind the material complete, it took a moment for her eyes to adjust. "Thalia?"

She felt something bump into her shoulder and gripped her knife tighter.

"I can't see shit in here," Thalia said.

"Next time spring for the glasses with headlamps. Just keep your hand on my shoulder."

Cat felt Thalia's hand settle into place. The stage was to the right, the only place she could possibly go was forward. Her outstretched fingers touched a wooden panel, and she slid her hand alongside it, scooting her feet forward and hoping she wouldn't catch her bum ankle on any wiring. A dim blue light appeared, looking as if it was floating in mid-air. Cat tracked it to a podium. She felt around expecting papers or a script or something, but when her hand came into contact with it, she was jolted back hard.

A voice breathed into her ear. "You never struck me as one who liked to crawl around in the dark."

Lights flooded the stage and temporarily blinded her. Not being able to see the threat sent her heart racing. She teetered back on her stilettos and landed hard on her backside. Thalia rounded the corner and shielded her eyes from the sudden brightness.

"Are you okay? I lost you back there." Thalia put her arms under Cat's and helped her to her feet.

Cat rushed back to the podium and searched for what she had felt. A small lump of cinnabar sat undisturbed. She searched for the source of the mysterious voice, but no one was there but the two of them. She held up her discovery.

"Is that?" Thalia reached out to touch the stone. Cat drew it away from her reach.

"Something you shouldn't touch." She slipped the stone into her clutch and kept a firm grip on her knife. Disappearing demons couldn't easily be vanquished with a small pokey object, but it still made her feel good.

The actors entered stage right. Cat knew that none of them were demons. Partially because of her sixth sense and also because no demon she knew would be caught dead or alive in the garb this ghastly crew wore. It soon became apparent that the *Creepshow* was exactly that, a reenactment of scenes from the horror anthology film written by Stephen King.

Cat and Thalia watched from stage left as the first story started, *The Lonesome Death of Jordy Verrill*. A man suddenly appeared at the podium, searching furiously for something. "The meteor, have either of you seen it?"

Cat shrugged, and the man slapped his forehead. "Guess we'll have to use the back-up. Not the same though." He shuffled off, and the two of them turned their attention back to the performance.

Jordy Verrill was a dimwitted backwoods yokel who thought that a newly discovered meteorite would provide enough reward money for him to pay off his bank loans. Cat watched as the man she had seen moments before handed a red rubber ball to an actor on the other side of the stage and shrugged. She realized the rock in her pocket was intended to be a prop. Maybe all of this was just in her head.

What she did know was that the goblins were probably out there. She should be searching the crowds or the faces of those around her, and instead, she was stuck watching the play.

An intermission was announced, and Thalia grabbed Cat by the arm. "I think that's our cue to exit stage left."

43

* * *

Cat escaped from the heat of the backstage with Thalia close on her tail. The fresh night air was like a splash of cool water to her fried circuit board of a brain. At the bottom of the steps, Aidan scanned the crowd, his hand shielding his face from the footlights. Tingling sensations prickled through the clutch at her side from the red rock. Cat had to hide it somewhere safe and away from any possible demons, even if all the ones backstage were only humans in costumes.

Vendors with carts of fried cherry fritters topped with fresh cream surrounded the venue. Intermission was in full swing, and the audience had emptied out of their seats to stand in one of several growing lines.

"There you are," Aidan turned, and his face brightened at the sight of them. "Did you see the performance?"

"We got stuck backstage, and they didn't want us to leave and disturb the actors." Cat conveniently left out the part where a phantom voice spoke to her, and she had taken the meteor from backstage. I was a little disappointed they didn't use the prop I gave Harold. It was a pain in the ass to take from work."

A pit formed in Cat's stomach. *Could Aidan have something to do with the exact thing she was looking for?* "What prop did you bring them?"

"Their meteor was supposed to be this hunk of red rock that we mine down at the Forge. It was near impossible for me to get Victor to approve checking it out from the line. We haven't had a rock that big come in a long time. Actually, that's part of the reason I called you for help."

"Hey, groovy chick," Norm called out to Thalia from across the green.

"Looks like Norm is waving me down, I'd better let him take me home." Thalia squeezed Cat's shoulder and gave her a mischievous wink.

"Home, where I'll call you shortly to make sure you got there okay."

"Yes, mother." Thalia skipped off and disappeared arm in arm with Norm through the cherry fritter infused crowd. Thalia was actually old enough to be Cat's great-great-grandmother, but there's no accounting for age and responsibility. A sweet breeze blew through the basin, and a groan echoed from Cat's stomach. She clutched it in embarrassment.

Aidan gestured to the line which stretched to the far end of the field. "Did you want one? I should have offered you dinner earlier."

There was a definite link between the Forge and the red rock. She had no excuse but to check it out. The worst part was that buckets of it were turning up on her doorstep and goblins were following along with it. If they were starting to ramp up production for something she needed to know what, so she could keep as far away as possible.

"Actually the line is really long, how about we go to my favorite Chinese restaurant? My treat."

"Yes, but there is one thing I would like to do before we leave." Aidan pointed at the large Ferris wheel that rose up high from the center of the fairgrounds. "I'd never forgive myself if I didn't show you the best view in town. And besides, I'd like to have a chance to explain to you why I didn't tell you my last name. What do you say?"

In the darkness, it was impossible to really see his eyes, but his voice sounded sincere. Despite Cat's reservations, there

45

was no way he could do anything to her on a Ferris wheel. She needed more information about the Forge and Aidan was her in. Going with him had nothing to do with any attraction she might have for him. Absolutely nothing.

* * *

They walked in silence through the thinning crowd. Most people had taken in the show and their fill of fried delicacies and were headed back home. Thankfully that meant fewer people who might approach him and frighten Cat away.

She didn't actually seem scared or timid in any way. And her friend, Thalia, definitely wasn't one to shy away from attention. But there was something walled off inside her. If he was going to get her to help him, he needed to get around that somehow. He needed to start by being honest with her if he expected the same.

"It's just around the corner."

She nodded and followed him to the bottom of the Ferris wheel where the last of the occupants were dashing out of the carriage, hands filled with giant lollipops and balloon animals. It warmed his heart to see people so happy and reminded him that if they were going to stay that way the jobs needed to remain in Ashton. A pit formed in his stomach. Including those at the mine.

"Looks like they are closing," said Cat. The ride operator stepped down from the booth and pulled a set of keys from his pocket.

"Do you think you can give us one last spin?" asked Aidan.

The teenager whirled around at Aidan's voice. He looked from Cat to Aidan and waggled his eyebrows. "Sure thing, Mr. Ash. Don't know why not."

46

His idea to bring her here was turning rapidly from bad to worse. Anxious to get this over with, he looped a hand around Cat's waist and guided her to the carriage. He took it as a good sign that she didn't slap his hand away. They took seats opposite one another. The door latched into place, and they were lifted into the air.

The cart wobbled, and Cat grabbed onto the sides. "I probably should have mentioned my fear of heights."

He seriously could not have done any worse. "Are you okay? I'm sure that I can get them to stop it once we go around."

She closed her eyes and inhaled a deep breath, her body going still as she kept her eyes clamped shut. "I'll be fine. Besides, I thought you had something to tell me. I don't necessarily need to see anything."

Aidan leaned back, letting the rigid plastic seat behind him act as his backbone. The feeling of anonymity he had for a few hours had been nice, but it was time to come clean. He had a perfectly good reason for not telling her, one that he could expose without giving the entire truth. "I'm sorry I didn't tell you right away who I was. To be honest, it felt nice to meet someone who didn't automatically know me. Have preconceived notions."

Her eyes flipped open in time for him to witness the rolling. She crossed her arms over her chest. "I don't know you or anyone from this town from Adam. There wasn't any reason to lie to me."

From below came the loud sound of gears grinding to a halt, which would be an apt metaphor except it actually happened. The cart swayed from their momentum and Cat grabbed onto the sides again. "What happened?"

Aidan peered over the side and saw the teenager giving him

47

the thumbs up from the both. The bright red light of the stop button blinked in front of him. The damn kid thought he was doing him a favor. But it would give him a chance to talk to her in a place she couldn't run away.

From across the valley, Aidan could see the red lights also blinking on the Iron Forge Mine. That scar wasn't always part of the skyline. Swathes of purples and oranges swept the sky. The wind kicked up, and a cool breeze blew through the cart.

Cat clutched her shoulders and shivered. "Are they going to get it moving soon? It's freezing up here."

"I think so. But it might be a few minutes. Can you open your eyes for a second and see the view?"

Cat pursed her lips and opened one eye. "What am I looking at?"

If he was going to get her warmed up to the conversation, he was also going to have to get her warm. "Mind if I sit next to you? You can share my coat."

She nodded, and he gingerly sat next to her, being careful not to jostle the carriage and force him to start all over again. He removed one arm from his coat and wrapped it around her shoulders. She snuggled into him, her body fitting perfectly next to his. The slight vanilla scent of her skin increased as their bodies warmed up to one another.

"That's the mine. This entire valley used to be farmland." He pointed to the area south of the mine, to his family farm. "You can see the delineations in the land. The places where the fields were demarcated and crops turned every season. Now it's all bare."

"That's why you work at the mine." She placed a hand over his, heat seeping through her skin and into his own. He wasn't sure why he felt a connection to this woman, but he wanted to know why.

Another gust blew through, and she tucked her body closer into his side. She looked up, and their faces were barely an inch apart. Cat's lips parted, and he pressed his own to hers. His right side went from scorching hot to ice cold in an instant. He opened his eyes. Cat had ducked out of his coat and retreated to the other side of the carriage, her gaze on some unknown point on the horizon.

"I'm sorry. I don't know what came over me." His lack of intimate relations with anyone lately was what came over him. How could he be so stupid?

She wiped at her lips with the back of her hand. "I think we are both just hungry and not thinking straight. Why don't we get that food I was talking about?"

The cart jolted and started its downward descent. Kind of like where he was headed with this woman. "Sounds like a good idea."

* * *

Miss Chow's was a hole in the wall on the side of another hole in the wall. The first time Cat laid eyes on the town it was close to midnight. She had walked the vacant downtown strip at 11 p.m. searching for a place to eat. The red neon open sign had summoned her through an alleyway that she wouldn't have chosen to venture. But the thought of a hot meal had beckoned, and she ended up finding her comfort food and a bit more.

A bell above the door chimed as they entered. She looked behind her. Aidan trailed sheepishly, likely ashamed that she had rebuked his advances. It wasn't his fault. Every man who had tried anything with her had gotten the same letdown.

49

Except for one thing, she hadn't let any of the rest of them get close enough to even try anything.

Inside the restaurant, the walls were painted a deep, vibrant red, bisected horizontally by mahogany wood paneling. The space was dotted with brightly colored paper lamps with golden tassels hanging down from them that diffused the room with a warm glow at any time of day. With everyone at the fair and the late hour, they were the only ones in the restaurant. Cat took two of the laminated menus, printed entirely in Chinese and settled into her favorite booth. With a perfect view of the front door and the comforting smells emanating from the kitchen that never rested, she felt immediately at ease.

Aidan settled into the booth across from her and inspected the painted over windows a throwback to when this place was a Chinese "massage" parlor rather than a restaurant that served the best crispy orange chicken Cat had ever tasted.

"I can't believe I've never been here before. Lived here my whole life and always thought this alley was a dead end."

"You're a nice man. You probably never came back here because until last year this was basically the town brothel. Miss Chow says her family owned it, but she was still in China until last year. When she found out what they were doing, she kicked them all out and opened this place up." Cat flipped open the menu and ran her finger down the list. She couldn't read a word of Chinese, but she didn't need to. Photos of mounds of Ginger Beef, bowls of Won Ton Soup and piles of fried rice sat next to each line of hanzi.

Aidan flipped his menu closed and looked around. "She should advertise in the local paper. I bet this place would be busting at the seams with hungry folks."

"Miss Chow fancies herself a fortune teller. She says good things come to those who wait, not those who advertise in the Penny Saver. The first time I met her, she clasped my hands and predicted good things for me in this town." Cat knew that magic was woven throughout this establishment, but Aidan didn't have to know as much. As far as he was concerned, it was as much smoke and mirrors as the performance at the fair.

Aidan leaned across the table, his cologne as enticing as the food. So far, Miss Chow had been right. The last year Cat had successfully built herself a fortress which had remained impenetrable until recently. Right now, she needed Miss Chow's fortune as much as her hungry stomach required her garlic green beans.

Much to her relief, the double-hinged kitchen door swung open and squeaked closed. In the formerly empty space appeared Miss Chow, a petite Chinese woman who looked about sixty and spoke like she was twice that. Cat knew better than to ask those with a supernatural spark their exact age. It gets a little dicey after one hundred. A bright fuchsia top stood in stark contrast to Miss Chow's pale skin. Large round wire-rimmed glasses were perched at the tip of her nose, a beaded chain draping around her neck held them in a precarious position.

"No like crowds. Take too long to cook." Miss Chow dug her fists into her hips. "You don't start any rumors now. I like customers I have. Who you bring here, Cat?" Miss Chow opened the doors to a small cabinet and brought out a tray lined with a bamboo mat. On it was a squat brown teapot, steaming with green tea and two handle-less tea mugs. She set the offering down between the two of them.

51

"I guess I'm not the only one in town who doesn't know you." The scents from the kitchen bolstered her spirit. Goblins might be skulking around town, but she had been through worse.

Aidan sat back in the booth and stared at the Chinese writing like somehow it would all make sense if he just kept staring. Miss Chow handed him a cup of steaming tea and took the menus from the table. "I know what you two need. Time. You have very little. I be out soon with food. Talk."

She scuttled away through the double hinged door. When the squeaking stopped the only sound you could hear was the buzzing of the neon open sign. Her comment unnerved Cat a little. Hopefully, she was only talking about the time between now and when she closed for the night.

Aidan rolled the hot mug between his hands. "She didn't ask what we wanted."

"Take a sip."

He raised his head. "I'm not much of a tea drinker, to be honest with you."

"For me."

Aidan shrugged his shoulders and brought the mug to his lips. Cat knew what he tasted, whatever felt like home. She wouldn't call what Miss Chow did witchcraft, at least not to her face, but beneath Cat's lips right now was the same "fresh" lemonade her mother always served. Shy on time, but not on love, her mother would open a can of pink lemonade concentrate before she got home, add water and ice, and serve it in a tall glass pitcher beading with the perspiration of a hot Detroit night. Home in a glass.

Aidan's eyes widened. He looked in the cup and wiped the moisture from his lips, staring at his fingers before setting down the glass and pushing it a few inches away from him. "I must be in dire need of sleep."

"Miss Chow didn't take our order because she always knows what you want." Cat raised her glass, knowing that even though Miss Chow had shown her magic to Aidan tonight, it didn't mean that it was safe to talk about it in the open.

Aidan spoke little about his family except to admit that he was the namesake of the town and that his family farm was in trouble. Empty plates littered the table, the two of them having devoured everything Miss Chow brought them. The restaurant remained empty the entire night except for the two of them.

"I don't like working for the Forge. It's what I have had to do to make ends meet these past few years. But this year, not even the Forge money can save the crop. I can only hope that my bonus gives me the seed we need." Aidan used his fork to herd the remaining green bean around his plate. "We've got enough saved for one bad year, but not two."

Miss Chow pushed a cart through the doors and cleared their table. She set a tray down with two fortune cookies. No bill.

Aidan pulled out his wallet. "What do I owe?"

Cat clasped her hand around the wad of cash in his hand. If he thought she was going to accept a dime from him after his story, then he must think her more heartless than she usually tried to come off as.

"I've got a running tab here. It's already been added. You can treat another time." She lifted the tray. "Pick a cookie, but don't open it yet."

Cat had brought him there for several selfish reasons, and one significant one was to see what the fortune inside this cookie said. Whether or not she was supposed to stick her

53

neck out for this town, or pack up and find another place to hide away.

Aidan watched her as she performed her ritual. Break off a piece of the vanilla wafer, eat a small bite, and then slide the little white slip of paper from its cookie sheath.

Man's mind, once stretched by a new idea, never regains its original dimensions.

"Aidan, what time can I meet you at your office tomorrow?"

Chapter Four

Being able to see the broad expanse of Ash Farms from his post at the Iron Forge used to bring Aidan comfort, now he stared over the barren strips of the unplowed field and felt the same sickness in his stomach that hadn't gone away since his father's accident.

He leaned against the ruins of the first furnace built on these lands back in the early 1900s when cinnabar mining was king in this area. The remains of the former condenser tube foundation and the old processing shacks now sat in the forested area behind the Iron Forge Mine, overlooking the road that snaked up to their place at the top of this small valley he called home.

Although his father repeatedly reminded him that he and the entire Ash Family should be grateful to the board for supporting the ongoing operation of the mine, despite every other cinnabar mine in the area being shut down for the last fifty years, Aidan only felt like it was a trap. A crutch that Ashton had relied on far too long, and now he feared the days of the mine operation were as numbered as his family farm.

On the road below, he saw Cat's late model Mercedes wagon entering the series of switchbacks before the main gates. He unclipped a walkie from his belt and depressed the PTT button. "Willy, there's a truck coming up the drive. Please let Miss

James in without too much trouble. Over."

The walkie crackled to life, transmitting a heckling laugh along with Willy's response, "Hoo-wee. Is that the gal with the wicked arm at the fair? I'll let her right in. Though you got to tell me what else she can do with that arm."

"Over and out, Willy."

Catherine James was a compelling woman, smart and independent, but he didn't need the complication of a relationship right now. Especially when he was so close to getting the bonus his boss had promised him. Aidan jogged the narrow trail. Beyond the town of Ashton, the Iron Forge Mine teetered like a lunatic on stilts, hovering above the River Rouge. He passed between the weed-strewn oak and creaking redwoods, humid from the mist evaporating off the wet stones at his feet. The night before a downpour struck just as he pulled his motorcycle into the barn. Luck was on his side, and he hoped Cat was bringing it.

Aidan keyed in the code to the back door, and a buzzer sounded. Just inside the back entrance was the employee kitchen and Norm rose his "69" mug to his lips and swallowed deep.

"Nothing like a nice cup of coffee in the morning after a nice night out with the ladies. You get yours home okay?" Norm winked and rose his cup to another co-worker who quickly grabbed a bagel and kept walking.

"You didn't give Thalia a hard time did you?" Aidan immediately regretted his question.

"Rock hard." Norm's hip thrust would have made Elvis embarrassed. "Actually, I told her she would have to wait for the Norm. He doesn't give it up on the first date."

"I'm glad to hear it. And I'd love to hear more, but Cat is

almost here, and I want to show her..."

"...your shaft?" Norm grabbed his gut, barely able to contain himself and his chortling.

"You stay here." Aidan knew Norm was more talk than action, but he didn't need his perverted jokes scaring Cat away. He needed her help. And although she was a strong woman, there was a vulnerability to her that made him wish to protect her. "Hey, have you seen Victor around today?"

Norm's countenance sobered immediately at the mention of their boss. A man who scared him shitless. "No, he said he was going into town to meet with the benefactors."

Good news Victor was gone, bad news that he was meeting with the benefactors. The people who decided whether or not this privately run mine would continue to stay open. Aidan was the one who was supposed to give Victor the report that said this operation was still profitable. He hoped Cat would be able to help him with that. He pulled at the collar of his shirt which seemed to be getter tighter by the second.

He reached his cubicle just as the receptionist, Betsy, dropped Cat off at his station. "Oh, and speak of the devil, here he is in the flesh. Are you sure I can't get you anything?"

Betsy went to touch Cat on the arm, and she drew back so violently she almost knocked over the potted plant sitting at the entrance to his cubicle. "No, I'm fine." Cat's brow sheened with sweat as if she had just run up the hill.

"We're fine here, Betsy. Thank you." She shrugged her shoulders and went back to reception. "Sorry if she was a little overbearing. She's from Texas and thinks if she can't get you to have a glass of sweet tea she has failed as a proper southern lady."

Cat released her grip on the olive bomber jacket clutched in her hands. "Where is the problem you wanted me to look at?"

Right to business. He knew that kissing her at the fair was too much. He'd scared her off and didn't even need any help from Norm. He sat down and swiveled over to one of the several screens lining his terminal. "What I want you to look at is part of the problem, but I'm not sure it's all of it."

She sat next to him, her perfume filling the small cubicle. Concentrating with her nearby was hard. He forced his attention back on the screen and tried to focus on something other than her. "These screens monitor the actual mining process. Iron Forge took advantage of two different methods of mining. Underground mining and river dredge mining."

He pointed to the screen that showed the network of rooms cut into the underground seam and the shuttle cars that pulled mounds of material from deep within the fertile volcanic soil surrounding Ashton. "It used to be that crystal forms of cinnabar were found down here. But that hasn't been the case for some time. The mine has been staying afloat by selling off the waste material from the mercury production. But then there's this."

Aidan pointed to one screen that showed a pontoon sitting on the river. Several men were working a dredge anchored to the shoreline. "The River Rouge has stood still since a dam was erected by the Forge. They found out that within the runoff in the river were chunks of the common ore of cinnabar that while not as precious as the crystals, still gave them the material needed to process the mercury."

Cat peered at each image, her stare as glassy as the screens. "I still don't understand why you need my help."

Aidan grabbed the stack of dot matrix printouts from his desk. "There has to be a bug in the program somewhere. I tried wiping the system and starting over, but it's still not working." He pointed to the values that were showing up on the reports a month ago and the ones from the past few weeks. "We aren't pulling even an eighth of the material we were. It's impossible."

His co-worker Lee walked by with an open box of donuts so sweet you could smell the sugar before he had even made it to Aidan's cubicle. With a mouthful of masticated pastry, he shoved the box in Cat's direction. "Want one? Fresh from the bakery this morning."

Flecks of fritter speckled his report on the red rock. Cat looked physically ill as she stared up into Lee's thick black plastic frames. His comb-over having long ago decided that it had given up reaching the other side of his head.

"Nice of you, Lee. We're good here."

Cat draped her jacket over the side of his cubicle and unbuttoned the top button of her white cotton shirt. A small thin line of her bra strap peeked out from beneath her shirt. He glanced up, embarrassed to be caught looking, however, her attention was definitely not on him. She refused to look Aidan in the eyes and motioned for him to slide aside so she could work on his system.

"What makes you so sure it hasn't just run out?" She clicked away on the keys, frequently stopping to rub at the back of her neck. Her hair was pulled into a loose ponytail, and small tendrils of her dark curls fell forward, shielding her from his direct gaze. He pictured his hand on the nape of her neck, his thumb sliding through the silky strands. "I mean couldn't the mine finally be dry?"

"I can't believe that." His mind floated up from the gutter. Aidan's thoughts went directly to the worst case scenario —

Ashton a ghost town. All its residents left without mining or farming, and he would feel responsible for both. "The numbers couldn't have dropped that fast. There would have been a steady decline."

In the reflection of the screen Cat's brow furrowed as she typed, each screen pulsing with strings of numbers before flashing onto another.

"Did you go to ITT or something?" The way her fingers flew across the keyboard impressed him. The fluidity reminded him of wheat in a strong wind, bending in a graceful rhythm.

"Self-taught." Cat continued to type as she talked. "I used to be a secretary for a big company, but they went belly up. Had to learn something new and had some time on my hands."

"The programs I've had to learn for this job are mind-numbing. I understand them, well enough, I guess, I'd rather be outside working the land. Something is satisfying about sinking your hands into the dirt and coaxing life from a small seed, a bit of fertilizer, and fresh spring water. To me, it is magic." *Much more than raping the land for its minerals.* He'd learned enough on this job to know they weren't just pulling out the cinnabar. Everything else came with it too.

"What I wouldn't give to be able to use my hands again." He stared down at his palms, and he barely recognized them. The evidence of nurturing, milking, thinning and weeding used to weave a tale in the tissues of his hands. Calloused, hangnails, muscles and cracks were now being replaced with smooth, unstained skin. Only shadows of his former self remained.

"He's not getting all handsy on you is he?" Norm leaned on the side of the cubicle.

The last in the line of co-workers who were likely eager to see what woman had gotten so near Aidan Ash. It was refreshing that Cat cared so little about small-town politics and was normal. Although she seemed spooked by social interactions and preferred to work alone, she brightened at his colorful friend's remark. "Norm! Great to see you, I hear you and Thalia had a good time."

Norm blushed. Not many people sought him out for conversation and Aidan could tell he had really taken a liking to Cat's friend. He tugged at his collar and took a nervous sip from his mug, turning the "69" so it faced away from Cat's view. "She's a peach. Hope we can all do it again sometime. I'll leave you two to the business of business." He hurried away.

Cat swiveled around in her chair and brought up a few screens. She pointed to lines of code that flitted down the screen. "You've got a daemon I don't recognize."

"Is that like a bug or something?" Aidan squinted at the screen, knowing that no matter how long he stared at it, it still wouldn't make any sense.

Cat gathered her purse and pushed away from the desk. "A daemon is a computer program that runs as a background process, rather than being under direct control of the user. It was probably put there by your boss. Maybe to track what you are doing. Look, there isn't anything else I can do from here. I've set a remote code so I can access your computer from home. I'll try to look into it more. I'm not even sure if it's affecting your reports, but I can check it out. From home."

Any chance of having his problem solved today was over and done with. He had already sent a soil sample to an outside lab to test the ppm, but it would be another week before he would see those results. And Victor wanted them yesterday.

"Let me walk you back to your car. I really appreciate you coming down here. I know you didn't want to." Cat had been

61

so jumpy he felt terrible for making her come down when she wasn't able to find anything. And he wanted to ask her what she meant about Victor spying on him. She seemed to know more than she was letting on.

"No, it's fine. I can find my way out. I'll...I'll call you if I find anything." She snatched up her jacket and whisked through the front lobby.

Seconds later Aidan's walkie crackled to life. "I swear whatever she was crying about, I didn't do it."

Aidan leaned back in his chair and stared at the screen. The first time he met Cat she fell at his feet with an injured ankle, not a tear was shed. Now she left his office crying, and they barely exchanged ten words. He didn't know what he was supposed to apologize for, but he couldn't help but feel her distress was somehow his fault. He rubbed at the sore spots forming at his temples.

The walkie crackled to life again. "Incoming. Over and out."

Nix that, he might be the one crying at the end of today. That was the signal that his boss was about to enter the building.

* * *

Cat flicked the windshield wiper out of habit, but the moisture obstructing her vision wasn't coming from the sky. She tugged her truck over and parked in the nearly empty lot of the Ashton Community Center next to Thalia's pale pink Vespa. Her friend attended her regular meetings on Friday mornings.

She pushed open the doors and peered into narrow a window cut into the classroom door where the meeting was being held. Thalia sat in the front row, a yellow pencil perched between her teeth. Evidence that her date with Norm had definitely pushed some of her buttons and this meeting was necessary. Cat turned to leave, but not before she caught the eye of the group leader. The man, who resembled Jack Nicholson, and probably had a lobotomy before he agreed to run this group gave Cat the creeps, but not in the same way Aidan's co-workers at Iron Forge had. There is definitely something wrong at that mine.

Jack waved at her and Thalia excused herself. Cat watched the leers of the other four members of the SAA group stare at her as she sashayed towards the door, her outfit of choice today being a grape-colored dress with a fitted bodice, dainty cap sleeves; slightly flared at the waist with a matching sash. Cat could only imagine how Thalia rode to the meeting on her scooter without flashing the town. Not that she hadn't done that on purpose several times before. Part of the reason Thalia had to attend these meetings.

"What's wrong?" Thalia gripped her by the forearms and Cat waited for the door to click close behind her before the dam burst again.

"They're back. Like you, but everywhere, back." Cat tried to gather the words she was looking for and form them into a coherent sentence, but she didn't even want to admit that the goblin was only the tip of the iceberg. Something much worse was happening in Ashton.

"Let's get out of here okay?"

Thalia followed Cat home and the minute she stepped over her threshold, she felt safe once more. Her senses were in overdrive, and the perimeter spell that Thalia placed around her home put her a little at ease. Though deep down she knew that if he were coming back for her, nothing would be able to stop him.

Cat sank down into her sofa. Thalia busied herself in the kitchen and brought out a tray of Little Debbie's Oatmeal

Crème Pies and a pot of chamomile. The crocheted peach cozy hugging the ceramic kettle was knit by Cat's grandmother and had been one of the few things to survive her time away. It reminded her of a simpler time and home. But unfortunately, a home that didn't exist anymore.

She sank her teeth into the layers of baked oats and cinnamon and rolled the crème filling around her mouth, following it with a deep swallow of the mild and flowery brew. She opened her eyes, and Thalia took the tray from her lap. The comfort of the warm tea kettle still cradled in Cat's hands. "Please tell me what you saw."

Cat closed her eyes and replayed the morning in her mind. She drove up to Iron Forge expecting bureaucracy and paperwork and instead got the shock of her life. The man sitting at the security gate was the same man who tried to finagle her at the fair, but he was changed. A soft red glow shone behind his eyes and Cat had felt the twitch of demon energy as she got closer to him. Willing to believe her nerves had gotten the best of her after sticking close to home the past year, she entered the complex. The rotund receptionist's smile beamed bright, as did her eyes. Red. When she was sitting with Aidan at his desk, another man came by, again with glowing red eyes. She was so overwhelmed with gratitude when Norm came by and had nothing but a lecherous stare to give her she was probably overly friendly to him.

She didn't need to explain all of this to Thalia, however. Thalia knew Cat's past. She knew Cat could sense demon energy. There was only one thing she needed to tell Thalia.

"Ashton is infested with demons."

The tray in Thalia's hand clattered to the floor, and a snack cake rolled under the couch. "I thought you said that was all done. I mean. Why would they come here?"

Thalia's particular affliction, while demonic in nature, was an entirely different species than the one Cat had experience with in the past and who she knew was here now. The red rock was proof. She made a mental checklist. *Next time you decide where to live, don't move next door to a cinnabar mine.* Cinnabar, demon stone, red rock. The same substance known by several different names. Mines across the United States shut down because of the utter toxicity of the stuff. There was a good reason demons liked it. In enough quantities, it increased their powers, and the Iron Forge was probably run by them.

"Would it be so terrible if I asked that we not talk about this right now?" Cat curled up into a ball on Thalia's lap. "I just need you to stay here for the night."

The one time she had decided to investigate, and she had found exactly what she didn't want to see. But if the Forge was running low on red rock like Aidan said, where had the bowl of the stuff on her porch come from? The only person who she could ask was the farm boy next door, Jeremiah.

Thalia brushed her fingers through Cat's hair. She was the one friend Cat had that she could confide in. Admittedly, there was one other person, but her relationship with her ex was complicated. Thalia gave a heavy sigh.

Cat pushed up from her coiled position and took her friend's hands. "I'm so sorry I stole you away from the meeting. How did things go with Norm after we left you?"

"Not good." Thalia squeezed Cat's hands tighter, the curtness of her response revealing all Cat needed to know. Thalia was on the verge of a relapse.

"Go ahead and do it." A year had passed since the last time Thalia had extracted life energy from Cat, she shuddered as she recollected the experience.

Thalia dropped Cat's hands and pushed back on the couch. "I won't do that again to you. I don't want to hurt you." She smoothed the front of her purple dress and took the pencil from behind her ear. She gnawed at the end so hard that it snapped in half.

There was only one thing that would calm Thalia right now, and Cat knew what it was. She also knew her friend wouldn't accept the offer without some convincing. Cat reached over and ran her hand up Thalia's bare thigh, leaning over to kiss her on the neck.

Thalia froze but didn't push her away. Instead, she un-buttoned the front of Cat's white cotton shirt and cupped her breast, nudging at her nipple. Tingles of sexual tension tightened in Cat's stomach, the energy Thalia needed to take the edge off. This was nothing but another form of therapy. Thalia stood up and scooped Cat up in her arms, walking towards the bedroom and kicking open the door.

She laid her gently on the bed and whispered into Cat's ear, "I'll just take a little." Thalia laid down next to her, sliding her fingers into Cat's inner thigh, coaxing a little more sexual tension before performing the ritual. She opened her mouth wide, and Cat's fell open, held tight by the strings of energy Thalia had latched around her. Deep blue waves of energy erupted forth from her body and poured out of her mouth. Spasms from her loins pulsated more and more until Thalia ripped herself away.

Cat shuddered, sweat forming across her brow. The last time she had done this the result was the same. Something inside Cat had prevented Thalia from draining her entirely. Had saved her. When she escaped her prison, she thought the influence her past had on her would stay with her captors, but something had followed her out. The same something that allowed her to see demons.

* * *

Aidan looked up at the clock. Time had moved faster than a rabbit chased by a hound dog. Everyone else had left two hours ago. The only two people left in the building were him and Victor. He'd tried everything to get the reports to run the way he wanted, but nothing was working. He stared at the screens that took continuous video of the rail cars at a standstill in the underground mines. It had been years since samples had been collected from so far below. Victor had come aboard and all but shut down that operation in favor of the pontoons. Admittedly the plan worked for some time. The amount of runoff material they were getting was far higher than what was left in the mines. Eventually, all the miners left town for other jobs. Now all that was left were the ones who worked the pontoons and everyone in the front office. Aidan longed to join them, to get the Hell out of this Hell he called work. All the other jobs from the mine were created by the process of making the mercury. Factory workers and scientists who processed everything at another plant on the Iron Forge property.

A door slammed, echoing through the cubicle farm where nothing grew but inboxes. "Mr. Ash, you have that report for me? I have a date that I don't want to miss."

Anyone who would want to date Victor Niro had to be certifiable. Although considering the debutantes that scratched at Aidan's door on a regular basis in the hopes of becoming Mrs. Aidan Ash, he supposed being arm candy of the seemingly wealthy Victor Niro wasn't bad either.

Aidan gathered up the last report he ran, he turned, and Victor was standing right in front of him. The stack of perforated papers started to slip, and he tightened his grip. He'd be damned if he'd allow Victor to startle him enough to drop them before his feet. "Mr. Niro, just in time for the report I printed off. I'm afraid it won't give you what you are looking for. I tried a variety of scenarios and nothing tangible. Even had a vendor here today looking at the system to see if there was something wrong. You don't know anything about a daemon do you?"

Victor's eyebrows shot up. "Should I know something about daemons?"

The skin on Aidan's arms began to crawl. He never liked being near his boss. Whenever he was irritated, he seemed to emit a pulse as uncomfortable as the high pitched whistle was to a dog. A person couldn't hear or see anything, but the physical reaction was unmistakable.

"It's probably nothing. The vendor I had here said that there was a daemon program running in the background and that maybe it had something to do with the reports. I won't know for sure until I get the sample back from the lab."

Victor brushed by Aidan and walked towards his computer. He ran his fingers along the keys and drew his hand back. An unexpected light of something Aidan couldn't quite gauge reflected from his eyes and the chills on Aidan's arm turned to raindrop sized goosebumps. There was something seriously wrong with this guy. "Who was this vendor?"

"She was on the list of those approved from Veritex."

"Her name." Victor came inches from Aidan's face.

"Catherine James. Or Cat, she goes by Cat."

Victor's shoulders relaxed, and a lazy grin crossed his face.

"Follow me."

Aidan trailed behind Victor toward his office. The buzz of the fluorescents overhead sounded like a swarm of wasp's waiting to attack some poor, unsuspecting victim. In this case, Aidan. Part of him hoped that Victor would fire him. If that happened, then at least he could tell his father he had tried as hard as he could. It was the truth. There was nothing else he could have done to change those reports.

Victor picked something off his desk and tossed it to Aidan. He caught the yellow hard hat in one hand. "Go down into the mine tomorrow. I want you to do some prospecting. See what you can find. And believe me when I say a lot is riding on this."

"There are million other people more qualified than me to prospect an old mine," Aidan said as diplomatically as possible. He had no idea what to look for down there, and he didn't want to tell Victor he was crazy.

"Aren't you farm types fond of digging in the dirt? And one more thing. I want you to give this message to Cat. You will be seeing her again won't you?" Victor handed him a sealed envelope with the Iron Forge return address in the corner.

Aidan definitely wanted to see Cat again, but he wasn't sure after her quick exit today if she would want to see him. "I'm not so sure I will. I could mail this to her if you want."

"No. You have to give it to her in person."

"What is it?"

"The information she needs about the daemon. But it is highly confidential." Victor sat back in his chair and crossed his legs atop his desk. "This is part of your job. You want to keep your job don't you?"

"Yes, sure. No problem." *Right?* Cat had freaked out the last time he saw her and was so anxious to leave his company, she practically ran. Trudging down in the mines would be easy in comparison to the difficulty of connecting with Cat. Aidan quickly made his way over the threshold. He'd better collect his things and leave before Victor could make any more crazy demands of him.

* * *

Cat sat in her window wrapped up in the flat sheet from the bed. She'd stayed awake after Thalia fell asleep and watched the last of the Perseid meteor shower streak across the sky. Observing the stars hadn't been possible within the confines of her prison. Every chance she had to do so became more precious.

The time fast approached when she must find more help than Thalia to fight the demon invasion. If there indeed were demons. There hadn't been any more signs of goblins or demons around her house today. Maybe she had imagined the whole thing. She hadn't exactly been getting very much good sleep lately. *Keep telling yourself that.*

She clasped the sheet, frustrated by the fact that she had to get involved to begin with. Other than Thalia, the only possible assistance to help was Miss Chow, the psychic. They would make some demon slaying team. A sex addict, an elderly woman, and a recluse that merely wants to bury her head in the pillow.

A headlight appeared, coming slowly down the road from the Iron Forge Mine. Her heart beat a bit faster. Was it Aidan? It had to be a worker. The only other thing past the mines were deserted canyons. But it was pretty late for anyone from the Forge to still be there. Business wasn't that booming lately. As it got closer, Cat noticed the familiar outline of a motorcycle

70

coasting down the slight incline. Instead of passing by it turned down her driveway.

Her lungs arrested and she stood stock still, like a deer in the headlights. As it approached, she saw the familiar outline of Aidan and remembered how to breathe.

Aidan rolled his motorcycle to a stop at the foot of the porch and flipped the kickstand in place with the toe of his black leather boot. Cat looked at the hands of the clock that glowed from her dark kitchen, almost nine o'clock. She observed the way Aidan checked his wristwatch and stood at the bottom of her stairs, his helmet in one hand and an envelope in the other. He was considering whether or not to ring her door. Under normal circumstances, she would retreat into her bedroom and wait for whoever knocked on her door to leave. In the first month, she had lived in Ashton she had several visitors. Nice neighbors or nosey neighbors, one or the other. They would leave welcoming baskets on her doorstep when she refused to answer their knocks. Jars of cherry preserves still sat in her cupboard from them remained untouched. She didn't know how to interact with the townsfolk and was even more baffled by the gelled fruit. What exactly was the point? One basket had a pickaxe keychain. She'd hung it from the hook by the door where she kept her eyes focused. Uncertain of what it meant then, she certainly knew what it meant to her now.

Why can't a mineral mine called "Iron Forge" be in the business of mining iron? Had she known how close the red rock deposits were, she would never have moved here. Although the reports Aidan generated said the mine had run dry, that wasn't entirely true. She had felt it the second she entered the mine. The Iron Forge was a powder keg waiting to blow. She shook her head, startled when he turned from the stairs and started to climb on his bike.

Aidan kicked at the ground and swung his leg back on his motorcycle. *He was going to leave.* Cat rushed to the front door and flung it open. When the cool breeze hit her bare legs, she remembered that the only thing between her and total nudity at the moment was a thin, white cotton sheet that had been on the small twin bed when she moved in. Threadbare and practically see-thru, it didn't leave much to the imagination. She scooted her lower half back inside the house.

"Hey, I didn't mean to wake you." Aidan's smile was brighter than the lights dotting the sky. He hopped up the few steps and stopped at the top of the porch. "Is it that late? I lost track of time at work."

"You didn't wake me. I was watching the meteor shower." Aidan turned to look toward the sky, and Cat noticed the envelope in his hand, her name written in a familiar scrawl across the front. "My payments go through Veritex. You didn't need to bring me anything."

Aidan stepped forward, and a telling flush crossed his cheeks as his eyes danced across her cleavage barely contained within her makeshift toga and came to rest on the house numbers above her doorbell. "You asked about the daemon program you found. My boss asked me to give this to you. He says it explains what you saw."

She glanced at his hand and spied the envelope. She felt her own flush and kept her attention on the delivery instead of his gaze. The second Cat's fingers touched the paper, the unique signature of one particular demon made itself known, and it had nothing to do with the handwriting. The radio sitting atop her pellet stove crackled to life, and Sammy Davis, Jr.'s voice sang out, "That old black magic has me in its spell, that old black magic that you weave so well..." Cat lurched towards the outlet and unplugged it before the next verse, but it didn't matter, icy fingers were already crawling up and down her spine.

"Is that the oldies station? I like a lot of that music myself." Aidan peered in through the open front door.

"It doesn't seem that old to me." Cat ripped open the envelope and pulled out the note. *Nice to know you are in town, maybe after my work is done we can meet up again. I'm much better in the flesh. Don't come, I will come to you.* Cat's hands shook, the paper turned into a crumpled ball in her palm. "Does your boss happen to call himself Niro?"

Aidan furrowed his brow. "People didn't usually "call themselves" something. But yes, Victor Niro. Do you know him?"

Too well. Her one-time captor had evolved into her lover, one she prayed never to see again. The fact that he showed himself might mean that he was plotting a way to snatch her back. The details of how she escaped were mired in false recollection. The black tinge of the nightmare returned, and she forced deep lungfuls of breath to keep herself upright. The time for delusions had passed. She rallied her nerves. She could no longer ignore the situation and had to find out more about the Forge before Niro succeeded in whatever warped plan he had hatched.

"I did a job for him once. After a bit more thought, I'm sure I can help you out. Should I meet you back at the office tomorrow?"

"Victor has me going down into the mines tomorrow." He shifted his weight and anchored his black booted feet firmly on the ground. "About today. I got this sense that you were uncomfortable with what I asked you to do. If you're afraid your job might be in jeopardy, then forget what you saw."

His concern warmed her in a way she hadn't felt in a long time. Something that pulled her to him more than a magnet to metal. While a nice man, he was dangerous in many ways. "The mine then. I'll wear pants."

"See you tomorrow." He waved, and she listened to him drive away before shutting the door and latching it tight.

There wasn't much more explaining she could do. What was she supposed to say? *Yes, I know Niro, we dated in the Underworld for a while. There weren't too many eligible bachelors to choose from. He might be a little ticked off I left without saying goodbye. Oh, and he's an asshole.* Speaking of, there was one former demon, also an ex, who she was going to have to call to help her sort this all out. As Thalia would say, she had the worst taste in men.

Cat picked up the phone and dialed the number, hoping his wife wouldn't answer. "Mane, it's Cat, we need to talk. I think they're coming to take me back."

Chapter Five

Aidan peered into the small mirror placed strategically on the wall of his cubicle, the frame angled to alert him of any visitors, namely his boss. Today he wanted to create the illusion of being well-rested when in reality he'd slept little. He tossed and turned half of the night thinking of Cat James, excited one minute and uncertain what the next day would bring. They would be alone again, the two of them in a darkened mine, not the most romantic setting but anywhere in the dark with Cat felt wicked. Granted, the chances of her being interested in him were about as likely as finding a new claim in the overworked mine. But a man had the right to dream.

Betsy had decorated his cubicle for Hawaiian Day with a tissue paper pineapple and grass skirt table. Under less stressful circumstances he might have appreciated her tongue and cheek homage to the tacky, today he had too much on his mind. Aidan pushed the objects aside and laid out the plans for the mine. He always figured that you dug a diagonal tunnel from the top of the earth and just kept going. Apparently, he assumed wrong. Much to his consternation, the mine consisted of six levels with each level following a grid pattern that focused on a cinnabar vein. His predecessors appeared to have been meticulous in their digging. If their guides were still in place, he might have a bit of luck. How could he – an amateur – discover what the top experts in the field failed to find, however?

"Good news and bad news." Norm leaned against the side of Aidan's cubicle, his garish Hawaiian shirt a miss-mash of at least three different prints all stitched together for a trifecta of bad taste. "What do you want first?"

"Damn it, Norm, does everything with you have to be as loud as that damn shirt?" The dull ache between Aidan's brows returned with a vengeance, and he took a swig of his coffee.

"The elevator into the mine broke a long time ago. No easy way into that joint anymore."

"And the good news?"

Norm made the ole poke your finger through the hole in an offensive gesture. "There's always another hole." He leaned over Aidan's shoulder and pointed to a place near the edge of the Iron Forge property. A place on the map marked *Emergency Exit.* "Right over here is a back door of sorts. It slopes down into the first level of the mine, and you should be able to access the rest through a series of internal ramps. The surveillance cams work, so we're getting electricity down there. No one has serviced the hydraulics since forever. It's probably just seized up, so you'll have to use some lube."

Aidan ran his finger over the map, noting the distance markers. "That's about a mile away from where we need to be. Are you sure it's safe to go in there?" While he looked forward to being with Cat, being stranded a half a mile under the earth wasn't his idea of a good time.

"Any hole is safe with the proper preparation. Lee, you got that equipment?" Lee appeared with two yellow mining helmets and battery packs and quickly shuffled away. "Everyone is so stand-offish today. Must be the shirt. They all know who's going to win the award, and it ain't you, my friend."

The black t-shirt Aidan wore wouldn't win best or worst Hawaiian shirt, but it would hide the dirt and the sweat. Perspiration caused by the pressure of making sure everyone at this factory had a job already dotted his brow. If the mine closed down, Ashton would become a ghost town. Inevitably the soil of his family farm, unanchored by crops, would turn to dust that the prevailing valley winds would blow into the clouds and blacken the sky. He had to find some answers. It wouldn't take a squad of zombies to start the apocalypse, only one more dry season and a failed mining operation. Both of which were on his shoulders.

"Why do you need two helmets anyway? You bring one of those science geeks with you?" Norm rubbed his palms together. "There's one gal, she wears this long white lab coat. Tight...ponytail. Would love to see what's under there."

Despite his lack of luck with the ladies, Norm had a vast amount of hope and imagination when it came to his future chances. Aidan wished he could channel Norm's optimism and apply it to his prospects and prospecting. "Every one of the employees in Sector Eight wears a lab coat, Norm. Cat is coming by. She's offered to help out."

"Oh, hey, I've been meaning to tell you something about her. Brother to brother." He pounded his fist on his chest in mock gangster fashion. He lowered his voice and leaned in. Not the usual level of tact Aidan was accustomed to from Norm. "I finally figured out where I've seen her before. The Community Center. You know I like to go there and make sure the ladies don't need a shoulder to cry on, plus they've got the best donuts."

"What meeting was she going to?" His curiosity about this

Cat was going to be his undoing.

"That's the thing. All of them. She either has a lot of issues or likes donuts as much as I do." Norm shrugged. The town of Ashton didn't offer much in the way of dating opportunities, and it didn't surprise him that Norm would be trolling the support groups. That didn't seem like something Cat would do, however.

He wasn't exactly sure how or why Cat seemed keen on helping, but it was only after she had heard his boss' name. Her enthusiasm was suspect. Had she simply dealt with Victor in the past, or was there more between them than employee to employer? A spark of jealousy ignited Aidan's blood. Victor was a swine, a blowhard bully. Some women liked that kind of man. Cat hadn't seemed the type but what did he really know about her? "Is Victor around?"

"In his office. Dang, even the mention of that guy gives me the willies." His friend's whole body shivered, and he smacked his lips like he'd just swallowed a glass of sour milk. He rallied quickly with a lecherous grin. "So you're off to penetrate the tunnel of love with Cat, huh? Just remember, those batteries only last for five hours. After that, you run out of light. Though being caught in the dark wouldn't be too..."

"Norm, please. I'm running out of time." He cut off his wayward pal. Cat was scheduled to arrive at any moment, and Aidan needed information on her relationship with Victor. Something wasn't right about the whole situation, and it suddenly became imperative he figure out what. "Cat mentioned doing a job for Victor. I need you to search through the company records, payroll, anything that might connect them."

"Sure thing. But I won't be doing it before she gets here."

Aidan swallowed his impatience. He didn't have the luxury of waiting. He was about to go into the mine with a woman who might be setting him up. He couldn't tell Norm his suspicions, however, not until he was sure. That didn't mean he had to be happy about it.

Betsy's southern drawl echoed through the lobby and into the open architecture of their office space. "Aloha darling. Nice to see you again. Would you like a pupu?"

"See what you can find out. We'll be back after lunch." Despite his concerns, excitement coursed through him at the thought of seeing her again. Aidan gathered the helmets and clapped Norm on the back. He wasn't sure what exactly he expected Norm to find. But there was a reason Cat had agreed to come back to the Forge, and unfortunately, it wasn't Aidan Ashton.

Aidan entered the lobby, and his mouth fell open. Cat reached forward to accept one of the egg rolls off the tiki head tray offered by Betsy. Upon seeing her in a dress at the fair, he thought he had seen her at her sexiest. He was wrong. Cat had perfected the farm town version of Lara Croft. Black cargo pants and a matching tank top, her long brown hair swept back into a braid. Attached to a thick leather belt was a knife holster which she openly displayed. At first appearance, she looked like a force to be reckoned, the elusion in direct contrast with the shy leg twirl she performed, one black combat boot tucked behind the other. Damn, she was gorgeous, and she had no clue what looking at her did to his pulse.

"Oh Aidan, your guest is here." The phone line rang, and Betsy put down the tray, which gave Aidan the opportunity to close his mouth. "Yes, Sir. I'll let him know." Betsy cupped her hand over the phone. "Mr. Niro would like to see you."

Aidan didn't miss the expression on Cat's face at the mention of his boss — a mixture of curiosity and fear. He tamped down his own impatience with her and with himself. Great, another reason to dislike Niro, the bastard. In the wee hours of dawn, he had determined the best course of action was to ask her about the kiss outright. With the doubts he had, perhaps it might be wiser to wait. It was more than apparent she held some sort of fascination with Niro. To what extent was the big question. "Tell him we'll be up in the afternoon. We've only got a small window of time to get down in the mine and report back before nightfall."

"If you need to meet with your boss, I can wait." Cat tucked her hands in her pocket and stared past Aidan's shoulder towards Niro's office without hesitation. *Like someone intimate with Niro and his affairs.* Or maybe she had been here before. Again, the fog of mystery around her thickened and his own ignorance played into his confusion. Or perhaps he was reading too much into a kiss, one he'd forced on her. He had no business being sidetracked from his goal, to save the town and his farm. He needed to focus on what was important. Bring her down to the mine, make sure she doesn't kill herself and get her back to researching the daemon program and gauging her progress.

"No, we've got our ride waiting for us. Besides, I still need you to see if you can work your magic now that you have that information from my boss on the daemon program. He did give you that information right?"

She gave him a blank look which morphed into a fake smile, like Violet Chanterelle and her ilk served up. "Sure, of course."

"You could stay here and work on the computers. I'm sure if you've done jobs for Niro in the past he won't mind if you set yourself up at my workstation." Aidan was feeling hot under the collar, and it wasn't due to the unusually humid summer that had been plaguing Ashton. All his life women had pandered to him, and he had done his best to fend them off. This was the first time he had experienced a woman who intrigued him and who barely gave him the time of day. The ego he tried his whole life to suppress felt a little wounded.

"I'd rather go with you. I've never seen an actual mine before. Sounds like fun." Cat stepped forward, claimed one of the miner's hats from his hands, deftly clipping the battery pack onto her belt, and balanced it on her head. If more miners looked like she did, the men would be inclined to stay underground longer. Great, Norm's dirty mind had really started to get to him.

Aidan stopped at his cubicle long enough to gather the map and turned his phone on do not disturb. Later, if Victor reamed him about not picking up when he rang, he could blame lousy reception on the mines. The two of them exited the back of the main building that opened out onto the vast expanse of open land, a man-made pit which extended for miles. Ashton's own Grand Canyon. An employee sat at the wheel of an all-terrain golf cart with nubby tires meant for the rugged landscape.

Cat hopped onto the tailgate seat and gripped the aluminum roof support.

He sat next to her, close enough to brush his upper arm with hers. The skin on skin contact struck like lightning. "You can sit inside if you'd rather. It can get a little bumpy across the trestle."

"I'm good." She studied the trellis, and he drank in the sight of her curious regard. "Are you sure this thing is safe?"

"The large wooden trestle was one of the highest in the

world. It took years to finish and used up all the trees in the valley. The locals were opposed to it until they realized how much work it brought in. Train cars full of minerals once passed over this trestle every day. It hasn't given out yet." He didn't mention it was also the fastest, and the bumpiest way across the wide stretch to the emergency entrance Norm had shown him on the map.

"I'm guessing living in this area you can tell me a lot about this mine." Cat used her other hand to grip the backrest and braced her feet against the footrest.

The cart pulled onto the beginning of the tracks, using the narrow lane alongside the rails to traverse the deepest span of the pit. One hundred feet off the bottom of the canyon, the ground dropped out from underneath them.

Cat's fingers gripped her thigh, her jaw tight and her green eyes vigilant. He experienced a touch of admiration for her pluck. This crossing wasn't meant for the meek. Rotting wooden planks, held aloft by rusty bits of wire, stretched out in front of them. The loose slats of the roadway clanked loudly while the bridge shook under their weight.

"I can tell you that they shut down the actual mining of this land about 30 or more years ago."

"Did your family work here?" Cat's voice warbled up and down as they passed over the center span.

Aidan wished the pang in his gut was due to a fear of heights, but he had none. He was feeling a stab at his pride. "No, I'm the first one. Every other Ash has worked in the farming business. The last few years have been hard."

"Oh." Cat focused forward. "The last few years were pretty hard on me too. I get it."

Guilt mingled with his wounded pride. Aidan hadn't even

asked Cat anything about her life before she came to Ashton. He wondered how such a smart and attractive woman had ended up alone in his small town. He loved Ashton, but they didn't have many people moving in. Most people were leaving for the bigger cities and better jobs. Even if he had a choice, he wouldn't go. This was his home. His father needed him. And so did the town.

They reached the end of the tracks, and the cart bounced over the last plank. Cat tumbled onto his lap, and he caught her around the waist before she fell off the edge. She was close enough he could smell the scent of her shampoo — wild and hauntingly beautiful, like the woman in his arms. Pitch pine with blackberries, cranberry, cedarwood, and tomato leaf. Inhaling deeply, he took in her essence. She smelled like a good day on the farm. Something he longed to have again.

"Sorry, I lost my balance there." She hopped off the end of the cart and wandered around the edge of one of the large gravel mounds built to prevent access to the mine site. If he didn't hurry, she'd probably go in without him. Even though she seemed independent, Aidan sensed sadness underneath it all. He wanted to know more, but he also didn't want her to shut down. What Norm said about seeing her at the community center made him think. She was there for a reason. Maybe she wasn't really living in Ashton, more like hiding here.

Aidan checked his watch, tucked the map under his arm and grabbed his cooler from the back seat. "Why don't you come back at 3:30? That should give us enough time to look around. Thanks, Mac."

He watched the cart rumble back across the bridge towards the Iron Forge complex until the sound of the rattling planks disappeared. The harsh noise faded into the bubbling song of the Meadowlark and the distant rush of the River Rouge that flowed free past the dam. Despite having been plowed down to nothing, the forest was reclaiming itself on the outskirts of the mine property, and he would love to see the whole town of Ashton recover its identity again as a good old-fashioned farming town. Many believed the key to prosperity rested down in this mine. Aidan disagreed. He dreaded the thought of the big monstrous boring machines that would destroy the saplings that took root after the miners left and were now tall enough to invite the birds back once more.

"Is there a way around this stuff?" Cat perched halfway up the loosely packed mound, her graceful limbs fighting for purchase.

"Up and over. They try and keep the kids out of here. Iron Forge doesn't want a lawsuit on their hands."

After climbing over a series of four mounds, each one higher than the other they reached the mine entrance carved into the side of a small hillside, pine saplings growing out from the top like a nurse log.

"Someone has a sense of humor." Cat pointed to some graffiti painted in white beside the door that said *Tunnel of Love*. "The kids can probably climb over those things easier than we can. What are you looking for exactly?"

Aidan pulled a set of keys from his pocket and checked over the lock on the door. The metal, flaked in places by years of exposure, was still intact. "We're looking for any signs this mine was abandoned before it was bled dry. Niro wants to make sure the shareholders get every ounce of minerals they paid for." There were no records of the end days of the mine. At least none he could find when he was looking through everything he had access too. Knowing Niro, he probably had the paper records in his office and was laughing behind Aidan's back. Nor had the man been forthcoming with information. Nothing like being set up for failure. But why hire him to do a job if he sabotaged the outcome?

Aidan yanked open the door. The sound echoed through the tunnel that quickly disappeared into darkness less than ten feet from the door. He reached up and flicked on the lantern on his helmet. "We have five hours, let's make the most of it."

He left his cooler at the mouth of the cave and considered the map. Cat clicked the light on her helmet and peered over his shoulder. "Looks like the old foreman's shack isn't too far down. Maybe you'll find something in there."

"You familiar with mines?" Aidan rolled up the map and tucked it into his back pocket. He was hoping to be in and out of this place as soon as possible.

"My Pop worked in the coal mines."

"Your Dad? Weren't most coal mining operations in the United States shut down years ago? Where did he work?" Aidan forced his mouth shut at his rapid-fire questions. He was used to barking orders on the farm, and now he had just done the same thing. "Sorry, I don't mean to pry."

"No, it's okay. I should have said my Grandfather. We called him Pops. He always had a lot of stories to tell. You know those Irish. Whiskey and tall tales."

Aidan tipped his head and inspected the rusted wire mesh above their heads, the only thing keeping the ceiling from coming down on them. "Of course. Let's check out the shack first, great idea."

They both walked carefully into the tunnel. Inspectors from the mine had checked out the supports holding this tunnel together less than three months ago and given it a clean-ish bill of health. Truth be told, the measurements had been fudged a little since no one was really too concerned about workplace accidents where no one worked.

The crunch of dirt under their boots was the only sound. Aidan glanced behind them and noticed the small square of light from the doorway getting smaller and smaller.

"Is it getting warm down here?" Cat paused, fanning her face and dabbing at her forehead with a bandana. "For some reason, I thought it would be cooler."

This far into the mine, the air was much colder than the outside. If anything, the goosebumps on Aidan's arm signaled a drop in the temperature. He shined his light to the right of Cat's face, so as not to blind her. "You look flush. Are you sure you don't want to turn back?"

Cat looked back to the small one-inch spot of light behind them. "No, I want to get to the shack."

Aidan cursed himself for not at least bringing his canteen. The least he could have done was have something for her to drink. "I'm sure it's not too far ahead. Just follow behind me."

His headlamp illuminated about ten feet in front of him. On the ground at his feet, he could see the outline of one thick red arrow, pointed to the right. They led to a large steel door placed into the side of the tunnel. "I guess this is the foreman's shack."

In the opposite direction was the start of the downhill grade to the next level of the mine. They had come to the end of the line. An invisible barrier of caution seemed to blanket him, and he hesitated. Somehow, the metaphor had taken on a life of its own.

* * *

Cat stepped up to the metal door and ran her hand down the cold steel. Shivers ran up her spine and zinged into her brain like an ice cream headache. The deeper they got into the mine, the more she felt the echo of the red rock which once used to be here. There definitely weren't any more deposits. She could tell Aidan that without taking any soil samples. But she couldn't tell him it was because she had spent the better part of the last few years before she came to Ashton in Hell. Actual, literal, Hell.

The fact that Niro was here and the red rock wasn't was further proof he was after something else. That something was most likely her. She yanked on the door in frustration, but it wouldn't budge. "Damn door is stuck."

"Here, let me help." Aidan stepped forward and pressed his full weight down on the lever. It squawked in protest. A grinding of rusted metal in this dank space.

Even though the surface of her skin was chilled, she felt roasted from the inside. A pulsing ache that threatened to melt her from the core. Panic started to set in and she wanted was to escape. In the darkness, her first days in the Underworld awoke from her nightmares and started to play out in the shadows surrounding her. Aidan kicked at the door in frustration, and the echoing clang vibrated through her bones. In the spaces just beyond the reaches of her headlamp, she imagined she saw movement. Unnatural and lithe. Old demons of the first class, with tails, and the hobgoblins and imps. A rustling, reminiscent of the exhales of the death horse, rushed by her ear. All the wicked things she had packed away into the closet in her mind came pouring out all at once, suffocating her in an avalanche of intense fear.

Cat barreled forward and threw her weight against the door,

87

knocking Aidan to the side. It gave a loud screech and swung open. She fell to the concrete floor and breathed deeply of the sanitized air within the space she'd invaded.

A light above her head flickered to life, and she turned to see Aidan with his hand on a switch inside the door. "Are you sure you're okay?"

He brushed the dirt from his pants. Cat envied his apparent ease and felt stupid for her overreaction. The artificial light banished the swelling panic within, and she got herself to her feet. "I guess I didn't realize I'm a little afraid of the dark."

She couldn't think of any other excuse, nor could she tell him the truth. They just needed to find physical proof of what Aidan was looking for, and they could get out of here. The sooner she could leave this town the better. If Niro wanted her, that meant he would have to drag her through a portal. No doubt that was why he needed the red rock, the one element that punched a hole from here to Hell. And she would be long gone before that happened.

"This looks like an old bomb shelter." He reached over to a small desk and dusted off a control panel. A small square of knobs and levers labeled with the words "solar," "temperature," and "waste" was dormant. Cat turned around, sensing the depth of the space behind her, which was lined on one side with shelves of non-perishables and another with two sets of fold-up bunk beds. Aidan picked a tin off the shelf. "Wow. I haven't seen these in years."

He showed her the canister, an antique print with the picture of a kind looking old woman on the front. *Aida Ash's Cherry Filling.* "Aida was my great-grandmother. This must have been down here a long time."

He cracked open the tin and inhaled deep. "You have to

smell this."

He passed her the container, and she peered inside at the swollen balls of fruit soaked in sugar infused syrup. Miss Chow was usually the expert at making her feel like she was at home. Back in the 1950s in Detroit, the time she had been stolen from. One of the first things Cat had done after Hell spat her out was to hunt down anything that would remind her of home. Connect her back to the person she used to be. Very little remained. It is the way of humans to progress and change, and after almost fifty years she found very little that could ground her. Clutched between her hands was a can of the very same pie filling her mother used to make her flaky, buttery crusted cherry pies.

"May I?" Cat's finger hovered over the contents.

"I'd say yes, but I think that spill you took might have dirtied you up a little. Let me help. May I?" Aidan held his hand out, and Cat relinquished the can. She became keenly aware of the availability of beds surrounding them and the knot tightening in her belly.

"My mother used to say that her grandmother's cherries could survive a nuclear war. I guess I'm not surprised that they kept some hidden down here." He dipped his thumb and forefinger into the jelly and extracted one of the plump fruits. The deep red color reminded Cat of her purpose for being there, not to get her jollies off. *But you couldn't be all business all the time.* Thalia would be proud.

She parted her lips and allowed him to place the fruit at the tip of her tongue. His finger lingered on the crease of her bottom lip for a fraction of a second longer than necessary. The heat she felt previously while under the grips of her panic attack returned, but far less alarming. She closed her mouth around the sweet morsel, and the juice burst forth, plummeting her back into memories of the safety she used to feel. And a new, delicious tension, that she associated with Aidan.

"What do you think?" asked Aidan. He raised his finger to his own mouth, licking off the remainder of the jelly.

I think you should have let me do that for you. The act reminded Cat of the brief kiss they shared on the Ferris wheel, and she wanted more. Wanted to sink deep inside the arms of this man. But she knew the moment she did, she would risk losing herself once more. Something she vowed would never happen again. She rubbed her hands on the side of her pants and straightened her shoulders, fighting to focus back on the task at hand. "I think I understand why you want to save your family farm so much. These are wonderful. Should we see if we can find what you were looking for?"

She scanned the small space, trying to keep her eyes off temptation, the jar of cherries and the man standing two feet from her. A metal filing cabinet underneath the desk caught her attention.

"I'm going to see if I can get this panel working."

Cat watched Aidan stare at the controls, apparently unable to make heads or tails of it all. Thankfully this was technology she was familiar with. This mine had been built during the advent of manipulation by fear and bomb shelters: her time. The controls had been converted somewhat, but she excelled at working with what she had and adapting it to fit her needs. Thalia said she was like MacGyver, whoever that was.

"Why don't you let me do that, and you can look through the drawers."

Aidan moved aside, pulling out the small wooden milking

stool stowed under the desk. Despite the looming presence of the mines, the fact that this town was a farming town reflected in every nook and cranny of this place. She squatted and concentrated on the panel in front of her. Aidan cracked open the drawer of the filing cabinet and began shuffling through the papers inside. She tried to ignore the feelings that stirred inside her as his hair fell forward across his cheek. This man was a real honest to god farm boy. Salt of the earth. Connected to this place in a way she had never felt connected.

Shaking her mind free, she concentrated on the panel before her, a combination of old and new technologies. The clearly marked buttons were affixed to a series of copper pipes that snaked up towards the ceiling, disappearing somewhere above their heads. A larger waste pipe, wrapped in black foam exited out the side. Cat followed it down and discovered a series of levers underneath the desk. Surprisingly, everything in this space was clean, like someone had recently been down here. If they were the only ones to have visited in the last twenty-five years, except the inspectors, she would be surprised. She flicked a few levers, and the lights on the panel glowed a dim orange.

"Hey, I think I got it working." She turned to Aidan who studied some papers. He ran a hand through his hair, eyebrows squished together like he needed a pair of reading glasses to understand what was in front of him. The sight was somewhat endearing, and she daren't contemplate why. "Did you find something?"

"I'm not sure. I'll bring these back to the office to study." He folded several of the papers and put them into his pocket. "You say you got that working?"

He changed the subject too quickly, and Cat sensed he was

hiding something from her. Darn it, just when he seemed like the perfect guy. I guess everyone has their secrets, and she was guiltier than most.

The generator which had probably been dormant for years squawked back to life. The walls of their tin cage rattled slightly, the smell of burnt dust puffed through the vents above their head as the system came back to life. "I can check the hydraulics for the elevator. Do you still need to get that sample?"

Cat was anxious to leave. She knew the red rock wasn't down here, knew he wouldn't find anything, and being in such close proximity to this much man was making her start to feel like she knew how hard it must to be for Thalia on a daily basis. Whatever Niro wanted, it was looking more like it might be Cat he came back for. Still, why now?

"We'll need to go down another level to do that. Do you think you are up for it, or would you rather stay here? I think we have another few hours before Mac shows up. Even if you get the elevator working, we should probably be there to meet him." Aidan pulled the zipper up on his heavyweight barn coat and shoved his hands deeper into his pockets. He glanced about the room, looking unsettled.

"You're right, that can wait. I'll go with you."

They entered the darkened cavern once more and switched on their headlamps. The solid beam of light pierced the darkness encircling them. Cat fought back the ever-growing discomfort, reasoning with herself that although they were going deep underground, she wasn't going into the Under-world again. Unlike the images her Catholic parents instilled in her as a child, Hell was not a place that rested somewhere below your feet.

No, Hell was very much alive, but only accessible through one of the many portals that occasionally opened up Earthside. You didn't go to Hell after you died if you were immoral. You went to Hell if the Hellmouth opened and the demons dragged you down with them. It was another world entirely, one of many, infested with beings that had their own agendas.

"I think we're almost at the first juncture." Aidan pointed to the tracks that appeared below their feet and the cameras mounted at the ceiling. A mix of the old and the new. He paused and rested a hand on her shoulder. "Look, I'm not sure why you wanted to come down here with me, but if this makes you feel uncomfortable at all just let me know and we can get out of here."

"Wouldn't that piss your boss off?"

Even though the space surrounding them was immense, Cat suddenly felt like the walls were closing in. His scent was vital and bold, a husky clove spice throbbing with sensuality. She was bewitched by the raw power he exuded and warmed by his gentle touch.

The difference in their height was slight. The only thing keeping their lips apart was a space of about four inches, necessary to avoid the clanking of their helmets. The need Aidan evoked in her was almost painful, Cat had to break off this connection before she broke down in tears. That first kiss had been a mistake, and she wouldn't do that again. She needed to face Niro and figure out his scheme. Being in the mines with Aidan delayed the inevitable confrontation. She hoped Mane would be able to help her, but she wouldn't ask him to sacrifice his life for her. *It was because of him you are in this predicament.* She shook her head. Yes, he had been the reason a target had been put on her back in the first place when his demon overlord decided to take over the earth. Mane had told her what he was from the beginning and had given her a choice. She had taken the risk and paid the price. As a rebellious girl suppressed by the restrictions of the 50s, she'd jumped at the chance for adventure and had gotten more than she'd ever bargained for. She had been given a second chance, but instead of living life, she had hidden away from it. Maybe she would better off returning to Hell, she was putting herself through Hell on Earth as it was anyway.

"I'll get what I need, and we can go." He slipped a cylindrical tool from his pocket and placed it against the bare soil of the wall nearest to them.

"What is that?" Cat had trained herself on all manner of technology when she returned, but this was something new.

"It's a hand auger, for taking soil samples. Honestly, I think this mine is dry. Every sign points to it. But I am not the one calling the shots. I'll just take a sample here, so we have something to bring back." He bent at the knees and pressed the probe into the soil, extracting the sample into the cylinder. He drew it out, leaving a two-foot hole bored into the sidewall. "Got it."

He showed her the sample, clutched between the prongs of the auger, and what Cat saw sent her tripping backward a few steps. The glint of red rock tipped the very edge of the tool. She brushed her hand over the place Aidan took the sample from, and a pulse struck her at the core. Hidden. Somewhere behind these walls, a stash of red rock was hidden, and they had just brushed past the tip of the iceberg. This town was in more trouble than she thought. Time to face the demon that might be responsible.

Chapter Six

The cart stopped at the back entrance to the Iron Forge Mine. Aidan never recalled a time when he needed to escape from a woman, especially one he had the hots for. Cat had thrown so many mixed signals she might as well have been speaking another language. The morning had turned to mid-day, and the growls that rumbled from his stomach echoed his thoughts.

"So what does Niro, think you'll find down there?" Mac drove the cart away, leaving Aidan alone with Cat while she continued the endless series of questions she had peppered him with since leaving the mines. Good news, he had gotten the sample, and the elevators worked. If he had to go back, he wouldn't have to brave the trestle again. Bad news, at least the bumpy ride prevented her from being too nosey. He was getting a distinct feeling that although he had intended to use her to help him, it was actually the other way around. Except he had no idea what she would want other than what every woman in Ashton wanted, a piece of the Ash family pie.

There were only so many questions you can ask when your first concern is falling to your death.

"What do you think he sent me for?" Aidan snapped. She dropped back from his side and fell in step behind him as he reached the door and punched in the entry code. Aidan clutched at his growling stomach and tugged on the metal handle, storming in ahead of Cat. She caught the door.

"The mineral deposits."

"Exactly." Aidan swiveled to face her, her animated color adding to his suspicion. She'd seen him take the sample and she knew how the mine operated. What game was she playing at? The time for guessing was over. "I know why I was sent down to the mines. Why did you come?"

Her eyes widened, and her mouth opened and closed like a fish out of water.

"I'm here at your request, remember? To help you." Irritation sent a wrinkle across her smooth brow, and her jaw tightened.

"Really, and Niro has nothing to do with your curiosity? Or are you 'helping him' as well? You appear to know him." He wasn't sure why he allowed jealousy to dictate his words but something about her and Victor together annoyed him to no end.

"We have met," she said, hesitation in her breathy tone.

There it was again, that softening of her features when she spoke of Victor. Irritation sparked his temper, and he crossed his arms and glared at her. "Why do I get the sense there is something more to that than you are letting on? What are you hiding, Cat?"

"Have you ever heard of the phrase none of your business?" Color flooded her cheeks and indignation etched in every jerky movement as she snatched her leather jacket from the hook and shrugged it on. "I didn't ask to get sucked into his. *You* asked *me* for help, and I stupidly said yes. I knew it was a mistake. Good luck. I thought we were making some progress, but apparently, I was wrong."

Her words extinguished the fury, and he clasped her arm, halting her withdrawal. "You're right, I asked you to help me."

She cast a pointed glance at his hand, and he became aware that he still touched her, the warmth of her body penetrating the leather under his palm. Decency said to release her, yet that tiny voice that wanted to seduce her whispered to swoop down and taste her lips. It was possible that he had misjudged her, that he could trust her, unlike all the other women in Ashton. She didn't seem like the type to care about wealth. Not like his family had much of that anymore.

"I'm sorry, this isn't any easier for me than it is for you. I really don't want you to see the ass-chewing Victor will, no doubt, be giving me, but if he has information you need to help get these reports sorted out, it would mean a lot. It would mean my job actually."

Cat tucked a lock of hair over her ear and looked up at him. The pain reflected in her eyes almost caused him to hand his handkerchief to her. She was on the verge of tears again, but this time it was definitely his fault. Despite all his shortcomings, at least Norm didn't make women cry. He might make them shudder in disgust, and possibly nauseate them, but there was a thing or two he could learn from his friend's lax approach to dating. The problem was, being around Cat evoked something primal within him. He had no idea where the idea to feed her cherries had come from. He had barely enough willpower to keep from using those abandoned cots down in the mines. Good thing he hadn't. That whole place was wired with cameras. Norm definitely would have pressed record.

"You guys are just in time for the dogs." Norm appeared in the doorway to the lunch room, a toasted bun between his fingers. Piled high with sautéed peppers and onions, jalapenos, and hot mustard, he had created his own hazard zone. "I call this one the *Home Wrecker*. Fifteen inches of pure beef. Want one?"

Norm made a hot dog every day for lunch, and every day Aidan refused his offer. Today his stomach betrayed him.

"No need to ask my man, consider your order taken. How about you Cat, you like dogs too?" Norm shoved about three inches into his mouth, way too much to chew all at once. He smiled and then started choking mid-chew.

Aidan cursed under his breath and positioned himself behind Norm. He reached his arms around his waist and place his fist just above his navel, grabbing his fist tightly with his other hand. If he weren't choking to death, Aidan would rather be punching him in the gut. This would have to do. He pulled his fist abruptly upward, forcing the air, and three inches of masticated beef from Norm's windpipe. It landed with a splat at Cat's feet. Her face turned from pale peach to slightly green. Norm had been forgiven, but Aidan still wanted to know what her intentions were.

"Damn, that was grade-A meat by-product." Norm bent down and collected his discarded meal between two napkins. "You guys still want one."

Aidan waved him off. "Nah, never mind. I'm no home wrecker. I like to keep things open and honest. No need to hide things." He turned his attention back to where he had left his conversation off with Cat.

"Oh man, speaking of hiding, you better do your best today. Bossman was all around this joint looking for you. I think he's pissed that you went down into the mines without talking to him first." Ever the adventurer Norm put another three inches of the Home Wrecker into his mouth, bits of sauerkraut sticking to his mustache. If ever there was a diet program that would work it would be watching that man eat because you were almost guaranteed to lose your appetite afterward.

"Incoming." Norm started to choke again but recovered enough to duck into the depths of the lunchroom.

Aidan felt the depth of his boss' stare before he heard his name exit his clenched lips.

"I see you decided to skip our morning meeting." Victor's voice echoed down the slender corridor, his lapels flapping open in response to his speed. "I have reasons for what I ask, and I expect you to..."

Victor skidded to a halt when he came face to face with Cat. Aidan watched her hand go to the knife at her waist, white knuckles gripping the handle. Her face turned ashen. This wasn't the reaction of someone with interest in his boss. She was scared, deathly afraid.

Victor jerked his head back, and his surprised reaction turned to one of amusement. He displayed a wide grin. "Well, a pleasure to see you again Ms. ..."

"James, Catherine James." Cat shrank back without moving, her shoulders rolling inward. Aidan couldn't help but notice she hadn't introduced herself as Cat. Something was wrong. "I don't believe we have met."

Victor laughed and slapped his leg like some lunatic. At that moment, his coiffed boss would have made the Nazis scared. "Silly me. Of course, working remotely you probably don't meet many of those you work with. And no, we haven't officially met. Cat."

At the sound of her nickname, the tension between them turned thicker than the air down in the abandoned mine. "Cat

99

is helping me with the reports. She accompanied me to the mine this morning so she could understand what we were dealing with."

Victor snatched Cat by the elbow. "I thought Aidan here was going to deliver my note to you. Obviously, you didn't get it."

Cat shook off his grip and crossed her arms over her body, her previous fear seeming to melt away into confidence. "I got it. It's why I decided to come down here. I needed to see the daemon for myself. How else was I supposed to figure out how to get rid of it?"

"You don't know what you think you found. You have no clue." Aidan sensed a deeper meaning behind the words.

"We can meet now," said Aidan.

Victor tipped his head to the side. He rubbed at his ear like Aidan's voice was a mere annoyance to him, the buzzing of a fly. "You get lunch, and after you come back, you *will* report to my office. Miss James will come with me. We have much to discuss."

Given her earlier fear, Aidan couldn't, in good conscience, allow Niro to manipulate her. Knowing he might regret it later, he cleared his throat and moved closer to Cat. "She hasn't eaten anything since the morning. We were just going out to lunch."

Niro's chuckle held little humor. "You go to lunch. Cat and I need to talk. Right, Cat?"

Before Aidan could formulate a rebuttal, Cat placed her hand on his sleeve. Their eyes met, and he spied the appreciation for what he tried to do coupled with resignation. "It's okay. I will meet up with you later."

Aidan slipped the sample from his pocket and watched them disappear down the hallway. He didn't trust Niro. The pang in his gut was from more than hunger. This just didn't feel right.

Aidan looked down at the core sample in his hand. Red dust coated the end of the auger.

* * *

"You don't have to escort me. I have no problem keeping up with you." The hand on her elbow brought back severe memories. Her last night in Detroit flashed before her eyes as she sped down the hallway after Niro.

She and Mane had been hot and heavy in the front of his Cadillac. The instant she'd met Mane at the Temple Hotel for her happy hour fix things had gotten serious. Known by the local gossips as a gay and lesbian hook-up joint, Cat often went there for the show and the attention. None of the more upscale customers would ever admit such things were going on under their noses.

Thick scrolling details graced the bar of the Temple Hotel. That night she had hooked her Mary Jane heels on the bar stool and ordered a whiskey sour. The bartender returned with the glass and a napkin, bearing a message. Before she could read it, the song "Fever" blared from the brass band on the stage. The Temple Hotel had the best cover bands.

You're more than you appear. So am I. Can we talk?

Cat glanced up and immediately met the gaze of a man in a navy pinstriped suit. Despite wearing the usual garb of the men she had to call boss on a daily basis, this man wasn't looking down at her, he was staring directly into her. Into her soul.

They quickly struck up a conversation and hours later, she was spilling to him her deepest desires. Never in a million years did she imagine she'd hook up with a real demon. The three whiskey sours were the only thing that kept her from bolting. She made him promise to never mention it again, and they started dating. The man was perfect, she didn't want to believe he was possessed, except that was what he was. He told her, and she didn't want to accept it as true. She taught him to control his impulses, taught him to be the lover she had always desired. He followed her lead. He wasn't a demon. He was an angel.

On the night she met Niro, they had been getting hot and heavy in the car. The windows had steamed over from their lovemaking session when the door suddenly opened. Before either of them could react, she was dragged from his lap, half-dressed, by men in masks. Kicking and screaming she looked back to the car and saw Mane, pinned to the seat by another. Horrified and shocked by the sight of her nightmares come to life, she was tossed into a waiting van. She thought all the terrible stories her mother warned her about strangers were about to come true. They would rape her and then kill her. That would have been preferred to what actually happened.

They drove for what seemed like hours until they were in a heavily wooded area she didn't recognize. The masked men jerked her out of the van and forced her to walk. She cried and begged for mercy, but her pleas egged them on. The rag they shoved into her mouth tasted like grease and sulfur, and the rope they tied it with burned her skin. She fought then, fought with every ounce of strength she had left while they dragged her through the underbrush, further into the woods. Sharp sticks and rocks cut at her bare legs. Despair replaced rage, and she started to feel the terror of someone about to be killed.

Daylight broke the horizon when they entered a clearing and dropped Cat to the ground. She lay helpless on her side, her arms bound behind her back. Mouth gagged. Naked. Cold. Two of them stood on either side of a large blackened circle on the ground that looked like someone had lit a fire, leaving a charred ring. The taller of the two swept back his hood, revealing a mop of bright orange hair. He turned to look at Cat, and his eyes flashed red. She was too stunned to scream.

He reached into his pocket, drawing out a handful of red dust that he sprinkled over the circle. The ground began to churn, and the ring became a swirling vortex. Cat blinked, disbelieving of what appeared before her eyes. A dark black pit that seemed to suck all the surrounding light. The wind whipped fierce, and the hood of the other man fell back. Well, not a man, definitely not human. The creature had deep plum skin, his canines protruding over his lower lip. And the eyes, the eyes were a dark red, just like the other man. The man she now knew as Niro.

During her first few days in Hell, or what seemed like days, he had pretended to befriend her. She quickly learned that you can't trust anyone in Hell. Should have been obvious, but when you are desperate, you cling to anything you can.

The tall, handsome man standing before her now little resembled the demon he was. She watched Niro tug on the collar of his stiff button down. She kept reminding herself that they were on her turf now, though with that red dust that could change in an instant. Mane had explained that demon circles occurred between worlds, most just hiding. Waiting to be found. The key to opening the portal was red dust. The discovery of the red rock meant that the means to open it lived right next door to her.

He went right to his desk. Cat slammed the door shut behind them with more force than necessary. She needed to keep a brave front and show no fear. Niro sat and kicked up his feet in the sanitized space which contained only a large wooden desk, green phone, a mirror, and a chair.

"You can try a little harder you know. Most *real* people actually have photos of their loved ones. Whose life did you ruin this time?" Cat stood in front of his desk, arms crossed over her chest. If Niro thought he could drag her back to Hell, he was in for a fight.

"What? This?" Niro pinched his chin between his fingers and checked himself in the mirror. "You have to admit though, finding another one with red hair...pretty brilliant."

Fury tingled throughout her body, and she refused to stand back and allow him to manipulate her. She decided to cut through the bullshit and call him out. "What are you doing here? What are all of you doing here? Don't think I didn't notice the rest of them."

Niro's relaxed demeanor morphed into a sneer, and he quickly stood tall. The distinct scent of sulfur wafted over the desk and seemed to fill the space of the small room in an instant, triggering a Pavlovian response Cat learned in all those years in Hell. She wanted to back away as far as she could and flatten herself against the door, but she forced herself to stand her ground. If she ever hoped to win, she needed to remain strong.

"Can't a guy get a little vacation?"

"You said it was work in your note." Her quick retort strengthened her resolve.

"Maybe a little of both. Especially since you are here." He closed the space between them, his body pushing hers until her shoulders met the hardwood of the door. "Just because you got a free pass Earthside doesn't mean you get to stay."

He grasped her face in his hand and pressed his lips against hers, pinning her in place. Her mind began to drift from her body, separating the physical from the mental and taking her away from the nightmare. In Hell, the less you fought, the quicker it was over, and you could get back to trying to hide so that you didn't draw any attention to yourself.

No. The stubborn side of Cat whispered. *You are no longer trapped, no longer weak. You have a choice this time, and it is to fight.* There was no demon portal in this office, and the mortal body in front of her could feel pain. She drew back and smacked him in the jaw. "Back off!"

Niro reeled back, a look of surprise on his face. His rubbed his sore jaw and grinned. "If you know what's good for you then you'll stay away. I'll be keeping my eye on you."

Cat swiveled around and tore open the door. A few people who had been milling about the hall darted away, and Cat realized the blinds had been open. Whoever had been walking by had seen their entire exchange. She prayed Aidan hadn't been one of them. She had to help him now. They were on the same journey whether he realized it or not.

If Niro were here to take her back to Hell, she sure would make it hard for him. She knew where he was stashing the red rock and if she could dispose of that then maybe she could wreck his entire plan.

* * *

Aidan caught himself on the edge of his cubicle, his eyes not quite believing what he just saw. After Victor dragged Cat down the hall, he kept his distance. She had a knife at her waist and obviously a discussion that she needed to get off her chest, and for once her anger wasn't directed at him. But with the door shut and the blinds wide open, he could see everything that passed between them. He knew Victor was an asshole, but this was worse. Cat was scared of him, and Victor forced himself on her.

He stood quickly as she slammed the door and raced towards the lobby. Strands of hair escaped her ponytail and plastered themselves to the side of her face. She was more out of breath and sweaty than when they were down in the mine.

He dashed toward her and was stopped by Norm. "Hey man, ran that search you wanted. Doesn't look like Cat has ever done a job for Victor before. At least not one that is on the books. If you catch my drift."

"Sorry, not now, Norm." He jostled past his friend, determined to get to Cat.

"A moment please, Aidan." Victor's voice boomed across the sea of cubicles. Aidan froze in his tracks. He watched Cat continue out the front door. If he wanted to keep his job, he would need to see what Victor wanted and try to prevent himself from punching him in the face.

Aidan turned, and Norm ducked back into the copy room he came from. Victor leaned against the door frame of his office, one foot crossed over the other. He crooked a finger in Aidan's direction and beckoned him inside.

The auger in Aidan's pocket knocked against his hip bone. He wanted to take the thing out and bounce it off Victor's arrogant jaw. To give him a taste of his own medicine. He plodded toward the entrance of his boss's office. The portal to Hell, if you will. It might as well be. It was the last place he wanted to be.

Victor gestured to the chair in front of his desk, closed the door and the blinds. Aidan had the horrible suspicion that

Victor had planned that little display for his benefit. Was this all about jealousy? Was Cat one of Victor's ex-girlfriends or something?

The silence was deafening. Not even Victor's Ferragamos made a sound against the plush carpeting as he walked around the desk. When he passed within an inch of Aidan, goosebumps broke out across his arms. His throat went dry. His body was responding in fear, and Aidan wasn't entirely sure why.

The second hand on the wall mounted clock ticked loudly, echoing through the barren office space. Aidan had never really taken notice of it before. Niro seemed a permanent fixture in the office, yet the office could have been unoccupied. It was too clean, too uncluttered. Not even a pencil looked out of place. No one had questioned when Victor Niro had appeared out of nowhere six months ago and set up shop. Maybe they should have.

Victor sat in his chair, steely gray eyes boring into him over the fingers steepled under his chin. "What am I going to do with you?"

"Excuse me?" Aidan swallowed the lump forming in his throat. He was so close to getting the bonus, the money he needed to make sure the crop was planted on time. He had done everything this sadistic asshole had asked him to do. Aidan's geology degree was framed and nailed to the inside of his cubicle. What did this guy have? A mandate from God?

Victor opened the desk drawer in front of him and pulled out a tablet. He pecked at the screen a few times, turning it around so Aidan could see. On the display were several windows, each showed a camera shot from inside the mine. He had been watching them the entire time they were down there.

"There were a few interesting things on this footage that, I must say, was very shocking to me." He double tapped on one screen, bringing up the image of him and Cat in the foreman's office. He watched as he fed the cherry to Cat, her eyes intent on his every move.

"We were hungry. Old memories. My grandmother..."

Victor held up his hand. "Please, I'm not finished." He tapped another screen, bringing up the moment in the first level of the mines when he and Cat had been close enough to kiss, except they hadn't. The problem with the camera angle was that it was behind Aidan's head. Their movements made it look as though they had shared an embrace.

"I can explain." Aidan's desire quickly evaporated. He shot up out of the chair, and the auger flew from his pocket, dancing across the desktop and plopping into Victor's lap.

Victor set the tablet aside and plucked the instrument from his pressed slacks. He brushed the errant dust from his dry clean only wardrobe. If nothing else, Aidan would have to foot the bill for that one. Victor looked from the auger and back to Aidan, his features hardening.

"Tell me who took this sample, was it her?" He shook the auger, and the dry soil inside cracked, the entire thing emptying onto his desktop. The particles of red rock were lost somewhere in the mess.

Aidan took a step back, just as Cat had done, whatever their exchange had been he needed to know about it. "No. I did. Cat was just there to watch and see if anything would be valuable to her finding out why we are having this problem with the numbers."

"We? We are not having problems with the numbers." Victor slammed his hand on the desk, and a cloud of dust rose into the air. "You are having problems with the numbers. And it is a problem you are going to fix. And fix alone. I let Ms. James go just now. She wasn't too happy about it, but I do not need unauthorized personnel roaming around the largest asset this mine has."

Aidan spied some of the red dust as the cloud settled. Perhaps all his efforts hadn't been for nothing, maybe something remained that he could show Victor and still walk away with his bonus despite all this mess. "Look, we did find something down there."

Victor didn't follow Aidan's gesture. He leaned across the desk. "I should never have sent you down there. And it doesn't matter anyway. The shareholders have made their decision. In a week this mine will be shut down."

All the hopes Aidan had cascaded like a torrential downpour from the place in his heart into a puddle at the bottom of his Doc Martins. All those years away from the farm. All that time in school so that he could provide a better life for his father. Gone. The sacrifices he had made meant nothing. He wasn't willing to believe that to be true.

"There's nothing we can do to stop this?"

Victor rubbed a pinch of dirt back and forth between his fingers, letting it fall back to the desk. "It's going to take a lot more than a little fairy dust to fulfill the contract."

Through the thickened air a flash of red crossed Victor's eyes, like the horrible after effect of an overexposed photo. Aidan rubbed the dust from his vision. These late nights were starting to get to him.

Victor sat down and picked up the phone on his desk. "You can go now. Oh, and don't go blabbing to everyone about the shutdown. If you do, I'll make sure yours is the first severance package to get cut." Victor pushed down on the call button to reception. "Get me somebody. I don't care anybody. And while I'm waiting, get me someone else."

Aidan took that as his cue to escape this strange confrontation. He resisted the urge to go to his desk and pack up now. He would be of more use working on the farm for one week than staying here and waiting for a meager severance. But there was still a chance. If he could get Cat to figure out this daemon program and search the mine again maybe they could find enough material to fulfill this contract Victor mentioned. Speaking of contracts, he remembered the folded paper in his pocket He would need to ask his father about that.

First, he needed to catch up with Cat.

Having the hum of the motorcycle engine between his legs focused his thoughts. If Cat were fired, she could still help him remotely. She probably had her ways, computers being what they are these days. He couldn't imagine the Iron Forge having much of a security system set up. The more significant problem would be trying to convince Cat to help him when she had some kind of past with Victor. Maybe now that she was no longer an employee, he could pursue a romantic relationship with her without complication.

It didn't take long to get to Cat's front door, but from the looks of things, he wasn't the only one. Not only was Thalia's pale pink Vespa parked out front, but 1958 Edsel convertible in mint condition. A car like that must have cost a fortune. If nothing else, he knew that whoever owned it wasn't a resident of Ashton.

Aidan pulled off his helmet and set it on the handlebar, unzipping his leather jacket before alighting the staircase. From inside the sounds of laughter and the low beat of music indicated a party, not a funeral over losing her job.

He knocked three times and waited for what seemed like an eternity before the door swung open. Cat appeared, breathless, on the edge of laughter. Her countenance sobered at the sight of Aidan. So much for providing a soothing shoulder in her time of need. While he was getting berated by Victor, she was apparently already toasting her detachment from the Forge. And it wasn't even dark yet.

"Aidan, what are you doing here?" Cat popped up on her toes, looking over his shoulder. "Are you alone?"

"Yeah, I'm sorry. I just wanted to catch up with you after you shot out of there. Victor can be a real ass. I didn't mean to get you fired."

Cat rolled her eyes and crossed her arms over her chest. She had already walled him out, and he hadn't even asked her the tough questions yet. "Honestly, I'm glad. I've dealt with him before on other projects. Not at the Forge, but another job I was on for an extended time. He literally made my life a living Hell. Needless to say, I wasn't too excited to see him."

Of course, that explained it. Aidan never even considered Cat's life before coming to Ashton. He'd lived here his entire life and only left for the years he was in college, going just as far as the University of Oregon so he could still come back to Ashton and help his father on the farm. You forget that anything exists outside the town border. He wanted to know more about this woman. If only he could get her alone, maybe they could focus on something other than the Forge for even a brief moment.

In the doorway behind her appeared a man about six inches taller than Aidan in his cowboy boots. Muscled arms bulged beneath a white cotton t-shirt and Levis. He cocked his shorn head to the side and hooked his thumbs in his belt loops. Aidan noticed the man assessing him, and he raised his chin a notch. "Sup."

"Oh, Aidan. This is Mane. He's a friend of mine. He came to help me with my equipment."

The man standing behind her looked more like Tarzan than a techie. An intimating figure to be sure. Were he and Cat involved? Is that why she was so distant?

"Mane, come pour me another glass," shouted Thalia from the living room. Definitely not a work meeting. Asking Cat for help now wasn't a good idea.

He held his hand out for a goodbye handshake. "Have a good night. Hopefully, we'll see each other around town."

He turned and hopped down the stairs without waiting for a reply. Jealousy burned in his chest, and he didn't want to stay and crash their party. He had a week to figure out what to do and wasting time was not one of those things. His next stop was his father and the contract. Finding an ancient looking document with the names of his ancestors in a drawer in the Iron Forge Mines was a mystery he wanted to solve.

Chapter Seven

Cat watched Aidan speed away on his motorcycle. Dust rose into the late afternoon sun as the bike struck the horizon, blurring her vision of him and whatever strange connection existed between them. It was probably for the best. If Niro was here to take her back, she didn't want Aidan to be taken down with her.

"Why did he leave in such a hurry?" Mane strutted back into her cottage. She knew him well enough to know he had guessed why Aidan had left. Because of him. Although he'd been granted a new life as a human, he hadn't lost his cockiness or his confidence.

"You know full well why he left? Kind of the same reason your wife isn't here right now."

Mane flopped on the couch and slammed his legs onto the barren coffee table. "Kit just started working at the station. Takes after her old man. She makes a great cop. Sexy as Hell in that uniform." He emptied his glass of wine and poured another for himself first, then Thalia who was curled up on the couch next to him, her legs tucked underneath her, elbow resting on the back edge.

Cat was happy for Mane. He had gotten his second chance. He was no longer a demon, but he still had all the memories of his past — hundreds of years of memories. She didn't like to pull him back into her life, but there was no one else she could trust. No one that owed her as much as Mane.

Mane handed her a glass so full that the red wine spilled onto her hand. She dipped down, licking the drops from her finger. Thalia let out a moan.

"Geez, Thalia!" Her friend was more keyed up than usual. Between the date with Norm and missing out on her SAA meeting, this succubus was on edge.

"Sorry. I promise I'll keep myself under control."

Mane leaned back, his biceps flexing. She threw a blanket over him. "Keep those under control too, Mister. You're not helping."

Mane snickered and wrapped the heavy wool around his shoulders. "Better? Now you were about to get to the details of why you hauled me out to this nowhere town. I'd go to the ends of the Earth to help you. But Kit does get a tad bit jealous, and now she's armed."

Cat returned to her previous activity and paced the length of the red runner that went from her front door to the middle of the living room, following the border of herringbone em-broidery set an inch from the edge. She was literally going in circles and making no progress with her feelings for Aidan or her dilemma with Niro.

Without stopping, she described Niro. Mane wasn't in Hell with her, and he didn't fully understand the extent of the tortures she endured. He was aware of some of the tortures she doled out. He had been on the receiving end. One day they would talk about that. Not now.

"Do you think he is here for me?" The question she ached to ask him since he walked through the door shot out of her mouth and fell flat to the ground like a stone.

Thalia untucked herself, setting her feet to the floor and moving to the edge of the couch cushion, ready to fold herself around Cat should the walls begin to crumble. Thalia, who Cat was closest to, hadn't even heard all the grisly details of her imprisonment. It was bad enough that when she was finally spat out of Hell, she had brought some of it with her. The ability to see the demons that walked the Earth. The one thing she wanted to forget and was what she was left with. Mane might think she was getting a second chance, but her Hell had never really ended.

"No, if he wanted you, then he would have taken you." He filled his glass again.

"But he's a demon and an asshole. He enjoys toying with me."

Mane emptied his glass and stood, looking as if he were ready to leave this nightmare. He rubbed the back of his neck and cleared his throat. "Niro is a collector. It's what I was when you met me. He was sent to bring someone or something back. The only reason he would still be here is that he doesn't have what he was assigned to retrieve."

Shock hit Cat in waves and sent her balance off. She tripped over the edge of the runner and fell into Thalia's outstretched arms. One benefit of being something other than human is quick reflexes. Breathless she started to put together everything Mane had just said.

"In Detroit, when you met me, was I the one you were supposed to collect?" Tears rimmed her eyes. Being in Hell, she was often reminded of her inherent evil. She had been wild. Lived on the edge and hadn't followed the rules of society. It was why she was chosen, why they hadn't killed her the second she arrived. Maybe there was something evil living inside her.

That was why she could still see the demons. What if she was one of them?

Mane stepped forward and wrapped his arms around her. He brushed a soothing hand up and down her back, holding her back from the edge of a breakdown. "No. Absolutely not. The reason they abducted you was to punish me. I've told you this before. I abandoned my job to be with you. It was selfish. I'll forever be sorry for putting you through it."

The shivering stopped and pulled back up into her core. The fear crawled back into its shelf in her heart and settled in for the long haul. No matter what Mane said, she still didn't believe that she was anything but evil.

Mane helped Thalia bring Cat to her feet again. "Look, you see all these things because you were captive for so long. The Black they injected into your body probably hasn't left you. But it isn't your fault. Look, if you want to figure out what Niro is doing here, you need to stay close to that guy."

"Aidan." Just saying his name soothed something inside her. She remembered the brief kiss they had on the Ferris wheel. The feeling she had as a regular girl kissing a regular guy. She wanted that feeling back. And she wanted to make sure that nothing happened to Aidan. He didn't deserve to suffer just because she had moved into his town.

She smoothed her hands down the front of her blouse and inhaled a calming breath. "I'll call him."

Thalia turned down the radio. Cat took the flyer with Aidan's number written on it and reached for the phone. It rang twice before the line picked up.

"Hello?"

His voice sounded agitated, but of course, he was. Cat couldn't blame him. She hadn't exactly welcomed him with open arms. Hadn't exactly been honest with him.

"It's Cat. Look, I wanted to say I'm sorry. I know your problem is serious and I probably didn't make things better for you by getting all upset at Niro. Can we meet up again to sort through everything? I'm sure with all the upgrades my friend helped me with I'll be able to sort through that data and figure out what is happening with your soil samples."

Her breath came out in a heavy pant. Everything she wanted to say flew out of her mouth in one breath. She hoped he didn't think her a blabbering idiot, or worse, a crazy woman. The sound of silence on the other line was deafening. "Hello?"

"Uh, yeah, I'm here." Aidan sounded hesitant. "I would appreciate any help. Can you come over to the house for dinner tomorrow night?"

"I'd love to."

* * *

Aidan replaced the phone in the cradle in utter shock at the conversation that had taken place. Cat was coming over for dinner.

He looked around the room and panicked. The Ashton Estate had once been a grand affair. Marble colonnades supporting two floors of opulence. Posh furniture and candelabras, not what you would usually expect from a farming family. But back before his father and grandparents, this place had been one of the first estates on the west coast. The Ashton family, tired of the backlash they were taking in the south because they owned slaves, pulled up their stakes, packed their wagons—or their slaves did—and moved out here. The Ashton Estate had been the grandest mansion on the entire west coast. Now it was a tomb, stuffed with all the old memories both good and bad.

Aidan didn't like that he lived under the roof of former slave owners and that those people had been his family. Even after a hundred or so years, the stigmatism of slavery still lingered. Violet Chanterelle was a prime example of that. She was a west coast southern belle attracted by the outer accouterments of this Estate and the Ashton name. Little did she, or any of the others, know the state they were in.

The last time the walls had been painted was about five years ago, about the time his father had been able to walk on two feet.

"Was that the little filly you were talking about?" His father readjusted himself in the recliner that sat in front of the fireplace. The fire was built a few logs high. Firewood was scarce these days, and they needed to save the majority of it for winter. Dad always complained of the cold, and his complaints seemed to worsen more of late, no matter the season. The doctors said it was normal. Aidan wasn't so sure. He set his book aside, removing his reading glasses to rub at the bridge of his nose.

It killed Aidan to see his father this way. Even at fifty, his father had been active until the accident. His mother had passed away three weeks earlier, and his father had pulled himself out of his depression, in the very chair he sat right now. He said he intended to check on the crops and hopped on the tractor, speeding off to the outer edge of the property before Aidan could even get his pants on.

It only took one gopher hole to catch the wheel and send the tractor over on its side. By the time Aidan caught up with him, his father was pinned underneath the green beast mumbling nonsense. "Take me, take me instead." He repeated it over and over. A man lost in his ramblings and grief.

Adrenaline had raced through his veins, and he shoved the gas giant off his father, all the while hollering for anyone to bring help. He scooped up his father in his arms. Never once did he think he would be in the position of taking care of the man who had always been so independent all his life. Now he was the one who needed to be strong and protect his father. He couldn't tell him Victor's prediction about the mine shutting down. As long as he lived, he would continue to fight for this land that every generation of his family had put so much blood, sweat, and tears into. His mother was buried in the family plot not fifty yards from the house, and his children would always know their family line.

"Not a filly Dad. This one is a wild mare." He settled into the chair opposite his father, his mother's chair. She loved to sit and watch all those silly crime dramas with his father at night until they were both asleep in their chairs. Aidan had to corral them up into their bed. "And I have no idea how to tame her."

"Am I ever going to meet this gal? I don't get out much, but the gals you got coming around here to make sure I eat have been talking." His father's skin was creased and leathery from his time out in the sun, and when he smiled, the deep creases in his skin made him look even more jolly than Old Saint Nick. With his mop of white hair and wispy beard, he had been offered the job as Santa at the fairgrounds the last few years in a row. It was one of the things that always brought a smile to his face, even after his mother died.

"Yes, Dad. You will meet her. But she's just a business associate. Or was, before she was let go today." A pang of guilt hit him in the gut, however, maybe he had done her a favor. At least she wouldn't have to deal with Niro anymore. Aidan remembered the muscular form of the man who was at her house when he showed up. Even without the complications, he might not be her type. "She has a lot of baggage."

"So do you, boy." His father replaced the glasses on his face and picked up a stack of papers sitting next to him. He thumbed through each one, and with every flip, his exhaustion appeared to increase. Despite Aidan's insistence that his father retire completely, his father insisted that he continue working the books and arranging the help. It wasn't a job that was any easier than the physical labor. Aidan could see that each time he reviewed the books his optimism faded. And they weren't even at the worst of it yet.

"Dad, you can't keep me in the dark. I know things are far worse than you say. Pablo keeps asking me when you are going to call his boys back to schedule the picking this year. I can't keep putting him off." The cherry blossoms were almost to peak. In a few days, all the pink petals would rain down, giving way to the fruit that ripened of its own accord. Blossoming red and full without the slightest effort on the farmer's part. Mother Nature worked her miracles, but mortal men pulled in the harvest before the crows descended and ruined everything like Niro threatened to do.

His father folded the paper, the parchment was brittle and crunched under his hand. Aidan palmed the paper in his pocket, the one he swore he was going to ask his father about. But it was just a stupid legend, and the last thing his father needed was to revisit the sins of his forefathers tonight. He already felt like he was responsible for the downfall of the farm.

"That's what you're working for. I'll call Pablo. Don't worry. I need to study the fine print on these old contracts and see if there ain't a way we can't come up with a little more time to get this farm back on track. The land is good. It needs to be reminded of that." His father grunted as he tried to push himself up to standing.

Aidan rushed to his father's side and looped an arm around his shoulder. "Let me help you, Dad."

He tucked his father into bed with little trouble. His frame was a lot lighter than it had been when he was working twelve hours on the farm.

Aidan sat back into his father's chair to keep watch over the fire until the coals died down. He looked at the piles that lay in each corner of the room. Memorabilia and boxes that were displaced after Mom died and never moved. Every time his father dug through another closet looking for something, the trail of destruction he left around the house remained and Aidan didn't have the energy to clean it up or the heart to tell his father that the one thing he was looking for he would never find. Mom was gone, and there was nothing that could bring her back.

Chapter Eight

She stared up at the ceiling, the crack that ran along the vaulted white plaster reminded her that something wasn't quite right about the situation with Niro. A thought had been nagging at her, and since she had the whole day available before she was set to meet Aidan, a bit of investigation might be in order. And she would start with the next-door neighbor and why he left the bowl of dust of her porch. Now was as good a day as any to confront the hellion. And she really hoped he wasn't actually from Hell.

Cat looked over at Thalia who snored in the bed next to her. Somehow, even with a typical human constitution, Mane had managed to drive himself to a hotel in the town over. Cat had stayed wide awake until he called to confirm he had made the drive back. The last thing she needed was Mane's wife mad at her. Sure, she might not be a selkie Queen anymore, but she probably had her connections.

She swung her feet to the floor and pulled on the nearest pair of jeans. A couple of sturdy boots and t-shirt later she was ready to face whatever the little bastard had to give her. She slipped the six-inch blade into the sheath at her side. Around town, no one blinked twice if you carried a knife. It was one of the good things about living in the country.

When she reached the doorway, she turned and looked back

at her friend. "Thalia," Cat whispered. "I'm going to the Harper's house."

She said it loud enough to assuage her guilt but not as forceful as she could have. Thalia would be upset that she had snuck out. But technically she had told her where she was going. Walking backward, Cat bit her lip when her boot heel clicked on a floorboard. Oh, who was she kidding, she didn't want Thalia to get in trouble in more than she wanted Aidan to get in trouble. Thalia had her own problems, and being tangled up in Cat's issues sure wasn't helping.

Cat passed by the disaster that was her kitchen and said a silent prayer that she hadn't been stupid enough to invite Aidan over to her house. She swore he had invited her over but had the opposite happened? Damn, she wished the throbbing in her temple would go away. Stepping out onto the porch the air felt crisp — possibility ripening in the air. She itched for one of Miss Chow's fortunes. She would have to make it back there soon.

There was a well-worn footpath between her house and the Harpers. Back in the day, the two properties had shared the horse pasture, making it impractical to erect a fence along the extensive property line.

The Harpers small cottage was nestled in a little vale a hundred yards from the road, the roof aligning with the Iron Forge Mine in the distance. The raped earth and cold, stone structure sent a shudder of revulsion along her neck and shoulders. She tore her gaze away, needing to stay focused.

Hazel Myers had told Cat at one of the community center meetings that Felicia Harper lived alone with her son, Jeremiah after her husband skipped town with some floozy years ago. It was obvious Hazel was the local gossip, and she might come in handy for the future. However, Cat didn't really want to know everyone's dirty laundry. She had enough to suffocate under, and she liked keeping it locked away. The stains were permanent. No amount of verbal bleaching would ever absolve her of the horrible things she had seen and done.

She alighted the stairs, each of the fragile boards creaking ominously under her weight. She hoped it wasn't a portent of things to come. The house was once a whitewashed clapboard cutout of Americana. Now the paint peeled on the west side where the afternoon sun had baked the siding. The porch was nothing but gray boards that still had flecks of red paint revealing that someone had once really cared about this home.

She was about to knock when the sound of a fight inside made her freeze, her fist inches from the door.

"Jeremiah Harper you get down here right now and pick up these comic books. I don't need your mess in here."

Cat looked down at the bowl in her hands. She'd erased all evidence of the red dust, but this sure wasn't going to make things between her and her neighbor any better. The last thing she wanted to do was to encourage Jeremiah Harper to make her life more difficult than it already was.

She knocked on the door and took in a deep breath.

"Who the Hell?" Cat heard from inside as the sound of chains and locks being thrown preceded the opening of the door. Felicia appeared at the doorway. The only other time she had seen the woman was the one time she appeared on her doorstep to "greet" the new neighbor. She had peppered Cat with so many questions that she had quickly made some excuse about work and practically shut the door in the woman's face. This interaction was bound to go badly.

Upon seeing Cat, she brushed her hands through her disheveled hair and threw her shoulders back, making the soft gray sweat suit she was wearing look high class just from the set of her shoulders. "To what do I owe this pleasure, Ms. James? Usually, people calling this early make it a point to announce their presence before landing unannounced on someone's doorstep."

Yep, not a good start. Getting past this gatekeeper might prove more difficult than dodging the demons in Hell. She lifted the bowl in her hands. "I wanted to return this. Jeremiah left it on my doorstep the other day. He brought over a present for me, and I wanted a chance to thank him. Is he around?"

At the mention of her son, the mother bear came out full force. She dug her fists into her hips and stared fiercely through the screen door, making good use of her short stature. "What do you mean a present? You tom catting after my boy? Considering you hang out with that floozy Thalia. He's just a teenager you know. You should be ashamed."

Cat blinked back the shock at the accusation. The last thing she needed was this nosey Nancy telling all the folks in town that she was a pedophile. "No, no, not at all. I thought maybe he was bringing something over from you. I simply wanted to thank him. I know I haven't been the best neighbor, but I just..."

"You can stay away from my boy." Felicia shook her fist in the air.

Jeremiah came down the central staircase and froze at the sight of Cat. His gaze went to the bowl in her hand, his freckled face paled, and he turned to high tail it back upstairs.

"Wait, Jeremiah!" yelled Cat. She needed to know where he harvested the red dust. Cat knew that the mines had a wealth of it somewhere and the boy was the key to finding it. She didn't have time to search through five levels of abandoned mine shafts to figure it out. This kid had to have some idea.

The screen door swung open, almost knocking Cat in the face. Cat looked down at the double barrel in Felicia's hands. The woman probably kept it by the door for protection, and now Cat was staring at the other end of something that could take her off this Earth forever. Suddenly this second life of hers was looking better and better. She certainly didn't want to die.

"I told you to stay away." Felicia reached out and snatched the bowl from Cat's hands. "You are demon spawn. I know it. I don't see you in church, probably because you are repelled at the door. You are luring my boy into temptation, and I won't have it. And to think I almost believed Mr. Ash when he came here to tell me my boy was causing you trouble. Now I know the truth."

She tossed the bowl inside, pumped the barrel, and propped the butt of the gun in her hip. Cat watched the bowl spin around on edge and come to rest upside down at the foot of the stairs. Her chance was over, and the only thing she could do was leave before she ended up with a chest full of buckshot.

She raised her hands and backed down the stairs. Felicia un-cocked the gun and shut the screen. Cat heard all the locks and chains being thrown over the door again. Then the shaking started. The fear that coursed through her veins rose to the surface, and she doubled over where she stood, unable to get her legs to move.

This woman had just accused her of being precisely what she was afraid of. A demon spawn. She had started this life out the same as everyone else, but when she was taken, she didn't know the transforming effect it would have on her. Mane had confessed that there were more reasons he refrained from rescuing her than his banishment. He knew that any human taken down to Hell was changed, their soul drained, and they were in effect a different person. Already dead if not soon to be.

She sucked in ragged breaths and tried to refocus on the scent of the wild grasses. Rusted iron farming equipment littered the Harper's lawn. White clover and daisies. Slowly she emerged from the sepulchral mist that separated reality and that space in her head that threatened to swallow her sanity forever. A permanent prison within her own mind.

Through the blur, she noticed someone standing at the edge of the path between her house and the Harpers. Thalia, clad in a deep-red dress, with a white Peter Pan collar set atop a column of decorative silver buttons. She saw Cat and took off, her black flats kicking up dust as she reached her side and wrapped her arms around Cat, pulling her to standing.

"You are lucky I can still scent you out. What were you thinking coming over here?" Thalia smoothed the hair back from Cat's face, equal parts anger and sympathy. Felicia's accusation had hit her hard. She needed to toughen up and push through her fears. Weakness wasn't an option she could afford, especially when she had no idea what Niro had planned for her.

Thalia wrapped her arms around Cat's waist, and Cat explained to her what had happened as she helped her back to the house.

"I'm really doing a bad job as a succubus if you are the one getting accused of being the demon spawn," said Thalia. They reached the front steps and sat down. Cat finally had to laugh. She couldn't let her fears get the best of her. Life was never

127

going to be black and white for her again, and she needed to find some solace in living in the gray area between the two. It would mean a certain level of uncertainty, but with friends like Thalia by her side, she could handle that.

"I think I'm coming to Step Two in my recovery process," said Cat.

Thalia hugged her tight. "What, you don't believe in God do you? Because you know that's a whole lot of flim-flam."

Cat laughed, but no humor rested behind it. After spending time in the Hell she knew existed, everything else was still questionable.

"No, but I do believe there is a power that can restore my sanity. I'm starting to accept things that seemed out of my reach before."

"Like the fact that we are all kind of fucked up," said Thalia.

"Fucked up and fucked if I can't get my shit together." Cat gave her friend one last hug and turned to go inside. "I've got a date with Aidan tonight, and I'm not going to waste any more time."

* * *

Aidan looked around the living room, the only room other than the dining room that he intended to let her see. Tonight was all about figuring out the next move. The place smelled fretfully clean, the same way he felt. Freshly-washed laundry, linden blossoms, soap suds, and a sprinkle of vanilla from the bread baked by Pablo's wife. She'd also left a pot of gumbo on the stove. These people depended on him and his family, and when his Dad fell ill, they all rallied around him. But it had been years, and they were suffering now too, he needed to pay them back somehow.

He tugged at the black and white sleeves of his plaid shirt and rerolled the sleeves. He'd dressed with care in a pair of dark washed fitted jeans and slid on his tan boots, hoping that his look didn't scream desperate, even though that's exactly how he felt.

All day at work he'd poured over the numbers from the soil samples. He'd even gone out to the pontoons and checked the set-up. He'd had some classes on mining when he was obtaining his degree, though his focus was more on pedology, soil study, not on stripping the land of the minerals, but how to determine if soil could support crops. As a farmer, he knew about crop rotation, but the Ash lands were sterile, as were the surrounding farmlands. Something much more complicated was happening here, and he was convinced it was all tied to the mine going barren also if that was even the case. The small sample he had taken from the mine showed levels off the charts, but the actual mineral was all particulate dust. It could have been a fluke. And since Victor wouldn't even let him go back down to the mine to check, he was out of luck. His only hope was that the program running behind everything was skewing the numbers on the pontoon run-off. The River Rouge wasn't called that for nothing. There was enough cinnabar dust in there that there was a moratorium against anything drinking from its waters. No fishing was allowed either.

A swirl of pipe tobacco flavored the air. Aidan's father was back in his chair, studying the papers. Whatever it was didn't seem to get any clearer the more he looked at it, but he also wouldn't let Aidan help.

The doorbell sounded, and Aidan started out of his thoughts. He rushed to the door and forced himself to slow his steps before he got too close. The last thing he wanted was to seem over anxious. He had already shown up at her house unannounced and had somehow not scared her away yet.

He opened the door, and his breath was taken away. Cat's curves were accentuated by tight-fitting blue corduroy jeans and a tan V-neck sweater with a modest silver tone corded rope necklace. The tips of her distressed boots peeked out from the bottom of her jeans. Elegant and down to earth at the same time. Those two things just didn't seem to exist inside one person in this town. At least it didn't exist in any of the girls he had met so far. Cat smiled, and he realized she had a small dimple on the right side of her face. He wasn't sure how he hadn't noticed that before. The pain that usually laced the space between her brows together was gone. He felt slightly guilty. Mentioning the mine and his problems would probably put those worry lines right back in place, and he certainly didn't want to be responsible for causing her any more pain than she had already been through.

"You look great, wow, come on in." Aidan held the door open, and when she passed, he smelled unexplored potential, sweet, raw tobacco leaves, and chamomile.

A blush crossed her cheeks, and she ran her hands through her auburn locks. "Thanks, you're not so bad yourself farm boy. This house is amazing." She looked to the grand staircase in the entryway. Aidan had left the lights dim to hide all the cobwebs and dusty chandeliers. This place was magnificent once. In the dusky light outside, she probably failed to see all the flaws.

"Thanks. I hope you're hungry. Had a friend come over and make her famous gumbo for us. I'll admit right off the bat, I'm not much of a cook." He directed her into the living room. Might as well meet his dad.

"Cat James, this is my father. Andrew Ashton." His father set his pipe into its holder on the small round table next to his chair where he'd abandoned his papers. Aidan couldn't help but notice the writing on the documents was similar to the one he found in the mine.

His dad reached out his hand. "Please, call me Drew. No need for formalities around here."

Cat came forward and clasped his father's hand in hers. "Nice to meet you, you have a lovely home. Thank you for having me over."

"It's nice to see Aidan with a lady friend." His dad didn't skip a beat.

"Dad, why don't we get you to the table?"

"No need. Rosita fed me while you were getting yourself all pretty for this one. Just get me to bed, and I'll get out of your hair." He took the papers from the side table and shoved them in his front pocket. So much for getting a look at them while he slept.

Cat stepped back as Aidan stepped forward and scooped his father into his arms. *A farmer without the use of his legs is useless. I'm a lame horse, and you need to just take me afield and put me out of my misery.* He was grateful that his father had stopped talking that way, but it didn't prevent him from keeping the guns locked up in a cabinet in his room.

"Excuse me, Cat. Please, have a seat, and I'll be right back."

Aidan set his father onto the double bed, the tarnished frame brought across the prairie by his great-grandfather. Before he got to the door, he called out. "Don't hide from this one, son. There's something special about her. I can feel it." His dad pulled the covers tighter around his chin and set his glasses on the side table.

"I know, Dad. I know."

His boots hit the last step, and he watched Cat examine the portrait of his mother above the fireplace. "She passed away five seasons ago."

Cat turned, setting the picture back down. "Seasons?"

Aidan released an embarrassed chuckle. He was so used to counting years by the seasons, he didn't even see it as a local colloquialism.

He ran his hand through his hair and took a deep breath to steady his nerves. "Sorry, years. Why don't we have some food? I know I can't stand just smelling that gumbo any longer. Believe me, you are in for a treat."

They walked into the adjoining dining room, and Aidan quickly stepped into the kitchen to serve up a few bowls from the stove. He returned and set them down, sitting across from Cat. "I probably should have asked what you like and don't like. I hope this is okay."

He watched Cat poke at the food on her plate with a fork and was afraid he'd made a big mistake like maybe she was allergic to shellfish or something. She paused and looked up at him, lost in her own thoughts. "No, oh, I'm sorry. I just feel like a real heel. I had no idea about your father."

She took a huge mouthful and gave him a half smile. Great, now she was feeling sorry for him. This was not going the way he hoped it would. "I don't like folks feeling sorry for me, so please don't. The accident happened after my mother passed away and we've had to make some adjustments. Like I never figured I would end up a geologist, though knowing about soil does help out around here."

"So, you didn't really want to work at the Forge?" She swallowed another bite, waiting for him to let her know everything. But it was difficult, he had never revealed any of this to anyone. Not even his father was privy to all the thoughts that ran in his head. He'd walled himself off from people for so long to protect his family's interests that he'd forgotten how to really communicate.

He looked around the room, searching for something he could show her. Words weren't his strong suit. He got up and took a picture from the top of the china cabinet. It was him as a child, dressed from head to toe as a traditional farmer. Overalls, cowboy boots, Stetson and a pitchfork, a long piece of straw perched between his lips.

"Farming is in your blood." She smiled as she looked at the picture and handed it back to him. An awkward silence fell between them, and Aidan returned to his food. There was so much more he wanted to show her. The town of Ashton was more than a home to him, it was a living breathing person. She patted her lips with the navy blue linen napkins Rosita had set out. "This is really good."

"Do you have a large family?" Aidan scooped the food into his mouth, noticing that he had a lot of catching up to do.

Cat's eyes went wide for a moment, like the question he was asking her was something shocking and not mundane. It had been a long time since Aidan had to make small talk, but he did want to know more about her. You had to start somewhere.

She swallowed hard and set her spoon on the table. "It's just me now. My family has passed away. I'm sure I have distant cousins, but I...my family moved, and I was isolated from everyone for so long. Once my folks were gone, there really wasn't anyone else I really called family anymore."

Cat was as wounded and isolated as he was. He wouldn't let her feel alone. "Seems like you've found friends here in

Ashton."

The smile returned to her face. "Oh, you mean Thalia. Yeah, she's a bit of an outsider like me. Probably why we get along so well."

"Honestly, I can't see you dancing up on the bars like that woman sometimes likes to do. But she keeps the gossips busy."

The furrow between Cat's brow deepened. "She's the nicest, most human person you'll ever meet. She's a little flamboyant, but life is here to be lived not looked at."

He put his hands in the air, hoping he hadn't offended her. "I completely agree. I'd love to show you more of your new home. I'm sure you haven't been up to the bluff yet."

A wide grin stretched across Cat's face casting a spell of infectious joy. "That sounds like some teenage make-out spot."

"Sometimes the kids go out there, but mostly they stick to the barns. Lots of soft hay." He stood up and offered Cat his hand. "Ms. James, I'd like to escort you to the best view you'll ever see. Better than any big city skyline."

She placed her small hand in his. "Well, let's go then, Cowboy."

He kicked his leg over the seat and waited for Cat to nestle in behind him. She wrapped her arms around his waist and hooked her boots over the passenger footrest. Overhead a ripple of pink waves graced the blue-black sky, haunting and beautiful, like the woman at his back. The heat of her thighs hugged him, her curves flush against his body. When they reached the bluff the light would be low enough for him to show her the spectacular skyline of Ashton. He revved the throttle and zipped up the narrow dirt road that led up the edge of the valley overlooking the town. The one place that overshadowed the Iron Forge Mine.

He rounded the turn tight and grinned when it had the desired effect. Cat squeezed her arms around his waist, and the weight of her cheek rested on his shoulder. A juvenile move, he realized, but all was fair in love and lust. Small rocks and dirt kicked off the side of the sloping path. One wrong turn and they'd be the ones sliding down, but he knew this path like the back of his hand. As a boy, he and his friends would take breaks from the farm by seeing who could race their dirt bikes up this hill the fastest. It didn't matter that it was dark and there were no lights, he could do this with his eyes closed.

They reached the top, and he skidded to a stop. Cat's death grip around his waist hadn't loosened. Maybe he had shown off a little too much. He lifted his helmet off and slung it over the handgrip, placing his hands over the top of hers. They were chilled to the bone. She gradually relaxed her fingers enough for him to slide off the bike.

She still hadn't said a word. "May I?" He gestured to the helmet, and she nodded, though he couldn't see her expression through the tinted visor. He slipped his finger through the strap at her chin and loosened the binding enough to slide the helmet off.

Tears dotted her eyes. "Oh God, I'm sorry. Are you okay? I didn't mean to scare you or anything."

"No, no. It's just..." She broke off and looked around, anywhere but at him. He'd forgotten she was such an introvert. They had more in common then he thought, what a pair.

He grasped her hand and assisted her off the bike, toward the edge of the bluff. "Let me show you what I brought you up here for." He gestured across the valley. The dim red glow of the lights of the Iron Forge Mine to the north, the blinking

Ferris wheel to the south, and the twisting River Rouge flowing between the two halves of Ashton.

She looked slightly confused. "I don't mean to seem rude, but everything is dark. You can barely make anything out."

A puff of warm air exited her lungs, creating a mist and she wiped the remainder of the tears from her face before tucking her hands deep into her pocket.

"Come over here, I'll show you," said Aidan. "Plus I have warmer pockets." He patted the deep pockets of his heavy flannel jacket.

She smiled and closed the small distance between them. Slowly she placed her hands in his pockets, and they were chest to chest. She looked up into his eyes. "Aidan Ash, were you just trying to get me alone?"

He hooked his thumb under her chin, and her lids became heavy. "I am going to kiss you, but there is something you need to see first. See how the sky is luminous with stars? When I was a kid, I'd lay in the hay bales and stare at the sky. To me, it looked like a celestial ocean of blackness. On nights when there was only the smallest sliver of moon, some stars shown dull while others flickered brightly."

"You sound like a romantic," she said. "How many girls have you wooed like this?"

Only you. Aidan couldn't bring himself to say the words out loud, not when things were so new between them. "A gentleman never kisses and tells."

"Is that the milky way?" she asked.

He nodded, pleased she was into his presentation. "The milky way is a river that flows into the ocean. For years I used to study the little dipper and the big dipper, wondering if Orion truly existed amongst the stars."

"You must love this kind of stuff a lot," she said.

"I wanted to be an astronaut. What did you want to be when you grew up?"

He looked down, and a single tear ran down Cat's cheek. Gently he caught it, rubbing the wetness between his fingers. She rose up on her toes and connected her lips with his. A sizzling heat rocketed from his belly up into the base of his skull where it shattered into ripples of energy that traveled into his fingertips. He dug his hands into her hair and pressed his body against hers. Soft curves bent to the will of his hard flesh. A small moan escaped her lips, and it was all the encouragement he needed to continue his exploration of her giving mouth.

Her leg wrapped around his waist and he cupped the pockets of her jeans, bringing her up into his arms. Wrapping his strength around her, closing in the walls around them. Her passion overwhelmed him for a moment, and he wasn't sure he had remembered to breathe. He broke off their embrace to look at her again. The last thing he wanted to do was to take advantage of a woman who was in a broken place. But when he looked at her he didn't see sadness, there were no tears in her eyes, only a burning desire.

"Don't stop," she whispered. She wrapped her other leg around Aidan's waist, rocking her pelvis against his rock-hard cock. The friction between them built up to a boiling point. The kiss they had shared at the top of the Ferris wheel was no fluke.

Her motions grew more urgent as she bucked harder against him. There was a wild spirit within this woman, and he craved sinking deep inside to discover every last secret there was to know about her. His tongue wrapped around hers, penetrating her mouth when he really wanted to penetrate the wet heat he felt between them. She pulled back from his embrace and grabbed the hair at the back of his head. She rested her forehead against his, keeping her eyes wide open as she gasped aloud, her mouth slackened, the delicious scent of her breath hot against his cheek.

Supple fingers inched down the bridge of his nose, rubbing her finger across the bottom of his lip. "You're right this is the best view."

Her legs dropped down to the ground, and he loosened his grip around her waist, but he didn't let her go. He didn't ever want to let this woman go.

Slowly they returned back to the reality of their surroundings. The night grew cooler, and despite the heat of their connection, a shiver ran through Aidan's back, his nose growing cold. Something was telling him he should be careful, that he really didn't know much about Cat other than she came from the big city, knew a lot about computers, and had some demons she wasn't telling him about yet. He took one last look over the bluff and the outlines of homes and small businesses down the main street. This was his home, and in a week it might not be there any longer.

Cat rested her head against his chest, her heart thrumming fast.

"I'd make a deal with the devil to save it all," he said.

Cat snapped her head up, almost knocking him in the jaw. "Don't ever say that. We'll fix this together."

Chapter Nine

Cat clutched the delicate porcelain stem of the teacup and downed her third serving of Miss Chow's ginseng tea. Soothing, but yet, her stomach still churned. She'd agreed to meet Aidan here after he got off his shift so that they could talk about what they were going to do. She figured it was a lot safer to be in a public place. She blushed for the hundredth time thinking of their bodies entwined on top of that bluff. She only hoped that he would actually show and that she hadn't scared him off by being too forward.

She had told Thalia about what they did, and her friend burst out laughing. "It's about damn time one of us got some."

And while Cat was very clear that they were both clothed the entire time it didn't matter.

"You fucking had an orgasm. It counts."

Cat was sure her face turned the color of the walls of Miss Chow's restaurant at about the same time the bell above the door chimed to indicate a new customer. She looked up from her tea to see the object of her desire strolling through the front door. While usually a little closed in and self-conscious, this man had an air about him today. Was that because of her? She wasn't sure whether to feel proud or a little used at being someone's conquest, which would be silly because she had been the one to initiate their interaction.

The motorcycle ride had rattled her nerves. Aidan's riding had been reckless, and while she had already been to Hell and wasn't afraid to die, she realized that she really didn't want to be the reason Aidan Ash met an early demise. This gentle soul was genuinely committed to this town and to his sweet father. Her core softened as he got closer. Dammit, she was falling for him big time.

Aidan gave her a two finger salute and slid into the chair across from her. He parted the small curtain in front of the window, providing a view of the shattered horizon. Criss-crossed swatches of orange and red. Always the red. He let the curtain fall and picked up the laminate menu waiting for him. Cat had refused Miss Chow's offer of food until Aidan arrived. She didn't want him to know she had actually been sitting here for hours.

She had run test after test on the systems at the Iron Forge. Even though Niro had fired her, they hadn't locked her out of systems access yet. Heck, it was probably someone at the firm she worked for that did that kind of thing for them. Cat didn't think Niro was that smart. Except when she discovered the program she had to think twice.

She looked at the stack of papers sitting next to her. She had every intention of telling Aidan, except she wasn't sure what to say. It all sounded like the ravings of a lunatic.

Miss Chow saved her the trouble by entering through the double doors of the kitchen. The few seconds that had passed since Aidan came turned into an awkward several minutes in no time flat. She had to put on her big girl panties and address two things. First, the fact that his boss was a demon. Second, she happened to have dated him at one point in time. Yeah, right, like that didn't all sound crazy.

"Need something stiff today." Miss Chow plunked down a bottle of baijiu. Sometimes infelicitously translated as "white wine," the clear drink was a strong distilled spirit about fifty percent proof. The brew fooled the senses with its light fragrance of rice and honey flavored with rose and crystal sugar, which quickly sent a burning path down your innocent esophagus with enough vigor to have you cursing the Gods for allowing it into existence.

She poured two servings into heated ceramic glasses, like making the fortified wine warm would make it any less toxic.

Aidan reached forward and swigged his glass before Cat could warn him that on an empty stomach, sometimes the baijiu made an unwelcome second appearance. He choked and sputtered as he set the glass down.

"That stuff is stronger than any farmer's moonshine." He wiped the back of his mouth with his hand and sweat broke out across his forehead. He squinted his eyes at the menu. Great. Cat hoped he hadn't ridden the motorcycle into town. She'd have to be the one driving him home.

Cat peered at Miss Chow who winked at her before disappearing back into the kitchen. She set her own glass down. A layer of orange chicken before any spirits or neither one of them would be making it home.

"I should have warned you, sorry." Eyes glassy, Aidan glanced from his menu to view Cat. She knew he didn't have a clue as to what he was ordering anyway. It was charming that he tried. "How was work today?"

The grin that had initially enveloped his face when he came into the restaurant quickly melted away. "Not so great."

The double doors burst open, and Miss Chow plunked down a plate of raw oysters.

"I didn't know you had raw oysters on the menu," said Cat.

"Fresh in this morning. Very rare here in cow town. You eat. You like." Miss Chow scuttled away through the double doors, leaving them in the very empty and very quiet space.

Aidan started to look a little green around the edges.

"You don't have to eat them if you don't want to." Cat's mouth watered a little around the edges. In Detroit, back in the 1950s, you just didn't get delicacies like this. If you did, it was the Maine oyster, an intense face-crumpling briny beast. The oysters from the west coast, off British Columbia, were gentle and sweet.

Raw oysters require nothing to be perfect. The baijiu would act as a wonderful palate cleanser. Cat lifted the oyster shell directly to her mouth, taking a deep inhale of the fresh briny meat, before slurping the tender flesh from its shell. She gave it a couple of committed, unhurried chews, paying attention to the flavor, urgently fresh, exciting, and utterly distinct. The raw stuff of joy, an unembellished and unmodified thing that is good. She washed it down with a swig of fifty proof.

Aidan reached over to the plate, gently picking up the shell like a newborn chick. "These are supposed to be an aphrodisiac right?" He winked before shucking the entire thing into his mouth. Cat was sure she would need to grab the nearest trashcan considering how green he appeared.

"You were smart to eat and then drink." Aidan leaned back in his chair and placed a hand over his stomach.

The double doors swung open again, and Miss Chow appeared with another tray of food. She set down the dish of sautéed chicken breasts swimming in a light brown sauce, tossed in red bell peppers.

"This isn't my orange chicken," said Cat.

Miss Chow patted her stomach and pointed to Aidan. "Ginger good for stomach. You eat Ginger Chicken." She put a large bowl of steaming hot white rice next to them and disappeared for a second time, somehow managing to put two glasses of ice water on the table without Cat noticing. Someday she would have to ask the woman what sort of sorcery she came from. She sensed Miss Chow wasn't in the demon class, but she wasn't normal.

Aidan reached forward and quickly piled his plate high with steaming rice and Ginger Chicken. Between mouthfuls, he explained how his day had gone. "None of the numbers are running right. There has to be something wrong. I just can't explain how the numbers could have dipped so fast. Did you find anything in the daemon program?"

She covered the papers on the side of her plate with a napkin. The information she had was enough to be dangerous. She required more evidence. She knew that what she needed would be inside the Iron Forge Mine. "I think if you can get me access to the mine again, I can help you."

She quickly regretted her words. Aidan's face lit brighter than all the stars over Ashton at her proclamation. The problem was, she wasn't exactly sure what she was going to do once she got there.

"In about a week the corporate office is coming for an inspection. Victor is really worked up about it. There will be lots of people. It will be a perfect time to sneak you in." He swallowed another mouthful of Ginger Chicken and poured a glass of baijiu for them both.

Both of them raised their glasses.

"One second." She reached for another oyster and Aidan caught her wrist.

"Let me." He plucked the delicacy from her fingers and rested the shell on her bottom lip. "Are you ready?"

Cat stared at him, not wanting to move her lips, not wanting to interrupt the moment.

He took her silence as consent and tipped the shell, letting the smooth flesh enter her mouth before it made its way down her throat. A soothing cool embrace to heal the spiked tonic of the baijiu.

After the second oyster was consumed, she raised her glass once more. The low light of the paper lanterns above their heads cast a glow over the both of them that was eerie and romantic at the same time. Seemed about right.

Cat slugged back the second glass of baijiu, and let the soothing warmth travel from her stomach into her toes.

The double doors slammed open once more, and Miss Chow appeared before the both of them with a single plate, two cookies. She set the tray before Cat, allowing her to make the first choice.

"This one important. You listen."

Cat repeated her ritual, savoring a corner of the wafer-thin cookie before reading the fortune.

An upward movement initiated in time can counteract fate.

* * *

After the dinner at Miss Chow's ended without even a kiss, Aidan was quick to invite Cat over to his house a second time. He looked into the mirror in the entryway and straightened his crème colored Stetson. His blue denim shirt was buttoned only halfway up, this white tank visible underneath. He adjusted the large belt buckle and hooked his thumbs in his belt loops. This time he would show her what Ashton meant to him.

Before she could dash out the door, he'd invited her to go horseback riding, and her eyes had gotten ten sizes bigger. It was a pleasure to find someone who was interested in the animals for more than their pedigree and how many races they had won.

He'd already procured the badge he would need to get Cat inside the Forge in a few days. There was nothing more they could do now then wait for the days to pass and hope that once inside, they would both be able to figure out what was going on. More than anything Aidan wanted to know why the soil around his farm was eroding. Even with the run-off and all the minerals sucked out of the ground by the mine, it should not have been able to destroy the soil five miles away.

His father wheeled himself across the entryway and headed towards his chair at the fireplace, a stack of papers in his lap.

"I really wish you would let me help you with those. We didn't pay through the nose to send me to college for a fancy frame." His degree was something to be proud of, sure, he was the first man in his family to get a college degree. But it also came with a bit of shame. He was also the first man in his family who couldn't make his way by living off the Ash family land. His fall back had been college.

"I...it's just a little historical project I'm working on. An old man's hobby. Nothing to concern yourself with." He started to wheel himself into the living room.

"Wait." He trotted over to his father's side and withdrew the paper from his pocket that he had taken from the mine. No use in keeping it. Maybe his father might find it useful. Aidan didn't completely understand his father's obsession, but he did know it was important to him. "Cat and I found these in the mine when we were down taking a sample. Looks a lot like what you got there. For what it's worth."

His father gingerly took the paper from his hand and set it atop the ones on his lap. He flattened the parchment and ran his fingers down the illegible lines of text. He looked up again, and there were tears in his eyes. "What are you planning on doing today, son?"

"Cat is coming over. I wanted to show her the Saddlers." His father stared into the distance, beyond his shoulder, like something was fascinating on the wall. Aidan knew that look, he was thinking of Mom again.

He clasped his hand over Aidan's arm. "You two have lots of fun now. Saddle those horses and ride like the wind. Heck, maybe ride to the next county. You could use some time off. You have been working too hard around here, son. Too hard. And you can't ignore a woman like Cat. You need to spend some time with her."

All his words spilled out so fast, Aidan felt like he needed to grab a bucket and a mop. His father was a mess. Whatever it was that was bothering him was starting to overwhelm him. It was too early in the day to insist that he go to bed and get some rest.

"Don't worry about me, Dad. I'll fetch you a cup of chamomile before I leave. Something to soothe your nerves. Go on into the sitting room, and I'll be right back."

Aidan strode into the kitchen, careful to select a non-descript white mug, not one of the fine bone china numbers that Mom used on a daily basis. His Dad wouldn't let Aidan get rid of any of this stuff or pack it away, but he sure wasn't going to try to calm his father's nerves by serving him a cup of herbal tea in one of the things.

He pushed back box after box of *Double Bergamot Earl Grey*

tea before finding a half-abandoned box in the back of the cabinet. With two men in the house, it wasn't often that either of them reached for the flowery brew. It was usually beer or coffee, and if they were feeling dainty, they brought out the Earl Grey. He laughed to himself at the thought of him and his father years from now, perpetual bachelors. This house would fall to ruin if it weren't for Pablo and Rosita. His heart skipped a beat again. He needed to bring this farm back.

He tried to shove the contents of the cabinet back into place, but the last box, the one that had been sitting on the counter, wouldn't quite fit. He took out a few boxes to see what the holdup was and brushed across an old timer that Dad received as a gag gift around Y2k. It was a countdown clock to disaster. Of course, since the digital thing was the one and only piece of actual technology Dad had ever touched, he wasn't worried. But that was over ten years ago.

The clock was still counting down. In fact, the deadline was four days away.

Aidan walked into the sitting room, a cup of tea in one hand and the countdown clock in the other, hoping to ask his Dad why he kept the thing around. Maybe lighten his mood a little. He looked up and saw Cat sitting on the sofa across from his father's chair, smiles lighting up both of their faces.

Cat wore a vintage plaid top. Soft and sturdy, the blue-, red-, and flax- hued shirt gave her a stylish cowgirl-chic look. Worn over tight blue jeans and boots, he about died when he saw the vintage bolo tie around her neck, polished stone-like pendant at the center.

"Is that..." He set the teacup and clock down and pointed to the stone at Cat's neck.

"Tiger's eye." She thumbed the small stone and raised it for his examination.

"Unlike cat's-eye quartz, tiger's eye is formed when parallel veins of blue asbestos fibers are first altered to iron oxides and then replaced by silica. As a result, it is more opaque and has a rich yellow to brown color, very similar to the eyes staring back at me. You have tiger eyes," he said before he realized the how lame his comment sounded. "I loved the study of mineralogy, it was one of my favorite topics in school."

Cat blushed at his words and allowed the stone to fall back to her chest. "I have to give Thalia all the credit, she's my stylist. Otherwise, you'd be seeing me in running shorts and a tank top every time you saw me."

Aidan definitely liked her in running shorts, a dress, un-dressed. He tore his mind from the gutter at the imagining of the feel of her body against his, the moans coming from her throat when she found release. The last time he'd seen her in shorts was the day he met her, running through the woods. He hoped that the Harper boy had finally left her alone after his talk with his mother.

"Is this here done? What is this a timer?" His father bent down and picked up the small clock Aidan had brought from the kitchen. The look across his face turned from one of confusion to shock. "Where did you get this?"

"I was about to ask you why you still had it. I thought Bud gave you that as a joke. It seems to have reset itself or something. It's counting down to four days from now."

Cat's smile turned into a tight line across her face. "Four days from now?"

"Yeah, well, I'm not going to wait four days to drink my tea." Aidan's father tossed the clock into the wastebasket next to his chair and transferred the tea bag from his mug to the plate.

"You two better get going before you lose your light."

Cat stood and put her jacket back over her shoulders. "I'm ready when you are."

Aidan remembered his love of the Saddlers again and led Cat out to the stables.

The stables were the most well-kept building on the property. Aidan and his father might not take care of themselves, but they wouldn't deny these horses anything.

He led her into the large barn from the south side where stalls lined up on a row along either side of the cavernous space. Above the stalls was a hayloft, and for a brief second, he wondered what might happen if he showed her the cozy hideout. Maybe a repeat of the other evening on the ridge, or a chaste encounter like the night at Miss Chow's.

A horse whinnied, drawing his attention where two American Saddlebreds peered out from their stalls. They had well-shaped heads with a straight profile, long, slim, arched necks that strained to catch a better look at the intruders.

"How beautiful." Cat stepped up to Aidan's chestnut mare and stroked a hand down its muzzle. "Does this one have a name?"

"Her name is Natara, Nat for short. It means 'sacrifice.' I'm not sure why Dad named her that."

A visible shiver ran across Cat's shoulders. There was no telling what was going on inside her mind and she still refused to entirely open up to him. She removed her hand from Nat's muzzle and kicked at the stray straw by her feet. "What about the other one?" she asked without looking up. His father's horse was a roan and had an even mixture of colored and white hairs that made his defined withers, sloping shoulders, and strong lean back look almost blue.

Aidan snatched the bridle from its hook and walked towards Nat. The filly whinnied a little at the sight of the harness, showing her excitement for a ride.

"That's Asmund. Means 'divine protection.' We love him, but he's a little slow. Never could take the clubhouse turn on the track." Aidan cinched down the cheek piece and scratched the sensitive spot between her ears. Nat blew air through her cheeks and tossed her head from side to side.

Cat perked up. "Looks like she likes that. I've never actually ridden a horse before."

Aidan saddled the horses with the lighter weight racing saddles. "I'll help you get up, and then you can let the horse lead. Like holding onto me on the motorcycle. Put your feet in the stirrups and take the rein. If Asmund gets off course, pull back, and he'll come to a stop. He likes to stop a lot anyway."

"Sure, sounds great." Cat put a hand on his shoulder. "I want you to know that I really appreciate you showing me around. It's been a while since I've felt like I was really a part of something. I'm going to do all I can to help you and Ashton."

Aidan's heart swelled. Here he was doing his best to win Cat over, and Ashton had done that for him. He knew this town was magical. He'd be damned if the mine was going to take away centuries of what good people worked for. He might as well tell Cat exactly what they were up against. She was already on his side. He didn't need to guilt her into it.

"You should know something." He slid the feed bags over the horse's muzzle, and she quickly dug into her oats. "The corporate office is shutting everything down. If the mineral is gone, then their job is done here."

"Wow! I can't believe it!" Cat tipped her head back and faced the sky. If he hadn't just delivered the worst news possible, he might think she was elated. She looked at him, mouth agape and closed her mouth back into a thin line, shaking her head. "I mean this couldn't come at a worse time."

"For the both of us, I know. But hopefully, we can shake out that bug and then we can all go back to normal." Though the life he had been living for the past few years was anything but normal. He needed to find out what was really happening in town before that day. If he were lucky, with Cat's help, he could do it. "Let's ride, I'm ready to show you the most beautiful thing you've ever seen apart from looking in the mirror."

Cat blushed, tucking a lock of hair behind her ear and popping up on her horse without any assistance. The woman was like an iceberg and he'd only seen the very tip. How he was ever going to reveal what lay beneath, he didn't know. "Ready when you are." She tapped the sides of Asmund with her heels, and he trotted out of the barn.

Aidan slung his leg over Nat's saddle, adjusting the cantle as best he could. That woman got him worked up and riding on a stiff horse saddle didn't agree with the stirrings down below. He quickly caught up, and they were side by side, trotting down the dirt road that led around the barn and down into the valley between their two properties. What he wanted to show her was just around the corner.

He heard Cat's reaction before he saw her face. A breathy gasp that he felt every time he saw the sight before them.

The cherry blossom tree is a sight to behold in full riotous bloom, and before them stood an entire orchard of flowering branches, each full of small pinkish-hued flowers. Soon they would be producing a bounty of the succulent, fleshy fruit of the cherry.

"Back when my ancestors came here they planted the first

cherry trees in this valley. In Japanese culture, the cherry blossom represents the fragility and the beauty of life. A reminder that life is almost overwhelmingly beautiful, but it is also tragically short."

"Yeah, and sometimes your life is cut even shorter." Cat had tears in her eyes as she spoke. Aidan didn't want to ruin the moment by asking her to explain. A little bit of the iceberg was surfacing, and he wasn't going to push it back down again.

She dismounted her horse and walked slowly towards the nearest tree in full bloom as if she was drawn by an unseen force. Aidan did the same, following behind her. He watched as she reached out and plucked one of the flowers from the tree.

She turned and looked at him. "I'm sorry, that was supposed to be a cherry right? I just couldn't resist. They are so beautiful."

Aidan slipped the bloom from her fingers and tucked it into her hair. "Now it's beautiful." He could practically see the woman before him blossoming before his very eyes. Something had happened in her past, something to make her want to work alone from her home. To make her want to hide away in a small town and not talk to anyone. He could only hope that she would someday feel like she could share that with him.

"Aidan, I..." The words appeared to stick in her throat, and rather than make her suffer through the composition of her thoughts, he pressed his lips against hers. The wind picked up through the valley, sending a flurry of pink petals around them. Cat's hair blew free, and Aidan felt like he could sail along the breeze with her. Their embrace intensified and he wrapped his arms tighter around her.

Aidan pulled back and stared into her eyes. With one finger he traced a heart onto her cheek. It was too soon for admissions of love, but he knew without a doubt that he loved this woman.

"I want to tell you everything. I really do." Her voice was choked with emotion, her eyes feverish and over-bright. She seemed desperate to tell him, but there was still a tall barrier between them that had been built up over many years, and he didn't expect it to fall down in one week.

"I'm not going anywhere, and I'm in no rush. This cowboy is on aloha time."

She laughed, then her eyes went wide as she spied something over his shoulder. "We have to go."

She detached herself from him and jumped on Asmund like a trained rider. She gave him a few taps, and the horse started in the direction of the barn and then quickly spooked, raising on his hind legs and kicking into the air. Aidan couldn't detect what startled the animal. He ran towards Nat who spun in a circle, trying to unhook herself from the quick lashing. Aidan quickly untangled her, but when he turned around, Asmund had already bolted across the field and was heading toward the property line—a sheer drop down into a cavernous canyon.

"Yah!" Aidan dug his heels into Nat, and the disciplined horse responded to his command. Aidan leaned forward, transferring his weight into the natural gait of the horse like he learned during those lazy summers of his childhood.

He pushed Nat to her limits. Asmund, though slow, had a scared rider as well as a headstart on them. He reached out, tipping forward on the stirrup irons, and grabbed the noseband of Asmund's bridle while giving it a sharp tug. The motion brought the stallion up quick, and Aidan had to rock back hard to avoid being thrown over the front of his own horse.

Both of the beasts were coated in sweat, puffs of hot air exiting their nostrils. Cat dismounted and crouched down on the ground, hugging her knees to her chest and burying her head in the space between. Aidan bent down and wrapped himself around her, not releasing at all until her body stopped shaking.

He whispered into her ear, "I'm so sorry. I have no idea what could have caused that."

Cat laughed a little and raised her head. "A weasel. I think he saw a weasel."

"Really? Doesn't seem like quite the season for them yet." Aidan looked around and noticed that they were five feet from the edge of the cliff. One second more and they may have both gone over the edge.

"I've seen a lot of weasels around here lately."

* * *

Aidan stared at her like she was a crazy person. She stood and dusted herself off as best she could, trying to regain her composure. There wasn't much she could do to salvage this date, but she could figure out where that goblin had gotten off to.

"Yeah, we see a lot of them around the property, but not usually until later. Maybe it's global warming or something," Aidan said.

She gripped the reins of her horse and reached out to stroke his muzzle. She knew darn well that the brave beast hadn't been spooked by some dumb weasel. But a goblin who dripped ooze and stench would definitely frighten anything that could see it. Besides the supernaturally inclined, animals were sensitive to otherworldly beasties as well. They were both in the same boat.

The sun had started its descent and Cat listened to the sounds from the sprigs of brush surrounding them. Nocturnal insect chirps mingled with the ambient noise made by the chattering of demons. They were not alone. If they didn't get back to the farmhouse soon, she would start to hear the whispers in the darkness and feel the cold breath of her past upon her neck. Being out at night was the worst.

Aidan had taken a brush from a satchel attached the horse's saddle. He began to brush Nat down, and the horse leaned into Aidan's strong strokes. Cat could easily understand Nat's reaction. If that man lavished the same attention on her, she'd be able to forget some of the evils she had witnessed. The realization struck her hard. *Was she actually falling for this guy?*

She stared at him, demons buzzing in her ears. Every man she'd fallen for had been a demon. How could she possibly have rewired her circuits to accept affection from a farm boy? It didn't seem possible.

"We are losing our light. We should probably be getting back." He stowed the brush into the satchel, and that's when Cat smelled it.

Black smoke, crackling flames, and smoldering ashes. Death. Cat turned her head towards the heat. Fire rose into the air off the branches of the cherry blossoms. The last hope Aidan had for his family farm was ablaze.

Her stomach knotted as realization dawned. *Niro.*

Aidan jumped on his horse. "You should stay here where it's safe." He kicked his heels into the filly and raced back to the farm.

There was no way Cat was about to let Aidan fight this alone. This was all her fault. Niro had lied to her. He was trying to get back at her and to think otherwise was hopelessly naïve.

Asmund grunted when she swung her legs over his heaving sides. He stared into the nearby brush, where Cat was sure the goblin was hiding and fought against her tug on the reins. She soon found out how difficult it was to force her will on a two-ton animal that refused to be strong-armed.

Clouds of smoke funneled against the stark blue sky, the acrid stench choking the air as it drifted on the wind. While she wanted to push Asmund, Cat called upon every bit of patience she had, and she bent over and stroked its neck, running her hand over the crest and withers. He relaxed into her lead. Cat whispered into his ear, "Trust me. I want to get away from them as bad as you do."

She righted herself and tapped her heels into his flank. The mighty beast shot off after Aidan's horse.

Aidan had taken the northern path. As she circled the field, tears welled in her eyes at the destruction. Blackened trees had burst into flames like the fabled spontaneous combustion, yet the surrounding grasses remained untouched — confirmation of Niro's duplicity.

Aidan brought his horse up sharp and raced towards a large metal wheel. His muscles flexed, his jaw clenched, as he struggled to loosen the wheel. A screech echoed. Water slowly spewed from pressured guns mounted on rotors and gained in momentum but it wasn't far reaching enough.

She could sense the hopelessness in Aidan's frame, both knowing that the platform wasn't near enough to the blaze. Aidan pushed his whole body against the center pivot, his thighs straining in his bid to save the orchard. Cat barreled in next to Nat and dismounted Asmund in a matter of seconds. She ran to Aidan and pressed against the other side of the wheel. Using every bit of strength, she gripped the metal, the rough, rusty, surface digging into her palms. She watched Aidan as she worked, his face flushed beneath the layer of soot that fell about them like tainted snow. Desperation brightened his eyes, and she responded by putting more of her weight into the turn. Between the two of them, they were able to maneuver the power guns close enough to put out the live fires. This attack was directed at Aidan and the heart of Ashton. These cherries were their lifeblood, and now the very symbol of their town had been snuffed out.

Sirens wailed in the distance, and fire trucks sped up the driveway and raced across the field toward the black smoke. An SUV stopped before the house, and the fire marshal climbed out.

Cat turned and spied Aidan's father in his wheelchair on the porch. He'd probably seen the fire and called the fire department. How horrible it must have been to watch his farm go up in flame when he could do nothing to save it.

She turned to look at Aidan, his white t-shirt soaked and clung to his chest. The skin around his eyes bunched, his breath heavy. His hands stuck out from his sides, and he clenched and unclenched his fist. Her eyes never leaving his anguished ones, she wrapped her arms around the tense muscles of his back and held tight.

Night had fallen, and his dark brown eyes appeared black, pupils wide in shock.

"I'm sorry." He broke away from her embrace and rushed past the fire marshal and his father and into the house.

More engines arrived, probably every last one in Ashton and

a few from the surrounding towns. The men stood around the periphery of the field, like an impromptu memorial service. Hoses limp in their hands, there was nothing more they could do. The fire had died out and the soul of this town with it.

Cat's heart beat fast, thrumming in her chest like it might burst, and she hoped that maybe it would. She'd brought death and destruction to this small town. How could she ever live with herself again? She grabbed her coat from the porch. No one noticed her. They were all too busy talking about what could have happened. Lightning strike? Firebug? None of them knew what she did. This fire reeked of demonic energy, and she meant that literally. Fiery, bright and thick with sweet sinfulness—a scent to entice men to perform evil and perfidious acts.

She raced toward her cottage, away from the destruction. The cold chill of night wrapped itself around her arms and legs, making each step harder than the next. The freezing air stole the breath from her lungs. She gasped, tripping over a branch and catching herself again. The gleeful titters of the goblins drifted from her right. They were tracking her, chasing her. Fear caught in her throat, and she pushed harder, struggling to make it inside the protection circle.

She caught sight of her front porch. Thalia stood, hands on hips, struggling to see what all the commotion was coming from Ash Farms. She had promised to stick around and wanted full disclosure on their date. She'd never been so grateful to have her overprotective friend watching over her.

Thalia caught sight of her, raced inside, and came back out with a baseball bat. She ran down the steps as Cat reached her. "Get inside."

Cat turned to see about ten goblins coming after her. Thalia took a swing and batted the first one across the lawn, it landed on the side of her car with a splat, sliding down to the ground and disintegrating into a puddle. The rest of them caught up and surrounded her friend. Gnashing and snarling, they closed in around her, jumping and taking swipes at her.

One of them caught the edge of Thalia's red and black polka-dot flare dress, tearing the fabric. "Dammit, I just got this dress." She hauled off and sent the goblin into the brush. Five more jumped on her back. She wasn't going to get out of this fight easy.

Cat snapped out of her daze and drew the six-inch blade from her side. She severed the throat of the nearest goblin, an orange spray of viscous fluids signaling its demise. Thalia was trying to bash the one on her back by smacking at it with the bat.

"Hold still," yelled Cat. She grabbed the beast by the small clump of hair between its bat-like ears and shoved her blade into the side of its head, killing it instantly.

Cat surveyed the yard. Piles of steaming goblin flesh littered the grass. No need to obsess about the clean-up since they were the only ones who could see them.

"Are you okay?" Thalia wrapped her arms around Cat, the knife still clutched in her fist.

"I'm fine. Turn around so I can check your back." Thalia sighed and swiveled around on her three-inch heels. A large angry welt had formed between her shoulder blades. "One of them got you."

Thalia looked over her shoulder and shrugged. "It's just like a nasty mosquito bite. Dammit, I really don't have time for this." She tried to brush the dust from her skirts, but there was no salvaging it. "What happened over there? I saw the fire and heard the engines. Please tell me it was just sex, plus candles in a barn, definitely fun but a no-no."

Cat opened her mouth to tell her friend everything and instead the thing that came out was the last thing she wanted. "I have to break it off with Aidan. I'm not sure what we're doing exactly, but it has to stop. That was all Niro's doing I know it. The closer I am to anyone the more they are in danger. You're in danger too."

Thalia's eyes flashed blue, anger and her succubus power swirling behind the soft veil she shielded herself with. "I'm going to go inside and change. And you are going to worry about you, not me. I'm a big girl. And I'm not referring to my weight."

La Cucaracha echoed from the far end of the driveway. Norm pulled in, running over one of the piles of goblin goop. His car bucked slightly. Norm parked and got out, walking around to see what he'd run over. "Hey, Cat. I think you got a big pothole around here or something."

He froze, staring at the knife in Cat's hand and Thalia's torn dress.

A sly grin crossed his face. "Looks like Norm missed a good time. I'd be happy to watch a replay though." He leaned back against his car, reaching his hand out and pressing play on his make-believe remote control.

Thalia turned, that look in her eyes that said she would drop everything for Cat right here, right now. But she didn't need sympathy and Thalia needed to go out with Norm. "Go, I'll be fine."

"You need to think about this. Don't make any rash decisions," said Thalia. She walked toward the car. "I was going to change, but I think you can handle me like this." She sidestepped a pile of goblin muck Norm couldn't see and got into his car.

She hung out the window as Norm backed down the driveway. "Do everything I wouldn't do."

* * *

Aidan tossed the worthless broom to the ground. Wet ash pasted the brush bristles together making it ineffective. He swept the back of his hand across his sweat-laden brow. After the fire trucks had determined it had extinguished all of the hotspots, they had all gone home. He was left to stare out at the fields which now looked more like a battleground. There was still no telling what had started the blaze.

Cat had disappeared, and he hadn't bothered to call her. Truth be told, he was a little hurt that she had left so quickly when things got rough. Maybe that was a sign. Now that the trees were all burnt to the ground he would have no choice but to admit that the Ash Estates were bankrupt. That left only the mine which would probably close down by the end of the week.

Aidan's mind began to formulate desperate plans. What if he could fudge the reports? Show them that there was something there? He'd give the mine another month or two sure, but it would never work in the long run. He grabbed the shovel from the cart in his pickup and started to shovel the wet ash into the back. He'd clean this place from top to bottom by himself if he had to. All by himself.

"Looks like you could use something to eat?"

Aidan looked up to see Cat holding a white china plate piled high with squares in a rainbow of colors. Some coated in coconut and others in chocolate sprinkles.

"It's nice to see you." He said the words with caution as if he were testing the idea to see if it was true.

Cat was a vision of beauty in a sea of destruction. High waisted form-fitting capris and a red and white checked top tied in a knot at her waistline. Her auburn hair was pulled back into a high ponytail, a red bandanna holding back any stray hairs. Work boots showed her practical side.

"An old family recipe. I promise they are not as rich as they look." She took a few steps forward.

Her words reopened an old wound. Aidan wasn't as rich as he looked either. Was that what she was trying to get at?

"You sure ran off in a hurry last night," he replied sharply.

She set the plate down on the hood of Aidan's pick-up, and he watched as she took a shovel from the back and dug it into the wet ash. The muscles of her arms weren't those of a woman who spent all her time at the computer or in the kitchen. She sank to her mid-calves in mud and pressed her lips together. Her fists tightened around the handle of the shovel, and she leaned her whole body into the action. He couldn't help but imagine her pressing her body against his. Lean and taut lines of muscle beneath soft, womanly flesh that he could make out through the snug fit of her jeans.

He was mesmerized by her actions. Neither one of them spoke as she finished off what he had started. The circle where one of the magnificent cherry trees had once blossomed was now a circle of plain dirt, untouched by ash. Cleared and ready for replanting. She stabbed the shovel into the ground and went back to fetch the plate on the hood of his car.

She brought it over to him, and he noticed the slight tremble in her jaw. "I'm sorry I ran out. There's still a lot we don't know about one another. And I happen to have a thing about fire. It's a long story. I hoped to bring this over as a peace offering. Perhaps your father could use a little cheering?"

Aidan plucked one of the fluffy squares from the plate and brought it to his mouth. It collapsed all at once, like a piece of cotton candy and just as sweet.

"They are called instant rainbow candy. I figured you might need one. A rainbow that is. Look, I'm really sorry about all this, Aidan. I still want to help you out if that is at all still possible. I just think that right now..."

"I say, is that what I think it is?" Aidan turned around to see his father sitting on the porch in his wheelchair. It was the first time he had seen the man come outside of his own accord, other than their recent emergency. Usually, Rosita and Pablo would make sure he was wheeled outside to feel the sun on his face. "I haven't seen rainbow squares in over fifty years."

Cat smiled and walked over to the porch. Aidan couldn't help but notice the sway in her hips and the bounce in her step. She leaned over, and he watched the grin on his father's face widen as he took a treat from the plate. "Why don't you come in and join us for lunch. I was just coming out here to haul Aidan away from work for a bit and force him to eat. Glad you're here now. Maybe it won't be such a chore to convince him after all."

"I'd love to. That is if it's okay with Aidan." The hopeful glint in Cat's eyes melted away any lingering trace of animosity he had toward her for abandoning him. After all, she was right, they didn't know a lot about one another and that was something he wanted to remedy.

"Of course." Aidan tossed his shovel in the back of the truck and took the handles of his father's wheelchair to bring him inside.

"I can get it on my own. Why don't you show our guest where the facilities are so she can get some of that mud out from under her fingernails. Honestly, son, we're not so desperate that you have to be putting a filly like this to work for us."

She pushed back a wayward strand of hair out of her face. "No problem Drew, he didn't ask for my help, I just took up a shovel. I hate to see what happened here and I'll help in any way I can." She handed the plate to Aidan and turned toward the bathroom. "Excuse me, I'll be right back."

"Now isn't that a strange thing?" Aidan's father plucked another square from the plate and popped it into his mouth. "I haven't seen these things since I was a small boy. My Mom used to make them for us back in the 1950s. Haven't seen them since."

Aidan looked down at the plate in his hands and noticed that his father had the pages in his lap again, but they were shoved inside a larger leather-bound volume, jutting out at an angle.

"Was that page I gave you of any help?"

His father motioned toward the kitchen, dismissing his question. "Let's get some food in our stomachs before we talk about anything else. I'm starving. Rosita and Pablo had to leave early today. They got another job out at the Chanterelle house. Sure they are paying better than we are. At least anything is better than nothing. Can't say that I blame them."

The news hit Aidan hard. He sat down at the dining room table, his head spinning. It was coming. He had known they would have to leave at some point. Goodwill would only get you so far. Everyone had to pay the bills. Of course, the fact that Violet Chanterelle had been the one to scoop them up didn't sit well with him. The destruction of his family's reputation would be swift at her unrelenting hands. He'd have to pay her a visit and act nice if he ever hoped to keep his family name untarnished—for his father's sake.

They all sat around the table which was covered in a thread-bare doily crocheted by his mother a very long time ago. Somehow, his father had managed to put together three sandwiches and had them all set around the table along with three glasses of sweet tea. It wasn't anything fancy, but the quicker, the better. He wanted to get more work done on the clean-up, and he wasn't sure how much time he wanted to spend talking to Cat.

She slid into the chair next to his father and eyed the stack of papers Aidan had been itching to talk to his father about for the last week. "There are some interesting lines of text there. Didn't Aidan find something like that down in the mine?"

Drew pulled the papers off the table and shoved them in the side pocket of his wheelchair. "Just a little research I've been doing. Sorry about that. Didn't mean to leave any more dust around than we already got."

The three of them ate in relative silence. Aidan didn't feel much the host. Cat finished her sandwich and stood, crossing her arms over her chest.

"I should probably get back. I have some more work to do today." She offered her hand to Drew. "It was a pleasure, Sir, I hope to come back and help out some more. I can't imagine the loss you must have suffered."

Aidan watched his father flinch. He didn't like anyone feeling sorry for him. Neither of them did. But Cat's comment went deeper than she realized. Sure, they had lost the crop, but they had lost a wife and a mother not too long ago, and she wouldn't ever be coming back. Aidan was determined to bring back their farm and their livelihood.

"Come around again. It's nice having someone so hardworking and kind around here." He jabbed a finger at Aidan. "This one is hard working, but he makes me go to bed early like some small child."

His father's joke lightened the mood, and they all chuckled before he walked her out the door.

"Well, I guess I'll see you later."

Cat turned, and he cupped her elbow. "You were about to tell me something when my father came out on the porch." He was waiting for it, the "it's not you, it's me" speech or the "we should just be friends." Heck, that would probably be best for him right now. He didn't have time in this life for the complication of a new romance. Especially not with someone so closed off.

"Yeah, well..." She stared at the ground, rubbing at the dirt with her work boot and tucking a lock of hair behind her ear. "I just wanted to make sure you knew that I would still help with the mine. I still want to help. Look, I want to make this place my home, and that means making sure...the mine...is safe. So that everyone in Ashton still has a job. Am I right?"

Of course, having Cat help him sure would make things easier at the mine. And if anything could go right for him, it was now. He didn't have too much more time for anymore screw ups. "We should get together soon. Talk about what we're going to do in the next few days."

"Sure, call me, and we'll arrange something."

Chapter Ten

A pop from the log on the fireplace startled Aidan awake. He clutched the edges of the recliner and wiped at his sweat pricked brow. The cracking hickory warmed the family room and filled it with the scent of burning wood. The last thing he wanted to remember. Eyes open or shut all he could see were the flames that had destroyed everything he had worked so hard to save.

Above the mantel was an oil painting his mother had done when he was young. He remembered watching her with the palette knife and artist palette as she scooped wedges of color and transferred them onto the canvas.

He stood and ran his fingers along the ripples of pink that represented the petals of the cherry tree in full bloom. Below, the bright kelly green patches of grass peeked out between the fallen petals. His mother had always been able to capture the movement, and he stared at the out of focus composition until suddenly he felt dizzy.

"Not enough sleep." Aidan picked up the clock on his father's side table. Seven o'clock. It was still early although it was pitch dark outside. He reached for the phone, his first instinct to call Cat. He did need to speak with her about their next meeting, but he wasn't sure if it were wise given the current situation. Calling Cat might be awkward, but the discomfort he might experience was nothing compared to the uncomfortable call he had to make.

He cringed as he picked up the receiver and dialed. On the other end, a message machine picked up. Aidan let out the breath he was holding. He didn't want to deliver this message in person and getting the machine was a relief. In a casual tone that he hoped belied his sick stomach, he began to speak. "Mr. Niro, its Aidan. I'm going to need any extra work you can give me. I'm sure you've heard of the fire? I'll be in first thing tomorrow morning."

Relieved to get that over with, he flopped back down into his chair. Above his head, the ceiling boards creaked on the second floor. His father had gone upstairs early, claiming there was something he wanted to study. Aidan wished he could immerse himself in something other than his obsession with saving the family farm. He sighed and geared himself up for another task, speaking to his father about a plan of action. Unless he had a treasure buried somewhere on the property, they had to face the reality of losing the farm.

Hand on the worn wood of the banister, he crept to the top of the stairs, his feet leaden with the burden of it all. A sliver of yellow light spilled from the crack beneath the master bedroom and fell across the hex shaped black and white tiling that covered the second-floor landing. Another contribution by his mother who was obsessed with Victorian-era stylings.

Aidan reached the door, hand on the knob when a rush of night airbrushed by his face, the sensation followed by a spectral mist. Fingers of white snaked above his head and rushed toward the ceiling, increasing his disquiet. Something was moving to and fro inside the room. Concern for his father overrode his unease, and he pushed the door open.

168

At his desk his father had fallen asleep, his head resting atop his arms crossed over one another. The window to his room was open, the wind blowing it ever so slightly causing it to creak on its rusty hinges.

If his father was asleep, where had the noises come from? Careful to keep himself between his father and any potential danger, he inspected the hallway. The mist had evaporated, and the space looked normal as if the fog had been a figment of his imagination. The rustling of papers behind him startled him, and he swung around. His father slumbered on, but the documents he never seemed to be without, and that once rested under his arms, sat in a perfect stack on the edge of his desk.

How the Hell did that happen? Man, he was more tired than he thought. He approached the desk and grabbed the stack. The paper crinkled in his hands and had the distinct scent of old yellowed parchment. It reminded him of his days at the university amongst the library stacks.

Tight black calligraphy covered the page, but most of it was illegible. A magnifying glass sat next to his father's elbow, and Aidan picked up the bone handle. Even with its aid, he couldn't make out the words. He flipped through the stack until he came to the last page. It definitely was a contract of sorts, at the end were the signatures of not one, but several of his ancestors.

Addie Ashton was born several generations before and had been a strong woman. The stories he had heard of her reminded him of Cat. She was an independent thinker in an age when women weren't allowed to have thoughts that strayed from child rearing or plans for Sunday dinner.

Her tale was indeed a tragic one. Forced into marriage and

raped on her wedding night she had conceived a son who would go forth and make the Ashton Estates into one of the most productive farms in the Pacific Northwest. Addie Ashton hadn't been much of a mother. She'd carried the child to term and foist him upon the nannies to raise. Her husband, Ben Ashton, was rumored to be as big a monster. Addie had descended into hysteria. It's typically a part of the history the Ashtons like to skip over at family reunions past, at least that was what Aidan had been told.

And here were all their signatures. Addie Ashton and Ben Ashton, along with other prominent families of the time, all long gone. But the Ashton names were more prominent than the rest, long curved lines showed no mistake that these were their signatures even after so many years past. The rest of the document was no longer legible, except for one phrase at the bottom of the last page.

The sacrifice of our future will ensure the prosperity of the present.

Aidan read the phrase aloud, and the mist crept in through the window outside. A spectral fog that snaked around the legs of the table his father slept on and shot upwards, knocking the pages from his hand.

Panic hit at the phenomenon, and he rushed to the window and latched the shutters, trying to keep whatever weird ass mumbo-jumbo outside. From behind him came a gasp and a short snort. He turned, and the door to his father's room stood wide open. He rushed to the hall and saw a shadow cross the light, then head down the stairs. The curved stairwell hid whatever slinked outside Aidan's reach. He rushed downstairs but caught only the bare whisper of whatever it was that thudded down the stairs in front of him. Morbid curiosity and a general agitation dogged him as he rushed down the stairs.

The front door stood wide open, and Aidan ran out onto the porch. Nothing. Not even the thick layer of fog greeted him. Above his head stars twinkled in the inky black sky, a perfectly normal night yet there was nothing ordinary about what just happened. Inside the phone rang, causing him to jump at the unexpected noise. He stood stock still. Another ring. The shadows remained frozen. Another ring.

"What the heck boy? You going to get that?" His father yelled from the top of the stairs.

Aidan came back in, his mind a whirl of questions. There was something strange going on. First, the trees go up in flames, and the fire chief has no idea how. Not even a local lightning storm to blame. Then some weird mist opens his father's window and some animal he can't see can apparently open doors. *Was he going crazy, or had that really happened?* He definitely needed to get to bed early.

He walked in and picked up the phone on the fourth ring. Maybe it was Victor telling him he had more work for him. He needed some good news.

"Hey, buddy. I'm in trouble." Norm's nervous voice grated against the last nerve Aidan had.

"Spit it out, Norm. It's been a rough day." Aidan raked his hand through his hair. He hadn't taken a shower since he finished the clean-up and his hand was coated in the dirt and ash he'd kicked up.

"Shit, man. I know. You think I would have called you unless it was an absolute emergency. I'm totally freaking out here."

Norm usually took nothing seriously, so the fact that he was freaking out about something made Aidan pay attention.

"Sorry. Please tell me what's going on."

"She just passed out. Cold. Like as in locker room cold."

"Who?"

"Thalia."

* * *

Cat sipped slowly from her cup of dandelion tea and tried to focus her mind on her mission. She needed to get into that mine and find out what or who Niro was here to collect and why he hadn't acted yet. There was definitely something there she wasn't seeing.

She picked up the note from the coffee table. A handwritten note from Thalia who must have come over when Cat took a little nap.

Don't want to wake you sleeping beauty. Out for the night with Norm. Don't wait up. The bottom of the note had a stamp of red lips. Thalia was getting pretty cozy with Norm. Too cozy. She'd have to pay more attention to her friend's activities. With everything going on Thalia had been spending a lot of time with Cat and not enough time at her meetings.

The phone rang, and Cat choked on her tea, sending it splashing over the side and onto her white t-shirt. "Dammit."

She looked at her Timex, she was definitely off the clock. The only other people who had her number were Thalia, Mane, and Aidan.

She picked up the phone, and before she could finish uttering her standard greeting, Aidan's voice came over the receiver.

"Cat. I don't have time to explain, I just got a call from Norm. Don't panic, but does Thalia have any medical condition? Something that might be triggered by excitement...or...?"

Aidan didn't need to say another word. She knew what had

happened. Thalia had fallen off the wagon.

"Yes. Um. Sort of. Is Norm okay?" For Thalia's sake, she hoped so. The first time Cat had met the succubus, she had that part of herself mostly under control. She remembered the promise Thalia had extracted from her if she ever reverted back to her old ways and couldn't be talked down. *Promise that you will kill me.*

Cat had demanded the same courtesy, the pact cementing their friendship.

Cat had wished there was someone who could have offed her when she was trapped in Hell. Stuck doing horrible and unspeakable things. But Cat had seen Thalia's good side. She hoped that side would listen to reason.

"Fine, just freaked out. Can you meet me at his apartment? I'll text you the address."

She grabbed her keys, adjusted the blade strapped to her belt and tore outside to her truck. Norm's apartment was located in the heart of the downtown district. Several years back a few apartment complexes had been built to support the influx of workers for the mine. Now they were mostly empty.

The road was devoid of cars as she sped across the bridge that spanned the River Rouge. The moonlight reflected off the surface, the bright light illuminating the banks that ebbed and flowed with the tide. She slammed on her brakes on the abandoned bridge and jumped out of her car, leaning over the edge to get a better look. The shores were lined with them. Hundreds. Goblins and other beasties of every shape and size, sipping from the water. *Where were they all coming from?* There had to be an active demon portal in the mine somewhere, and someone had apparently opened the door.

A chill of horror skittered along her spine, and she looked

around, sure she would be pounced on at any moment. Thankfully, the bridge was devoid of demons. Heart hammering, she jumped in her truck and drove like the hounds of Hell were at her heels. Fingers stiff from gripping the steering wheel, she skidded to a halt in front of Norm's apartment building. Aidan's motorcycle was already out front. Rushing up the steps two at a time she reached the third-floor door to the apartment and pressed her ear to the wood. If Thalia were going crazy in there, it would pay to use a little caution.

She was only met with silence. She knocked twice before she heard footsteps thudding towards the front door. She stepped back when the door flung open. Norm was standing there in a red silk robe that came down to just below indecent. A giant dragon was embroidered across the front. On his feet were white socks, one slouched down to his ankle and the other tugged up to his mid-calf. Painfully unappealing, however, completely unharmed.

"She's back here, follow me." Norm raced down the hall. Cat entered Norm's bachelor pad and tried not to look when Norm's robe flipped up in the back as he ran down the hall, revealing his bare backside.

At least it seemed they had been getting intimate. So why was Norm the one standing up straight?

"Is she okay?"

Norm froze at his bedroom door and pointed inside.

Cat peered through the open door. Aidan was perched on the side of the bed, his back to the door. Thalia's wrist was in his hand, and he had his eyes on his wristwatch. He was testing for a pulse.

"What were you doing before this happened?" asked Cat.

To his credit, Norm had the decency to blush for once. "We

were having a good night. I invited her back to my place, and I wasn't even going to make a move on her, I swear. I talk big, but Norm usually strikes out with the ladies. And I like Thalia. A lot. I wasn't eager to get my heart crushed so soon. She made a move on me. It got a little hot and heavy and then she just passed out."

Aidan placed Thalia's wrist back on the bed. "She's okay, but her pulse is weak. You said she had some kind of condition. Did you bring her medication?"

Aidan and Norm gave Cat the full stare. Right, she was supposed to have brought the answer. Flustered and a tad bit embarrassed, she patted her jacket pocket. "Right in here. It's probably best if I do this alone. Do you mind waiting outside? It will help to have a little privacy."

"Do you need me to call a doctor?" asked Aidan. He leaned against the doorframe, his hair still slick with dirt likely from the clean-up efforts at the farm. His white tank top showed off the tan muscles of his arms and Cat ran her gaze to the worn spots in his jeans. He had such a calm confidence about him it scared her. She had always been attracted to demons and the bad boys. *Could Aidan be one of them and she just didn't know it yet?*

"No, she'll be fine. This always works. It shouldn't take too long."

The door clicked shut, and Cat stared down at her friend lying underneath the Dungeons & Dragons bedspread on Norm's bed. Her chest rose and fell ever so slightly. She was still breathing. Cat lifted the blanket. "And you're completely naked." She dropped the blanket and scanned the room for Thalia's clothes.

She lifted a pair of underwear from a giant light-up Borg

cube, her bra from a lightsaber mounted to the wall and her dress from a Star Wars Wampa rug. Norm was a geek who was really into this fantasy and magic stuff. Cat wondered how he would react if he knew it really existed.

There wasn't really a protocol for waking up a sleeping succubus. Cat dumped the pile of clothes next to her friend and drew her knife. She leaned over Thalia's sleeping body and gave her a hard pierce on the arm.

Thalia screamed. "Ow, that hurts." She rubbed at the abused spot and groggily looked around the room.

"Everything okay in there?" asked Norm through the closed door.

"She's fine. I'm just not that good with needles," said Cat. She leaned in close to Thalia as to not be overheard and whispered, "Get dressed. I don't know what you did, but we need to get out of here. And apparently, I'm going to have to tell them you're diabetic or something to cover for you."

Thalia rubbed her eyes and started to pull on her clothes. "Wow. I have no idea what happened. I just took a small sip. He's amazing. That or I am a total lightweight now."

"You're supposed to be abstaining from that." Cat crossed her arms over her chest. She didn't like having to be the secret holder, the one who would have to lie to Aidan about this to protect him. Nor did she wish to kill Thalia if it came to that. But she had been lying to him already. Mane was just her "friend." She used to "work" for Niro. The lies were piling up. There would be no way to have a real relationship with Aidan if this continued. Just another reason why she should break things off with him.

"Just like you were supposed to be breaking up with Aidan tonight. How did that go?" Thalia stood up and crossed her arms over her own chest, mirroring Cat's actions. She knew Cat too well.

Cat flopped down on the bed and hugged a stuffed Pokémon to her chest. "I need to break up with him. It's not safe for him to be around me."

Thalia sat down next to Cat on the bed and put her arm around her friend. "Aidan is a good guy. Do you think it's safe for him to be at work with Niro? You being close to him is probably the best thing right now."

"You're right. I need to see this through and being close to Aidan is my only ticket in right now."

"So what symptoms am I supposed to have if I just came out of a diabetic coma?"

"You're supposed to be pale, have a rapid heartbeat, and be soaked in sweat."

"Kind of like what a good romp does for you. Speaking of which, doesn't seem like the Earth is going to explode any time soon. You should really 'get close' to that one. If I can't indulge, I would love to live vicariously through you. And don't skimp on the details."

They exited the room and Thalia did her best acting job with Norm. She leaned against the wall and made her apologies for ruining their evening. Norm, surprisingly, was a complete gentleman. Aidan escorted Thalia to the Cat's car and helped fasten her into the front seat.

"I wanted to tell you that I really appreciate you coming by yesterday and helping with the clean-up."

Cat fastened her seat belt and placed her hands on the wheel. She thought it took courage to face the beasties and the demons, but the real courage was to live in the world outside of that. To actually be normal. She wanted that more than anything. "Yeah, well looks like you could still use a lot of help."

Aidan looked down at his shirt. "Yeah, I kind of just ran right out of the house. I would like to see you again, but you don't have to put in any labor. There isn't a lot we can do right now anyway. Not the time for planting seedlings. I just can't stand to see the devastation. You sure she is going to be all right?"

Thalia was slouched down in her seat, eyes closed and mouth hanging open. She snored a little and turned her head towards the other window. *Don't oversell it, Thalia.* While she appreciated her efforts, her play acting was downright embarrassing.

"I'll make sure she sees her doctor in the morning, but she'll be fine tonight. That was really nice of you to hurry over here. You didn't have to do that." Cat was glad for the cover of night. She was uncomfortable with the fact that every time his gaze met hers, her heart turned over in response. A few more of those looks and he just might jump-start her into actually falling for him if she hadn't already.

Aidan leaned into the car, his scent undeniably warm and sensual. She ached to crush her body against him.

"I have some medical training with the animals on the farm. People aren't the same, but animals and humans alike have a pulse." He ran his finger along her forearm and rested it on the veins inside of her wrist. "Your heart is beating fast. Are you going to be okay?"

Her heart was about to burst from her chest. If this continued, she might need his rescuing from a medical emergency soon. She tilted her head and caught his eyes in the light. A warm glow flooded through her, wrapping her up in his protective gaze. Without realizing it she reached out and placed her hands on his chest, pure need guiding her towards the object of her affection. He dipped his head down, pressing his lips to the pulsing hollow at the base of her throat. She let go of the breath she had been holding, and it came out in a gasp.

Soft kisses scorched a path up her neck. Her cheeks burned, and she began to shiver. Aidan drew back and brushed a gentle kiss across her forehead. "It's late. I won't keep you. We've got four more days until the inspection."

"I'll be in touch." Cat straightened herself back in her seat. He was reminding her of what they were up against, and he was right. Time was running out. The glow of the moonlight against the River Rouge created an eerie tinge to the air above the town.

After I figure out what the Hell those things are doing here.

Chapter Eleven

Aidan rounded the corner to his cubicle and stopped dead in his tracks. Sheaves of print-outs weighed down his desk, miles of reports to sift through and make sense of before the big wigs arrived. He eyed the pile, tall and intimidating, a roadblock to success, one of Niro's making. Damn it, why had he given into the self-indulgence and taken the three few days off to process what had happened at the farm, when he needed to keep his head in the game? The crops would grow back with labor and love. The money would buy the seeds. Thus it was imperative he save the mine. But why had Niro insisted on sabotaging its success by doing everything in his power to ruin it? Was he getting a kickback from a rival mine? Sneaky bastard. Well, Niro might have his own agenda, but so did Aidan.

Irritation caused by lack of sleep, coupled with the fast-growing obsession with Cat shortened his temper. He un-shouldered his bag, scooped up the offending reports from the chair and plopped them onto the desktop with a loud *thunk*. Thinking about Cat and the lack of progress he had made only worsened his mood. He sensed she wanted to open up to him, he felt it every time they were near one another, right before the inevitable withdrawal. He wasn't sure it was a real sense of intimacy, or merely wishful thinking on his part; the part that resided in his pants.

"Thought you could use an extra pick-up me today." Norm appeared, two cups of coffee in hand. Both mugs were free of any obnoxious saying. A first for Norm.

Aidan accepted his before he inhaled the rich brew. Dark and strong, nothing added, just like he liked it. "These mugs are a little on the vanilla side. You feeling okay today. That was quite a scene last night."

Norm slumped and leaned against the side of the cubicle. "Man, it's been forever since I've been that close to a woman and she almost dies. I'm starting to think that maybe it's best if I remain asexual Norm."

"I can't imagine that being a possibility." Aidan remembered the first night he and Norm had gone out after work. Norm had managed to find a cowgirl bar a few towns over that Aidan had never heard of. After a few lights beers, he had been the one riding the mechanical bull. He hadn't laughed that hard in a long time. Norm meant well, he just didn't have very good direction. "Did you call Thalia and see if she was okay?"

"She called me." He took a swig of his coffee and wiped his mustache with the back of the sleeve of his brown sweater. Even his clothes were on mute. "Said she was doing okay and that we should get together again soon."

That was a better response than he had from Cat. When he leaned in to kiss her, he felt an overwhelming urge to pull her out of her seat and press her body against the car. Something inside him wanted to be closer to her even though he knew very little about her and she wasn't one to give things up about her past too quickly. A mysterious past that included Niro. There was a story there, one he wasn't privy to.

"You're doing better than me." Aidan scanned a few of the papers that reported the numbers coming from the dredge of the river, useless reports meant to distract him. He wasn't buying into that trap. "Hey, Norm. Have you seen the report come in from the soil sample I took? I expected it to be here by now."

Norm pulled a paper from his back pocket. "I thought I would bring it to you myself. I've been sitting on it for days." He set his cup on the desk and worked to smooth out the wrinkles on the page before handing it to Aidan. "Literally."

Aidan ran his eyes down the report, incredulous. No, this couldn't be right. He started at the top again. "These numbers are off the charts. There hasn't been a concentration this big since...since..."

"Since the days the mine first opened." Norm handed an internal memo to Aidan which summarized the historical data from the mine. "Must be some badass report. Niro has been hounding me for days, wanting to know where it was. I played dumb. He treats me like an idiot, so I acted like an idiot. I've been trying to stall him, but he's going to want to see it soon."

Everything that the shareholders would need to know about the mine and its rich deposits rested in Aidan's hands. But that still begged the question, why was the mine closed if it still had cinnabar and why were they working the dredge and not the mine?

"Norm, I need you to pull the reports from when they closed the mine. I want to know what they said. This isn't making any sense."

The bombshell in his hands burned a path of excitement through Aidan. There were a few days before the shareholders showed up, enough time to launch a counterattack against Niro. But where to start? The mine was the obvious choice, but he couldn't do it alone. He'd have to ask Cat to help. At the thought of her, he suppressed a sheepish grin. Any excuse to spend time with her would be welcome.

As if reading his mind, Norm leaned in close and lowered his voice. "Okay, so me and a bunch of the guys are going to raid the mine. Wanna go?"

"You are going into the mine?" he asked, rolling the idea in his mind. This was way beyond Norm's usual shenanigans and more along the lines of what he had been considering.

"You know, my LARP group. I got the keys to the place from Bob, and he's going to turn off the surveillance cameras. Should be fun right? I mean you were down there, and I looked at the safety reports. Shit man, this is going to be real." Norm bounced on his heels and coffee sloshed over the side of his cup.

"LARP?" Aidan asked, the idea gaining merit. He had to admit, Norm might be onto something.

"It's an acronym. It stands for Live. Action. Role. Play. We dress up in costume and pretend to hack at each other with foam swords. And mead. There will be lots of mead."

Aidan rubbed at his chin. If they were in costume then even with Niro's backup surveillance cameras they could get in, look around and be out before he was the wiser. They would only have a limited window of time though. He would need Cat's help to make sure they got the proof they needed.

"Can I bring Cat?"

"Ey, we be needing some service wenches. See if Thalia be up for it too will yee?" Norm squinted and hobbled on one leg. Apparently now they were storming the mine as pirates.

"I won't ask them to come dressed up as wenches, but yes, I'll ask."

Norm pulled a flyer out of his pocket and handed it to Aidan.

In the center was a black griffin in a circle and around the edges it said, "Dargarth Wargame Rules."

"So it's a medieval fantasy combat roleplay. Full garb and padded weapons. You create a fictional character for yourself, get a weapon, and start swinging. If you pick a magic user you have to recite spells, but you can always bring a cheat sheet," Norm said, although he appeared disdainful of such an act.

Aidan rubbed at the vein that started to throb in his forehead. This sounded like it was going to be more than he wanted to sign up for and definitely more participation than he was comfortable with.

"Sounds a little complicated, Norm. I mean, if I'm going to invite Cat and Thalia I need to make it easy for them."

Norm twirled the end of his mustache as he considered the idea. "I have plenty of weapons. Just tell them you'll be fighters and to wear something comfortable. They'll have newbie bands on their arms anyway so people will be gentle with them. I'm a level five cleric so I can heal their wounds if need be."

The mischievous grin returned to Norm's face, a sign that things were getting back to normal for him. After the scare at this apartment with Thalia, Aidan was glad to see a little of the old Norm.

Aidan picked up the phone. This really was their best chance of getting into the mine sooner rather than later. "I'll call Cat. Tell Niro the report was delayed by the lab and won't be in until the beginning of next week."

A light bulb seemed to go off over Norm's head, and he rubbed his hands together in mock glees. "But that's after the shareholders show up, cheeky bastard."

"Exactly."

* * *

Cat tightened her grip on the wheel as Thalia fussed with the shoulder pads she had shoved into her shirt to create fake biceps. "I think this looks ridiculous."

Thalia cocked an eyebrow. "We're going into the woods and down an abandoned mine with a bunch of guys pretending to be medieval warriors, and you are concerned about looking ridiculous?"

Cat took the shoulder pads from her arms and shoved them into her bra. "They'll be looking here anyway, might as well give them a show."

Thalia laughed and continued to paint her face like some kind of warrior princess. Rouge for the lips and swooshes of black under her eyes. Apparently, you needed to look good going into battle.

"Are you sure you are going to be okay? I don't like what happened with Norm, and he'll be there you know."

The lipstick Thalia was holding fell into her make-up bag. "I will be fine, Mom. It was just a little slip. As long as he doesn't hold me down and ravish me in the woods, I'm sure it won't happen again." She gave a wiggle of her eyebrows. "Aidan will be there too. Should I be worried?"

"I told you, we're working together to get this thing figured out. Work being the operative word. This is business, Thalia. Aidan and I, we aren't going to happen on any level but work." The words were no sooner out of her mouth than she was questioning herself.

As if Thalia could read her mind, she spoke the question out loud. "Why not?"

"It's complicated." It was always complicated. Every man Cat had ever fallen for had been a total demon, and that wasn't being figurative. They actually had been. She was so drawn to trouble that she herself had become trouble. Aidan was a good man, and he deserved a good woman, not someone tainted by the evils of the world.

"He's not like your usual guy, you know. I mean I get why you think you should stay apart. But I think he's more your type then you realize." Thalia blotted her lips with a tissue and patted the curls at the end of her hair, looking like the supernatural goddess she was. She usually did a better job hiding it. Cat wished she could hide her feelings for Aidan better.

Heat pooled in her core at the memory of her thighs clamped around him, the motor purring between her legs as he took the curve up the hill a little too fast. Fast enough to make her stomach drop, like riding on a roller coaster and starting that steep dive to the bottom. At the bottom was where she was afraid of being again.

"I'll take it into consideration." She swiped her blades and fastened them through the straps on her outfit. At least she could bring her weapons to this party. Even though you could only use fake ones, she had the excuse that they made her outfit look better. She was supposed to be a fighter after all. She was just hoping that the beasties stayed away. Though if what she suspected was right, that there was a large concentration of red rock still in the mine somewhere, then it wouldn't merely attract a few, it would attract all the beasties within the city limits. A potent demon drug that she hoped they wouldn't get their hands on.

The wheels of the Jeep bounced up and down the rocky path to the outskirts of the mine. Cat turned onto the same backroad that she and Aidan had taken the first time. She had expected to have to turn off right away and hike over the large mounds, but the piles of dirt had been cleared.

"Something is going on here." Her sixth sense kicked into overdrive and she peered through the windshield to study the roadway reflected in her headlights. "There are fresh tractor tracks on the road."

"Sure, I bet they needed to clear a path. I'm glad, I was really hoping I wouldn't have to mess up my cute new shoes." Thalia kicked her stiletto heeled boots onto the dash and gave Cat a wink.

Cat ignored the gestures and clenched the steering wheel while she rounded the next corner. The breath she held hissed through her teeth. It was the same, freshly plowed road.

"So much for secrecy. A red flag would draw less attention." Under the distraction of the game, she and Aidan were supposed to search the sample site. Given what she was looking at, Niro would figure it out. Fear for herself and for Aidan twirled her gut.

Thalia sat up straight in her seat and opened her window. She hung her head outside and closed her eyes as she took in a deep breath. "We're not alone out here." A flash of red eyes in the side view mirror chilled Cat. "Damn, I knew I should have brought better shoes. Every time I want to look pretty, I get demon guts all over me. You know how impossible it is to get out that smell?"

"It lives on the very air, like out here." Cat rolled down her window and continued to creep down the dirt road with her foot hovering over the brake pedal. Fear whispered to turn around, run back to her house, and lock herself within the safety of the protection circle. Damn the rest of the world. She wouldn't go back. Couldn't go back to that Hell.

Thalia settled a firm hand on her arm and gave it a reassuring squeeze. "We got this. No one else can see them besides us, right? We'll just be 'extra' theatrical tonight. Heck, we might win an award or something."

They came to the clearing in front of the entrance to the mine. There were about ten other cars parked outside, and the door to the mine stood wide open.

"Everyone must already be inside," said Cat. Every sound seemed magnified, even the chirps of every insect. The sound of the diesel hum of the dredges working around the clock on the river miles. Everything masking what she really wanted to hear—rustling in the brush, the snorts, and swallows of hungry demons waiting to pounce. She could hear every one of them, in her dreams and in real life.

A note was taped to the door. "Ye intruders beware."

"Was this a medieval thing or a pirate thing? Please tell me I am not dressed wrong." Thalia looked at the note over Cat's shoulder. "That's Norm's handwriting."

Cat scanned the face of her cell phone and noted the time before her anxious eyes settled on the non-existent bars. No signal. *Shit.* She couldn't call Aidan. The need to find him proved stronger than her fear and she stepped inside.

The familiar terror returned twofold, and she pressed through it like wading through tar. Attached to the walls were battery operated sconces that flickered an unnatural light against the floor and ceiling making shadows dance in the corners of her eyes.

Panic settled in, and Cat moved her head back and forth to track the black specters that taunted her, the effect dizzying. Something inhuman lurked here, a being that hadn't been present when she and Aidan visited before. It was new, and it was searching. But for what?

Oblivious to her fear, Thalia trailed right behind, using her cell phone to light the way.

"Dammit!" said Thalia.

Cat swiveled around, expecting trouble. She found her friend leaning against the wall, one leg crossed over the other while she examined the bottom of her shoe. A wave of relief rocked through Cat. She needed Thalia safe and whole, now more than ever. Exasperation lessened panic's hold, and she relaxed the slightest bit. "What happened?"

She held up her broken heel. "New shoes. Brand new."

"Boo!"

Cat whipped her blade from her side and shoved it under the neck of the person who had appeared behind her, pinning them up against the wall.

"Hey, little lady. Already getting into character I see. Would you mind backing off the artery slicer?" asked Norm.

The pinpoint focus Cat had on the flesh under her blade widened, and she saw Norm's large pupils staring back at her. He was wearing a large black wizard-style hat, gloves, robes and a black shirt, wide legged pants cinched with a belt, and in his left hand, he was holding a spell rod prop painted cherry red. He's not a threat. Back off Cat. Her mind reasoned with the fear that kept the blade in place. Not a threat. *Not a threat.*

She slipped the blade back into its holster. "Shit, I'm sorry Norm. You scared the crap out of me. I was beginning to think we had come upon some illegal drug ring or something and got the night wrong."

Cat quickly covered for herself. It's something she had gotten good at over the years. Covering for the neurotic impulses that made her react with violence without thinking.

Something she never seemed to be able to shake.

"Well, then we've set the stage right. I made sure the electricity stayed off so that the surveillance equipment at the mine wouldn't catch us messing around out here. It's just flashlights...sorry, I mean torches, from here on out." Norm took a few off the wall and handed one to Cat and another to Thalia. "And no actual fire, there are probably still a few sticks of dynamite around here. Wouldn't want to blow anything up. Follow me we're just down another level."

"Hi, Norm. Good to see you again." Thalia hobbled over. She had broken the heel on her other shoe so that at least she was even.

"I'm glad you're feeling well enough to come out."

An awkward silence passed between them. Cat felt bad. Her friend was having boy troubles, and she had been too busy with all her own thoughts and problems to pay much attention. She was wrapped up in her own little world, a selfish act by a desperate woman. Hell, she hadn't even pressed Thalia to explain what happened with Norm. Some friend she turned out to be.

"I made sure my blood sugar was fine, and I've got medicine with me just in case."

"Let me help you down." Norm offered his arm to Thalia, and they continued to descend the slight incline to the next level. The same level that Aidan and Cat had found the sample high in cinnabar concentration. If she could get rid of the others, she could locate what she was looking for and leave this place. Unfortunately, it would prove challenging to snoop around while everyone was hanging out in the same corridor.

Norm started to explain the rules as they continued. The game was simple. Act like you were your character and help end the storyline by nights' end. The only mystery Cat wanted to solve was where the cinnabar was coming from and why Niro would be hiding it here instead of continuing to mine it.

The incline increased and prevented them from seeing the group of players until they were completely inside the open space. Everyone was bent over maps talking strategy. From the corner, a tanned, shirtless man approached Cat. His face was masked by a metal helmet which he removed as he propped a foam battle-axe onto his shoulder.

"Aidan." His name escaped her lips in a breathless whisper. Time spent on the farm had done his body justice. A body that she'd curled her legs around and pressed up against him to the point of ecstasy, but she somehow had yet to see him completely shirtless. The man definitely didn't miss his workouts.

"I told you he was your type," whispered Thalia in her ear. "I'm going to take a look around. Make sure not to lose your head, we've got company down here."

"Hey, you guys made it. I'm glad. At least I'm not the only one with the ridiculous get up. Though I have to say, you look pretty much like you always do." Aidan smiled, and his pearly whites almost seemed to glow in the low light. Lanterns were spread throughout the space casting eerie shadows upon the walls.

Demonic energy bounced off every wall in this place and Cat couldn't get a bead on where it was coming from. It was possible that the concentration of red rock was high enough to mess with her evildoer sensors. "So, your boss doesn't mind Norm using this place as his play space?"

"This is definitely not sanctioned activity. I only hope the electricity being off gives us enough time to find what we're looking for. Even without it, I think Niro has his ways of keeping his eyes on this place." Aidan rubbed the back of his neck. "Why don't we cut over to where we got the sample while everyone is preoccupied?"

Finding the source of the red rock was more important than the walls that felt like they were closing in on her. More important than Niro finding her here. More important than the feeling that she was in a situation worse than when she was dragged down to Hell.

She nodded, following Aidan towards the entrance to the corridor that led to where they had retrieved the sample.

A hand clasped her upper arm before she could make it two steps. Cat whipped around to see Thalia, eyes wide. "We have a huge problem that I'm not sure we can handle."

She gestured behind her at the collection of players who were standing in front of Norm receiving their final instructions for the game. At first, nothing seemed out of the ordinary. No weirder than a bunch of grown men dressed up in costumes and playing like they belonged to a medieval order bent on destroying each other. And then she saw it. Their eyes. A soft glow of red lit up every one of them, except Norm. She swung back to Aidan and saw the same thing.

Cat took a sharp intake of breath and covered her mouth. She tried to force the bile back down in her stomach. They were possessed. Every last one of them except Norm. Killing them wasn't an option. They had to get out of there. Fast.

"Is everything okay?" asked Aidan.

Cat refused to look into his eyes. She stared at his feet and wiped the sweat from her brow. She had failed. She hadn't done her job, and now Aidan was possessed along with the rest of the town. She had been foolish enough to think that the only thing she would need to kill down here were goblins no one else could see. The temperature increased in the small space, and she fanned herself furiously.

"I need to get out of here, or I am going to faint. Claustrophobia. You should see what you can find. I'm sorry, I can't help you right now."

She grabbed Thalia's arm, and they jetted up the steep incline to the main entrance. Before she left, she looked again at the crowd of players. Every one of them had their eyes pointed at her. Niro didn't need actual cameras, he had the eyes of those possessed employees. And now he had gotten to Aidan too. She couldn't help the town if its savior was already a goner. There had to be a way to dispel the demons, she just needed to find it.

They exited the mine and the chilly midnight air struck Cat hard, sending her body into spasms and racking her senses.

"I want to get out of here." Cat wrapped her arms around herself and sunk to the ground. "But I need to find a way to get that demon energy out of them. Out of him."

"I can help." Thalia pulled Cat to her feet and hugged her close, tucking Cat's head under her chin. "But I'm not sure you'll like it."

"How?" Cat pulled back hard and almost knocked Thalia's jaw. "Whatever you can do, you need to do it."

"We can go back and play their game." Thalia smoothed her hair back into place. "And I'll just have to do what I do. Norm isn't infected, so it shouldn't be a problem."

"I never asked you. Why was Norm a problem for you? Why did he make you pass out?" asked Cat.

The cold night air was like the slap in the face she needed. A burst of reality that sharpened her senses and made her see what was in front of her. Her friend. A woman who had stood by her when she fell apart and wouldn't leave her house for months at a time. If it hadn't been for Thalia and Miss Chow's Orange Chicken, she never would have survived. Thalia needed her as much as Aidan did, as much as this town did, and no one was above anyone else.

Thalia put her hands on her hips and blew a stray hair out of her face. She looked like a fierce warrior in her costume, but something troubling brewed under that facade.

"You'll think I'm stupid and we don't have time for me to explain." Thalia started to walk past Cat, and she caught her by the arm.

"We have time, and you need to tell me. We can't be going into battle if I don't know what is going to make you pass out on me." If she couldn't appeal to Thalia's feelings, she would appeal to her common sense.

Thalia shirked Cat's grasp and folded her arms under her ample bosom. "Fine. Love. You happy now? Actual love can really screw with my mojo. I can have plenty of noncommittal wham-bam, thank you Ma'am, but love tosses me on my ass."

Cat didn't know why she hadn't seen it before. "But you just met him. How can you be in love?"

"Are you telling me that you don't believe in love at first sight? That you don't believe in a connection so strong that you feel like you would move heaven and earth just to be with that person?" Thalia's arms dropped to her side, and she stared off into the distance, focused on something in her mind's eye that Cat couldn't see. "That if that person was to drop off the face of the planet and never speak to you again that you might drop off with them and disappear forever into the blackened abyss."

Thalia sat down on a fallen log and put her head in her hands. "This is not good."

Cat tucked herself in next to Thalia and wrapped an arm around her shoulder. She knew exactly what Thalia referred too. Her whole world had disappeared when Mane walked into it, and she had completely lost herself in him. Her passion had blinded her to the danger in front of her. She never wanted that to happen again. Her love for that man had landed her in Hell and Thalia looked like she was dangerously close to being there herself.

"If Norm is meant to be then it will happen. Just don't lose yourself. I've been there. It's not pretty."

Thalia lifted her head from her hands, the moonlight reflected the tears in the corners of her eyes. Even in the dark Cat could see the pain emanating from her. "Hear me. I really want you to listen this time. No going into the dark recesses in your mind. No traveling back into the Hell you were in. Love is real. Believe me, I have a physical reaction to it that leaves no doubt. Maybe all this time the curse I thought I had wasn't a curse at all but a blessing. I might have to live with lustful thoughts and the occasional person I might suck dry, but at least I have no doubt when true love comes knocking on my door. I know. I only wish I could give you part of my curse and not the other. And then there is that whole thing with you actually being human and me being born a succubus."

Thalia straightened her shoulders and patted her hair back into place. "Now come on, let's use the bad part of my curse for good."

Cat insisted on taking the lead. The power to dispel these demons might lie with Thalia, but she was the one with the sharp pointy weapons, namely the six-inch blade now grasped tightly in her fist. If Thalia couldn't knock the demon out of these civilians, she would have to disable them somehow. Thalia held her cell phone aloft from behind Cat as they crept down the dank passageway. All of the sconces had been taken, and they had been plunged into darkness. "Where do you think they all went?"

"Probably playing whatever game Niro sent them down here for," said Cat. *Living in their own kind of Hell.* Bile rose up in her throat as she recalled the spell she had been under for an untold amount of years at the hands of her captors. The evil things she had done while they had a hold on her caused a cold sweat to break out across her brow. Where the others drugged like her? She recalled being pumped full of a substance akin to heroin, the Black, which she was certain was probably being pushed these days by the same demons who had her at one point. It was fed through her veins on a daily basis, mingling with her blood and absorbing into her every pore until she became a mindless zombie. Well, not entirely mindless. A sober witness to all the horrors she was forced to perform on a daily basis. Flaying the flesh from the innocent. Torturing the already tortured souls with stories that still haunted her nightmares. Watching everyone around her go insane while she was kept sane enough to be locked inside a Hell of her own making. Everyone else got off easy compared to her.

She placed a hand on the cool stone wall to get her bearings. The meeting place had been abandoned, and scraps of paper littered the floor around the few boulders that the "players" had been stooped over moments before.

Thalia picked up one of the papers from the floor and shone her light over it. "One of their LARP maps which shows the layout of this place. Seems like they would need these." She passed her light over the rest of the discarded debris. All of them were the same.

"They don't need the maps if they are being told where to go." To open the portal demons needed magic. The catalyst for that magic was the red rock. This mine should have provided enough of the stuff to let every demon in Hell come pouring through. But yet, Niro hadn't used it for that. Why? Instead, the demons only route in was through possession. They couldn't manifest physically, but they could inhabit the body of some hapless soul.

Aidan was one of those hapless souls. If Thalia couldn't do what needed to be done, then she would have to rid Aidan of his suffering. A new sort of Hell sent chills along her spine and tears threatened to fall. *Would she have the nerve to do what must be done?* There is no telling what he would be made to do under the control of Niro. Heck, Niro would probably have him jump off the nearest bridge just to torture Cat further. She wouldn't let that happen.

"There is only one direction they could have gone." Thalia gestured to the passageway before them. She knew it well. Red rock alley.

A wave of dizziness caught Cat off guard. The floor seemed to tilt at an unnatural level under her feet, and she reached out to the stone wall to steady herself. Thalia grabbed her around the waist. "Are you okay?"

Before her, the narrow passageway seemed to narrow further. Cat shook off the optical illusion associated with her claustrophobia, and she took a step forward. "I'll be fine. We just need to keep moving."

The passageway declined into another level of the mine below them, the darkness so complete that it glowed an eerie purplish hue. From the depths echoed a low growl that was at first barely audible, a distant rumbling like the gathering of electrical energy before lightning strikes. A thunderous echo belched from the belly of the beasties before them and traveled through the cylinder of rock surrounding them. Cat fought the urge to clasp her hands over her ears at their piercing sound.

"We need to break up this party stat," said Thalia. She stepped forward, and Cat stopped her.

"Norm is the only one not affected. I can distract him, but you are going to have to perform some serious suckage to rid all of them of the possession. There were at least ten guys in the group from what I remember." Plus Aidan, she couldn't forget about Aidan.

"I have experience with gangs." Thalia pulled a ribbon from her outfit and secured her hair in a high ponytail. "This could get a little messy. But it sure will be a lot of fun."

Thalia's own eyes turned red, and Cat was reminded that, while they were both there to help these people rid themselves of demons, Thalia was one herself.

"Are you going to be able to pull out of this?"

Thalia flashed her ruby reds at Cat and pointed to the blade in her hand. "As long as you can keep Norm safe then he will be able to bring me out of this without you having to use that."

"I'll keep Norm safe." Cat released the death grip she had on the cotton sleeve of Thalia's tunic. "Please keep Aidan safe."

A simple request for an innocent's life to be spared. That was all she was asking. But deep down she knew that it was something more, and that thought scared her almost as much as the thought that they might not be successful. Thalia's words echoed in her head. The blackened abyss that threatened to swallow her whole would be a worse Hell than the one she had already experienced. She knew that now. She only wished she hadn't taken so long to realize it.

"Partner swap. I like it."

Nervous laughter escaped Cat's lips. "Now you're even starting to sound like Norm."

"What can I say? He's grown on me. And in me." A slight snort escaped Thalia's mouth lightening the mood enough so that Cat could bring her focus back on their mission.

A chill crept up Cat's arms, like the legs of a thousand millipedes were coating her skin and heading to the base of her spine to nest. Freezing temperatures made the inner sanctum of the mine an ice box. Her exiting breath formed a cloud in front of her, and it took an instant to notice the fog settling around their ankles.

"Dammit, already some pretty heavy shit going on down here. We better break it up fast." Thalia sped ahead, and Cat kept to her heelless heels. Thalia stopped short, and Cat skidded to a halt, dirt grinding under the soles of her boots. Thalia's head whipped around her finger to her lips in a nonverbal gesture of silence. Cat gripped her knife tighter, an oily texture forming under the pads of her fingers from the combination of heat and pressure on the leather wrapped handle. And then she smelled it. Blood. Hot blood hitting cold air, turning the ordinarily copper tang into a flinty metal spike that pierced the veil, parting this reality from another one that felt all too close.

"I didn't know you guys got squibs. And how are you making your eyes glow like that? Glow in the dark contact lens or something?" Norm was utterly oblivious to the fact that he was bearing witness to a demon ritual meant to open a portal to another dimension. One that definitely needed to stay closed.

His association with Thalia must have made him immune to demon possession. This was one time when Cat wished her friend had fucked her boyfriend. Was that what she and Aidan were? Boyfriend and girlfriend?

The circle of cherry eyed zombified LARPers all turned toward them at once casting a red horizon across Cat's field of vision and making it impossible to sort out which one of them was Aidan.

"Hey guys, you're just in time for the sacrifice." Norm waved them over.

A half dozen limp-limbed walkers headed for Thalia, jostling past Norm who seemed to still think this was all still a game. He followed behind them, raising his arms and pretending to be as mindless as the rest of them. "Claim the warrior princess, Thalia!" shouted Norm.

This seemed to whip the rest of them into a frenzy, and they closed the gap, leaving several feet between them and the hoard. Stagnation wafted from their skin as if the possession had already begun the process of decay on their feeble human forms.

"Do it now!" shouted Cat. She held her knife in front of them and shielded her eyes from Thalia's face. She didn't need to be taken in by the succubus spell. She needed to keep Norm safe so that once Thalia had sucked all these turkeys dry, she would have a sobering cup of Norm to bring her back to her senses.

"Come a little closer boys." Thalia grabbed the lapels of the nearest fiend and opened her mouth. The light in the man's eyes dimmed and disappeared through his open mouth into Thalia's outstretched lips. A wavering spectral haze floated in the air. The man dropped to his feet, and Thalia grabbed the next in line.

"What's going on up there?" Norm, not gifted in the height department, jumped up and down to try and see over the tops of the heads of his gangly co-workers.

Cat skirted the crowd who all seemed to be pulled in by Thalia's demonic energies and corralled Norm to a small antechamber between this floor and the next, hoping to keep him from view. "Thalia is vanquishing the hoard. We need to capture the treasure before it is lost to the underworld," said Cat, urging Norm onto activities other than wondering why his girlfriend was sucking face with half a dozen guys at once who were literally falling at her feet. And she still needed to locate Aidan and the red rock.

"Right! Onward!" shouted Norm.

As she passed over the center of the room, Cat saw a circle of the red dust sprinkled around the floor. She kicked at the dirt, and it entered the air. Particles floated up and caught on the dimming glow from Norm's torch that he still had clutched in his hand, the only source of light in the room.

Cat turned and scanned the backs of the few that still stood in front of Thalia. None of them had Aidan's broad shoulders. And then she saw him. Standing at the side of the room. Mouth hanging open as if he had just witnessed every nightmare in Cat's head come to life. His head swiveled to Cat, eyes bulging with fear. He had seen everything, and there was no glow in his eyes. Either he had never been possessed, or he wasn't anymore. And there was no hiding what he had just witnessed.

The last of the LARPers dropped at Thalia's feet, and she stepped around them, eyes bright red, looking both sensuous and frightening at the same time. She came to a halt and stared at Aidan as if he were her next snack. Without any demon energy present, Thalia would just be sucking out Aidan's soul, and that would leave him dead, not passed out with the horrible hangover the rest of these creepazoids were going to have in the morning.

"The warrior princess has vanquished all the defenders. We must stop her with a prince's kiss." Cat tugged at Norm's sleeve and pushed him between Thalia and Aidan's line of sight. Thalia immediately clamped her hands on either side of Norm's face and pressed her lips to his.

Aidan's frantic gaze settled on Cat, his mouth opening and closing without a sound. Too horrified to speak. He spied the exit behind Thalia and stumbled over the arm of one of the LARPers. This only further increased his speed, and before Cat could stop him, he was already running up the passageway.

"Wait, Aidan. I can explain." But could she really explain? Could she tell him all about the supernatural world that existed and that she was a part of it? There wasn't much to say that wouldn't alienate him further. She had a taste of the normal. A taste of real life at his lips and that was all she was going to get. Perhaps all she deserved.

Cat halted her pursuit before it even began, her own demons having already caught up to her and sucked out her resolve, leadened her feet, turned her heart back to black quicker than the tar that used to flow through her veins in Hell. This was what she feared she deserved, and now it had happened.

Chapter Twelve

A memory of one of the most horrible days in Aidan's child-hood came flooding back to him as the wheels of his motorcy-cle skidded along the gravel road. The chilled night whipped his hair into a frenzy. In his rush to escape the nightmare behind him, he'd left his helmet attached to his motorcycle. His nightmares insisted on following him anyway.

He'd been picked on a fair amount back in school. Being the namesake of the town might have made his elders think he was immune to typical childhood bullying. Heck, he should have been the most popular kid in class. Back then the testosterone flew with reckless abandon and the guys weren't worried about whether or not Aidan Ash could make things easier for them later in life, they only knew that all their girlfriends had a crush and they wanted to take him down a few pegs.

That day he had been walking through the sports fields at the back of the school, dust billowing around his feet as he made his way home. Earlier in the day, he'd been called to the nurse's office and handed a phone.

His father's words still rang in his ears. Something was wrong with his mom. She'd been sick. It seemed that every other week she was laid up with a different ailment and every time she was having a harder time getting better. She'd been to the doctors in town multiple times. That day Aidan's Father and Mother had gone into Portland, to meet with a specialist and run some tests. While he was anxious to get home, the rebel in him wanted to stay for practice. He just wanted a few more minutes to pretend that this semi-normal life he had was going to stay that way. Not get more complicated. He'd had a hard time fitting in, and now he had finally earned enough respect so that they would stop sacking him at every practice for no reason. It was only every other practice at that point. If he skipped practice that would put the target back on him. He just wanted to blend in enough so that he could stop living day to day in survival mode.

His mother. Something was wrong with his mother.

Billowing clouds of yellow dust rose around the wheels of Aidan's motorcycle as he transitioned from the mining roads to the narrow strip of road that led to the farm. The same billowing clouds of yellow dirt that he had kicked up around him as he walked past the practice fields and past his teammates who were running drills. A few of the worst of them were milling about the outskirts, knocking each other in the shoulder. Playing some game of who was tougher when they spotted him. Aidan looked forward, toward the break in the fence where he could scoot out past the boundary of the field. If only he could make it there, then they would leave him alone rather than get called out by the coach.

A pair of dusty black cleats appeared in the dust in front of him. He'd been so focused on his escape that he had failed to notice the worst of the bunch had circled around the back of the bleachers, escaping the coach's notice. Chester Cawling had been Felicia Harper's older brother. He'd since joined the military and had been killed in the line of duty, but Aidan hadn't shed any tears for him.

"Looks like you're quitting the team." Chester balled the front of Aidan's shirt in his hand and pulled until Aidan heard tiny tears from the cotton neckband being stretched to its limit.

Aidan tore his shirt from Chester's grip and took a few steps back only to bump into one of Chester's gang. The coach wasn't on the field. He'd left one of the seniors in charge of the drills, and there wasn't anyone left who would stop the inevitable from happening.

"I'm not quitting the team," said Aidan. "I've just got some chores to do at home. I'll be at the next practice."

The gang pressed in on him from behind, pushing him further forward until he was again within arms' reach of Chester who pressed his finger into Aidan's chest as he spoke. "No, you don't get it, do you? This guy is stupider than he looks, eh boys?" The peanut gallery had let loose a chortle and Aidan could smell their stale breath. Spittles of chaw rained down on him. "You is gonna quit. You'll be telling coach tomorrow. You see, we can't stand to looks at you no more."

"Little Aidan Ash has to go home and milk some cow titties." The thug to his left thought he was funny now. Thought he could get Aidan to take a swing at him. The last thing Aidan or his family needed right now was him to get involved in a fight.

"Naw, I think he's still sucking at his Momma's teet, that's why he's got to go home."

At the mention of his mother, Aidan had snapped. The focus of his world had sucked down to a small pinpoint that was aimed directly at the nose of the nearest bully who had made the offending remark. With reflexes he didn't know he possessed he struck out, cracking the boy square on the nose. Before he could raise his hand to his face, a cascade of blood started to pour from the disfiguration left on his face. He stepped back, and the remaining three filled in the gap and began to rain down retribution on Aidan for messing with one of their cronies.

Quickly overpowered, Aidan had shrunk down into a ball to protect his vitals. Tears poured down his face, but not from the pain. His imagination had taken him out of the moment. But instead of bringing him someplace happy he had begun to think of his mother and what might be wrong with her.

The news was not going to be good. There would be no cake and candles waiting for him at home in celebration. Only his mother and father, solemnly delivering him the news he didn't want to hear. He'd rather continue receiving this physical beating than to take any more strikes to his psyche.

Aidan slid his motorcycle to a halt in front of the farmhouse, ending the painful trip down memory lane. He pulled his helmet off and caught a glimpse of himself in his rearview mirror. Red eyes. Like the eyes of all those men in the tunnel. What the Hell was wrong with him? Was it a trick of the light or was he possessed?

Everyone except Cat, Thalia, and Norm. He looked up and saw the small red beacon atop the Iron Forge Mine glowing in the distance. Trying to get ahold of his rough emotion, he looked at his reflection again. His eyes were normal. Must have been his imagination. Maybe it was all his imagination.

Norm pulled in behind him, Thalia and Cat in the backseat of his pimpmobile. "Hey man, you alright? You looked really spooked."

"I just need a minute alone. I'll be okay." He needed more than a minute, he needed miles. Miles between himself and this town that seemed to be trying to suck him into something sinister.

Something evil.

He'd tried to deny it, but tonight it was evident. And Cat was definitely part of it.

"Aidan, I can explain." She exited the car and took a few steps toward him with her hands in front of her like he was armed and dangerous and she was afraid he was about to shoot.

He should have made an excuse. Anything to clamp down on the raw emotion boiling just below the surface. What he had to say—how he felt—hadn't managed to form into a coherent sentence. The pain was too deep. Looking at her was too much.

"What the fuck was all that? I let you in, and you lied to me." Adrenaline still coursed through his body and his hands shook as he spoke. "What are you?"

He didn't want to believe that Niro could possibly be the one in the right. That Cat could be some *Thing* that was here to collect the minerals he had been storing deep within the old mine shafts. But what else could explain what had happened tonight?

"I've just been through a lot. Seen a lot. There's a better time and place to explain everything. Look. You used me to get what you needed in the beginning, right? To help you figure out your numbers. You pulled me into this. Not the other way around."

She was right about that. But that still didn't explain the red-eye warriors and whatever otherworldly shit that Thalia did. "How do you explain her?" He pointed to the car where Thalia had remained.

"Well, she is a demon. But a good one, I swear it."

That was the last straw. "A 'good' demon. Do you even hear yourself right now? First, you're telling me there are demons.

Now you're telling me some are good and some are bad."

"Whatever shit you guys took tonight do you mind sharing because damn, stuff must be good." Norm leaned against the car. "I should probably get the girls home though. Make sure they're safe from the demons." He chuckled and opened the car door. "You guys are hilarious. I don't know why you didn't go LARPing with me sooner. You are total naturals."

Cat got within Aidan's sphere. Close enough so he couldn't deny her existence. Warmth radiated from the place on his forearm where she had her hand, her touch seeping all the way to his core. He already loved this woman. Which was why doing what needed to be done was going to be all that much harder.

"Look, Aidan. Before you asked me to meet you at the mines, I hadn't left my house more than a handful of times in the entire year I've lived here. I've been hiding out. Hiding from all the evils in the world, but it didn't work. They found me. But so did you. I could chalk that all up to coincidence, but I won't. Especially since Niro has set up shop in your mine."

Set up shop. She was acting like Aidan had put the open sign in the window and Cat was there to do some browsing. "Is that why you decided to come out? Because you learned he had the red rock and you need it?"

Cat's face screwed up in confusion. "Why would I ever need any red rock?"

"Power. Niro told me all about what that stuff can do, and I saw what you and Thalia did tonight. Niro says he is protecting the red rock from the likes of you and Thalia. He's offered me a place in his army. To help protect Ashton and everything else."

He shouldn't have revealed all that to Cat or the others. He'd been told to be discreet. Told that all the torture he'd been put through would be for some good in the end, for Ashton. But his gut told him that Cat couldn't be all bad. He didn't want her to be.

"I wanted to wait to tell you all of this. But perhaps I've waited too long already, and that's why we are here now in this situation." Cat motioned for Thalia and Norm to come closer. "Everyone here might as well know. If what I think is right, we will all need each other more than ever soon."

"So, you're saying all of what happened down there was real?" Norm popped up excitedly on his heels. Of course, *he* would be the one who would not be freaked out about the fact that there were actual monsters under the bed. "I knew it."

"It's not as cool as you think, Norm," said Cat. "Niro is a collector. A demon. He's been sent here by his boss to bring something back."

Thalia crooked her two forefingers and made makeshift horns on the top of her head. "Mr. Prince of Darkness himself."

"What is he here for?" asked Aidan. A pit formed in his stomach. If Niro was here for something, he had also been recruiting help. Including help from Aidan. He wanted the promises he made about saving Ashton to be as real as Cat being on the right side. But somehow he knew that one or both were too good to be true.

"I'm not sure yet. I thought it was the red rock, but if that were the case, he would have taken it and left by now. There's something else here that he is waiting for."

If Aidan was going to remain objective, he needed to place some distance between himself and Cat. Every time he looked into her hazel eyes he was drawn in again to the fantasy that he had finally found the woman he'd always been looking for. Before he could have second thoughts, he blurted out, "We should stop seeing each other. I think it is the best thing for both of us."

"Awkward." Norm backed up toward the car and Thalia followed him. They got in and closed the door.

"Look," said Cat. She looked up at Aidan, eyes glistening with unshed tears clinging to her lower lids. "I don't blame you. But I still want to help. We'll need to go back into that mine. Whatever he is hiding is there, I'm sure of it. But we need more information. There is a reason why he is hanging around the mines. I don't know, maybe he keeps something at his home. I've tried to hack into the work systems, and there's nothing. Do you know where Niro lives?"

* * *

Cat found it difficult to read the slip of paper taped to the top of her computer monitor through the tears that continued to rim her eyes. Blinking back the unwelcome reminder of Aidan's declaration, she recognized the words as her favorite Winston Churchill quote. "If you're going through Hell, keep going."

She'd actually been alive when the chubby, stoop-shouldered, funny-faced man with a speech impediment had uttered that phrase to rouse the people of London against the vicious and victorious Nazis. Churchill had been described as having a lion's heart. Her own wouldn't stop breaking. Aidan was right to distance himself from her, but it didn't hurt any less. And no matter how much she told herself it was impossible to fall in love in ten days, she knew now that was exactly what had happened. She had fallen in love with Aidan Ash, and now he had broken her heart.

Cat had convinced Thalia that she needed time alone to do some damage control. Norm was the weakest link. Although there weren't many people who would believe his far-fetched story about a bunch of beasties in Ashton, he was Norm, after all, just one panicked soul could ruin everything. Uncovering Niro's nefarious plans was enough to deal with. Despite Aidan breaking her heart, she cared about him deeply and could never live with herself if something happened to him.

Tomorrow, Aidan had agreed to show her where Niro lived. For tonight, she was glued to her chair, safe within her protection circle. The rest of the night and their relationship was over. Cat ran her eyes over the contents of her living room. She had finally made a home here, one she must abandon even if she succeeded in saving the town. When the mine shut down, so would her source of income. Even if she found a new position, living this close to Aidan would be next to impossible. Regardless of her feelings, she needed to protect him at all costs.

She picked up the phone and dialed the number of the only other man that had broken her heart. Mane was scheduled to go back to Seattle in the morning. His wife was anxious to have him return. Divine intervention had given him a soul and a real life.

Cat had a soul, she just couldn't figure out the real-life part. Of course, a lot of humans seemed to have the same problem.

"Mane, meet me at Miss Chow's. I need to talk to you."

Without waiting for his response, she grabbed her keys and darted out to her car.

The heat of the day permeated the air and darkness enveloped the road before her, feeding on the light from her high beams. At least this late at night she didn't have to worry that there would be any people walking the back roads between her house and the bridge over the River Rouge.

Her wagon hit the smooth pavement of the bridge. The waters below were inky black. Barely a ripple disturbed the surface. A sliver of a moon hung in the sky. The shores were barren of the critters she had seen before. *Where had they all gone to?*

The only business in town that still had its lights on was the corner gas station with 24-hour mini mart and Miss Chow's. Though Cat was sure only she and the "not so normals" could spy the neon sign in Miss Chow's window. Mane sat in his bright white '58 Edsel, silver pinstripes and silver roof, idling on the street out front.

When he saw Cat's car pull up, he turned off the engine and stepped out. "Are you sure this place is open?"

Cat was more unnatural than this man who used to be the devil's right hand. He'd been given a second chance at life, and she had no right bringing him into this again. He was no longer a demon, no longer the man she resented. "You know, this was a bad idea. I'm sorry to get you up so late."

Mane crossed the space between them and put his hands on her shoulders. He lifted her chin with a gentle hand to the light from the overhead street lamp. There would be no hiding her puffy eyelids from him. He would know that she had been crying. "You want to tell me what or who has upset you so much." Even though his powers had been taken, a raw power still emanated from the man before her. It was that power she had first been drawn to, the shred of the soul that had always resided in the man and was only made corporeal by divine intervention.

"Let's go inside, and I'll explain everything."

The bell above the door made no sound as they entered the restaurant. Miss Chow liked to keep a low profile, but something was definitely off as they opened the front door from the alleyway. The familiar red booths were covered in plastic sheeting. Faded shadows lined the walls where there used to be pictures hanging. The lights in the kitchen beyond the double doors were off. The hairs on the back of Cat's neck stood at attention.

If all the workers at the mine had been infected, then it stood to reason the townsfolk might be infected also. And if they became something other than normal they would be able to detect this place.

And Miss Chow.

A pit formed in her gut. If anything happened to the old woman, it was Cat's fault.

"Something isn't right here," said Mane.

It definitely didn't take a demon to sense that. Cat slipped the six-inch blade from the holster at her side. The cool steel glinted in the light from the bulb that swayed slightly above their heads. At the back corner of the room, the shadows seemed to gather and take shape.

"Shifter." The word hissed out of Mane's mouth, and he took a step to stand between Cat and the form rapidly taking place.

"Eh? Cool your horses. You no hot shit no more." Miss Chow stepped from the shadow dressed from head to toe in a dark red gown with wide open sleeves capped by thick brocade. The bottom of the dress pooled around her legs giving her the appearance of floating as she approached. Miss Chow had given herself a thirty-year face life, but it there was no mistake she was the same woman. And she was hot. She flipped her long dark hair over her shoulder and jerked her thumb at Mane. "Why you bring this one here?"

Cat pushed Mane to the side. "It's okay, this is Miss Chow. She owns the place."

"Owned. Past tense. I sell. Not safe here no more." She lifted a box from the corner and grunted while she carried it over to the one table that hadn't been covered yet.

Mane tried to take the box from her, but she batted him away. "Your kind the problem. Let me be. I live long time without no help."

"I'm not a demon anymore." Mane stood up straight, and Cat could see that Miss Chow had struck a nerve with him. He was proud to be rid of his past. Considering what she wanted to bring up, this conversation might not go well.

Miss Chow pointed to the empty booth. "Last meal. Then I get out of here." From the box she pulled a take-out container and the second it hit the air, Cat knew what it held. Miss Chow's Orange Chicken, a dish worth scalding her thighs over. The scent brought a slight bit of comfort and warmed her heart until the cold reality of the last time she'd eaten it hit. Aidan had been with her, here, in this very booth.

"You no snivel now. You need your strength." Miss Chow plopped the container in front of Cat and another in front of Mane. "Eat. I be back in minute when you done."

She floated back into the shadows, this time disappearing into the ether rather than through the double doors. There wasn't much point in keeping up appearances anymore. Shit was about to get real.

Mane started to get up from the booth. "Shifters aren't good news, Cat. We need to get out of here."

"Kind of like demons aren't good news?" Danger or no, Cat

wasn't about to pass up this particular meal. She took the wooden chopsticks from the paper pouch and sanded them against one another, a ritual she enjoyed and one she would savor especially if this was going to be the last time she did it. "Sit and eat. She is one of the good ones. Like you."

Mane snatched the other paper container of Chinese food from the table. "Broccoli beef. Okay, I'm listening."

"It seems Niro is here for the red rock." Cat took her time explaining what had happened in the mine. As the story unfolded, Mane's rate of food consumption slowed rapidly. "Not sure why he hasn't taken it yet. What is he waiting for?"

"He's here for someone, not something." Mane placed the now empty container onto the table. "He is a collector like I was. He isn't needed for sniffing out the mineral, that's up to the lackeys. And it sounds like he's probably closing in on whoever he's come for."

Cat pressed her back into the padded vinyl booth, but the cold surface offered her no comfort. "He's here to bring me back. I know it. He's toying with me." Fear turned to anger and then guilt. Maybe if she had insisted on going with Niro, she could have spared Aidan and the rest of the town.

Aidan.

The last time she saw him the red had faded from his eyes. Perhaps he was immune somehow to the effects of the red rock. Or maybe Niro was saving Aidan for last to torture her even more. Torture being the thing he had taught Cat.

A shiver ran up her spine at the thought of the last person she had on her torture table. The man sitting across from her. "I'm sorry. For what I did to you. I wasn't myself. I didn't mean to hurt you."

The words hung between them, ones she had owed him for

many years but was too ashamed to say. Mane had never asked for an apology, especially since Cat's involvement with him had been the reason she had landed in Hell in the first place. But she regretted the tortures he had endured by her hands. Even the memory of the joy she had felt while inflicting such pain made her ill. The delicious Orange Chicken threatened to make a reappearance.

Mane clasped her hand between his own. "I know that wasn't you. Believe me, I know what being down there can do to a person. I'm happy now. With Kit. We're happy. I only wish I could be of more help to you here. There really isn't anything I can do anymore. I can't protect you. You're on your own, and it isn't because I don't want to help. It's because I no longer can."

She looked into the eyes of the man before her. The first man she had ever loved, affection bordering on obsession until she lost herself. She had made so many mistakes, and instead of owning up to them, she had hidden inside a tiny house in a tiny town and hoped that she could pretend none of it had ever happened. She had failed to make amends with her own soul, and this was the consequence. Instead of pulling those around her down with her, it was time she stood on her own two feet.

"Thank you for your friendship," said Cat.

They both startled as Miss Chow appeared before them, a small black tray with two fortune cookies in her hand. "I know you do right thing. But I hate goblins that come with this shit. Shut door on your way out."

Cat took the tray from her hands, and Miss Chow vanished. She selected one of the two cookies from the plate and performed her ritual. Breaking the cookie, eating a morsel of the vanilla wafer, and unrolled the last fortune from Miss Chow.

Among the lucky, you are the chosen one.

Confirmation of her deepest fears and desires in the form of a two-inch strip of paper. This battle was for her to win or lose. A battle for the town of Ashton, but also a battle to finally find her own humanity again. There was no option anymore.

Mane stared at the slip between his fingers. "Maybe I better start out toward home tonight."

"Why? What does yours say?"

Mane gave her a smirk. The familiar bravado she had known still lurked right below the surface. "It says I'll be hungry again in an hour."

They walked out together and closed the door. When Cat turned around the restaurant was dark. Boards covered the windows as if someone was preparing for a maelstrom to hit the city. She inhaled deeply, and a sweet, pungent zing of an impending tempest filled her lungs. There was a storm coming all right, and she would be ready for it.

Chapter Thirteen

Aidan set the scroll he found in his father's room down on the entryway table and thrust his chin forward, using the mirror in the dim and narrow space to adjust his silk tie. The last threads of dusk filtered through the oval glass of the front door highlighting the cluttered corner of mud-encrusted overalls and farming tools he hadn't put away. Barely enough light to see by, but not dark enough to justify the expense of turning on the lights. Outside, engorged drops of rain struck the metal gutters which rattled against the side of the house. Another project to add to his list.

He ran a comb through his hair. Humidity thickened the air, and his formal attire felt suffocating. He wasn't even sure that his evening plans were a good idea. The call from Violet Chanterelle had been unexpected. He'd accepted her invitation thinking she would be a welcome distraction. And he was starting to feel desperate. Sure, she belonged to one of the most money-grubbing families in all of Ashton, but the Chanterelles had their own money, and maybe he could save Ash Farms if they would loan him enough to get through this season. Next year would be better, had to be.

He cinched the silk noose around his neck.

The spring storm masked the crunching of tires rolling up his driveway, and he didn't notice the vehicle approaching his house until a dark shadow fell across his reflection. His date was early. He pulled his cell phone from his pocket and checked his messages. He'd left a message for Cat about the investigation of Niro's apartment. He hadn't heard back. He'd much prefer daylight to face his demons and the fact that Niro would be at work, cushioned the chances of being caught. If they were going to do any reconnaissance, it would be better if there weren't a chance he would walk in on them.

The truth was, he wasn't sure he could handle seeing Cat again so soon. Being in her presence was intoxicating, and he didn't trust himself to be rational. Distraction was something he couldn't afford, he needed to make the right decision. And Cat wasn't part of his plan.

He grabbed an umbrella from the corner and opened the door to find a shiny black Escalade parked at the base of his front porch. The driver tilted his cap over his eyes and scrambled to the rear passenger door with a broad gray umbrella. A white satin heel touched down on the dirt and out emerged Violet, perfectly coiffed as if she was going to the horse races. A stylish derby hat covered in feathers and a fancy bow sat atop her shoulder-length blond hair as if some wild bird had come to roost. At least there was no chance of intimacy with such a mood-killer-slash-obstacle between them. The pressure of how he was going to bring up the money was already tricky enough. Violet had shown interest in him in the past, but he didn't want to lead her on.

He stepped onto the porch, and despite the rain, the scent of the burnt orchards hit him smack in the face. Violet had obviously smelled the same thing as she quickly pulled a lace handkerchief from her bag and held it to her nose. "My, my, they did put out all the fires, didn't they? I didn't think it

219

would still be so pungent." Her driver followed alongside her as she maneuvered the muddy potholes.

"It's only been a few days." Aidan tried to tamp down the frustration he already felt in Violet's presence. Maybe asking her for money was the wrong thing to do. Even after repaying the financial debt there would be a debt of gratitude with no expiration date. He met her at the bottom of the steps and exchanged cover of his own umbrella with that of her driver. "Why don't you come inside? You're a bit early. Our reservation isn't for another hour."

"Of course. I hoped we would have a chance to chat in private." Violet extended a gloved hand, expecting to be escorted up the stairs. "I do hope you'll help me navigate these barren boards."

Aidan surveyed the weathered planking that cried out for a fresh coat of paint. Last week he might have given a rat's ass. But then last week he hadn't known about the monsters. And if Aidan didn't figure out how to squash this hocus pocus, the upkeep of his farm would be the least of his worries.

Red eyes flashed across his mind's eye, and the pieces of the puzzle began to fall into place at the deadly image. The headaches he'd been having. The dreams. The scroll he found in his Dad's room that contained some kind of prophetic message. Not to mention the red rock. *What if they were all connected?*

The only person who remotely understood the extent of the evil around him was Cat and Niro. In auto-pilot mode, he took Violet's hand, and her driver scuttled back into the vehicle.

"I'm delighted you finally accepted my invitation to spend some time together. I mean, we've grown up alongside one another all these years. Don't you think it's best if we get to know one another better?" Her words, although delivered in an affected drawl of a Southern Belle, lacked sincerity. They had grown up alongside one another. Literally. The Chanterelle property bordered the south side of Ash Farms. While the Ash family farmed the land, the Chanterelle's pursued industrial ventures and were far wealthier because of it. They'd unsuccessfully tried to get their lands re-zoned for years, and the only thing between them and success was his father.

Violet scooted past Aidan and crossed the threshold into his house. He needed to go to Cat's house and bring her the scroll to see what she made of it. He followed Violet inside and grabbed his coat from the hook, sliding his arms through the sleeves. Perhaps honesty was the best policy. Lies he had told Cat and lies she had told him had only led to disaster.

"I'm sorry, Violet. I need to go see Cat about something very important. Could we postpone this until another time?"

Violet turned her head, catching a glance of the worn paper of the scroll setting on the entryway table. She reached out, brushing her fingers against the delicate parchment and a shiver traveled down her spine. Her eyes remained out of his view. "You're going to go visit the troll under the bridge? Whatever for?"

She spun around, and the breeze caused the parchment to fall from the table. Aidan bent down to grab it at the same time as Violet latched onto the end of the paper. He expected her to relinquish it, but Violet kept a tight grip. He studied her face that rested a few feet from his. She looked normal enough. But did the monsters possess her, or was she her usual stubborn self? At this point, he had no idea how far this had spread or how it spread.

"What did you call her?" Aidan held his end of the paper firmly.

"A troll." Violet released her hold on the paper and eased her features back into a casual albeit feigned fashion. "She's the one I saw you with at the fair, am I right? The one who moved here ages ago but insists on hiding herself away in that house?" She waved her gloved hand as she spoke and walked further into the house toward the dining room.

"She's been getting out more." Aidan shoved the parchment into the inside pocket of his jacket and followed behind her.

Violet sashayed over to the window, completely disregarding Aidan's request to leave, and parted the curtains that looked out over the now barren cherry fields. "You should get out more too, Aidan. Talk to the townsfolk. I'm not sure you would like what I have been hearing. What with the cherry fields burned down now and the mine hiring fewer workers each year, there aren't many options for folks wanting to find work."

He pressed the paper to his chest. The document with the signatures of all the founders of the town. The message. His time was running out. "It's just one bad year. We can bounce back. Ash Farms has been part of the Ashton since it was founded. We'll find a way. We always have."

With her gloved hands, Violet plucked a sealed white envelope from her leather clutch and placed it on the dining room table. The table his mother used to serve grandiose meals to vast swathes of the community, opening Ash Farms during certain times of the year to feed any who wanted to taste the bounty of their hometown like it had first been presented by the founders. "I had wanted to go over these with you over dinner, but that can wait. My father made the changes Drew agreed to. Hopefully, everything is finally in order, and we can start construction by the first of June."

The way she set the envelope down and used his father's first name in such a perfunctory manner made every muscle in his body tense. And what was this about construction? She better mean a taller fence between their properties. He didn't realize his fists were balled at his sides until Violet spoke.

"Something tells me that Drew did not tell you he was speaking to us about his plans for the future of Ash Farms?"

Violet Chanterelle liked to play the part of a dim-witted femme, but she was more a femme fatale. She knew before she set the paper down that Aidan had no clue what it was about. He was certain of it.

"You can be sure that before my father signs anything, I will be reviewing whatever this is." Aidan snatched the envelope from the table and ripped open the seal. In his hands was a contract. A contract to let the Chanterelles use the entire south side of their land to develop a shopping center.

For a split second, Aidan forgot how to breathe. His entire life had been about this farm. Working the land. Learning about the land. And now saving the land. This wouldn't only destroy the farm it would destroy the town. Local merchants could be affected. Small businesses driven out. He didn't have to dredge up history to figure out how this had happened, he just didn't know his father had become so desperate. The last page of the contract showed an artist rendering of the sprawling mega shopping complex which would span the length of the Chanterelle property all the way to the edge of their homestead. Instead of looking out their back porch at horses grazing in the wheat fields they would be squinting back from the phosphorescent glare of the lamps from a parking lot.

He gripped Violet's upper arm and steered her toward the front door that had been left open. "We'll be talking very soon. There is no way I am going to allow this to happen."

Violet shrugged out of his grip as they reached the threshold. "Soon you'll have no choice. Have you not been paying attention to the papers? Your property is going to be put up for auction soon. Taxes haven't been paid in years. It's this, or we take everything at auction. But think about what we could do if we partnered instead."

A thunderclap erupted from the heavy gray clouds, and a bolt of lightning snaked a horizontal path across the sky toward the Iron Forge Mine. Violet placed a hand on Aidan's chest and leaned into him, changing her tactic from hard sell to trying to make him hard. The cloying, powdery scent of her perfume infiltrated his senses and caused him to sneeze.

"Why bless you," she said.

Her words sent a shooting pain through his skull. The last thing this woman brought to him were blessings. Aidan squeezed his eyes shut and stumbled backward a step. Violet wrapped a surprisingly sturdy arm around his waist, keeping him upright. Slowly the ache in his head subsided enough for him to crack open his eyes. A red glow flashed before him, and he grabbed Violet by the shoulders, pinning her against the door frame. "You're one of them."

"What the Hell, Aidan?" Cat's voice rang out, cutting through the low rumble that had somehow transferred from the sky into his mind. Was he hallucinating the sound or was Violet mimicking Cat to mess with his mind? She was infected and using her evil to influence him. He couldn't trust anybody.

"Aidan, snap out of it!" Cat's hands tugged at his arms,

dragging him back to reality. He looked up to see the orange glow of the setting sun bleeding through a break in the clouds. The red light he thought he saw. His hands dropped to his sides.

Violet's eyes were as wide as saucers. "You need help, Aidan Ash. And I don't just mean with this farm. You need medication." She ran her hands over her rumpled dress. "And I'm sending you my dry cleaning bill. My father will expect to hear about that contract soon. If not, then we'll see you at auction."

Aidan watched her stomp down the steps into the rain and fling open the car door. Her flustered driver raced around in time to have the door shut in his face.

Norm's car was parked next to his motorcycle and from inside Thalia and Norm had their faces pressed to the steam coated windows to watch the show.

"Are you okay?" Cat wiped the rain from her face. Her brown leather jacket was soaked, and her boots were coated in mud. "What was that all about?"

"I left you a message." Aidan stuttered, watching Violet's car being steered down the road along with the last plan he had for saving his farm. He crammed all his grief into a box and shut the lid tight. His farm was only one piece of Ashton. The rest of the town's fate might rest in what Cat knew, and he wasn't going to give up yet. "I'm sorry if you didn't get it."

"No, I got it. I just came anyway to see if we could catch you before you left. We've got a plan to figure out what Niro knows. Looks like your plans have changed for the evening. Are you in?" The enthusiasm in her voice gave him hope and that also translated to desire. "I promise I'm only trying to help. This isn't a date."

The wet t-shirt beneath her open coat clung to her body, reminding him of the first time he had met her. And she was still a mystery to him. He would change that. The first step was to trust her. And get her to trust him. Niro's voice echoed in his mind. "Don't let her get to close to you. She'll get inside your head."

The only voice that wouldn't leave his head was that of Niro, and he wanted to figure out why.

"I'm in."

* * *

Cat slammed her SUV into gear and revved the engine as Aidan slid into the passenger seat, too furious to even speak. She snapped her jaw shut while trying to control her jealous rage. The cloud of dust from Violet's car still lingered, the pungent dirt reminding Cat of Aidan's betrayal. If he could start screwing some other woman before the dust settled between them, then he wasn't the man she thought he was. She pulled out of the driveway and followed Norm's taillights toward the city.

She had a job to do and getting sentimental over what wasn't meant to be might possibly get Thalia killed. Her friend had come up with a plan to use her succubus charm to lure Niro out for a night on the town. Stiff drinks and karaoke at the local bar. Norm would make sure Cat and Aidan knew when they were on the way back to his apartment. Cat figured they should have at least a few hours, enough time to figure out why Niro was hoarding red rock and who he had come to collect. Adding to the urgency of the task, she sensed they were not alone on Aidan's property. Somewhere close by lurked more creatures. For once, her ability to detect them proved handy. She knew they had to get out of there before whoever or whatever caught up with them and tipped Niro off to their plan. Their time was almost up. They had one shot at this.

Aidan drummed his fingers on his thigh. He'd changed out of his suit and pulled on some jeans and a cotton tank. His gray bomber jacket hung open, his eyes straight ahead on the road. Cat patted the front pocket of her black cargo pants to check for her cell phone and her knife. A tight ponytail held her hair from her face. She was dressed for the job, not for a date like Violet seemed to be.

"So, what was Violet doing at your house?" she demanded with more force than she intended. While she wanted to play it cool, she was pissed off and wasn't going to suppress her irritation.

"Do you really care what she was doing there?" His tone was slightly teasing. He leaned his elbow on the window and studied her profile.

"I care to know why you were viciously attacking another human being. What the Hell were you thinking? Do you get your thrills attacking women?" When they had pulled up to Aidan's house, she thought she was witnessing an intimate embrace. She had alighted the stairs, jealously boiling below the surface, before seeing the panicked look in Violet's eyes. She knew that look. She had caused that look in many others before.

Aidan slammed a fist on her dashboard. "Violet Chanterelle and her family are out to destroy everything that has always made this town what it is, and they took advantage of my father to try and work a deal behind my back."

Cat felt slightly relieved that they were talking business. Maybe he wasn't ready to move on after all. But something was definitely off about him. "So, she dresses like that all the time?"

"We were planning on going to dinner," said Aidan. "I wasn't planning on having her drop a bomb on me."

Cat jerked the car to a stop as Norm and Thalia pulled in front of the bar and Norm hopped out to take his place inside. "You were going out on a date?"

She choked back the disappointment in her voice. She had never taken Aidan for the type to be interested in such a plastic woman, but who was she to judge? It wasn't like she was better for him. She was much much worse.

"I wanted to find a way to ask her for a loan to help finance keeping the farm afloat another year. But I realized I was ignoring the bigger problem."

Thalia pulled her car in front of Niro's apartment complex. Cat drove past and parked several cars down in a darkened section of road across the street, the location giving her a prime view of Niro's apartment entrance. The moment they left, she and Aidan would sneak in and hack into the mine's computer systems from Niro's PC. Cat knew from her work on their systems that he had remote access. She also had his password.

"The bigger problem?" Cat squinted in the darkness and watched as Thalia exited her car in her hot pink patent leather pumps and matching halter dress splashed with white polka dots. Her black hair was swept into a formal updo and her cat eye glasses perched on the edge of her nose. She looked like she had been plucked right out of a 1950s high school prom. Her familiar style was one of the reasons Cat had taken an immediate liking to her. She wished she could be transported back in time. Everything had been a whole lot simpler.

Aidan took a rolled piece of parchment from his jacket and handed it to her. The second her fingertips brushed the coarse vellum, a surge of energy rushed into her core and stole the breath from her lungs. The paper fluttered from her hand onto the floorboard. "What the Hell is that?"

"What's the matter?" Aidan retrieved the document and offered it to her again, but Cat waved him off.

"That thing is infused with demonic energy. Every fiber of it. Like I mean it is not from here." The thing brought back memories of the vast libraries within the confines of her otherworldly prison. Books of the many contracts made with humans. "Where did you get that?"

Aidan handled the page like it was nothing. And now that she was aware of it, it was like a jar of spiders in an enclosed space with a claustrophobic arachnophobe. "Apparently, it's been in my family for years, and I was hoping you would be able to tell me what it means. My father has been holding onto it. Hiding it from me. But honestly, when I look at it, I can only understand half of what it says, and the other half is so faded it's illegible."

"It's not faded. The contract hasn't come due yet." This was bad. Very bad. If Aidan's family possessed such a document, it meant that someone in the past made a deal with the devil. Staring at the document, her heart thudding painfully in her chest, she knew what Niro was after, the Ashes. Was the document about Aidan or his dad? The problem was, the words wouldn't reappear on the contract itself until it came due. The terms had been agreed upon by those long gone. "Hold it out so I can see it, but I don't want to touch it."

Aidan held up the paper and Cat slipped her cell phone out of her pocket and flicked on the flashlight app. Black, dripping tar oozed from every page, an aura of pure evil that sent chills of panic along Cat's spine. While she knew it was an optical illusion, the sight struck terror in her heart. Using every bit of concentration she could muster, she focused on the legible text.

At the bottom of the page were half a dozen signatures. "Who are these people? Do you know them?"

"The elders of my family. My great-grandfather and his brothers."

"You have other family here in town? I thought you and your father ran the farm."

Aidan shook his head and tucked the scroll back into his pocket. "It is the two of us. My great-grandfather was the only one who stayed in town. My grandfather told me once that his aunts and uncles all moved away. The farm had some spectacular seasons around the time this was signed. They made their fortunes and decided to try to branch out. Make a home for themselves in a more prosperous valley. But misfortune befell every one that moved away from Ashton. Disease. Accidents. None of them lived more than six months after they moved away."

"But you moved away to go to school. Didn't you?" If Aidan's family were cursed, then he probably would have died once he left the farm. But he had been able to go to school without a problem.

Aidan leaned back in his seat and ran a hand through his hair. The cogs and wheels in his mind were trying to put the pieces of something together. "Yeah, but I was never gone for more than a few months at a time. I always came back during breaks to help with the harvest and the planting. But Mom..."

Aidan took a sharp intake of breath and pointed out the

window. "Looks like they are on the move."

Thalia's hot pink dress swayed from side to side. There was no mistake that Niro would know she was a succubus. They were counting on it. Thalia intended to lure him to the bar Norm was at to find a victim to play with. A devilish delight that they hoped would attract the demon in human skin that had had to play nice for far too long. It looked like he had fallen for the bait. The actual bait would, of course, be Norm since he seemed to be able to keep Thalia in her "right" mind. The one that could control her urges and didn't cross the line into killing that is.

"I think you should probably keep that in here." Cat reached over and popped the glove box.

Aidan shoved the contract in the box and clicked it shut. They both watched as Niro slid into the passenger side of Thalia's car and they both drove away. Easy. Too easy. The fact that Niro had agreed to go with Thalia meant that she would have to drive him back and could make an excuse for them to stay out longer if they needed more time.

The paper in the glove box practically had a heartbeat that Cat could sense was growing faster. Whatever the paper said, Niro was definitely here to collect on it. And it had to do with Aidan. Her Aidan. "Let's go."

Niro lived on the third floor of the newest construction in Ashton. A modern condominium, the building's bottom level was supposed to attract chain businesses like Starbucks and Subway. Except, they hadn't found the sleepy town of Ashton yet. If Violet's plan went through that would all change, but Cat was afraid that if the prophecy came, true "going corporate" would be the last of this town's worries.

They slinked through the dim phosphorescent lamplight.

The moon was barely a sliver tonight and although the stars showed brightly in the country, in town the streetlamps drowned out the pulsing glow of Venus and the Big Dipper.

They hit the darkened cover of the stairwell, and she withdrew her knife. Its smooth surface caught the reflection of the dark circles under her eyes. She had not had to face such a direct threat in a long time. Had taken great care not to. And here, in this sleepy town where sleep eluded her, she faced her worst nightmare with the man of her dreams trailing right behind her.

"I'll get the door open, and then you need to let me go first. You won't be able to see them. I can." There wasn't a lot of time for explaining. She hoped with all Aidan had been thrown in the last few days that he would accept that there were things beyond his explanation or comprehension and go with the flow. Of course, that would be too easy.

"What do you mean you can see them? Besides, I'm not totally useless you know."

Aidan held in his hand a silver key. "I swiped it from his key ring on a lunch break and made a copy. So are you like one of them?"

There was so much of her life story that Aidan didn't know. That she wanted him to know. But they had so little time. She could only hope that he could trust her. "I can't really explain how. I lived some of my life around these creatures, and now I can sense them. But I'm not like them. Honestly, it's a skill I wish I didn't possess."

"It's why you keep to yourself, isn't it?" The look in Aidan's eyes was wholly sympathetic. The type of emotion that would elicit tears in someone who was looking for a hug, but Cat was beyond that. Had been for a long time. She wanted her life back. Her normal life.

She took the key from his hand. "Don't worry about all that. You ever been in a fight before?"

The soft demeanor that had come over Aidan turned in an instant, and his shoulders stiffened. "Don't worry about me."

Unfortunately, she had to. Aidan wouldn't be able to see the beasties, which meant that if they even so much as touched him, he would feel the effects. Fear. Terror. Enough to send him running out of the room. It was like an allergic reaction that all humans naturally have against demon contact. A way for both species to co-exist and kept clear of one another.

"You will feel fear without knowing why. You will want to bolt. Don't be afraid. Just don't leave. Once I take care of them, the fear will subside. I promise." She needed him to help sift through the data once she found it. Cat worked on the back end of the system, but Aidan was used to the daily reports and numbers. Maybe he could find something she wouldn't be able to notice. And they were short on time. He might be even shorter on time.

Cat slipped in the key, turning the deadbolt with ease. The door swung open without so much as a creak. The hairs on the back of her neck stood up. Too easy, way too easy. She glanced around the cavernous space that lay beyond the door. Devoid of furnishing, the minimalistic loft apartment was much more expansive than she had imagined would be possible in this small town. Niro had obviously spared no expense. Cat's footsteps were muffled by the plush Saxony carpet under her feet. Cat led the way into the dimly lit space and waited for the inevitable trap. After a tense second where the only sound that she heard was Aidan's breath behind her, no man-made alarms sounded. Niro had gone for supernatural protection.

"Holy shit." Aidan hissed from behind her. "He's got a guard dog."

"You can see that?" Cat gripped the knife tighter and eyed the black wolf-like creature with matted fur and red eyes. His mouth hung open to reveal a gaping maw of yellowed teeth. The beastie before her was not a possessed earthbound creature but a demon pet straight out of Hell.

"Unfortunately, yes," Aidan said.

Before Cat could ponder this anomaly the beastie made its approach, a low growl emanating from deep within its chest. Battling demonic creatures in this realm gave Cat the advantage. They were vulnerable to regular weapons. She just needed to get a clean hit in before being hit herself.

"Don't let it bite you. I'll take care of it." Cat lunged at the creature before it could do the same to her and aimed her knife for the heart.

The massive dog jumped up and over her as she was taking aim and she landed on the floor, her knife escaping from her hand. Now the creature was between her and Aidan, and Aidan was the next target in its sights.

Aidan backed up and leaned against the closed front door, searching around for some kind of weapon. "Hey, doofus, over here," she yelled.

The dog stepped a few feet toward her, and she lunged for her knife. As she did so, the dog turned and jumped toward Aidan. Aidan ducked, and the dog landed on the floor next to him. He held his hands in front of his body, and the dog sniffed at him. It gave a yelp and backed away a few feet, seemingly afraid. It turned around again to focus his attention on Cat who now had her weapon.

It took another leap and Cat brought the blade into its soft underbelly. A loud screech and it dissolved into a cloud of black ash that disappeared before it hit the floor.

"Was that what I was not supposed to be able to see?" Aidan stood up and quickly looked out the window before pulling the curtains closed.

"Yes." Cat realized that even though the creature was gone, she could still sense something. Something was not quite right. She stepped toward Aidan and put a hand on his arm. A tremor of power surged through her body, nearly knocking her backward.

Aidan gripped her around the waist. "Are you going to be okay?" He stared into her eyes and Cat watched for the red glow to follow, but it didn't. However, there was definitely something present within Aidan that was not there when she first met him. Something growing.

She shook off the tremors and refocused on their mission. "I'll be fine. I think that was probably the only one, but we should still stick close to one another."

Aidan tightened his grip around her waist. "I think I can handle that."

She planted her feet firmly on the ground and gently loosened his arm from her waist. "Just follow me." She felt her cheeks flush from the close contact. The last thing she needed was lusty thoughts clouding her judgment.

They headed down the long hallway. The first three rooms were empty, that left the door at the end.

"Do demons sleep in coffins like vampires or something? Why all the empty rooms?"

Aidan followed close behind her. Close enough for her to feel the heat of his flesh. Perspiration broke out across her brow. The air was cool, but being this close to Aidan, and alone, was starting to make her hot.

Cat put her ear to the door at the end of the hall and tried to avoid making direct eye contact with Aidan. For whatever reason, he was having an effect on her. If he was starting to exhibit some demonic influence, the last thing she needed was for him to work his mojo on her, even if it wasn't on purpose.

The space behind the door was silent. Cat brought a finger to her lips and gently eased it open. Niro may have skimped on the furniture in the other rooms, but he definitely had his bedroom taken care of.

In the center of the room was a large four poster bed with lacquered wooden black posts, each fitted with its own hardpoint. Niro the demon was apparently a little kinky. The bed had a black satin comforter and enough matching pillows for a whole harem. In the corner near the window sat a small desk with a computer. Mission accomplished. Now, if they could just make it past the bed.

The charge in the air was electric. Against Cat's better judgment, she turned and looked into the blue eyes of Aidan Ash. The dam that had been holding all her feelings shattered. She felt her desire welling up from inside her at an uncontrollable rate. *Damn Niro had a booby-trapped bed.*

They stood at the foot of Niro's bed, satin sheets beckoning. "I had no intention of doing anything with Violet other than asking her for money. I wanted you to know that." Aidan loosened the band holding Cat's ponytail and let her hair fall loosely around her shoulders.

"That's good because I really didn't want to have to kill her." Cat flipped her knife closed and put it back in her pocket. She unburdened Aidan from his coat and ran her eyes along the curve of his neck to his broad muscular shoulders. The scent of earth emanated from his pores from all the work he'd done on the farm. She inhaled deep of the warm, soft, ruddy scent and was slapped with a wet sweetness. A swelling undertone of something lecherous leering at her from just below the surface. Instead of scaring her it drew her in further. Whatever was warring within Aidan had not won. His humanity was stronger than the dark forces surrounding them, and she craved his humanity.

As if hearing her thoughts, he brought her in closer, his tongue tasting the tender flesh of her lips until she opened up and invited him in deeper. With deft hands he undid the buttons of her blouse and slipped his hand inside, cupping her breast with one hand and her ass with the other.

The closer they got to the bed the more uncomfortable Cat became. All this heady lust didn't erase all her common sense. If they fucked in Niro's bed, he would know about it.

Aidan freed a nipple from the confines of her bra and elicited a moan of pleasure. She was rapidly losing the ability to think at all. "Not the bed."

She pulled him down to the jute rug on the floor. The scratchy texture dug into her bare back as he pulled at her belt and tugged her pants down. Aidan rose up on his knees and Cat watched as he pulled his tank over his head and tossed it to the floor. A stray curl of brown hair hung in his eyes, and he paused to rake his gaze over her body.

"You're gorgeous. I wish we had more time." He loosened his belt and released his erection from its confines. The man didn't even wear underwear. He pulled a condom from Niro's side table and ripped it open between his teeth. "Did you want to help me with this?"

Cat rose up on her elbows and took the condom from his

hands. It had been years since she had sex with a man and she wasn't that great about being careful. She fumbled with the awkward device, and Aidan quickly took charge, seeing that she was having difficulty.

"Let me show you." He pinched the tip and unrolled the thin latex over his girth. He cupped her cheek in his hand. "There's so much I want to show you."

Gently he laid her down and pressed his length against the wet cotton of her panties. With one deft finger, he pulled aside the fabric and plunged into her core. Her arms wrapped around his waist, guiding him to just the right spot. Insatiable desire coursed through her veins, revitalizing the spirit she thought had died in the Underworld. This man was of this world. Real. She grasped onto his biceps, feeling the muscles flex under her grip. She arched her back, ignoring the bite of the jute on her flesh, and collapsed into sweet release under his pulsing thrusts. Her core swelled at his impending orgasm, and she held him as he reached his peak and jolts of pleasure rippled through his body.

For a moment they stared into each other's eyes, mouths slightly agape, breaths coming in rapid pants. Vibrations coming from Cat's pocket interrupted their reverie. Her cell phone. Thalia. Holy crap, this place was oozing with some mojo that completely made her forget why they were here. She tried to shake her head clear and looked up to see Aidan staring at her dreamily.

"Snap out of it Prince Charming, we've been had." Aidan sat up, looking confused and she took the vibrating phone from her pocket. Across the screen read a message that had been sent ten minutes ago: *I'm headed to the slammer. Long story. Send bail money. And oh, get the fuck out of there, he's coming back.*

"Are you having regrets already?" Aidan pulled his jeans back up, and Cat tossed his tank top at him as she put herself back together.

Even though she should feel regret—should feel like she'd been had all over again, she didn't feel that way. She did regret doing it in Niro's room, but she didn't regret the feeling in her heart. The love she had for Aidan. That was real. And she wouldn't let anything happen to him.

She reached out to him and put her hands on his shoulders. "No. Don't ever think that. The message I got was from Thalia. Niro is on his way back. We don't have much time, and I think besides the familiar Niro left to guard this place, he also left a charm that causes feelings of lust and disorientation."

As she said that her eyes continued on their path down Aidan's chest. Before she knew what she was doing her hands were pressed against his biceps.

"I see what you mean." A wry smile graced his lips. "The computer. That's why we're here, to see if he has information on his computer about why the mine has gone dry all of a sudden and why he's storing the red rock."

"Right." Cat swiveled around and headed straight toward Niro's desk. She powered up his laptop, shoved the memory stick into the USB port, and entered his password. She typed the name of Niro's boss, and a shiver ran up her spine. She never spoke the name out loud and certainly didn't think it when she could avoid it. Voldemort had nothing on the real thing.

The computer screen blinked to life. She clicked through a series of folders on the desktop. One of them was labeled "Junk." If there was anything she knew working in tech is that everyone kept their secret documents in a junk folder on their desktop. It was a way to keep the snoopers away, but have your most important documents right at your fingertips. While the download of the mineral reports from the last year was transferred to the thumb drive, she double clicked on the folder.

"Why does he have a ton of shit on me?" Aidan leaned over her shoulder, and she could tell the effects of the spell were still strong.

"You need to lean back."

"Right, sorry." Aidan switched to the window and parted the curtain to watch the street.

She copied and pasted the contents of a folder labeled "Aidan" to the thumb drive. It contained videos, photos, and documents. There was no telling how much time they required to do the equivalent of a smash and grab at this point.

Aidan let the curtain slip from his fingers. "He's here, and he's running up the stairs."

The last of the files finished transferring, and Cat ejected the thumb drive and powered down the computer. "Hide."

They crowded into Niro's small closet, behind his rack of identical black blazers and pressed pants.

"What are we going to do now?" Aidan folded his legs closer to his body, but the two of them would not be able to stay long. Certainly not the night. There had to be another plan, and fast.

The front door clicked open, and Niro called out to his hellhound. His voice stopped short. Cat pressed her finger to her lips and searched for Aidan's eyes in the darkness. "I need you to trust me."

Aidan wrapped his hand around hers and squeezed. "Right now the only thing that I'm certain of is you."

Cat tried to calm the swelling surge of emotion that followed Aidan's admission. He wouldn't like what she was about to do. Between the two of them, only she stood a chance against Niro. And even if not, she wasn't going to let Aidan sacrifice himself. "I'm going to take care of Niro. When we leave, I need you to find out what happened with Thalia. She may be in jail. I'll meet you back at my house later tonight."

He nodded, and the bedroom door clicked open. Cat watched Niro enter through the openings in the thin slats of the closet door.

He paused as he got to the center of the room and ran his hand over the smooth surface of his comforter. A sly grin appeared on his face, and he turned toward his computer, repeating the same gesture across the top of his laptop.

Niro spoke with his back to the closet. "Catherine. I know you are here. Why not do us a favor and come out, so we don't have to play hide and seek? I've had a long night."

Aidan gripped Cat's wrist as she moved toward the front of the closet. "I trust you," he whispered.

She was glad he trusted her because that trust was about to be tested.

Chapter Fourteen

Somewhere deep inside his lizard brain, Aidan debated his options. He could stay put and remain quiet while he watched his asshole of a boss seduce the woman he loved or he could take one of the Venetian crocodile skin loafers currently being crushed under his weight and shove it down Niro's throat.

His blood pressure rose, and the thrumming in his ears masked the conversation between Cat and Niro. Eyes locked on the couple, he noticed how her fingers trailed up Niro's arm as she tried to coax him out of the room. Temper near boiling, he reminded himself that she had asked him to trust her. She was trying to get information. Nothing more.

A part of him believed in her, yet a nagging sensation in the back of his mind distrusted the sentiment. Blind faith only went so far, and Cat had yet to prove herself worthy of his trust. God help her if she failed to do so. He startled at the uncharacteristic surge of vindictiveness that curled his hands into fists and focused instead on Cat. Something about Niro's house gave him the creeps, and the sooner they left it, the better.

"You can't blame me for being curious." She cocked her hip to one side and her head to the other.

"You broke into my apartment and killed my guardian. Do you know how difficult it is to get a good guardian these days?

He'll be irreplaceable. How do you expect to repay me?" Niro crooked his finger under her chin and brought her within an inch of his face. For a moment Aidan thought he was going to kiss her and then he bit her lip. Hard.

Her scream muffled his movement in the closet. Before he could free his foot from the tangle of belts and kick open the door, she pushed Niro off of her. Aidan froze.

"Are we even now?" Cat wiped the blood from her mouth and spat the residue onto the carpet at his feet. She left the blade in her pocket. "Or do I owe you for a carpet cleaning bill?"

A red glow emanated from Niro's eyes as he licked the blood that coated his lips, and for a moment the demon man mesmerized him. Unexpected bloodlust shot through Aidan's veins, and a deep longing to feel Cat's blood slid down his throat while he fucked her luscious body nearly overwhelmed his imagination. Murderous thoughts penetrated his mind. The thought of Cat's blood coursing down his own throat caused blood to rush to other areas of his body. Sounds of feet pounding on the pavement and whimpers of fear played a loop in his ears while a movie of Cat running away from him played before his eyes. The black and white reel flickered and paused as she turned toward him, a look of horror etched on her delicate features before the celluloid dissolved into nothing.

A click of Niro's fingers brought Aidan back to his senses with a horrific start. He'd just fantasized about Cat's demise at his own hands. His tongue felt thick in his mouth. The walls of his temporary hiding spot seemed to close in on him. Cat needed to get Niro out of the room before Aidan did something stupid like burst out of the closet in panic. Cat warned him he would feel this way, at least she hadn't been lying about that.

Niro unwittingly came to his aide. "Come with me to the circle. I'd love to have you by my side when our guests arrive."

"There is a circle in Ashton?" The color drained from Cat's olive toned skin. "You're going to bring him through."

Less a question and more of a statement that Niro neither denied nor confirmed. He led the way out of the room and Cat trailed behind him. To her credit, she never looked back toward the closet door.

The click of the front door lock echoed loud in the near-empty loft and Aidan burst free of his confines.

He parted the bedroom curtain and watched Cat slide into the passenger side of Niro's sleek black town car, the tinted windows like black eyes in a soulless night. Niro shut the door and turned to look at the building. Aidan flattened himself into the shadows and remained still, not daring to make a single move. With the bedroom lights being dim and the view from the streetlamps, Aidan was sure Niro wouldn't be able to see him. Still, that brief pause was an invitation of pursuit that he couldn't turn down. There was no way he was about to drive to Cat's house and just wait for her to return.

Aidan waited until Niro slipped into the driver's seat and drove away before he shot into action. He palmed Cat's car key and raced down the staircase, taking the steps two at once until he hit the street in time to see Niro's taillights disappear toward the mining road. Niro might have a head start, but this country boy knew the backroads. He could probably be at the mine twenty minutes before them and hide the car before they showed up. That is if he was right.

He raced to Cat's car and popped the SUV into gear. Making it to the mine before them would require some off-road driving

CHAPTER FOURTEEN

and he could only hope Cat's wagon performed as well as she did. He could still feel the soft curve of her hip against his hand while he sank into her warmth, the heated rush of her breath in the throes of passion. He brushed the image away. Getting distracted wasn't the best way to save Cat. Once this was over, they'd talk again, and maybe things would be different. Maybe.

He whipped out his cell phone and punched in Norm's phone number. Thalia might still be in jail, but at least she was safe there and hopefully confined. Cat might be in real danger.

Then again, so might he.

Norm picked up after the third ring, panting for breath, like the pervert that he is.

"I didn't catch you at a bad time, did I?" Aidan pulled the steering wheel hard to the left and dodged the half gate meant to keep cars off the forest roads.

"Aidan! Are you two okay? Man, that was an utter shit show." Norm's voice caught up with him. "I'm jogging over to the police station. They hauled Thalia away in cuffs. I think she's in major trouble. Did she warn you that Niro was on his way?"

Branches slapped the top of the truck. The suspension jarred against a pothole in the road and the glove box popped open. The scroll rolled out onto the floorboards reminding Aidan of Cat's strange reaction to the document. She had been very elusive as to the extra-sensory perception she seemed to have when it came to all this weird shit. Maybe he was the one being led into a trap and not her. Maybe she and Niro were in this together the whole time, and she was leading him on. "Yeah, and he showed up before we could get out. Cat went with him to the mines. I'm trying to beat them there."

"Oh shit. That means that Thalia is still in jail doesn't

245

it?" Norm's breath hitched, and Aidan could tell he had commenced jogging again. "If we don't get her out of there then the entire prison population might end up a pile of dead bodies. Something bad happened at the bar, Aidan. Really bad. I have to go."

The line went silent. Aidan chucked his phone onto the seat. When he hatched this plan to save the town, he hadn't thought that Cat might already be a part of it. Now Thalia was in jail, and the whole town was infested with demons. And the scroll rolling around on the floorboard might have more to do with the evil surrounding him then the thumb drive of information they pulled from Niro's computer, except he couldn't read what it said.

He came to the fork in the road, literally. Take a right and he would make it to the mine before Cat and Niro. Take a left and he could make it to the police station in a few minutes. He couldn't do both.

* * *

Despite the cool air pumping through the vents, Cat's sweat-drenched back clung to the leather upholstery. She had spent years reintegrating into society and now she might be headed straight back. Adding to her unrest was Aidan and what he must think of her now. She'd like to play it off as some screwed up D/s dynamic which would seem strange enough, but the truth was even stranger. At least BDSM was mainstream now. Demons from Hell were still make believe to most people.

Niro turned onto the main road leading north of town, a roundabout way to the mine. Cat could only guess that he was avoiding the bridge over the River Rouge. *But why?* It was the fastest way. "You are definitely a bonus find on this project.

He will be very surprised once he sees you."

"You mean you haven't told him yet?" It didn't seem like Niro to miss an opportunity for advancement. He pretended to help her several times in the Underworld only to take credit for exposing her treachery. It didn't take long for her to lose all hope of escape. "I'm surprised."

Niro loosened the tie at his neck and slipped the car into a lower gear. "I didn't want to promise him something I could not deliver on." He pulled the car into the shelter of the copse at the side of the road no doubt in an attempt to camouflage the black car from prying eyes. A click of a button on the driver's side console and all of the doors locked shut.

His hand clamped on her thigh followed by a sharp prick. "But now that isn't an issue."

She glanced down and spied the syringe embedded in her leg. Her vision blurred and she fought to bring the images in front of her into focus. Black residue coated the inside of the plunger. The heroin of the Underworld was back in her veins.

"I didn't say I was bringing you back alive."

* * *

Aidan flattened the accelerator to the floorboards. The wagon dipped slightly in the roadside ditch and flew onto the asphalt, fishtailing from side to side as he fought to regain control and maintain his speed. Jogging about fifty feet in front of him on the left side of the road was Norm. He laid on the horn and slammed on the brakes. Norm rushed to the passenger side and flung open the door.

"What about Cat?" Norm grabbed the door and struggled to close it as Aidan accelerated again.

"I'm not even sure that Cat is on our side anymore." He

shifted from third to fourth gear. The road widened, and Aidan could see the lights from the police station up ahead. He could also see that there were several cop cars from neighboring counties parked out front, their emergency beacons flashing red. Cabins empty and car doors open like they had been in a hurry to exit. "Tell me what happened at the bar."

Norm gripped the dashboard. "I tried to stop her. I tried. But, this guy. This guy started to bug Thalia when Niro was in the head. He'd had a few too many and Thalia wanted him out of the way, I think. She started doing her thing to him, and it just got out of hand, the guy passed out. I wanted to help him, but Niro grabbed my arm. I think she killed the guy."

They skidded to a stop in front of the station. "How were they able to get her here?"

"The Officer hit her with a taser, and she went down."

Even the wind had ceased to blow outside the police station. Aidan expected to arrive at a scene of chaos. Now he wasn't sure how to approach the situation. Black ops were not something you learned as a geologist or a farmer.

"I know that you seem to have an effect on her. Something that calms her down. Maybe if we can get you close to her, then you can keep her from hurting anybody else."

Norm nodded and opened his door, as he did so, the scroll that was on the floorboards at his feet fell onto the ground. He quickly picked it up and handed it to Aidan. "Is this important?"

"That's the million-dollar question."

* * *

Cat fought to keep conscious. She used to have an extreme tolerance to the drug, but that was a long time ago. When they first fed it into her system, it would immediately knock her out. They had to give her more and more to keep her compliant. At some point, she just pretended to go along with them so she could wean herself off the stuff. She pressed her back against the passenger door, attempting to get as far away from Niro as possible.

"Don't you think he'd rather have me alive?" Although she would rather be dead then go back to Hell, being dead was not going to help Aidan. "I'm sure we can work something out."

Niro leaned over the stick shift, his hot breath a few feet from her face. "You have already caused me enough problems on this job. The only guarantee I have that you won't continue to be a problem is to get rid of you."

Cat remembered all those unending nights in Hell. All the time she had fought to hold onto the last shred of herself. The meditations she had gone through to keep herself intact, burying deep down her independent spirit and putting blinders on her soul so that she could someday return to the world she knew and still be able to function. One of her captors was in front of her and threatening to take it all away again. Forever. She hadn't let him crush her before, and she wouldn't let him do it now. She eyed the toggle switch for the door locks below Niro's left elbow and calculated her chances. He already intended to kill her. What did she have to lose? "How are you going to do it?"

"With these." He shot out and grabbed her neck with both hands, tightening around her windpipe.

Adrenaline flooded Cat's veins, and she grabbed his fingers, making sure to keep his grip away from her carotid artery while she swung her feet around and kicked out. She made contact with his thigh. "Damn bitch!"

Niro clamped down harder. Her head swam with dizziness. The adrenaline from her fight for survival turned into a fearful panic. If she didn't get the door open, Niro would succeed in his plan. Her world started to dim, and she kicked out again in one last desperate attempt. Would Niro's sly grin be the last thing she was going to see before she died?

Her heel made contact with the toggle switch. It unlocked with a noticeable click, but she was too late. Panic turned into peace as the last bit of air exited her lungs in a forceful exhale.

Tapping on the window disturbed her exit from the world. Niro loosened his grip, a look of fear crossing his face. He released her neck and raised his hands as if he were a common criminal with a gun pointed at him. At this point, Cat realized breathing was again an option and took in shallow gulps of air through her battered windpipe. She could see Niro's lips moving, talking to someone, but the only sound she could hear was the thudding of her blood in her eardrums. He shook his head back and forth.

Behind her, the door opened, and she was grabbed under the arms and pulled backward out of the car. Her back end hit the ground with a thud. Niro exited and opened the trunk, pulling out a long blade. The sound of the metal pulling free from the scabbard brought her back into consciousness. Her legs felt wobbly, but the drug was wearing off.

"You hurry. You run now. I take care of this one." Cat looked up into the eyes of Miss Chow. The voice was the same, the eyes were the same, but she looked very different. Covered in shimmering black scales, Miss Chow was now a Campe. A monstrous she-dragon with the body of a serpent and a fearsome scorpion tale. Now she knew why Mane had been so uncomfortable dealing with a shifter. She was just glad Miss

Chow was on her side.

Weapon in hand, Niro challenged Miss Chow. "Stand down witch, this one belongs to me."

Miss Chow elongated her massive snout, yellow teeth bared and released a ferocious shriek that blasted the surrounding air with its shrill pitch. She turned her massive head and roared a command at Cat.

"Run!"

Cat scrambled to her feet and shot into the nearby woods. Tree limbs slapped at her face, and thorny branches scraped her arms, but she didn't look back. She heard another shriek followed by the hollow snapping of giant wings as Miss Chow took to the air. With each lift and drag, her ominous form morphed into a bat. The small creature swooped down and brushed against the top of Cat's head.

Miss Chow spoke in a rush of wind before she lifted in the air once more and disappeared from sight.

"Run! He is coming!"

That meant that she had won or run. Perhaps she had taken her own advice. Niro wouldn't be too far behind her. In her weakened state, she wouldn't be able to run much more.

Cat broke out into an open expanse. In the distance, the series of buildings that made up the fairgrounds came into view. If she could make it there, perhaps she could find transportation to the mine. Stop whatever Niro was doing. Whatever it was, it wasn't going to end well for any of them.

* * *

With the scroll tucked into his jacket, Aidan hefted the service rifle that he snatched from the front of one of the sheriff's cars. Norm refused to take one, saying he'd probably end up shooting Aidan in the back if he used it. If they hurried, he and Norm could still get back on the road and make it to the mine. He might not be there before Cat and Niro, but he would be right on their heels.

Aidan checked his cell phone. There was no message from Cat. Guilt gnawed at his conscious. He should have followed her. Niro was dangerous, and yet he had seen Cat in action.

She is no match for us.

A voice, not his own, echoed in his head and set Aidan's temples pounding. Until this moment, he didn't want to admit he heard the odd, lilting rasp that filled his mind with thoughts of pure evil. He didn't want to admit that he had not been feeling himself lately. He tried to blame it all on Cat, these demons, and his family farm going under, but there was something other than devilish fantasies swirling around in his head. Some strange being possessed his mind, and at times he felt like it might succeed. Or worse, what if in a moment of weakness, he gave into the voice?

"It's too quiet in there, man." Norm peeked out from behind Aidan, one hand on his shoulder. "You think we're too late?"

A sheriff's deputy bolted from around the corner, handgun raised in his trembling hand. Aidan recognized the guard as one of the boys who bullied him in high school. The man hesitated at the sight of Aidan, gun in hand. Aidan eyed him back, and the wicked voice whispered to pull the trigger, to take his revenge for the many days he'd gone home bruised and swollen.

The deputy appeared to weigh the danger of his old foe versus the nightmare in the holding cells. A low, keening wail made his decision for him.

Aidan raised the gun, the sight resting on the man's barrel

chest. The deputy froze, face pale as chalk.

"What are you doing?" Norm asked, the voice of reason cutting into Aidan's brain.

Aidan raised the gun higher, aiming over the deputy's shoulder. "Get out of here before I do shoot your sorry ass."

Another door slammed, and the deputy dropped his gun hand and sprinted past. "Get out. You have to get out. She's coming."

"Protect and serve, my ass," snorted Norm. "You think..."

He stopped mid-sentence. At the end of the hall stood a woman, completely naked except for a G-string. Her long black hair shielded her bare breasts while a serpentine tail with a forked end snaked around her hip. Most impressive of all were her leathery bat-like wings, and the curved devil horns erupting from her forehead. Her eyes glowed a deep red and a smirk crossed her familiar yet alien face.

In a voice dripping with seductive poison, the creature spoke. "If you want to live, you will leave now."

"Thalia?" Norm stepped from behind Aidan's taller frame.

Aidan caught the man by the shoulder. If this was Thalia, she may no longer have any qualms about eating her boyfriend.

Norm shrugged off Aidan. "It's okay man, I've got this."

"She's not herself anymore. You can't risk it." Aidan tried to reason with Norm, but there was one problem. You can't give someone advice you aren't following yourself.

"Kind of like you putting yourself at risk for Cat?"

The reminder hit home and put him on track once more. Their mission was simple, tame Thalia, find Cat, and kill Niro. And the only person that could control Thalia was Norm. He gripped the stock of his gun, but something told him that conventional weapons didn't work on her. The police had no doubt found that out.

Hips swaying, Thalia took a halting step toward them, her face contorted in a mixture of seduction and pain. "I don't want to hurt you."

"I don't want to hurt you either." Aidan raised his weapon and fixed the site on the spot between her eyes. If Norm's plan fell through, shooting her might delay her long enough for them to get away.

Norm raised his hands and strolled down the hall, each step punctuated by the idle and inappropriate chatter he was infamous for. "Hey babe, you're so hot you'd make the devil sweat."

Thalia cocked her hip to one side and smiled, sharp teeth gleaming white against the blood red of her lips. "I dated the devil once. He was a total ass."

"Is it hot in here, or is it just you?"

The blinding red glow of Thalia's eyes dimmed at the lame joke. Could it be possible that cheesy pick-up lines were the key to exorcising a demon? I suppose not even the devil wants to stick around for lame comedy hour. Her wings folded behind her back and the woman she once was became more noticeable in the lines of her face.

"It's bad, Norm. Really bad." She raised her hands to her face and sobbed. "I didn't mean to hurt anyone."

"It's not your fault. I think Niro knew what we were up to and turned off your filter. It'll be okay. We'll figure it out together," said Norm. Only a few feet separated him and Thalia.

His filter. *Is that what Niro had done to him?*

Norm reached out and touched Thalia. Her aggressive stance melted away, and she collapsed into his arms. He slid his jacket off and put it around her shoulders.

"You want to see what is left back there?" asked Norm.

Norm's comment reminded Aidan of the reasons he was at the police station in the first place—to save the people of Ashton from the demon menace. The last thing he wanted to see was that he was too late, but he didn't have much choice. He nodded at Norm and walked toward the cells at the end of the hall. Collapsed on the floor at the door was a guard. Aidan checked his pulse. It was faint, but he was still alive. He unsnapped the security card from the guard's belt and unlocked the door separating him from the holding cells.

Inside were several other guards passed out on the floor, all of them with shit-eating grins on their face. If they were dead, they had all died happy. Aidan checked each one, pleased that they were all alive. He took the phone off the wall and dialed 911 to call in the medical emergency. At this time of night, help would need to come from a county over, which would give them enough time to clear out. But these men would live.

Aidan rushed out of the room and back to Thalia and Norm. "They'll live, but we need to get out of here now."

Thalia looked up her eyes back to their normal electric green color. Even without her demon in charge, she appeared otherworldly. "Where's Cat?"

"I'm about to catch up with her now. She went with Niro. I think they're headed to the mine. He said that he was bringing her to the circle. Does that mean anything to you?"

If anyone knew a thing or two about the obscure references Cat and Niro had made, it would be Thalia. She clutched the opening of her coat, and her hand trembled. "It means that more of them are coming."

* * *

Heart thudding in her chest in a staccato rhythm, Cat scanned the tree line for any signs of Niro. Although she couldn't see him, she sensed he was out there somewhere, waiting to kill her. She shivered at the memory of his fingers on her throat and increased her pace. Exhaustion pounded at her body, but she kept going.

If Niro had gotten back in his car, the only way she was going to be able to see where he went is if she got up somewhere high. The roads surrounding the mines were exposed. Niro could hide the way he was getting there, but if the mine were indeed his destination, then he wouldn't be able to conceal his approach.

After an indeterminable amount of time, she arrived at the fairgrounds. Between her hiding place in the woods and the entrance was roughly one hundred feet of uncovered space. Could she bolt fast enough across the green to make it to safety or was this a trap? She eyed the landscape and gauged her chances. She had everything to gain and nothing to lose. *Except for your life.* Gathering the last of her energy, she sprinted.

Cat rattled the gate to the fairgrounds. Locked. Panic gave her the strength she needed, and she scaled the fence, dropping to the other side. As her feet touched the ground, her legs crumbled. The damn drug had taken more out of her then she thought. She steadied herself and took a deep breath before getting back to her feet. If she passed out here alone, then no one would know to look for her here. She patted her pocket and retrieved her cell phone. There was only one bar showing, and it faded in and out.

She sent a text to Aidan to let him know where she was, hoping it would go through. The little icon on her phone scrolled around and around attempting to send her message.

The blue circle of death. Circles were not good things in this world or the Underworld. She pocketed the phone and headed toward the highest spot on the fairgrounds.

The Ferris wheel. The first place she and Aidan had kissed. Had he taken her advice and gone back to her house? And if he did, would he would be safe there? The protection spell would keep Niro and any other beastie from getting through the front door.

For now.

If Niro had access to a circle and the power behind it, then he could easily break down such low-level magic. Throughout the years she spent alongside the demon, no matter how much she tried, she could never tell when he was telling the truth or when he was bluffing.

She stared at the Ferris wheel, knowing she had to climb to the top. Every muscle in her body screamed in protest. She ignored the desire to sit down and sleep and placed her foot on the first of the many steel ribs holding the Ferris wheel together. As she worked her way up, she hoped he was bluffing.

The power to the ride was controlled by a key she did not possess. However, that would not deter her. Ever since she had returned to this plain, she had spent her time in hiding. Hiding from people, from experiences, from emotions. Now she had the chance to really make a difference in the life of not just one person, but an entire town. She'd seen too much destruction to let that opportunity slip out from under her.

Morning dew coated the metal lattice and her left foot shot out from underneath her on the wet surface. Fear lanced out, and she gripped the bar above her head tight, forcing a calm while she readjusted herself.

All of her concentration on the climb, she ignored the

buzzing in her pocket that signaled an incoming message. Her mind screamed to check it. What if it were Aidan? The incentive to know pushed harder at her determination and she continued to climb. Although the sun peaked from the horizon, she could feel her body rapidly giving into the darkness. Sleep. The drug she fought so hard against, was dragging her into the silky depths and soon there would be no battle. It would win. Days of no sleep and even less nourishment crashed down on her.

Above her head one of the carriages swayed back and forth, the vibrations from her ascent giving it a life of its own. More than anything she wanted a life of her own. Something apart from all this madness—away from all these demons and beasties. Mane had been gifted a normal life and allowed a normal human existence, and his sins had been equal to hers.

Or were they?

Mane had been born a demon, a creature without a soul. He'd been given a soul, and when he proved worthy, he had been granted a new life. She had been born with a soul, and she'd allowed it to blacken, to give in to the evil that she knew was wrong. She'd known right from wrong and had chosen evil. Did she even deserve a second chance? There was no question in her mind who did. Aidan Ash. The man was good, pure, the type of man that any 1950s girl would be proud to bring home to her parents.

Except this wasn't the 1950s. And Cat's parents had been dead and buried for a long time.

She grabbed onto the bottom of the cart, and her fingers came away wet, compromising her grip. The heavy cart swayed back and forth, leaving her little time to gather her strength and find purchase with her foot inside the safety of the carriage.

The cell buzzed again, the motion giving her the energy she needed. If she let go now, she would plummet to her death. And she wasn't sure what awaited her on the other side.

Heaven. Or Hell.

* * *

Aidan turned onto the gravel road, the car bumping along the rough track. He turned off the headlights and allowed the pale glow from the rising sun to guide him. Cat was somewhere ahead, in who knew what condition. He gripped the steering wheel against the panic that threatened caution, his palms slick with sweat. While every instinct screamed at him to turn around and seek out Niro, to uncover the truth, the message he'd received from Cat dictated his next move. Finding her eclipsed any other desire.

The circle is a portal to Hell. A direct link. If he can open it up, then all Hell will be unleashed into Ashton.

Thalia's words echoed in his mind. He's seen enough to know she wasn't bluffing. He'd be naïve to think for even a second that she would lie about something so outrageous.

"I'm sure she's okay." Norm tried to reassure him.

When we get there, you will stay in the car. The last thing I need is to worry about the two of you."

Loud snores emanating from the backseat gave him a touch of relief. Thalia had apparently overloaded on sexual energy, and like an oversexed man, she'd passed out for the night. At least he hoped so.

"If you're not back in twenty I'm coming to look for you."

"Shouldn't take long." Aidan slammed the door shut and approached the guard's booth. Aidan had been up for 24 hours, and while exhaustion dogged his every move, he had to keep moving, or else Cat might lose her life. Although it would be less complicated to jump the fence, it would be a lot easier to convince the guard he had official business.

"Hey, Hank."

The old man looked up from his morning paper, his wire-rimmed glasses perched on the end of his nose. Steam rose from a paper cup next to him. This was his life. Pure and simple and Aidan wanted to help keep it that way.

"What are you doing out here this time of the morning, Mr. Ash?" Hank looked past him to Cat's car. Norm waved from the passenger seat. "I heard on the police scanner there was something happening up at the police station. Ain't safe for no one these days. I tell ya."

Aidan brushed his hands through his hair and pulled the scroll from his vest pocket. "I've got some official business I hoped you could help me with, Hank. The mine wants me to compare these old surveys with an aerial shot, except we don't have the money to hire a helicopter. Thought maybe if I could get up on the wheel, I could see what I need to. A good excuse not to be in the office, if you know what I mean?"

Hank took the bait and the master keys from the hook at his station. "Sure thing."

Aidan eyed the wheel. Cat's message said she was going up the wheel to track Niro, but she hadn't returned any of his other messages. He could only hope she was still there or that he would be able to find a clue as to where to go next. He didn't have to look too hard.

A slender hand dangled from a carriage at the top of the Ferris wheel. The sight of the pale fingers curled in a vulnerable position felt like a punch in the gut. Was she dead? Or had he gotten to her in time?

"My, God. Who's that?" Hank had seen the same thing before Aidan could try and distract him. He shot over to the control panel and inserted the key to start up the power. The massive wheel turned slowly, bringing the carriage down to the bottom.

Hank gasped. "I'll call the ambulance."

"No." Aidan turned and grasped Hank's wrist a little harder than he meant to. "I'm sorry. I mean, this is my Cousin from out of town. My Dad will kill me if he learns I let her out of my sight. I've got her medication back at the house."

Aidan leaned forward and placed a finger to Cat's pale neck to check for a pulse. A steady thrumming that signaled she was very much alive rewarded him. Hank seemed too shocked by the appearance of a half-dead woman in the Ferris wheel to ask about the coincidence. Aidan planned to be far away from here before the man stopped to think too much about it.

"Thanks for your help." He slung Cat over his shoulder. The last time he had been this close to her had been in her embrace. He had also been under some kind of mumbo-jumbo spell in Niro's lair.

Norm popped out of the car as soon as he saw Aidan. "Is she okay?"

"Yes, help me get her in the back."

Norm prodded Thalia awake. She looked like she was back to her usual self. The wings and horns seemed to have disappeared. Just a half-naked woman in the back of his car. Yep, everything was normal.

Thalia scooted over and assisted Aidan with Cat. Her limp body slumped in the seat, and Thalia lifted her eyelid. "We need to get her back to the house. I can help her from there."

"What about this circle?" Aidan started the Jeep and pointed it in the direction of Cat's cottage. "Should we be worried?"

"Of course. But they won't be able to do anything until nightfall. Opening the circle is one thing, but those demons need the cover of night."

The sun had risen higher in the sky since they'd arrived the fairgrounds. Aidan rubbed his eyes, his vision blurry from lack of sleep. None of them had slept all night. He was grateful they would at least have a few hours before the world ended.

When they hit the bridge over the River Rouge, he noticed something bizarre.

"Man, the river isn't red anymore." Norm pressed his face to the glass.

"There are already a lot of reinforcements in town. They must be using it as a feeding ground. Damn bottom feeders. As low as you can get really," said Thalia. Aidan looked in the rear view mirror and saw her stroking Cat's hair gently. He was comforted by the slight rise and fall of her chest. Now if only Thalia could help the nagging pain in his head. As they crossed the bridge, the pain intensified.

The walls of his vision started to close down to a narrow path. If he couldn't control it, he might black out entirely. "Norm, I need you to take over."

Whatever was hiding in the back of his mind took the reins, and he ripped the wheel to the left and pointed the front of the car at the railing separating traffic from the depths of the river several hundred feet below.

* * *

Cat's body jerked to the right and slammed against something hard. The last thing she remembered was seeing Niro's car headed out from the cover of the forested areas surrounding town in the direction of the mine. She had wanted to text Aidan. To tell him where to go, but she had a compelling urge to close her eyes. Rest for a moment.

So it was quite a surprise to find herself in the back of her car with Norm and Aidan fighting over the wheel.

"Will someone hold him?" yelled Norm.

The car skidded back and forth across the bridge as Norm fought to keep them in the right lane and Aidan pulled the car to the left. If he was trying to avoid danger, Cat couldn't see what it was.

"Aidan, what the heck are you doing?" asked Cat.

He paused long enough for Thalia to grab onto his arms. "Aidan isn't home at the moment."

Norm steered the car straight, and Aidan twisted his head toward Cat. His eyes glowed bright red.

"He's been taken over. Oh, shit. Aidan, I'm so sorry," said Cat.

Aidan had taken his foot off the gas, and the Jeep rolled to a stop. Norm jerked the emergency brake while Aidan continued to struggle against Thalia's grip. "Don't think you're getting away that easy. My batteries are fully recharged, and I don't have anything against knocking you on your ass."

He relaxed a little, his gaze still fixed on Cat. "Safe. Somewhere safe." A cryptic message from the mind of Aidan, trapped somewhere within.

Cat shook off her shock and tried to gain her bearings. It was daylight. They were over the River Rouge, and the car was pointed at her house. "Norm, can you help get Aidan into the back seat? I'm good to drive."

The glow in Aidan's eyes stayed strong, but he stopped

struggling and sat rigidly between Norm and Thalia. Cat threw the car into gear and punched the accelerator. If she was right, the only thing that would bring Aidan back was to get him to her house. Inside the circle of protection. She only hoped whatever possessed Aidan hadn't completely taken over.

When she was taken down into Hell, she wasn't supposed to come back. No "human" that enters the Realm gets out with their mind intact, except for her. The boss man had wanted to make sure she stayed aware of everything she was doing, as much to torture her as to torture his nemesis, Mane.

The roads were clear, almost like they were in a ghost town. The city of Ashton was completely unaware of everything going on in their little town. The mine would open soon, but she didn't think Niro would be surprised if Aidan and Norm didn't show up for work.

She skidded to a stop in front of her house and looked in the rearview mirror, so much for the guards. Thalia and Norm were both crashed out, each with their head on one of Aidan's shoulders. Whatever was residing inside Aidan seemed to find this amusing. "They are supposed to keep me under control?"

Cat took a mental inventory of her options and didn't care for any that sprang to mind. The press of her knife mocked her as much as the demon inhibiting Aidan's body. If push came to shove, would she be able to hurt him? He wasn't in his right mind but could she risk saving his life at the expense of thousands of people? If she were Aidan, the answer would be no. His selflessness was the trait she loved best about him. She wanted to be a better person, and he'd made her one. There had to be a way to save him while purging the demon from his soul. If she needed to, she could reach the weapon in seconds. "Are you still Aidan?"

"He's still here. For now." The demon crossed his arms over his chest. "The time draws near when I will completely inhabit this body, and he will be cast aside. It's all in the contract."

Eyes as red as fire met hers while the demon handed the scroll to her. She worried the hilt of her knife, unsure if she dared to accept it or take the opportunity to end this before it escalated.

She scanned the familiar face, hard and unyielding in a way that Aidan wasn't. Still, she hesitated.

He thrust the scroll at her, daring her to resist. With reluctant hands, she grabbed the parchment. Her stomach lurched. Where before there was only faded lettering and signatures, now the intent of the contract was made clear.

And if she didn't find a way to void it, she would lose Aidan forever.

Chapter Fifteen

Aidan's mind stayed strong within his body, but none of the words exiting his mouth were under his control. He hadn't felt this helpless since his mother died. He'd gone mad, drowning in a pool so deep he couldn't see the surface, couldn't find hope. Cat's face pulled at him, an anchor in a sea of terror. He had to fight this, for her and for himself. But how would he find the strength when he was imprisoned in his own body, a slave to the voice in his head? Had he gone mad? If so, Cat was on the same ride. Cat looked at him suspiciously and handed the scroll back to him. He wished he could tell her to tie him to a post outside and not let him in.

"Sounds like your boyfriend is into some kinky stuff. I'm going to like this body." The sound of his own voice mocking him sent him into a spiral of frustration. He wanted to punch the asshole, and yet he was the one who was the asshole.

Thalia startled awake and wiped at a thin line of drool on her chin. Naked from the waist up, she definitely didn't look like a threat. "Nice tits."

"Looks like we're going to have to knock some sense back into him. I totally volunteer." Thalia rolled her eyes and opened the car door.

"Are all your friends into kinky stuff or am I having a lucky day?" Honestly, thought Aidan, if anyone had a roll of duct tape now would be a good time to tape this bastard's mouth shut.

Norm let out a loud snore and pressed his face against the glass. His mind was probably on overload. And they were all suffering from lack of sleep. All except him with a demon presence at the helm.

"Why don't you go inside with Thalia and I'll try and rouse Norm," said Cat.

Aidan watched whatever had taken over his body do a once over on Thalia's curvaceous figure. The thoughts running through his head were not at all respectful. He was afraid if he went inside with Thalia he would definitely do something he regretted. He tried with every ounce of his free will to force a warning from his mouth, but it was no use. He was still here, but he was completely walled off from himself.

Soon you won't have to worry. When the portal opens, I'll have complete control over this body, and I'll make sure to kick you out nice and quick. Like pulling the plug. No more pain. I can't say the same for these two. I'm going to fuck them till they beg me to stop, but I won't.

That did it, the extra jolt of anger he needed to fight back. For a brief moment, he was able to tear through the boundary and screech out a warning. "He's going to hurt you."

Seconds later it felt like he was slammed against a wall. His breath knocked out of him. *I admire your strength but shut the fuck up.*

Thalia looked into Aidan's eyes. "Hit me with your best shot, body snatcher." She sashayed up the steps, and he followed. As he crossed the threshold, he was suddenly thrust into his skin. His senses flooded back, overpowering him. He went down on one knee and clasped the doorframe.

The breeze blowing through the open window smelled of the crumbling, charred black remnants of his cherry orchard. Thalia touched his arm, and his skin felt raw, sun-scorched.

"Give yourself a minute, and you'll get your feet back under you." Thalia knelt by his side, a blanket wrapped around her shoulders.

The pounding of feet coming up the stairs behind him thudded too loudly in his skull like he was coming off of an all-night drinking binge.

"Is he okay?" Cat's voice sounded tinny and distant. The floor appeared all too close and all too far away at the same time. Any moment now, he would probably pass out.

"He will be. Norm, help us get him inside."

Norm's spindly limbs curled under his shoulders and Cat scooted inside and cleared off the couch as they set him down. Cat tucked a fuzzy blanket under his chin, and the soft fabric gently caressed his skin, like dozens of feathers flickering over an overstimulated bundle of nerves. Slightly painful and exquisite at the same time. A sigh escaped his lips. He deserved to have them chain him up after what he had done.

He looked up into Thalia's eyes. A knowing smirk crossing her face. "He's coming back quick. Don't worry, that spell I bought was premium." She reached up and stretched her arms above her head. "You two mind if we pass out in the bedroom for a few hours? If we're going to make any moves, we need to have a little of our strength back."

Norm laid his head on her shoulder, all but sleeping standing up. He was very unaware Aidan had been temporarily possessed. He deserved to keep his ignorance a bit longer. Soon, all the cards would have to be on the table. But he wasn't the only one that hadn't been himself lately.

Aidan pushed himself up to a seated position and winced against the pain. "Are you going to be okay in there alone with him?"

Cat turned her attention away from Aidan and seemed to realize Thalia had been half-naked since they got home. "Did something happen?"

Thalia half draped an arm across her bare bosom. "It's a long story. But believe me, Niro has some payback coming his way. I'm under control now. I wouldn't allow myself to be alone with him if I thought I would hurt him."

Aidan collapsed back onto the sofa. Cat waved them off without speaking. She walked over to the door and kicked it closed with her foot, her entire body hanging loose with exhaustion. She fell into a Papasan chair and curled into a tight ball.

"You don't have to sleep there, we can switch." Aidan sat up again, noticing how his body felt less sore but still exhausted.

A gentle snore sounded from Cat. He got up, placed the blanket over her body, and went back to the couch. If he thought he could keep the demon at bay, he would leave now. Get as far away from Cat and the others as possible. But he was more dangerous now away from them than by their side.

He rolled over, and the parchment made a crinkling sound in his pocket. He pulled it out, and his mouth fell open wide. The lettering clearly legible. Generations ago his family had made a deal with the devil, and he was the payment.

* * *

Not me. He's not here for me. The reality crept across her consciousness, spreading like the warmth of the sun rays across the blanket tucked around her shoulders. Relief quickly turned to guilt. If she wasn't the target, she had undoubtedly been the bait. Cat shifted in the chair where she had passed out. Aidan lay tucked in a ball on the couch, his back to her. Safe by her side. As she sat up a piece of paper flickered to the floor.

Thalia's elegant handwriting was scrawled across the paper in red lipstick. You had to be resourceful these days. *Gone out to gather reinforcements. Don't leave without me.*

Cat didn't have much choice. Aidan had to stay within the circle of protection or else he might transform once more into a demon. She mustn't let that happen. He might be safe, but that also meant Niro could go about his plans undisturbed.

She cradled her face in her palms and rocked back and forth, feeling helpless. She might be surrounded by a great gang of people, but would what she brought to the table be a help or a hindrance? Memories of the portal that swallowed her into Hell remained fresh in her mind, and she had to reconcile the fact that there might never be a time when she wouldn't remember. She wanted to do something to make sure Aidan and the rest of the people of Ashton never had to experience what she had.

"How long have you been awake?"

Cat raised her face and dropped her hands. Aidan sat on the couch, hair gently messed from the few hours of sleep, and rubbed his eyes.

"Just now." She gestured to the paper in her hands and cautiously searched Aidan's face for any sign of the previous possession. Nothing but pure chocolate brown eyes met her own. "Thalia went out to get us some help."

"Listen," said Aidan. He leaned forward, face pale before he quickly leaned back as if burned. Color flushed his cheeks and pain darkened his eyes while he raised his hands in supplication. "There is something wrong with me. You have to believe me. Everything I said and did wasn't me."

"I know it wasn't. I've had a lot of experience with these types of situations. I understand what it's like to lose control of your actions, even your mind." While a certain weight was lifted because Niro wasn't there for her, she still couldn't rest easy. He was there to put Aidan in the same prison she had been in, and it would probably be for life according to the contract. "Do you still have the parchment from your house? The one signed by all the townspeople."

Aidan tossed the paper onto the coffee table between them. "Yeah, it's really messed up. But it's really happening, isn't it? It's why the land went dead, the mine dried up. All because of this contract...with...with the..."

"With the Devil." Cat had known him by another name during her time in Hell, Ravanna, but the name didn't really matter. What mattered is what Aidan said was true. According to the contract, the town of Ashton hadn't started out as a prosperous farm town.

Aidan's ancestors had settled in the area and found them-selves victims of disease and famine. A village elder had promised a sacrifice in exchange for saving the people of Ashton. Grant Ashton prosperity and health and the townsfolk would protect the red dust. The mineral allowed the demons to open portals to this world. If ever the dust disappeared, then payment of the soul of the last of the Ash family line would be collected.

At some point, the land stopped supporting crops, and the mine was opened to keep the town afloat. No one knew or would take this "deal with the devil" seriously. They did what they needed to create jobs. But then the mine had run dry, and now the contract had come due.

"Yes, but this says the mineral has to disappear. Until the other day, there was plenty of cinnabar in the mine and the river to keep this land saturated for generations. There is no explanation for why it suddenly dried up. That's why I called you to begin with."

Aidan paced the floor in front of the window. He was right. There was no reason for the mine to have run dry. In fact, the core sample they had taken proved it was still down there, hidden. But for what purpose?

Maybe Niro did have something to do with this after all. Maybe it was still personal.

"When did Niro take over operations at the mine?" asked Cat.

"It was about a year or so ago, why?"

The room started to spin, pressure squeezing the sides of her head until she thought it might explode. Her worse nightmare had come back, confirmed by the evidence before her.

A year ago.

That was when Cat had driven into town and seen the quaint little one-story whitewash house she now resided in. It seemed so perfect. Hidden away from everything. From people, from traffic. No one was supposed to be aware of her location. Of course, she still had to pay the rent. Still had to have a presence on the internet, even if only for her job. And after everything she had lost, the one thing she refused to change was her name.

"Niro has orchestrated this whole thing. The mine hasn't run dry. He's made it seem like it. The sample we took proves it. He is still trying to get to me. He thought destroying my new home would be great, but now that he has seen me with you he figures he had to destroy my relationship too."

"Relationship?"

Aidan approached her chair, hands tucked into the pockets of his jeans. They had all been running around town for far too long, but he was still smoking hot in his tattered white tank, bare toes poking out from the bottom of his jeans.

Cat stuttered, the explanation in her head starting and stopping. "I guess we never really talked about it."

Aidan perched on the coffee table and positioned Cat's knees between his own. He grasped the tops of her thighs. "I thought what happened at Niro's was all a spell. Or at least I thought that would be your explanation. I know it was more for me. At least I want it to be."

"I have this tendency to fall for guys who aren't really good for me." Cat pulled her knees up to her chest and hugged herself tight. "Guys who are literally demons."

Aidan brushed a hand through his hair. "And now I fit into the same category, right?"

"Unfortunately, yes."

Aidan gently took her hands in his own, his voice barely above a whisper. "Didn't you once fit into that category as well? You can't give up on this. Those other guys you fell for started out as demons. I'm, I'm, heck I have no clue what's happening but I know I was born in the hospital the town over, my mother and father raised me on the farm bearing this town's name, and I would do anything to save it from being destroyed. Does that sound like something an evil demon would do?"

He was right. Of course, he was. There was nothing to keep Cat from trusting Aidan other than her own fear. She would push everyone away for one reason or another, be it their failings or her own. If she couldn't take a risk on being happy, how could she ever expect anyone to take a risk on her?

Slowly she leaned forward and pressed her lips to his. Aidan's lips parted, and a low moan escaped his throat. She threaded her hands through his hair and clasped them together behind his neck. She pressed her lips to his, and he remained still yet unresponsive. Was he waiting for further invitation or would he push her aside?

"You can kiss me back if you want."

It was the signal he needed. Aidan scooped his hands underneath her slight frame and brought her onto his lap. Beneath her, she could feel his excitement growing.

Cupping his face in her hands, she searched his eyes for anything that could give her a reason not to let go, not to give herself to him. Not to let those barriers down inside her soul that she had held onto for what felt like an eternity.

"All I want to do is hold on to you forever."

His arms wrapped around her and the barriers crashed down with such force the wind seemed to be knocked forcefully from her lungs. She gasped for air and Aidan pressed his lips to hers, filling her with the warmth she needed to jumpstart her heart.

"It's been so long." The words exited her mouth before she could explain. Sure, she had had sex with men after she was absconded to Hell. Even after she had been spat back out. But she had never let it mean anything. Never allowed those motor neurons in her brain to assign an emotion to the physical act of sex. But here and now those walls were being torn down. She didn't even have to give orders. It was happening all on its own.

Aidan tucked a lock of hair behind her ear and rubbed his

thumb down her cheek. "I won't let anything happen to you. So help me, as long as I control this mind and this body no harm will come to you."

Cat ran her hands over the cool cotton of Aidan's tank and grasped the bottom of his shirt. She pulled the fabric over his head and admired the ripples of muscles shown in the morning light. Eager hands brushed over his abs, feeling the heat, feeling the beat of his heart.

He grasped her hand and placed it in the middle of his chest, the rhythm matching her own. "For you. I've never felt anything like this before."

"Neither have I." The words were flowing freely from her. No more filter. No more hiding behind painful memories. This man was normal and deserved a normal life. Whatever Niro was doing she would die rather than let him take this beautiful man.

The angst she had been feeling transformed into carnal lust. Her body pressed against Aidan and there was no ending or beginning. She felt the clasp of her bra release. His thumb and forefinger searched out and found her nipple. Pleasure coursed through her body as he stroked her.

She kneaded her fingers through his hair and brought him closer to her chest. Beneath her, she felt his cock swell which increased her need to have him inside of her. The Papasan chair listed dangerously to the side. Aidan scooped her up and planted her on the couch.

"Are you sure you are okay with this?" He locked eyes with her. She might have been unsure of his motives before when he was possessed, but now he was trying to suss out her intentions. See if she was the real deal. His heart was just as much on the line, and both of them had seen enough pain.

"Yes." Her answer was just above a whisper, but it was all he needed. Quickly her shirt was pulled over her shoulders, and her jeans were around her ankles.

"I've wanted to do this for a long time."

The first few strokes of his tongue threatened to take her into another realm, but she held fast to the present. It was too good to miss. With meticulous precision, he brought her to the edge again and again. Bringing his tongue so close to where she wanted it to be and pulling away.

"Please." She forgot who she was, another voice answering for her needs. Her carnal needs.

He answered without speaking, bringing his mouth down on her. Soon she was taken to a peak that evoked all of her emotions. All of her feelings which came flooding down, crashing through the dam that had been built up inside. If ever she had felt love, she was confident it was now.

"Aidan." His name a breath on her lips. She raised and worked to undo the buttons of his jeans.

The look in his eyes was animal, but all Aidan. He reached into his pocket and pulled out a condom before pushing down his jeans. His erection was freed from its confines, and she felt another rush of heat between her legs at the sight. He leaned over top of her and captured her nipple in his mouth. He gently pressed his length into her wet heat.

A moan escaped both of their lips at the same time. Sweat beaded over her forehead. Aidan scooped her up and turned her over, grabbing her by the hips. She angled her body to receive even more of him and gripped the side of the couch as he thrust into her.

He moaned and pressed one last time into her before collapsing.

"Hey, good morning...oh, I'll give you a second." Norm turned around in the doorway, but she caught his lecherous grin before he disappeared behind the closed door.

Aidan grabbed the blanket from the chair and handed it to Cat. "I'll never hear the end of that."

He tossed the evidence of their encounter in a nearby waste bin and pulled his jeans back over his hips. Cat groaned internally. If they could save the world, she swore she would spend an entire day in bed with the man, stopping only to use the bathroom and eat Chinese take-out.

"I hope he gets the chance to kid you about it." She pulled her jeans back on and quickly fastened her bra, the action brought her back to harsh reality. "If Thalia doesn't come back soon, I have to go to the mine and see if I can figure out how the red rock is mysteriously disappearing. Niro is hiding it somewhere and finding it may be our one chance to save you. Niro is plotting something else, I can feel it. He's been camped out here too long to just be waiting for the time to open the portal and bring you through. There are too many beasties hanging around town."

Aidan looked in the direction of the mine. "I don't want you to go alone."

"Is it safe to come out now?" said Norm from behind the closed door. "Or are you starting Act Two? Because I could pop some popcorn and watch the show."

"Norm, get out here you perv. We need to talk to you anyway." Cat pulled on her tank top as Norm exited the bedroom. He looked no worse for wear despite being in the middle of a full-blown supernatural disaster in the making. Ignorance is bliss, but he was about to have his life altered, so he needed the raw truth.

Aidan continued to peer out the window, but this time he shifted his attention toward his family farm. "I need to get to my Dad. He's been hiding this from me, and I want to know why. He's been studying that document for years and never said anything to me. Why would he keep something so important to himself?"

"You can't go anywhere right now," said Cat.

"Damn." Aidan cursed as he peered out the window. "They are going to get to him before me."

"What, is it Niro?" Cat jumped up and searched the road. Two black sedans with tinted windows bumped along the drive into Ash Farms.

"No, worse. It's Violet Chanterelle and her father."

Chapter Sixteen

Aidan felt clear headed. It pained him to have to stay inside Cat's house while the vultures descended on the remains of his family's legacy. Of course, if what Cat was saying was accurate, then the whole town of Ashton was going to suffer a far greater tragedy than an influx of chain retailers.

He continued to watch for Thalia's return as Cat filled Norm in on the status of the world as we know it, which included a detailed explanation of the existence of supernatural creatures that could possibly drag you into Hell and whose intended target was Aidan. Everyone in the town of Ashton might already be possessed by demons which would mean they would be in a fight against their own.

"Man, that's really messed up." Norm sat back on the couch, his manner upbeat considering the craziness around him. "What's our plan?"

"Hopefully, she has the answer." Thalia barreled down the driveway and skidded Cat's Jeep to a halt in front of the stairs. A plume of dust kicked up in her wake. She raced up the steps and plowed through the door as Aidan held it open.

A sheen of sweat covered her brow, and she was breathing heavy. "I got...I got..." She held up a bag and dropped it onto the coffee table.

"Did you find something to help Aidan?" Cat opened the

bag and stepped back from whatever lurked inside. "What the Hell?"

The smell of raw sewage and rotting meat permeated the room. Hand over his nose, Aidan reopened the door and inhaled the fresh air.

"Close the door. I don't think they can get through, but I'm unsure how long it will hold."

"Who can get through?" Aidan inspected the empty road. Nothing except for the plume of dust hung in the air.

"Them." She pointed, drawing his eye.

Dozens of them. Coming from the road. Walking with slow, deliberate strides toward the house. A few became ten, which then became more. The townsfolk of Ashton, but they were no longer themselves. Red eyes glowed through the dust.

Aidan slammed the door shut and threw the deadbolt, embarrassed by a sense of overwhelming panic. He'd grown up with this people. His Sunday school teacher led the pack, her usual cheerful demeanor gone, pushed aside by an evil spirit. "How are we going to get rid of them? I don't want to hurt anyone."

"I'm hoping we can get out before killing becomes necessary. And I'm hoping Cat can remember some of her otherworldly skills."

Aidan watched as the first zombified townsfolk reached the edge of Cat's porch. They tried to take a step up and quickly bounced off what seemed like an invisible dome around the property.

"I hope the barrier goes all the way around the house." Aidan saw some of the herd veering off to find another way in.

Thalia put a finger to her lip. "Yeah, I'm pretty sure it does. But let's not test the theory, shall we? Cat, do your thing."

Cat stared into the bag, mouth agape. "I haven't had to manipulate the dark matter since I was trapped in Hell. I just had to deal with expelling it from my system. I can't..."

Wild eyes met his as she backed from the table and rushed into the kitchen, a sob drifting to his ear. The sound hit like a fist, and he started to follow her, to offer her comfort. Thalia grabbed his arm. "You need to get her to be okay with this. Sooner rather than later."

Aidan nodded. He wanted to help, but he also didn't want to ask Cat to go through any more trauma. Inside the kitchen, Cat banged the cabinet doors.

"I swear I had more tea in here." She filled up the tea kettle and set it on the stove, flicking the burner on high and returning to her frantic search of the cabinets.

"You came here hoping to hide out. Hoping you'd never have to deal with demons again. I'm sorry you're in this position." He didn't know what else to say. It was most certainly the truth.

Cat laid her hands on the tile countertop and inhaled a sharp breath. "I'm not entirely convinced part of this doesn't have to do with me. And I'm not entirely convinced that me being here isn't making things worse."

Aidan stepped into the kitchen and pulled Cat into his arms. With a gentle hand, he pressed her head to his chest and stroked her hair. "You being here definitely isn't making things worse for me."

He felt her shudder in his arms, his chest beneath her face became slightly damp, and she wiped at her eyes. "Well, I certainly won't let that start now."

She straightened her shoulders and stumbled walked into the living room.

"You got anything to eat? Norm's been getting busy and getting busy makes Norm hungry." Norm was the least fazed of all of them. His primary urge to feed and tell dirty jokes remained on full force.

"Take whatever you want in the kitchen." Cat waved him in the general direction, focused on the bag on the coffee table. A lingering scent of death hung in the air and she looked at Thalia for answers. "First, tell me where you got this."

"The same witch who sold me the protection spell. She owed me a few favors from a long time ago. I think at this point I might owe her something."

"I can manipulate this, but I'm not sure how effective it will be."

Aidan watched as Cat lifted a glass vial of black liquid from the burlap sack on the table. Even looking at the stuff made his skin crawl, but he wasn't sure why. Whispers crossed his ears, and he feared the voice was trying to make a return. "What is that stuff?"

Thalia grasped the hem of her skirt as if she were trying to keep her hands from reaching for the stuff. "Pure evil," she said.

"Well, then why the heck is Cat handling it?" He swiped for the vial in her hand.

Cat pulled it closer to her chest. "Because I had this living in my veins for fifty years and somehow didn't end up a zombie. Whatever quasi-possessed state they kept me in helped train my body. After a time, I learned how to I simply absorb as much evil as necessary to justify my horrible actions and still remain sane. But it was a choice. That's what I've come to learn anyway."

Thalia slung an arm over her friend's shoulder. "I knew

there was a reason you kept me around."

"I keep you around because you're loyal, not evil, and are the best friend I have ever had. That said, back away from the juju she-devil."

Thalia raised her hands and took two steps backward. No matter what their intentions were, this stuff seemed to be very attractive to demons. Even more than the red rock.

"Anyone want a hot dog?" Norm's pervy laughter followed him taking a large bite into a raw hot dog he had unearthed from Cat's fridge.

"I would never have taken you for the type to eat processed meats."

"We all have our faults." Cat winked at him, and he was pleased to see her sense of humor returning.

From outside, the noise of the gathering townsfolk increased. Surrounded by innocents intent on murder, they had no option but to fight their way out with one glaring issue. Each and every one of them might fall under whatever spell Niro cast and become part of the walking dead. A rock shattered the window near the door and Thalia jumped back, barely missing the cascade of shards. It rolled to a stop at Norm's feet.

"Guys, we need to get moving." He shoved the rest of the hotdog into his mouth and started pulling on his shoes.

"What was the plan, again?" The anxiety inside Aidan was building.

"If I can absorb enough of the evil, it won't affect you guys. You can wear it, and it will act like a mask. The demon magic will think you are already possessed. At least that's the way it's supposed to work."

"And if it doesn't?" asked Aidan.

"I turn into the evilest thing who ever walked this town, and you all are screwed."

Cat popped the cork without any further ceremony. The time for indecision had passed. She pressed her palm over the opening and closed her eyes while letting her head fall backward.

Veins of black crawled up her arm, twisting up her neck and across her face. She appeared otherworldly, and yet Aidan wasn't afraid. Like Thalia and Miss Chow, Cat was one of the good guys. He wished whatever had possessed him didn't feel like the spawn of Satan. Even now he could sense it. A beast rattling against a cage within his psyche. Hopefully whatever Cat did would keep it that way.

Cat swayed back and forth, but she didn't appear out of control. Euphoria parted her lips, ones he'd just kissed. The thrust of her breasts, while she inhaled, made him want to sweep her into his arms and make love to her again. Damn, she was beautiful, and he wanted to be with her for the rest of his life. Slowly the lines across her skin faded. When she opened her eyes, they were normal. A smile crossed her face. "I have to admit, that felt pretty good."

"Don't get used to the drug, Hun. I certainly know what road that leads down." Thalia rose on her toes and peered through the peephole. "Better get going."

"You first." Cat faced Aidan and, dipping a finger into the vial, applied it like eye black. Capable fingers touched his skin, gentle and delicate. He experienced a thrill at the contact and wanted to clasp her hand in his own. She moved away before he had the chance and Aidan watched her with hungry eyes while she applied the salve to Norm and then Thalia.

The stuff tingled, like sore muscle balm, and smelled about

as bad. "I really hope this works."

"You will be carrying the whole bottle with you. I'm pretty sure it won't be enough otherwise." She corked the vial and pressed it into his front jeans pocket, her fingers slipping deeper into the material than necessary. She was tempting him, and he loved the freedom in which she did it. Was there hope for them yet? They still had a lot to work through.

She stood on her toes and kissed the bridge of his nose. "It'll work for a while." Let me grab one more thing and then we can go. Aidan watched her bend over and pull her boots on, her firm backside taunting him. The face paint definitely didn't dampen his naughty thoughts.

Cat slipped into her bedroom, and Aidan peered out the window. The townsfolk had stopped moving. Apparently, word spread they couldn't find a way in, so instead, they were just waiting them out. They were three deep in a circle around the house.

"How the Hell are we getting out of here?"

"Hey, maybe if we blast some Gloria Estefan we can get a conga line going." Norm paced back and forth, peering out from behind the sheer curtains. From the kitchen, the tea kettle whistled loudly. "I'll get it."

"Are you at all worried about him?" Aidan gestured to the kitchen. "He'd be safer if he stayed here."

Thalia shook her head. "This barrier isn't going to last forever. The only way he'll be safe is if he stays by our side."

"Got it." Cat stood in the bedroom doorway, a pair of handcuffs dangling from her finger.

"Hey, now we're talking. Anybody want tea?" Norm didn't miss a beat.

"Are we planning on taking Niro into custody?"

Cat strolled across the living room and pressed the cuffs into Aidan's other front pocket. "No. If you feel like the stuff is wearing off. If you start hearing anything, you find the nearest steel pole, and you get yourself attached to it quick. At least then you won't be putting yourself or anyone else in danger."

"Good plan. What's your next one?" He pointed out the window. "Wait a minute. Is that who I think it is?"

* * *

Cat followed Aidan's gaze, her attention caught by a strange sight. Behind the gathering horde at the edge of her driveway stood the neighbor boy who had caused her so much grief. Jeremiah waved his arms as if to get their attention.

"What's he doing?" asked Thalia.

A plume of red entered the air as Jeremiah tossed a hand full of red rock dust above him. The horde was definitely interested and started to turn away from the house to investigate.

"I'm not certain why, but he's creating a distraction. Grab whatever you need because we're going to make a break for it."

Right at the bottom of her front porch was Cat's Jeep. If they could all make it inside, they could get away fast and not have to worry about hurting anybody.

Aidan tilted his head, gaze locked on his family farm. "I need to check with Dad. You guys head to the mine, I'll meet you there. I swear."

Cat wondered if the black magic would work. She'd done her best, but there was no telling what this prophecy exactly entailed. She wasn't sure he could really take care of himself.

"It's not safe for you to go alone."

Desperation crossed his face. "I can't leave him there. You

don't understand."

But she understood all too well. Cat knew all too well what it was like to lose everyone close to her. It had happened in an instant. "We'll go with you."

"What?" Thalia protested. "Look, we have a small opportunity to act here, and if we can't figure out what's happening with your ex, we might as well spend our end of days having a last good fuck."

Norm raised his hand. "That's how I would prefer to go out."

Jeremiah continued down the driveway, leaving a trail of red rock dust for them all to follow and it was working. In a few seconds, they would be able to make it to the car, and they didn't have time to have a logical discussion about what their plan was going to be.

"We're going to stick together. I'm driving, and you guys are all coming. We need everyone on this. Are we good?" They all nodded. "On three."

"One." Cat gripped the door and pressed her eye to the peephole. The horde was definitely headed off, but they were also busily trying to scoop up what they could of the red dust dropped by Jeremiah.

"Two." She turned the knob and studied her friends. Aidan's eyes appeared clear. She hoped once they all got in the Jeep he wouldn't become evil. That would make things difficult.

"Three." She pressed her shoulder into the door and raced down the steps, pushing her key fob and unlocking all the doors as she hit the last step.

Cat watched the townspeople while she raced to the car. Climbing inside, she started the engine and looked up in time to see Norm trip off the last step into Thalia, his arm knocking over a flower pot. The thing hit the hood of the car with a loud bang. The Sunday school teacher swirled her grayed head, and red eyes blazed brighter. She turned on her heel and headed toward them.

"Get in the car, now," Cat urged as the zombies started to notice the actions of their leader. Thalia dragged Norm into the car and Cat stepped on the gas, hands on the wheel tight. She swerved to miss the teacher and saw the back door swing open and Norm's skinny arm flailing from the force of the turn while he tried to remain in the car.

The teacher grabbed his arm and Cat yelled into the back. "Get him inside."

As soon as she heard the last door click shut, Cat slammed on the gas, peeling in a tight circle to turn the car toward the road. She pulled the wheel tight to miss the townsfolk who turned with their eyes shining red, looking a little confused.

"We have to go to my house," said Aidan. "I have to get to my dad."

"I'm sorry to tell you, Aidan," said Thalia. "But I think your dad is probably possessed as well."

"Right," said Norm. "Shouldn't we go to the mine and see what's going on there? I mean isn't that where everything's happening?"

"You don't understand," said Aidan. "I saw them going to the house."

Plumes of dust covered the back window making it difficult for Cat to see if they were being followed. She could see, however, that Aidan who sat in the passenger seat next to her, was still himself, his eyes their natural color. And she knew what it was like to lose your family. If she had any hope of keeping his demon at bay, the best plan would be to go to

Ash Farm and see about Aidan's dad. No matter the outcome, Aidan would be hurt by what they found.

Her fingers gripped the steering wheel and sweat beaded her brow. Her first thought was Niro. As they approached the house, two black sedans were parked in the driveway. They looked just like the car that asshole drove, but she knew it wasn't him. She would have sensed him before they even got down the driveway.

"Since when did you get such a fancy car, Aidan?" asked Norm. "You get a raise I don't know about?"

Aidan had his hand on the lock and was opening before Cat could come to a full stop. Her fear increased at his actions, and she reached across and put her hand on his shoulder.

"Wait. We're doing this together, or we're not doing it at all." She waited, breath held, for the demon to flare in response. To battle back. If he were possessed, she would rather it be in the car than inside the house. "Did you say you know whose car that belongs to?" she asked.

"Yes." His jaw stiffened, but he stayed in control. "It belongs to Violet Chanterelle and her father, both of whom are trying to take away our land. They made some sort of deal with my father under my nose. I tried to get him to listen to me, but he just doesn't understand. He thinks that he can sell the land and somehow still keep Ashton the way that it always was. But that mistake was already made long ago. The townsfolk thought they could make a deal and now look what's happening."

"Well, we will definitely find out soon enough," said Cat.

If Aidan's evil side took over and he hurt his dad, he'd never forgive himself. The only one who would be able to help would be her and Thalia. The best thing for Norm was to stay in the in the car, but she wanted everyone close by in case the magic charm wore off, and the demon possession crept in. The worst thing any of them could do right now would be to let down their guard.

"On the count of three, we book it to the house. Ready?"

At the collective yes, she opened her door, and the others followed her lead. She was the first to place her foot on the stoop.

Cat put aside her newly acquired manners and turned the knob. It wouldn't do any good to knock. Plus, if anyone inside were possessed, they would already know that she was out there. On the porch. Waiting for them. As much as she could sense the demons, they could also sense her. Her power was a bit of a double-edged sword. The good news was, other than her friend Thalia, she wasn't sensing much of anything.

"I think we'll be ok," said Cat. "Just follow my lead."

Cat opened the door and waltzed in as if she belonged there. "Hello? Is anyone home?"

"What the Hell, Cat?" Aidan put his hands in the air. "Aren't we supposed to be, you know, sneaking up on them?"

"I don't think we have much to worry about," said Cat.

She walked further into the house, the other three trailing behind her. As she got toward the dining room, she heard the familiar clink of antique China and smelled the earthy tincture of a fresh pot of tea. *Darn, my tea. Did I remember to turn off the stove?* She shook off the ridiculous thought. She bit back hysterical laughter. That was a minor issue in the grand scheme of things.

Violet Chanterelle looked up as they entered. She was dressed like a Southern Belle, her hair in perfect curls. Her bodice tight. And her ample bosom spilling out the top. This woman didn't miss a chance to show off. Especially when it was when she was trying to get what she wanted.

"Well, well. What a surprise," said Violet in her affected drawl, one as genuine as the faux diamond she wore. "You never told me that we were expecting others."

Aidan eyed the woman with disdain. "This is my house, and you're not welcome."

"That's not what you said the other night when you tried to seduce me," said Violet, picking the papers up and holding them to her bosom.

Aidan blanched at the reminder of his coarse actions.

Cat resisted the urge to roll her eyes. "That's not how I remember it."

Violet's expression steeled. "Oh, it's you. Trailer girl. Don't they have showers where you're from? You might want to wash your face, but then cheap doesn't always scrub off."

"What part of the south are you from again?" Norm asked.

"Southern Oregon." Aidan recovered his wits. "I told you not to come around here with those papers unless I was here. I told you that. What's wrong with you?"

Cat could think of a lot of answers to that question, but one of them wasn't that she was possessed. For whatever reason everyone in town has been affected except for them, Jeremiah and the Chanterelles. It wasn't adding up. She was missing something, and Violet had the answer.

Without being asked, Cat took a seat. She smoothed the lace tablecloth, running her fingers over the embroidering and gesturing to her friend to sit next to her. Violet's father sat on the other side of the table. His eyes hadn't moved from Cat since they entered the house. He wasn't a demon, but that didn't mean he wasn't creepy. "Yes, well, we were stopping by because Aidan wanted to check in with his father, so why not stay for some tea. Thank you. I take mine black. So what brings the two of you to Ash Farms today? I'm guessing the answer isn't for pleasure."

"How is this your business?" said Violet's father.

Aidan made to rise from his seat and Cat put her hand over his knee to settle him down in his chair. "She's here because I asked her to be. I've already reminded your daughter once. This is my house. So while you can refuse to answer her questions, I certainly expect that you would answer mine."

Mr. Chanterelle leaned back in his chair, nonplussed. His hands folded behind his head, a smirk across his face. "Well, of course, I will listen to Mr. Ash, Junior. Though I'm not certain that you have a lot to add to this conversation. An agreement has already been made."

He put out a hand toward Violet. She quickly thumbed through the papers in her hand, pulling one from the center of the pile and placing it on her father's outstretched palm. He pushed it across the table to Aidan.

Aidan settled his fingers over the document, his expression giving nothing away. Cat wished she could be as calm. She had to bite her tongue and not order him to turn it over.

Once he performed the task, she wished he hadn't. His face paled, and her heart went out to him. In a low, hurtful voice, he met his dad's eyes. "What did you do?"

A tremor passed over the tea in Cat's cup. The eye of the storm had drifted past, and the winds of war were about to whip into a frenzy. Aidan's anger was translating into telekinetic movements, which wasn't a good sign. The demon inside Aidan was stirring. She might be keeping it at bay, but not for long.

"Son, we can speak about this another time. We have guests

in this house."

Norm peered over his shoulder and looked out the window. He bent over and whispered to Cat as Junior and Senior were exchanging words. "Looks like we're going to have quite a few more guests if we don't get moving."

Cat followed Norm's line of site. The hoard must have finished their power-up meal courtesy of Jeremiah and was heading back toward the main road. They were still several miles away and walking slow, but they were coming.

"Aidan, why don't you let me look at that while you talk to your father in private. My dad was a lawyer once." It was a total fabrication. Or maybe it wasn't. It was hard to recall anymore the details of her life before this one. Maybe that was a good thing.

The instant Aidan disappeared, Thalia rose in her chair. "I think I'm going to find the restroom. You never know when you're on the move when you are going to have another chance."

"Me too." Norm followed closely behind her.

Cryptic, but effective. Thalia knew they had to go soon as well. While Cat realized the importance of leaving to save their hides, she still had one burning question. Why were the Chanterelles normal? Well, they were anything but normal, they were annoying as Hell. But they weren't possessed. They were only obsessed with getting Mr. Ash to sell his land to them.

Violet took her seat beside her father and sipped her tea, pinky up and nose tilted downward at Cat as she scanned the document. The ink on the contract was still wet. Aidan's father must have signed it right before they got there. As deals went, it seemed pretty reasonable. No mention of demon possession anyway.

"So why are you both so anxious to close the deal on the land? Seems like you wouldn't be able to start building soon anyway. Isn't the land still being used for crops? If you don't mind me asking." Cat had no idea where she was going with her line of questioning, she just hoped to get the Chanterelles talking. Even if Mr. Chanterelle wouldn't let anything slip, she was sure that Violet would.

"Now you're a smart girl," said Mr. Chanterelle. "You know my business isn't in crops. No money there. You and I actually have more in common than the rest of the hillbillies in this town. Computers."

A chill skittered across the surface of Cat's skin, and not the pleasant kind. He wasn't a demon, but he sure gave her the creeps. "You'd have to make a pretty good deal to make the land worth anything to you out here then. I mean, it's not like you're going to open up another Microsoft in the middle of a small town like this."

He leaned across the space. "Yeah, you'd have to make a deal with the devil."

* * *

"Dad, I thought we agreed that you were going to wait until I was able to make this decision with you."

"Son, you haven't been around much lately, and the time was past due to make a decision. Especially after the fire. You'll see. I'm only looking out for you in the long run. You don't want to be stuck in this small town, and I don't think you should be. Why do you think I was so glad when you decided to attend the university?"

It struck him all at once. The picture he had of his father

before his mother died. The strapping, muscular man who worked the farm tirelessly and whose skin always held a golden sheen was gone. In his place was a pale and frail old man, who could barely use the bathroom without help. Aidan couldn't imagine having all that taken away and still want to try to live a life you knew wasn't possible anymore.

"I came back because I love this land. I love this farm. I never intended to leave you here all alone. I only wanted to learn more so that I could come back and make this place even better than it ever has been. Selling off part of the property to the Chanterelles, especially the part they know holds the most value for our crops, isn't going to make this place better for me."

Aidan's father ran his hand through the wisps of his remaining hair. "I was hoping I wouldn't have to tell you the truth of it all."

"How did you think I wouldn't find out? I sure as shit would have noticed when they started their bulldozing."

"Not that. Dammit, Aidan. You need to listen to me this time." It had been years since Aidan's father had raised his voice to him. It wasn't in the man's soft-spoken style, but something had him agitated. Something other than the property dispute. "I tried to get you to leave because I've been trying to protect you. You see, there is this curse..."

Aidan pulled the prophecy from his pocket, and his father's voice trailed off. "I've wanted to discuss that too."

His father dropped his face into his hands. "You think I'm an old fool now, don't you? Well, put me in the nut house, I don't care. You must promise me you'll leave this town and never come back. I couldn't bear it if anything happened to you."

Choosing his words wisely, he inhaled a breath for courage. "What exactly do you believe will happen to me?" Silence followed his question, and he stared at his dad, waiting. He had to know if the only person he thought he could trust one hundred percent had been keeping something from him.

Tears welled in his father's eyes, and he adjusted the blanket over his lap, his once strong hands shaking with age and despair. "It was just a story my own father told me, one for years that I didn't believe. Who would? The tale is outlandish. A town making a deal with the devil seemed like a ghost story some man made up to scare kids at the campfire."

"Only it's a real prophecy. And I'm the last victim before the credits roll."

"From what my father said, the town leader, your great-great-grandfather, had been desperate to save his family and the other settlers of Ash after drought hit and a cholera epidemic spread like wildfire. He convinced the other founders of this town to make a pact with the devil to save their families and their land. The demon would keep the red rock, and we'd get to keep our land. But if ever the red rock ran dry, then the payment for all of the years of prosperity would be the soul of the last born to the Ash family line. That's you, Aidan. I don't know what happened to the mineral. This shouldn't have happened for many generations. I thought if I sent you away, you'd never know. I'm so sorry."

"So he sacrificed his future ancestors to save his own skin."

"If he hadn't, we wouldn't be here, and I'd never have had you."

Aidan bent and embraced his father. He was trying to protect Aidan like Aidan had tried to protect him all of these years.

"I wish you would have told me sooner. I hate that you have

lived all these years with such a burden."

"No man in his right mind would believe such a farce."

"I have to admit, you're right." He couldn't fault the man for not telling him such a crazy story. There is a good chance he would not have believed him even if he did. Now that the truth was out, it was up to Aidan to end the curse or die trying. "Do you know why you haven't been infected? Why the Chanterelles haven't been infected?"

His father shook his head, eyes bleak. "I have no idea how any of it works, and I'm afraid it's too late to figure it out."

Aidan paced the room, rubbing at the back of his neck. Like his father, he had no clue how they were going to get out of this. He peered through the window in the foyer. The crowds of townsfolk were getting closer. In twenty minutes they would probably reach the edge of the driveway and block them all in.

He was startled when a stone *thunked* on the glass. Jeremiah stood right under the window. He gestured for Aidan to open up. He unlatched and pressed it open. "What are you doing out there?"

"I thought you guys could use my help. I got them away, but I ran out of the red stuff. I went back to get more." He lifted up a bag and dipped his hand in, pulling out a handful of chunks of red rock, cinnabar. More than he had seen the mine pull out in months.

"I need you to show me where you got that. Can you stay there?"

The boy nodded and sat down on the porch to wait.

"Dad, we can talk about the contract later, but I need to go check something out. It could be the out we are looking for. Promise me you'll stay here."

His father nodded his head. "Please be safe. I don't think I could handle losing you too."

Aidan helped his father get comfortable in his bedroom and made sure he locked the door behind him. Pressing his hand to the closed door, he said a silent prayer hoping that leaving his father behind was the best decision.

He was the one the demons were after. While he wasn't sure where his next steps would lead him, he was sure it wasn't going to be anywhere safer than here.

He turned around and almost ran right into Cat.

"We have a problem," said Cat.

He heard the front door open and close and brushed past Cat in time to see the Chanterelles cars bolt down the driveway. "They have the right idea. We need to get out of here."

"Did someone say it's time to get going?" Thalia smoothed down her hair and checked her watch. Norm exited the room behind her and finished buttoning his shirt. "Because we are definitely burning daylight."

"Listen," Cat blocked the path to the front door. "The Chanterelles have made some other kind of deal. It's why they aren't infected like everyone else."

Aidan thought about his father and quickly chased the idea out of his mind. There was no way his father would sell him out to save himself.

Why do you think he sold the farm, you idiot boy? Aidan dug his hand into his pocket and pulled out the vial, reapplying the salve to his cheek. He listened for a moment, but the voice didn't return.

Cat stared into his eyes. "Tell me if you are not okay. We can't risk you flipping."

"I'm fine. We need to get outside before that hoard makes it down the driveway. Jeremiah is out there, and I think he can help. Here take this." Aidan handed a rucksack to Norm. "Go into the kitchen. Fill it with some food and make sure to fill the water bottles. I'm not sure how far we will have to go."

Norm ran into the kitchen and Thalia parted the curtain on the front window. "We have five minutes before it becomes too late for us to get down that driveway."

"We won't need it." Aidan flung open the front door, taking the steps two at a time. Jeremiah popped out from the corner of the house. Cat was on him in a matter of seconds, her hand twisted into the front of his shirt and her faces inches from his.

"What are you up too, Jeremiah? Why have you been stalking me? Who put you up to this?"

"Cat, wait." Aidan had known the boy his whole life, and while he was a troublemaker, he was mostly harmless. He didn't believe he would actually be instrumental in any of this. Although he wasn't infected either.

"Back off, Aidan." Cat didn't give him an inch. She held firm to the boy's shirt looking as though she was about to tear the answer out of him. He hoped that the black stuff wasn't getting to her.

"Look at what he has in his hand."

Cat snapped out of her trance and snatched the satchel from Jeremiah. She opened the bag, and Thalia immediately sniffed it out. "What the heck is he doing with that much red rock?"

"There's a whole room of it. Mom's been selling it on eBay. But I'm not taking much. They don't even notice with all that is down there."

Cat let go of his shirt and stepped back. "Show us where."

Chapter Seventeen

Cat loosened her grip on Jeremiah. Despite what Aidan and the others might think, she wasn't losing her grip on reality. She had to see his reaction to anger or violence when provoked. If they were going to be following him to a stash of red rock, she'd needed to be cautious.

Tree limbs cracked in the distance signaling that the hoard had started to make its way across the field directly to the house. Forget the road, they were escaping via the straightest route.

Thalia opened the driver's door. "Get in then we can discuss the specifics."

Everyone scrambled toward the car except Aidan.

"What if they attack the house? My father is still in there."

"You needn't be concerned. I think they are trying to get to you or me." Cat walked over, placing her hand in Aidan's. "We'll make it through this. As long as we have the red rock, they will follow us."

They are after Aidan and me. The thought rolled around in Cat's head as they headed down the drive. Norm held onto the *oh shit* grip as Thalia took the sharp corner onto the road at high speed. It was strange. Why wouldn't Aidan's father be the perfect person to possess? If he could get to Aidan and bring him to the portal, this would be all over. Aidan would

300

never have suspected his father. Niro was up to something else. And it had something to do with the Chanterelles.

The late afternoon sun dropped lower in the sky, signaling the upcoming night. It was only 5:30 p.m. and they had three more hours of daylight. After that, the possessed would be at full power, and then death would be imminent. No more trundling along like zombies. They would morph from their zombie-like state and come into their full power. The devil's minions would complete their master's task. Was Niro their leader, or was he also tasked by a higher power? She shivered at the thought. Niro might be dangerous. His boss was deadly. In a nuclear option kind of way.

"Take the side entrance." Aidan pointed to a service road. "I can get in there with my key."

Thalia went to pull off in that direction, but someone stepped out from behind the trees.

"Look out," Aidan yelled.

She swerved the Jeep, and the backend fishtailed from side to side.

"Are you trying to get us killed?" Norm asked from the back seat.

"Shut up!" Thalia fought with the steering wheel and tried to steady the vehicle. They came to a screeching halt. Nobody spoke. The only sound in the car was their harsh breathing.

Cat grabbed her knife, ready for trouble. The dust cleared, and a sheriff's vehicle came into view. The officer stood, gun drawn.

"Turn off the car and come out with your hands up. Now!" His agitation was clear.

"If I had to hazard a guess, this is one of the officers I recently drained," said Thalia. "Except he is awake now and

301

not feeling too friendly."

"What do we do?" asked Norm.

Thalia looked at Cat. "I have to go. You can do this without me. I'll give you some time." She snapped Norm's badge from his waistband and handed it over. "I bet Norm hasn't been shut out, go through the front. It's the least expected anyway, right?"

"Hands up! Get out now!" The officer was growing increasingly agitated, gun shaking in his outstretched hands.

"He's alone. Probably patrolling the perimeter when he saw us. We can take him out without hurting him," said Cat.

"No, I'll go. No need to ask for further trouble," said Thalia.

"Thalia, Cat's right." Aidan held her shoulder.

"Honey, if you want to get yourself sucked dry you can keep touching me like that. Don't worry, Norm will come with me to keep everyone safe. Right, Norm?"

"Of course." Norm undid his seatbelt and put his hand on the latch.

"Aidan, you switch places with Thalia. I'm pretty sure the sheriff won't shoot at you when we throw this thing in reverse," said Cat. She turned to the scared boy in the backseat. "You stay put. You'll be okay. And after this is all over, so will your Mom."

Jeremiah nodded and hugged the satchel of red rock between his legs. She didn't envy the boy getting caught up in the middle of a literal war of the worlds, but he was their only hope of finding the stash. She only hoped once this town was put back together they would forget this ever happened. Though a spell of that magnitude would bear a hefty price tag. One that might cost someone their life. There was only one person who might be able to help her if it came to that and he was the last resort.

She grabbed Thalia's arm as she made to exit the car. "When you get that one phone call, do me a favor. Call my ex. He might be able to help."

"Seriously?" Aidan's eyes flashed red for the briefest of moments, but it was enough. Before she could make a move, he stole Thalia's place behind the wheel. Norm and Thalia ran toward the officer, hands above their heads.

Aidan glared at her in the rearview mirror and threw the car in reverse and made the sharp turn back onto the road. Jeremiah flew against Cat in the back seat, pinning her against the door.

Aidan stared through her as he spoke. "One little hiccup and you have to call in your ex? What is it with you and these ex-boyfriends? Isn't having Niro, my boss, you know the one who is here to kill me, enough for you? No, you have to call another one in."

She ignored his rambling discourse and tried to get him back on track. He was an instrumental part of the drama surrounding the mine and needed to be a part of the solution. And she just plain needed him. Needed him to make it through this or she wasn't sure if she would.

Aidan brought the Jeep to a shuttering stop.

"Do you have the salve?" The car was pointed in the direction of the front gates of the mine. If he were this agitated when they got to their destination, security would know something was wrong.

He took a deep breath and reached into his pocket, hand trembling. "I don't think it's working too well anymore."

He was right. Cat was hoping it would last long enough for her to find the stash of red rock. "You'll be okay a while longer.

303

Just take a deep breath." She reapplied the face black.

"What's with you and the football black eye?" Jeremiah sat back up in the car, appearing more intrigued than scared. "It looks weird."

"You're right. It doesn't look right. Let me fix that." Cat smeared the face black on Aidan's cheek and forehead, doing the same to herself. "Now you. It will protect you from all that has been going on. So you don't end up like the townsfolk."

Jeremiah allowed Cat to apply the face paint. "Mom said I should stay away from your house. She said it would only get me into trouble. But I seen that friend of yours do magic. I seen her, and I know she's a witch."

Cat thought back to the day Thalia had put the protection spell around the house. The circle had been lit, and Jeremiah had run out from the back of her house and kept going until they couldn't see him anymore.

"You were hit with the spell. The protection spell. It's why you're not like the others. At least something is making sense around here." She handed the vial back to Aidan. "There is a little left."

"Hopefully enough." He shoved it back in his pocket, and as he put the Jeep into gear, his former anger seemed to dissipate.

Another realization clicked into place in Cat's head. Of course. Thalia had drained the officers, and the one they had just encountered was obviously not possessed. Thalia had also drained Norm and herself. Something about the succubus suck must have made them immune. Maybe she could do the same thing for Aidan. But now she was on her way to lock-up. If she could shut down the portal opening, she might be able to still help Aidan even if Niro was the one pulling the strings and not the prophecy. Hope struck a chord, and she prayed this was the case.

Aidan slowed the Jeep as they approached the mine. The security booth was empty, the straight bar still down blocking the road. They came to a stop, and Aidan swiped Norm's badge in front of the security panel. Nothing. No lights.

"I'll check inside." Cat pointed to the booth and exited the passenger side. She crossed around back and slowly approached. Her heart pounded in her throat. She remembered very little about her escape from Hell, but she knew she had a moment of clarity down there. A moment when she realized what she was doing and where she was. It was very clear to Cat at this moment she was walking back into her Hell.

Habit made her look for the lever to open the gate. Forget being captured, she was seeking a way in. She must love Aidan to risk her own sanity again.

She tried to shake the thought from her mind and find the manual release for the gate.

"Are you okay?" Aidan shouted over the idling vehicle, his face a mess of black. The same shit she used for evil down in Hell. Now Cat had made it work for her. She felt the ground, solid underneath her for the first time in years. She wasn't helpless anymore. Not the same naïve waif that was dragged into the Underworld.

She retrieved the knife at her side and used it to pry open the locked control panel. "Yeah, I found it."

The bar rose as she turned the crank and she quickly jumped back in the car. As they wound up the curved drive, she noticed the parking lot was full of cars.

"There is no reason why that booth would be empty. This place is packed." Aidan leaned forward and peered through the window. "Something isn't right."

He pulled off the road into a copse of trees, hiding their vehicle from sight, and killed the engine.

"Where exactly is the stash of red rock?" asked Cat.

Jeremiah pointed toward the old mining operation. "Out there."

* * *

"Why would Niro agree to still have the board of directors come here in the middle of this shit storm?" Aidan kept himself hidden behind the trees, eyes trained on the front of the building. The parking lot was full, but there were no signs of life.

Cat wavered a little before she steadied herself on the tree trunk. Aidan offered a hand, and she waved it off. "If what I am feeling is any indicator, then that entire building is full of demons. And not just townsfolk who are possessed. Some of them must have already come through. They must have already opened the portal."

A deep sinking feeling settled into his gut. They were here for him. To collect him. And their only hope of preventing that from happening was to keep the portal closed. And it was too late. All he wanted to do was to save the people of Ashton from a fate they never signed up for. He was the key. If he gave himself up, maybe they would all leave, and everyone could go back to living their normal life.

Aidan stepped from the tree and placed a foot on the road. "I'm going to give myself up. It's the only way. You two take the Jeep and head back to your house. Stay behind the protective circle. It's your only hope."

The crunch of gravel under tires sounded. Another car was coming up the drive. Cat snatched his arm and pulled him back into the trees. He landed with his body flush with Cat, her back on the ground. She put one hand over Aidan's mouth and another finger to her lips. He wanted to kiss those lips one last time before he gave up his life.

"Ugh, guys. I don't want to see that stuff. Kid here." Jeremiah put his hand over his eyes.

"Shut up and stay down," said Cat.

The car passed by them and weaved slowly up the rest of the drive. Aidan recognized it immediately. The Chanterelles. Gideon Chanterelle pulled the vehicle to a halt before he exited. He straightened his tie and after checking his reflection in the window, started toward the front door. Finally, there was an answer of movement from the inside.

Niro rushed out the door and stood in his path in a state of agitation. "What the Hell are you doing here, Gideon? Now is not the time." Although Aidan was new to the whole demon thing, he could tell Niro's grip on humanity was fading, his eyes smoldered and his normally coiffed appearance was in a state of disarray. "This was not our agreement."

"Right. I just wanted to make sure that my interests were protected during this board meeting. I mean, if I am to take over this property once the mine is shut down, I need to be sitting in on these meetings."

A shot of alarm sent chills up his spine. He never liked the guy, but the way Niro licked his lips was like what a predator does when he spies his prey. He certainly didn't want to see him killed. He tried to untangle himself from Cat's grip, but she kept her legs firmly around his waist and mouthed the word, "No."

"Your presence here right now would raise suspicion. You and I have a signed deal. Leave now." He took a menacing step toward Gideon. The elder stood his ground.

"See here. Planting that program to make it look like the mine was in slow decline while you stole all the red rock was a big risk. I can't just leave and hope that this meeting goes the way you want it to. You might have experience running a mine, but I know how to run a business."

"You stopped the program too early. You are the one who risked this entire operation. I told you I needed until the end of the season." Niro became agitated, gripping his hair as if he were going to pull it out by the roots.

Gideon took a step toward Niro and planted a finger in his chest. "You were the one who ran the mine dry quicker than planned, then let Aidan get too close to the truth. You're lucky I was able to get his father to close the deal or I would have to start knocking on your door for my share of the profits from the red rock."

Niro gripped Gideon's finger in his fist and quickly bent it the wrong way. An audible snap proceeded Gideon falling to the ground, his hand clutched to his chest.

"I'll make sure they all know what you did. You'll never get away with this. No one crosses Gideon Chanterelle." Even as he stared right into the eyes of Niro's demon, he didn't realize the truth.

"Shit, that guy is going to kill him," said Jeremiah.

Niro's head snapped up and scanned the trees where they were hiding. They were far enough away that any normal person probably would not have heard him. But Niro was not a normal person. He stopped and focused in on their exact location, the corners of his mouth coming up in a malicious grin. "How convenient. Looks as though lunch has been delivered."

He gripped Gideon by the shirt collar and dragged him back toward the front door of the office. He yelled inside to someone behind the one-way glass. "Get them. They're hiding in the trees."

"Shit." Aidan jumped to his feet and pulled Cat to standing. He directed Jeremiah to the Jeep. "Get in the car and stay down."

From the front door came several of Aidan's co-workers, Betsy, Lee and the receptionist, Cora, no longer themselves.

"Wait," Cat held Aidan's arm. "They have weapons."

Betsy and Lee had axes, the kind kept in mining tunnels for emergencies. Cora had a two-barrel rifle.

"And if they run, shoot their legs. I need them alive, but I don't mind them being crippled," ordered Niro as he pulled Gideon inside kicking and screaming.

"Fuck, I don't want to hurt them." Aidan stood his ground as the group of three approached. He didn't want to hurt them but what choice did he have? It was kill or be killed. He hated the thought of either scenario. His own fate was already written and had been the second his ancestor signed the contract. The sun was lower in the sky, and they were moving at a decent clip. There was no use running with the shotgun pointed at them.

"Let them take us," said Cat.

"Are you fucking crazy?" asked Aidan. "If we go in there we die."

The three minions stopped before them, weapons at the ready.

"You heard, Niro. He wants us alive. We need to get inside and see what we're up against. It's the only way."

The nagging tingle at the back of Aidan's neck returned.

309

Whatever was inside him was still there, and he feared that he wouldn't be able to keep it at bay for long. "Cat, I'm not sure how much longer I am going to be myself."

She reached out and clasped his hand. "I've got a lot of experience in that department."

The double barrel was pointed at their chest, and they gestured for Cat and Aidan to follow them inside. They were about to go into the belly of the beast.

Chapter Eighteen

Nothing but inky blackness emanated from inside the office building. Even with the door open, Cat couldn't make out what existed beyond the threshold or didn't exist anymore. If the portal had already been opened, then Hawaiian shirt day it was not. Her senses tingled. Every person standing around her was possessed. Even Aidan. If she walked through that door, she might as well be walking right back into the prison that stole the last sixty years of her life. But she was done running.

"We're coming peacefully." Cat put her hands up. Aidan followed suit, though he didn't look happy about it.

The minions patted down Cat's pockets and extracted the blade from her holster. Although she would rather have some form of protection, at least this way, she didn't have to worry about accidentally killing someone.

Arms of darkness reached out and pulled Aidan into the building. She froze for half a second, and the butt of Cora's gun dug into the small of her back. "You next."

She steeled herself for the familiar brush of black matter that once stole her from this world. One touch and it slinked its way up her arm. Icy veins swallowed every inch of bare skin and poured over her body. Her soul pressed back as it tried to wrap around that too, something she learned to do during her stint in Hell. Aidan's only salvation would be the repurposed black matter. Though the possibility still remained that the rest of this mission she might have to finish on her own.

She landed on her knees in the lobby of the Iron Forge Mine. The windows were covered in black matter. A filmy light filtered through and combined with the flickering of two fluorescent bulbs that swayed from the ceiling. A wave of dizziness struck Cat hard, and she put both hands on the floor to steady herself. Through the din, she saw Aidan standing against the wall, his hand on his stomach. A second later, he vomited on the floor, and it was all she could do to prevent herself from doing the same.

The three Stooges were right beside them but seemed to have no problem with the transition. "Cleanup on aisle three. You guys going to get us something for this or are we expected to visit whoever your master is and vomit all over his or her feet?" asked Cat.

"They can't leave now. Go get, Niro. Tell him we got them." Cora stood her ground, barrel still pointed at them and directed the other two down the hall.

Aidan stumbled over and offered her a hand. "Don't worry, this one is clean."

Warmth spread back into her limbs at the sight of his face. Still normal. For now. She accepted his gesture and pulled herself to standing. Even on two feet, she could still feel an immense weight on her shoulders. It meant he was close. The big boss. The main dude. He who should not be named and who had been given many different names over the years by many different cultures.

"Why does the air feel so heavy?" Aidan asked.

"The portal is open. He's here." Cat kept her eyes trained on Cora. She had her own nickname for the evilest thing that could ever walk this plane of existence. "The asshole."

"Any ideas how we could not run into him? I have a feeling that our introduction might mean my last day on Earth. We're still on Earth, right?"

"Very much so. But the portal has been open long enough to enclose this space. If it's left open much longer, then none of the people of this town will return to normal. They'll all be sucked down along with you and whoever else they are here for."

"Like you." Aidan brushed his fingers through his hair.

"The thought has crossed my mind."

Cora plopped down in the receptionist chair and swiveled back and forth. Even demons get bored. She sat the gun on the desk and pointed the finger at Cat. "You used to be one of us. I remember you."

"Do you? All good things I'm sure." Cat flicked a glance from Aidan to the gun at Cora's elbow. Their only chance of departing before anyone else's arrival depended on stealing the weapon from her.

The grimace that crossed Cora's face told her otherwise. Being the devil's slave, the one who doles out his bidding, doesn't make you all too popular in the Underworld. Only down there, they couldn't do anything about it. "You screwed me out of a job. I was supposed to get out of there years ago, and then you put me in the back of the line. Said I didn't have the right qualifications."

"Looks like you have a breather now. Things are looking up." Cat took a step toward the hallway, drawing Cora forward.

"Yeah, and I got a breather's arms and legs and fists." Her eyes flashed red, and she stood and took a step out from behind the desk. "And I think I'd like to try them out on you. Boss said

313

you needed to be alive. Didn't say you couldn't be bleeding a little. Or a lot."

Cat put her arms up, but she didn't bother to dodge the blow. The portal's power kept any mortals from moving very fast under their own power. Cora was completely possessed and moved without restriction. She'd win in a running game. In a second she was flat on her back, tiny fists of steel pummeling her body.

The sound of the barrel ratcheting back on the gun was a welcome relief.

"If you want to keep that body you'll get off of her. Now."

The demon struggled against the binds of USB cables and network wiring they tied her up with. Aidan swiveled the chair. "I think we have this one wrapped up for now."

A strip of duct tape kept the demon from yelling too loudly, though her muffled swear words weren't too hard to interpret.

"Where to?" Aidan palmed the rifle and shoved the box of shells Cora had in her purse into his back pocket.

"We need to shut down the portal, and the only way to do that is by using the red rock. We've got to get to the mine. And into an enclosed space where the circle of Hell is open. Oh, and there might be some minions along the way," she said.

"Of course there will be, why make this easy," Aidan said, sarcasm oozing from every word. "I'll lead the way."

Aidan snaked through the sea of abandoned cubicles. As they rounded the corner, he froze and pressed his back to the wall. "There's a bunch of them having some kind of meeting. We need to go past them to get out the back."

Cat peeked over Aidan's shoulder. The marble conference table supported the elbows of probably a dozen or more demons wearing their new human suits. Liquid black eyes all focused on the head of the table. Cat felt a sucker punch to the gut.

Under her breath, she couldn't help but utter the words at the tip of her tongue. "Asshole."

She pressed her back to the wall next to Aidan and tried to gather herself. Warm fingers intertwined with her own.

"You okay?" He looked back the way they had come.

Soon Niro would realize they were missing and had a weapon, which might not kill him but could cause a lot of damage. Time was short. But not so short that she couldn't tell Aidan what he meant to her. It might be her last chance.

"I will be. Look, I need you to know something." Cat wrapped her arms around Aidan's waist. She nuzzled at his neck and tried to remember the scent of him. Anything to get her to force out the words she needed him to hear. Anything to cling onto in case the worst happened. She pulled back and looked into his eyes. "There is a chance I might have to go back. To close the portal, I might need to be closed up with it. And if that happens, then there is a good chance we won't see each other again. I doubt Asshole would ever let me escape again. He'd probably kill me. But I need you to know that for the short time I was back, you were the best thing that ever happened to me."

Aidan pulled her in tight, crushing her body to his chest. He leaned down and whispered into her ear. "I'm never letting you out of my sight."

She choked back her response. The last time she ended up in Hell, Mane had abandoned her there. She had forgiven him. Mane had been a demon and thus hadn't the same morality as a human. Aidan was all man, a loyal and unwavering friend who would lay down his life for her. If it were in her power, she couldn't let that happen.

Shouts came from the opposite end of the corridor. Aidan released his grip and grasped her hand. "We have to go!"

He ducked down and pressed himself to the wall just below the conference room windows, making sure to keep his body down and out of view. If they could make it to the door, they could get to one of the vehicles. The demons were limited by the bodies they inhabited. No super speed or passing through walls. They could only lumber along as fast as their skin suits would travel.

The shouts increased. Cat couldn't tell if Niro's voice was one of them. It was possible that the other two stooges had discovered their friend's mistakes and were rescuing her. Thank goodness her grandfather had taught her the bowline. The more they pulled, the tighter those knots would get.

They continued to slink past the solid conference room door. Just one more corner and they would be out the back. The sounds inside the conference room became heated. Some kind of argument had broken out, but the voices were too muffled to make out what they were saying.

Cat pressed her ear to the door. Crouched down on his haunches, Aidan took a quick peek around the corner. The conference door swung open practically smacking Cat in the face. She stifled a scream of protest at the rude action, and her hand went automatically to the empty sheath at her waist. Two suits exited the conference room.

"Dr. Pepper is definitely the best. Hands down. No question."

Cat caught the edge of the door with the toe of her boot. She and Aidan were barely hidden from view, but revealing themselves would mean coming to face with these two and the rest of the conference room. Then there would be a much bigger problem than the soda wars.

"Coke is best. Why do you think they made like a zillion flavors of it? There's a machine down the hall. Let's settle this now."

The two suits lumbered down the hall toward the lobby, backs to them. Cat let the door close to the conference room. In about thirty seconds, they would be coming upon the three stooges.

Aidan pulled Cat around the corner and swiped a set of keys from a hook on the wall. He pressed against the door to the outside. She felt the tension of his hand on hers. They both stood in shock.

Spectacular shades of scarlet, fiery orange and red bounced off a layer of purple-gray clouds dotting the sky. In minutes, the sun would set, but the hold of the Underworld had already started to take effect. In the valley between the Iron Forge Mine offices and the mine itself, Cat could see the shadows taking shape. Forms of those stuck in Underworld.

Violet Chanterelle thought she was building a mall. Looked more like someone else had designs on this piece of land and it was going to Hell.

"What are all those things?" Aidan asked. He rubbed at his eyes and squinted as if he were trying to bring them into focus.

"If you can see them then we really need to hurry." She slipped into the passenger side of the motorized cart, and Aidan followed.

No sooner had they started across the tracks, then Cat heard the sound of the back door slam open. She turned in time to see all the suits pouring out the back, fingers pointed in their direction. Two stooges were pushing Cora who was still stuck to the office chair. Asshole appeared behind all of them, dwarfing everyone by about six inches Typical Asshole, picking the tallest body to show his status. His arms were crossed over his chest, and even though they were putting more distance between themselves and the offices, Cat could feel the smirk on his face.

He wasn't worried. And that worried her more than anything.

"At least they are all behind us." Aidan slipped the cart into the highest gear. The wooden tracks rattled under the tires, and they skidded to a stop before the entrance to the mine. The door hung open. Not a soul around.

Cat pressed forward. There was no one here because they were all back at the offices. If all they had to deal with were a few lackeys, then she could employ a few sleeper holds. Once the portal was closed, the demons in the boardroom would all be sucked back down with it. The only problem was the prophecy. She still had to figure out a way around that if she was going to save Aidan and the town. "We need to get to the red rock. It opens the portal, but it can close it too. Hopefully, Jeremiah was right, and Niro kept his stash down here. If he was keeping a stash, then maybe the prophecy really hasn't come to pass."

"Cat, you don't have to worry about saving me." Aidan stopped and held onto her shoulders. "Don't you think I know that if the prophecy comes to pass, then they will go away? All of this. The town will be safe. You will be safe. As much as you think I am the best thing to happen to you, you are also the best thing that has happened to me."

Visions of the Hell she had lived in for sixty years flooded back into her consciousness. Her mouth opened and closed, but nothing came out.

"Why don't you listen to lover boy here, Cat? He's got the right idea." The words, spoken in rapid-fire succession tore at her gut even more painful than a bullet blast. Fast as the snake he was, Niro captured her waist with one steely arm and pulled her off her feet. She tried to push the arm away, but it only constricted further. He bent down and whispered into her ear, and she felt a blade pressed against her throat. "You are not going to stop me from getting out of there. Permanently."

Aidan stepped forward, his face a mask of fury. "Let her go. It's me that you came for and I'll go with you willingly if you just let her go."

The blade dug into the tender flesh at her neck. "Stay there. This will all be over for the both of you soon."

"I can't let you kill her." Aidan cocked the rifle in his hand and pointed it at his own head. "I believe I am the one you need to complete whatever plan you have."

"Aidan, no." Niro walked back slowly, dragging Cat inch by inch further away from Aidan.

"It's the only way." Aidan looked ready to pull the trigger. Cat searched his face. Would he really go through with it or was he bluffing? Against the backlight of the sun, she could only see the hard line of his jaw and the intensity in his eyes.

"If you do that then your father becomes the target."

Aidan relaxed his grip on the rifle, and it was the split-second Niro needed.

"I'd say thanks, but I don't really give a crap about you." Niro jerked her backward into the next alcove. On the floor, a red ring glowed around a black pit with no end. The entrance to the Underworld. Wisps of smoky shadows poured forth, and one of them reached out and twisted around her ankle.

A blood-curdling scream pierced her hearing, and she realized it had come from herself. She turned in time to see Aidan rush into the room and aim the gun at Niro. The man ducked as the shot fired above his head. He bent down and took Aidan down at the knees and a second shot ricocheted off the ceiling.

Then everything went black.

Chapter Nineteen

A vise-like grip seized Aidan's skull and squeezed until every corpuscle was on the brink of bursting. He attempted to open his eyes, but some unseen force kept them shut. The wind howled past his ears. The world he knew left behind.

His sight gone and his hearing distorted, he lost track of time and space. The more he dropped into nothingness, the more his memory became a blur. He tried to hold onto his thoughts, but they faded as quickly as he journeyed down the rabbit hole. His body clattered to the floor, and the breath knocked out of him. Cool, damp stone quenched the fire that burned all over his skin, and prickly heat made him break out in a sweat. The next moment, he shivered, trying to remember where he was and where exactly he had come from. A fog bank rolled into his mind, clouding his memories. Opening his eyes, he stared at the ceiling of the circular room where he landed. In the middle, a black circle scorched the ground. He rolled over and reached out to touch the strange marking.

"I wouldn't do that if I were you." A woman leaned against the wall clad from head to toe in a tight white ensemble. She appeared young and beautiful with flowing black hair, a profound look of grief etched into her lovely features. He watched her, uncertain of who or what she was. Caution whispered in his head, and he clenched his fists, preparing to fight if the need arose. He had no idea why he shouldn't trust this woman, but gut instinct told Aidan he should be distrustful of anyone he met in this strange place. She chewed and sucked on some kind of twig. No weapons were in sight.

"Why shouldn't I?" He rubbed at his temples to quell the throbbing pain and tested his legs. He could stand, but he felt like he had run a marathon. "Who are you?"

The woman stepped out from the archway that formed the entrance and surveyed the space from left to right before she ducked back inside. "We came in hot, and you'll feel more pain than you already are in if you touch the portal. I'm Dorothea. We had a deal. Remember?"

"No, I don't. Refresh my memory," he said, trying to recall anything.

"Chew on this, it'll help." She pulled another stick from her back pocket and passed it to him. He considered the twig, unsure if he dared follow her lead. He had no idea where he was or if Dorothea were friend or foe.

"You promised to bring Cat back to your world before the bitch stole my man. We don't have all day. Would I be doing the same thing if it didn't? You're going to lose everything if you stay down here too long."

The sour stick turned at once into a familiar taste. Miss Chows' Orange Chicken. *Cat.* Memories flooded back in with a rush, and he doubled over, hands on knees, knocked off guard by both the intensity of the recall and the fear he had over Cat's life. He came to bring her back. "Yes, I remember now. But you're not getting anything if you don't help me find her."

Aidan tried to take in their surroundings. If this was Hell, it wasn't what he expected. The air was dank and moist like they were underground. Nothing like the dry heat he would expect of a world encased in fire and brimstone.

"That's just what they say up top. It's nothing like that." Dorothea motioned for him to follow her.

He skirted around the circle, one hand trailing along the cool stone wall to help guide him in the low light. *Did I say that out loud?*

Laughter met his silent inquiry. "No, silly mortal. Rules are different here. That's why it is near impossible to get out. But we might be able to capitalize on the momentary confusion. His focus will be on Niro right now."

They entered the hallway which appeared to go in both directions and contained an infinite number of twists and turns. Torchlight flickered, and shadows of unknown figures danced up and down the hall.

"If we came in here, why isn't Cat somewhere nearby?" With every turn, he was getting farther and farther away from the only door he knew existed between this world and his own. He grasped his hand on his pocket and inhaled a sigh of relief that the small bag he had brought with him was still there. "Would she be wandering these halls all alone?"

Dorothea stopped, her hands on her hips. "For many years, she escorted the Damned through these halls herself. Participated in tortures at His side and took all the glory. She knows her way around. The person you should be worried about is yourself."

Cat had told him humans that entered Hell didn't come back. She was an unusual case, spared at the time because she was being used as a pawn to get back at another demon who had pissed off the big guy. What about now? Was she still immune? And how long would he last down here before he became no good to her at all?

"We had a deal. You won't get what you want unless we find her and I take her back with me." His resolve swelled, sharpening his senses enough to notice movement at the intersection of the next two halls. "There."

Cat stepped from the shadows and into the light. Blood trickled down the side of her head, and she dabbed at it absentmindedly. He winced and gritted his teeth, trying to hold back his anguish in seeing her in such a state. If he was going to get her out of here, he needed to stay strong, for the both of them. The full breadth of her injuries was highlighted by the sconce on the wall. Her face was covered in scratches, and a more significant wound on her forehead wept. Her skin, red and raw, looked as if she had spent too much time in the sun.

"Cat." He stepped into her path.

She paused for a moment, looking up at him without a hint of recognition, and then proceeded to try and step around him.

Aidan followed behind her, fearful of touching her tender-ized skin but more fearful that he was too late. Maybe he'd already lost her. "Can you hear me?"

"I need to get home." She stumbled and put a trembling hand out to the wall to steady herself before she continued on her path.

He stepped into Cat's path. Aidan had literally traveled to Hell to fetch her, and he wasn't leaving without what he came for. "Cat, it's me, Aidan. You need to let me help you. I have a way out."

She swayed before straightening to her full height. Cat grabbed the back of her neck and winced as if in pain, but quickly seemed to collect herself. "No one can help me. No one. I'm going back home." She pointed down the hall into the blackness.

"I told you she wouldn't leave. I knew it." Dorothea pushed Cat in the back, and she fell against Aidan "Don't think you're taking the position I worked so hard for."

Cat whipped around, energy renewed, and growled at the demon with teeth bared. The hard cast of her jaw and the feral gleam in her eye was foreign to him. "I'm going home." She pushed past Aidan, knocking him into the wall.

Aidan reached out and snatched her arm. "I am here to take you home."

She looked from his hand back to his face and shook her head vigorously, wrenching her arm from his grasp and crossing both her arms over her chest while shuffling backward. "You don't know what you are talking about. This is my home."

"No, it's not," Aidan said in a reasonable tone, determined to get through to her before it was too late. "You don't belong down here."

"You don't know anything about me. I've lived here longer than any place in my life. I have a purpose here."

"No, you *had* a purpose here, now it's my turn. You need to leave," said Dorothea.

Aidan stepped between them and ignoring Dorothea, stared hard at Cat. "I know you're a good person and a fierce friend. You helped save hundreds of lives. You don't belong here."

"No, you're wrong. I used to thrive on torturing people, loved to hear their screams and agony and I was good at it. Damn it, I was good at it." Pain lanced her words and anguish twisted her lips. She might have been brainwashed into thinking she was evil, but Aidan knew better.

"I was never meant to leave. If you stay, you'll become just the same. Leave while you can."

Her steady, sober voice supported a rapid-fire rationale void of passion.

Was this truly the real Cat? He couldn't believe that to be true. "I know that isn't what you want. You don't belong here. You know that." Emotion choked his voice, and he grabbed onto her while a tightness formed in his chest. This could be the last time he held Cat in his arms. The thought sent his heartbeat racing and his mind into action. There had to be a way to convince her.

"There is nothing for me up there. Nothing. Wherever I go, they follow me. They came for me, and if I stay down here, you can be safe up there. I'm not going back." She pounded her fists into his chest, making the barest of efforts to disentangle herself. Tears dotted the rims of her eyes. She sucked in a deep breath and yelled at the demon woman. "And you can suck it, Dorothea. Just get used to being number two."

"Soon there won't be any choice. Damn, I thought you said you would be able to get her out of here. Told you it wouldn't work. She likes sleeping with the devil too much," said Dorothea. She unsheathed a knife hidden in her waistband.

"She dragged you down here?" Cat glared at the demon woman. "I'll make sure to make her pay for the rest of my years."

Dorothea twirled the dagger in her hand, a haughty laugh erupting from her throat. She flipped the cascade of black hair over her shoulder and pointed to a long jagged scar that ran the length of her neck from her ear, disappearing into the fabric draped over her shoulder. "I still bear your marks, bitch. If you think I'll ever let you get close to me again, you are mistaken. I didn't want to say anything before, Aidan, but be careful with this one. She'll make you think she cares and then she'll stab you in the throat. Literally."

Cat bucked against Aidan's grip, doing her best to finish what she had started. Aidan wasn't about to let her travel down that road again. He turned to Cat, desperate to get through to her. He wouldn't leave without her, but he couldn't force her to do anything against her will. She had been forced against her will enough in her life so far. She needed to make the choice herself.

"Dorothea is the demon that was hanging around in my body the last few weeks. I asked her to bring me down here. To come for you. It didn't hurt that she wanted to be accepted into the position you held as the object of affection for the senior asshole down here." Aidan released his hold on Cat. She stumbled backward a few steps, one hand against the wall. She took in deep breaths, her eyes focused on Dorothea, her body taut and ready to pounce. His head was pounding. Fists tight, his fingernails bit into his palms, but he ignored the pain. The pain of losing Cat was far worse.

"Listen to me. Everyone was fooled. Niro wasn't sent for you. He was there for himself. If anything, your presence messed with his plans. His only plan for you was to get you out of the way so he could take over the portal in Ashton." A blast of heat traveled down the hall and passed over all of them. Rancid heat that swirled about their bodies and left behind a sickly film. Something was coming.

"He's out." Dorothea's eyes widened. "Our deal is done. I can't help you any longer." The echo of her footsteps disappeared into the darkness of the labyrinth of passageways. There was a distinct possibility he might never make it out of here.

His revelation temporarily shifted her focus. "It was not

pure coincidence that I was in the same town as a mine full of red rock and a portal. I know now, this place will always be in my blood. I'll be attracted to it, and I won't be able to stop it. You need to get out of here."

Cat grabbed his arm and ran forward, into the maw of heat which increased with every step.

She had to know that she had more control than that. He knew it. He had seen it. Aidan reached into his pocket and pulled out the bag of red rock he had brought with him. He held it at arm's length, and she froze in place. Ahead of them, the darkness threatened to swallow them whole. So black and thick it appeared to take on a shape of its own. The farther they traversed down the hall, the louder the noises came. Sounds of those wallowing in depths of misery he could not even imagine. And this woman had lived through it. His heart bled at the thought and yet he knew that the woman he had met had overcome all those horrors. To the extent one ever could. And he wanted to help her get back there. Not become forever entwined in the vicious brutality of what existed beyond the Black.

"I don't want it, take it and go." She released her grip on him and sank deeper into the Black. The left side of her body completely disappeared. Aidan grabbed the nearest sconce off the wall and shown it into the dark. Squeals of pain erupted, and the curtain retreated. A living blackness settled on all sides of them, pressing closer.

"Don't you see? You might be attracted to it, but you have control over that. It doesn't control you." He took another step, and she stood still. A rosy hue returned to her cheeks, the whites of her eyes visible again. Perhaps he was getting through.

"You lived beside the mine for a year before you knew. If it hadn't been for you, we might never have found the stash in the first place. Because of you, the entire town of Ashton has been saved and the mine sealed forever. The prophecy will never come to pass. That's what you did in coming to Ashton. You saved it. You saved me."

Cat shook her head. "I've killed you. Now that you're down here, even if you get out, you may never be the same."

"I'm not leaving without you." Aidan kept the sconce close, shining the light into her eyes. Flecks of green and gold sparkled in the light. She was still in there, and she was listening to him. "I love you, Cat. It's why I came after you. It's why I always will."

Cat gazed down the hall in the direction of the blast, eyes fixed on some unseen spot in the blackness. She swiveled back to Aidan and searched his expression. "Are you sure that you can handle whatever is leftover in me? What if I turn back into something evil someday? What if I really should be down here to keep you safe? I don't want to hurt anybody else."

That was the only reassurance Aidan needed, he reached out his hand. "We'll figure it out together."

She reached out to take hold of him. "I love you too."

* * *

Cat could read how the din of this place rested heavy on his brow. He couldn't understand why she hesitated. Curling arms of the Black pressed upon them, barely contained by the light emitted from the sconce in his hand; the flicker that lit up the confusion and hurt etched on his face. Whatever happened, Cat had to make sure Aidan returned to Ashton in one piece.

"Keep the light close and follow me." She didn't wait for

his response. Taking hold of his bicep, she hurled toward the portal. Piercing the veil of black, she was immediately immersed, surrounded by memories of what held her here all those many years. The comfort of the constant. She bled for this place. She made others bleed because she longed to belong.

Each twist and turn of the corridor she knew by heart. However, knowing your prison like the back of your hand doesn't mean you will always belong there. She'd been confused when she'd been sucked into Hell, and she was confused now, but one constant kept her going. Aidan.

The gnawing and gnashing sound of the Black increased as they approached the portal room. Her heart thundered in her ears, and the whispers of a thousand souls called out to her. She ignored them all, the firm flesh of Aidan's arm beneath her hand grounding her mind. Only twenty feet to go, twenty feet until she could send him back home.

"Cat."

Cat's fist closed down on itself as Aidan's bicep was ripped from her grasp. She spun on her heel in time to see his legs come out from under him and the sconce clatter to the floor at her feet.

"Get out of here, hurry!" Pulled backward by some unseen force, Aidan clawed at the dirt, leaving lines in the floor.

The Black wanted him. He wanted him. And whatever he wanted he got, that was until the day she decided to leave this place. Fear ricocheted inside her mind and the animal instinct to hide warred with her need to save Aidan. He wouldn't get Aidan. Her heart ached at the thought of losing him. Losing his presence in her life. He was her tether to the normal, but he was more than that. He was the one who loved her even though he knew she was damaged. Even though she could only give herself to him in bits and pieces because to give over her whole self might mean losing herself again.

She flung herself down, clasped her hands over his forearm, and hooked her foot in the doorway to the portal. The strength of the Black pulled back hard, threatening to rend her spine from her body.

"Fight back. Please."

Aidan stared into her eyes and clamped down on her forearms, teeth gritted. He pushed up on his elbows and fought to free his legs from the sucking force of the Black. The muscles in his chest bulged beneath his tank top as he wrenched his body free. Scrambling to his feet, Aidan scooped up the sconce in one hand and Cat in the other, tossing her over his shoulder in a fireman's carry before he plunged through the doorway into the portal room. They both crashed to the floor.

Waves of blackness crashed into an invisible barrier at the curved entryway. The liquid glass quivered and shook in response to the assault. But it wouldn't penetrate it. Couldn't penetrate it. Cat pushed herself up and walked toward the barrier.

"What are you doing?" Aidan followed close behind, breath hot on the back of her neck.

Cat pointed to markings at the bottom of the doorway before she knelt down to place her fingers over the grooves. Her fingers slid with ease into the rough furrows, and the fog on her mind cleared.

"I remember."

Since she had left this place, she had forgotten how she escaped. Now it all came flooding back, each excruciating detail and with it a raging emotion almost too intense to bear.

Cat remembered everything she did before she got here, everything she did while she was here, and everything after landing, naked in the middle of a portal in the forests of rural Washington, but she didn't recall her actual escape.

"I fought back. I didn't want to be here anymore. The evil. I didn't want it." The realization spread through her like wildfire and sent renewed energy into her resolve.

Aidan put a hand on her shoulder. "I always knew you had it in you. That you could save yourself."

She had saved herself. She had always saved herself. She freed herself from the confines of her restraints. From the recall of the sheer force of will, she had to exert to extricate herself from this place. It had taken all of her strength and many years, so many years, to finally find her way to this room. But this time was different.

Sand crunched beneath her boot as she swiveled around to face Aidan. He reached a hand down to assist her in standing. Face to face with the man who risked his life to save her.

"You sacrificed your life to come down and save me. You didn't have to do that."

He crooked a finger and ran it down her cheek. "You're right. I didn't have to. I chose to. I love you, Cat. If I couldn't be with you in Ashton, which is my preference, by the way, I wanted to spend eternity trying to figure out a way to save us both. Heck if we've been down here long enough, maybe when we go back it will be like *Star Wars*."

"Star Trek." Cat punched him playfully in the shoulder. "Norm would be very ashamed of your geek." Her stomach dropped at the thought of her friends. "Norm! Thalia! Are they okay?"

"They're fine. You just worry about yourself. Are you ok?"

He placed a gentle hand beneath her chin. A bead of sweat trickled down his forehead, and she noticed cuts on his arms where he had fought to free himself.

"You're bleeding." Cat felt through her pockets and pulled out a handkerchief to dab at his wounds, but her hands shook so badly she did more harm than good.

Aidan gently took the cloth from her hands. "I asked if you were okay."

Behind her, she could hear the cries of the Black, the same shrieking that used to send her under the covers for days, hiding in her room surrounded by empty containers of Chinese takeout. Now she was calm. Calm in the arms of the man staring back at her. The one who had come to save her when others hadn't. The one who had always believed she had saved herself when she continually doubted it.

Cat slipped her arms around Aidan's waist and laid her head on his chest. She focused on the steady heartbeat thrumming beneath her ear. The live man in her arms. Not a soulless demon. Not some shell of a man. A man that loved her and one she loved back. "You think I saved myself, but if you hadn't come down here, I don't know if I would have had the strength to get back by myself again. You saved me."

He rested his chin atop her head and gave her a quick squeeze. "You're stronger than you think."

A loud boom echoed through the space. Dirt fell from the ceiling, raining over them. She had decided she would leave with Aidan. This place would forever be a memory. The problem was, they needed to get out of there first.

Shrieks pierced their ears, and they dropped to their knees. The Black might not be able to make it inside, but the things that lived down here would be drawn by its calls and could

333

certainly cause them trouble. Cat yelled over the noise. "Do you have the red rock?"

From his pocket, Aidan pulled out the small pouch. He started to hand it to Cat, and she instinctively drew away. His words were still fresh in her mind. *Her strength would get them out of this.* The red rock, the Black, none of it mattered. Snatching the bag, she walked the circle. Red dust fell into place along the burnt outlines. She stopped short of connecting the circuit.

"What are you waiting for? Do you have enough?" Aidan rushed to her side and peered into the open bag. A quarter size lump of red dust rested in the bottom. Enough to complete the circle. Enough to say goodbye to this place forever. Her gut told her to hurry yet a tiny voice inside, the one that hid in the dark and convinced her she was no good, held her hand.

"Cat, what is it? What's wrong?" Aidan cupped her cheek, his dark eyes encouraging.

"I remember being here, in this very spot. I was...I was so scared, but I couldn't do it anymore. I couldn't Aidan."

"It's okay, Cat. You're okay," Aidan kissed her cheeks, his lips warm against her skin. "We need to close the circle."

"What if I can't. What if I haven't changed?" She choked on a sob and shook her head. She spied the marks again, and an echo of her former self, like a ghost, appeared before her eyes. A wild woman. Dirt streaked face. Gown in tatters. Tears running down her face and blood running down her arms from where her fingers bled. She had held onto that doorway until the Black had moved on. Until it found a new target and she had been able to get inside. But even then, it wasn't over.

"You're no longer that woman, Cat. You're beautiful and strong and stubborn, but you're not evil."

She had hidden in the shadows until the portal activated, flinging herself inside to wherever it led. She could very well have ended up in a very different world than her own. But then it didn't matter. She would have rather ended up dead. Here the Black wouldn't let her die. Now she needed to get this right. She and Aidan must get back home.

"We both need to mentally focus on the same place. We need to pick a location, or we could end up in very different places."

Aidan placed his hand in the bag and took the last of the red rock. Their ticket home. "I know where we're going. Just think of your house. The porch swing. The view of my cherry orchard."

A pang of guilt swept through her. "There's nothing left of your farm."

He clasped her hand and stepped to the edge of the circle. "It will all grow back. With love and attention, everything always returns to normal, even if it's not the same."

He sifted the red dust through his strong fingers and completed the circle. The instant the last particle hit, a rush of heat and sound emitted from the sand, each sparking off the other until they lifted from the ground and intertwined in a swirl of light, forming a powerful vortex. Cat nodded to Aidan and clutched his hand tight. In her mind, she imagined the rickety porch, the creak of the wood beneath her feet. She brought forth the memory of the almond-scented blossoms, luxurious pink and white blooms sprouting forth from the branches of the cherry trees.

Cherry blossoms represent the beauty and fragility of life. A reminder of how overwhelmingly beautiful life could be but also tragically short. She would take each last moment and spend it with the ones she loved.

"Let's go home," she said. Together, she and Aidan stepped into the abyss, his loving arms wrapped around her body. She sank deep into the cocoon of his embrace and imagined her final destination.

Chapter Twenty

The early morning sun streaming across the bed woke Aidan from a particularly pleasant dream, one where he held Cat in his arms. Except for the reality of her was even better. She snuggled next to him, and he couldn't help stroking her hair and listening to the sweet sound of her breathing. He'd almost lost her, and the fact that she was in his bed was a blessing he'd be grateful for his whole life. Ever since they'd returned from Hell, he had been having nightmares that he hadn't been able to convince her to return. This was the first night in weeks that the dream had been different. Closer to reality. He glided his thumb over the soft flesh of her cheek and raised her face, intending to continue where his dream had left off and kiss her awake when the door flew open.

"It's time, it's time," shouted Thalia. Cat rolled away from him and buried her head while Thalia ripped the duvet off the bed leaving him with only the top sheet and giving him no time to cover the fact that he was about to have sex with his girlfriend. The succubus didn't miss the visible signs.

"Looks like someone has already risen this morning. But now the both of you have to get up. They are about to do the ribbon cutting! We don't have all day, Mister!" She hopped up and down on her platform shoes in a freshly pressed white dress dotted with cherries, rouge lips jutted out in a firm pout.

She was helping with his plan for the day but was none too smooth about helping him execute it.

In the weeks since the episode at the mine, all the staff at the sheriff's office had recovered from her attack, so Thalia was in the clear. With some help from Norm's geek friends in IT, they were able to plant a security alarm breach in their system, which indicated that the building had been flooded with a gas which caused hallucinations. The whole bizarre episode was chalked up to some childish prank.

Norm appeared in the doorway with his ugliest shirt yet.

"What are you wearing?" Aidan turned his body and rose up on his side, smirking at Norm's shirt that boasted a series of mustache icons down the front.

"It's a 'stache bash. We're on our way to a party right? And I also plan to have a little party of my own with this one later." He wrapped his arm around Thalia's waist. She playfully elbowed him, giggling.

Another moan from the other side of the bed announced that Cat wasn't as enthusiastic as these two were. If these two would only leave, he had an excellent way to perk her up.

"I'll let you deal with Miss Cranky Pants." Thalia tugged at the blanket.

"Leave me alone, demon." Cat snatched it back and buried her head deeper into the covers.

But not her heart. She hadn't reverted back to that state when they had returned and hidden from the world. She had flourished, delved head first into becoming a part of this community by his side. Love had changed her as much as it changed him. Warmth enveloped his heart, and he smiled, satisfied with the way his life had turned out. Anything was possible with Cat by his side.

Thalia appeared to have no intention of giving up on her goal. She swooped over to the side of the bed and fished her hand underneath, obviously giving something a sharp squeeze by the yelp that emanated from beneath the blanket pile. "I'll forgive you for that because you haven't had your morning coffee and because it is true."

A muffled term of endearment answered from the cocoon. Thalia and Norm left and closed the door behind them.

"Are they gone?" Cat's head peeped out, eyes peering out from the blue blanket framing her face. If Aidan had his way, he'd stare into those eyes forever and never leave this bed. Sadly, the whole eating thing often got in the way.

Aidan rolled back toward her, arm stretched out, intending to draw her to his side. He couldn't go another minute without touching her, kissing her, making love to her. "You know we need to make an appearance today."

"And I agree. I just think that maybe we need to make sure we are properly awake." A lazy smile curved her lips as she inched the sheet down, the pale blue slowly sliding along her skin, flesh he longed to explore. He swallowed, anticipation increasing his heartbeats. The cotton shifted, exposing her chest and draping across her hip bone. He wanted to rip it off to reveal the treasure beneath but waited instead. Waiting was a wicked aphrodisiac. "I read this article that morning sex is better than a cup of coffee. Do you think it's true?"

"In the name of science then." Aidan flipped his half of the blanket down and greeted her with his naked body. A throaty laugh exited her mouth and was enough to close the gap between them. He wasn't sure if she had reached for him, he had reached for her, or they had reached for each other. All he knew was that she was in his arms and he never wanted to let go.

He planted gentle kisses along her neck and across her collarbone, letting his finger glide along the curve of her side, exploring all the curves and hollows until his hand palmed the firm flesh of her backside. He squeezed and elicited a breathy cry followed by a lusty moan. God, he loved this woman. How had he ever survived without touching her, tasting her, loving her? She was his world now, and he intended to show her every day how much she meant to him. He snaked his hands around her waist and pulled her closer until he could feel her heat through the twisted sheet that separated them.

"We need to move that. Now!" Cat panted her words as he tugged and nipped at the tender flesh of her nipple. She wrestled her arm free and pushed at the offending fabric. His impatient little flirt wasn't going to get her way this time. He wanted to take it long and slow, to savor his new found peace with her.

"No, we don't." Aidan snatched her wrists and pinned them above her head, lengthening her torso and giving his mouth free access to the luscious swell of her breasts. "I'm going to make this last at least another fifteen minutes."

She bit her lip, her eyes closed and head back. "Fifteen minutes? That's way too long."

He grinned at her complaint, his own need gaining in momentum but he held back. For her. For them. "Only you would say something like that. Most women would beg for this kind of attention so lay back, shut up and let me love you. The only thing I want to hear coming from that pretty little throat are moans."

"Such a charmer. Now fuck me." She writhed under his grip, giving in to his seduction, letting him hold her. Letting him take care of her, and he would take care of her as long as she would allow.

The instant he released her wrists, she wrapped them around his shoulders and pulled him in tight. His erection breached her, and she gripped her thighs against his. When she began to pump against him, he clasped her hips and halted her movements, determined to slow things down if it killed him. "It's not a race, Cat."

"But I..."

He placed a finger on her lip and shook his head. "Not a word. Let me love you, Cat. The way you deserve."

Tears formed in her eyes and her aggressive stance softened. He held her gaze as he began to move, each stroke a connection between them, one he never wanted to let go of. He loved this woman, and he'd spend the rest of his life proving how much.

Kissing her sweet mouth, he skimmed his hand between them, pleasuring her both inside and out. The moans he asked for emitted from her throat and built in intensity, the same way the pleasure built inside him. When she cried out, her body convulsing beneath him, his own exploded in response, the muscles of her heat tightened around him and pulsated around him.

She fell back onto the bed and turned toward the clock, a decided huskiness to her voice. "I think you only lasted five minutes there hot stuff."

"And whose fault is that?" She fell into giggles as he wrapped her up in his arms. "You were quite impatient for someone who didn't want to get out of bed this morning."

Cat detached herself and searched around the floor, seeking out a pair of pants and pulling them on. "I just wanted to get rid of them, so I could get in a quickie before the ceremony.

Aren't you excited to see how well the spell worked? Think the town will buy our story?"

"They'll have to. Nothing strange ever happens in this town, remember?"

They had their work cut out for them when they returned. Miss Chow had returned, and with her help along with Thalia's contacts, they were able to get everyone to forget that they had been possessed and the entire town almost overrun by demons.

"Yeah, but do you think your Dad can keep his poker face on?" She pulled a white ribbed tank top over her head and freed her mane of hair from the back, swinging her head back and forth. His body stirred at the sight and he wanted nothing more than to draw her back into bed, but they would have plenty of time to revisit this morning later. She was right, this was an important day — the rechristening of the town. And a few other surprises he had up his sleeve.

"I told him if he didn't then he wouldn't get to ride the tractor ever again. That set him straight." Aidan had worked hard to repair the relationship between him and his father. He was glad they were back to being able to trade verbal jabs with one another. He snatched his Levis off the back of the chair and buckled his belt. When he turned around Cat was lacing up her running shoes.

"I'll race you there." She grabbed her sweatshirt and dashed out the door.

Dammit. She was going to ruin the surprise. He grabbed his boots and ran out after her, leaving his shirt in a ball on the floor.

* * *

The mid-morning sun was at a point in the sky that made it difficult for Cat to see. She continued to jog forward on the path that ran from her cottage to the Ash family farm. Behind her, Aidan yelled out something and hopped on one foot while trying to fit his boots on. Ever since they got back, she hadn't left his side. And it had been blissful. Even running out ahead now she trusted that he wasn't far behind. Finally, she had found a man who wouldn't abandon her.

She had insisted on keeping her cottage though. Aidan's first priority needed to be the town, and she didn't want to distract him from that. His father had been one of the hardest to deal with since they returned. The guilt that weighed on his shoulders almost sent him to the hospital. But he hadn't been the one to sign the contract. He'd only hidden it, and why not? Who in their right mind would believe that magical portals actually existed? She sometimes wished she had never known, but everything she had been through up until now brought her to this moment, and she wouldn't let that go for anything.

She jogged through the familiar path and reached the fence where she had first encountered Aidan while she was chasing down a beastie. The fiends had all been banished when they'd finished the ritual closing of the portal, something Miss Chow had insisted on before she would move back. There were two things in this life Cat didn't want to live without. Aidan Ash and Miss Chow's Orange Chicken.

The delicate aura that surrounded anything supernatural was still visible to her and would likely always be. But now she saw it as a blessing instead of a curse. Something useful that would allow her to protect her friends and her family.

In the distance the pink blossoms of the cherry trees were breathtaking. She pressed a hand to her chest to quell the rise of emotion. She didn't ever want to shed a tear again. Happy or otherwise. She had cried enough for two lifetimes and had lived two lifetimes already. The sweet almond smell wafted through the air and made her stomach growl. Morning sex might have been a substitute for coffee, but she still needed food. And that was the confusing part. There was supposed to be a ribbon cutting here. A big ceremony for the whole town to celebrate the return to their roots. Except the only thing adorning the fields were the magically restored cherry fields. What's been destroyed by magic can be undone. They were lucky it actually wasn't a natural disaster.

"Wait. Wait." Aidan yelled out from behind her. She turned to see as Aidan rounded the corner, sweat glistening on his naked torso.

"Did we sleep through an entire day or something? Where is everyone?"

Movement in the distance caught her eye. The slowly revolving Ferris wheel was turning at the fairgrounds across the River Rouge, now not so red anymore. The fine silt had been gathered and locked away deep inside the mines, guaranteeing that the prophecy that called for the soul of Aidan Ash could never be collected upon. Now the river could feed the many farms that had sprung up along the banks again. Ashton didn't need the mine, it just needed the people to believe in the power of the soil again. Just like she believed in the love again.

"Did they move the ceremony? Seems strange they wouldn't tell you," said Cat.

Aidan doubled over, hands on knees. He held out a finger asking for a moment to gather his breath. He was used to working on the farm, but the boy needed some cardio. Cat had been running all her life. This man before her had taught her how to fill her heart and for that she would be forever grateful.

She placed a hand on the fence line. The same fence she had first met Aidan when she had literally fallen at his feet.

"I hope you don't mind I do this here." Cat turned again, and Aidan was down on one knee He shoved his hand in his pocket and brought out a ring. Several brilliant diamonds sparkled in the simple antique silver setting. "It belonged to my mother."

Suddenly it was Cat who felt she couldn't breathe. She leaned against the fence railing for support. She never imagined she would ever find peace again, let alone someone who would be able to accept her and all her demons. Literally. Tears welled up in her eyes, and she gave them permission to fall. Welcomed them. Forget all the rules. She didn't need them so long as she had Aidan Ash.

"Will you stay with me, Cat? Forever? Marry this country bumpkin and help me keep this town free from beasties? I can't guarantee they won't ever come back, but I can guarantee I will never abandon you."

"Yes!" The words left her lips, and she knelt down beside him, putting out her hand to accept the precious gift. "Will your father approve? I know this has been hard on him."

Aidan rose up and brought Cat along with him. "He's the one who gave me the ring." He looked over her shoulder and gave a thumbs up. His father had rolled out onto the porch and waving at them.

Cat's voice caught in her throat. She had felt pure evil for so many years that pure love threatened to overwhelm her senses. "What do we do now?"

Aidan pointed toward the fairgrounds. "Now we go to our engagement party. And start our new life together, free of any

345

prophecy hanging over our heads. Every day after today we get to choose our own destiny."

Thank you

Thank you for reading *Daemon Rising*.

If you enjoyed *Daemon Rising*, please consider helping others to enjoy this book as well.

- **Recommend it.** Please help other readers find this book by recommending it to friends, readers groups, and discussion boards.
- **Review it.** Please tell other readers why you liked this book by reviewing it at one of the following websites: Amazon, Barnes and Noble, or Goodreads.

About the Author

Nicolette is a mother, wife, paralegal, writer, knitter, traveler, violinist and anything else she can get her hands on. She turned to writing stories at an early age, when filling out Mad Libs just wasn't enough.

She enjoys watching dark comedies, warped fairytales, and cheesy 80s comedies. Her interest in music spans from George Winston to Thrill Kill Cult to Bel Canto and U2. She loves to travel, and plans to do more as her son grows older. In her younger days she loved to go out dancing, and you may still, on occasion find her shaking her booty during 80s or goth rock nights at the few clubs they still exist at. She is constantly picking up new hobbies and interests. She knits socks, grows mini cucumbers in her garden, and played the violin for 5 years. She has a pug dog with a nervous temperament and speaks a little Spanish. She's eclectic.

www.nicolettereed.com

You can connect with me on:

🐦 https://twitter.com/nicolette_reed

📘 https://www.facebook.com/missnicolettereed

Also by Nicolette Reed

FAE HUNTER (The Soulstealer Trilogy, Book #1)

Valora Delos is a Hunter, charged with tracking the treacherous Soulstealers and bringing them to justice. Unlike the other fae of her kind, Valora was born with stunted wings that render her flightless, driving her to prove herself in the eyes of King Aric, with whom she has been infatuated since she first set eyes on him as a young prince.

She descends to Earth and finds herself trapped in suburban Seattle after the portal to her world closes. With the help of a sexy half-fae named Dooley, Valora must find her way back to save Dell'Aria. Dooley uses his own brand of magic to help Valora discover memories buried deep within her, which produce more questions than answers- questions about her growing attraction to Dooley and her devotion to her King. Uncovering who the Soulstealers are and who is behind the destruction of Dell'Aria brings Valora a truth she may not be able to handle.

MANE ATTRACTION (A Soulstealer Novella, Book #1.5)

Being a demon trapped in an elf's body seemed a prison at first, but Mane has gotten used to his new home in the Riparian forest amongst the elves. When the waters of Lake Mavrovo start to run red it seems a sure sign that the demon king that cast him out may rise again. In order to investigate he will need to navigate the dominion of the selkie, and they aren't known for playing nice.

Going from an apartment in the suburbs of Seattle to living in a castle at the bottom of a lake in the Realms was one change that Kit had to get used to, being half-selkie was another. Now she has to get used to the changes she undergoes after the selkie sleep, one that involves bloodlust and lust of a whole different kind. A problem she is hoping Mane will help her with.

FAE GUARDIAN (The Soulstealer Trilogy, Book #2)

Dealing with wedding day woes, naked elven rituals, a best friend with a biting problem, dragon battles, and a war brewing between the selkie and the fae are only the beginning for Valora, the Fae Guardian.

Valora needs to get Aric out of her mind if she's going to live happily ever after with Dooley. But nothing is ever easy with magic. Tying herself and Dooley to Aric becomes a matter of life and death, not just for them but for all of the Realms and even those beyond the portals to Earth.

But can Valora handle the affections of two half-fae brothers? She has to if she wants to save the Realms — a world filled with cloud cities, volcanic mountains mined by dwarves, deserts inhabited by dragons, and lakes teaming with ferocious selkie. And getting the two of them to get along may be her biggest battle yet.

MANE CHANCE (A Soulstealer Novella, Book #2.5)

Mane, a demon trapped in an elf's body, has never been one to wait for the action to come to him. Sitting in the cloud city of Dell'Aria while he watches the red waters of Lake Mavrovo churn and boil is enough to get him moving. His old boss, the Demon King Ravanna, is on his way to the Realms and he may be the only one who can stop him.

Kit's selkie mother has done her best to ruin her life, but Kit's human side fears for her safety in Mavrovo. Her and Mane are the only two who can venture through the infected land unharmed. Unfortunately, they probably won't get too much alone time.

FAE WARRIOR (The Soulstealer Trilogy, Book #3)

Valora Delos – a fae of Dell'Aria – has spent her life battling the unknown foe responsible for her mother's death. Now she is racing against the clock to keep Ravanna, the Demon King of Acheron, from invading the Realms. Drowning in the affections from two half-fae brothers in a tricky magical triad turned love triangle doesn't help matters. Cryptic prophecies and cagey spells take Valora through hell and back. As if that weren't enough – someone else's agenda could prevent Valora from being the one to "save us all."

www.ingramcontent.com/pod-product-compliance
Lightning Source LLC
Chambersburg PA
CBHW050539260626
47157CB00002B/360